"You wouldn't be doing it for me," he emphasized. "You'd be doing it for Mattio. What's a few weeks out of your life? The poor kid hasn't had much continuity in his so far."

Even a compulsive liar had to speak the truth occasionally, Maya thought sardonically as her half sister's words floated through her head. *You don't know what Samuele is capable of.*

Well, she now knew one thing he was capable of after this breathtakingly blatant attempt to play on her feelings for Mattio.

"For future reference," she told him crisply, "I don't respond well to moral blackmail. Not that there will be—a future, I mean," she tacked on, wincing, because the only thing she'd managed to do was make it sound as though they had a past.

They didn't have a past, present or future.

It was just the entire off-the-scale hothouse weirdness of everything about the last few hours that had fed this strange feeling of intimacy, utterly misplaced intimacy, between them, she told herself.

Kim Lawrence lives on a farm in Anglesey with her university-lecturer husband, assorted pets who arrived as strays and never left, and sometimes one or both of her boomerang sons. When she's not writing, she loves to be outdoors gardening or walking on one of the beaches for which the island is famous—along with being the place where Prince William and Catherine made their first home!

Books by Kim Lawrence

Harlequin Presents

A Ring to Secure His Crown
The Greek's Ultimate Conquest
A Cinderella for the Desert King
A Wedding at the Italian's Demand
A Passionate Night with the Greek

Spanish Secret Heirs

The Spaniard's Surprise Love-Child
Claiming His Unknown Son

A Ring from a Billionaire

Waking Up in His Royal Bed

Visit the Author Profile page
at Harlequin.com for more titles.

Kïm Lawrence

THE ITALIAN'S BRIDE ON PAPER

HARLEQUIN®
PRESENTS®

Recycling programs for this product may not exist in your area.

ISBN-13: 978-1-335-56904-2

The Italian's Bride on Paper

Copyright © 2021 by Kim Lawrence

This edition published by arrangement with Harlequin Books S.A.

For questions and comments about the quality of this book, please contact us at CustomerService@Harlequin.com.

Harlequin Enterprises ULC
22 Adelaide St. West, 40th Floor
Toronto, Ontario M5H 4E3, Canada
www.Harlequin.com

Printed in U.S.A.

THE ITALIAN'S BRIDE
ON PAPER

PROLOGUE

Eighteen months previously, Zurich

Maya and Beatrice had set out early, not alone, as the minibus ferrying tourists from the small ski resort to the airport in Zurich had been full of fellow travellers. They had all been stranded by the severe storm front that had resulted in the ski slopes being closed for the previous four days.

The storm was over now but *early* as a strategy had not worked—the minibus had been diverted before they'd even reached the terminal. The update texts the sisters had received so far from the airline had not been particularly encouraging or helpful and the details of the *airport security issue* mentioned in news reports remained worryingly vague.

There were rumours floating around on the Internet and also in the hotel bar situated within a short taxi drive of the airport where Maya and Beatrice had decided to wait out the delay.

They were not the only stranded travellers to take this option; the place was full of easy-to-spot tense, grumpy and frustrated airline passengers, who were waiting to be given news.

'A response some time this side of Christmas would be good.' Beatrice's remark was not leavened with any of her normal humour. Her smooth brow was creased in a frown as she acquired a spare bar stool and sat down, arranging her long legs with casual elegance before turning her gaze back to the screen of her phone, as if willing their airline's promised update to appear.

'I might just go and check—'

'Fine,' Bea snapped, tight-lipped, without looking up.

Maya sighed. No sign of a full thaw just yet. They'd had the biggest row ever back at the ski resort, and, although they'd made up, the atmosphere was all a bit frigid. Some of the things her sister had said to her... Maya just couldn't get them out of her head; they kept playing on a loop.

'Really, Maya, relationship advice from *you*— what a joke! You've never even *had* a relationship. As soon as any half-decent guy gets within ten feet of you, you push him away,' Beatrice had said accusingly.

Maya had been stung. 'I dated Rob for months!'

'And you sabotaged that one just like all the others—and there have hardly been any others, have there? So *you've* never had your heart broken, for the simple fact that you won't take a risk—'

'*You* took a risk and look where it left you!' Maya had regretted the hasty words the moment they'd left her lips, and her swift efforts to de-escalate the situation had not exactly been a success. 'Sorry, Bea, but I hate to see you so unhappy. I know you chose to leave Dante, but he is clearly still messing with your—'

'Do not badmouth Dante to me...' her sister, who had spent the last few days doing just that herself, had growled back. 'Yes, I left him, Maya, but people do sometimes leave! And people die, we both know that too. It's called real life—and at least I have one.' Tears suddenly filled Beatrice's blue eyes. 'Sorry... I'm so sorry. I didn't mean that.'

After that final riposte, they had hugged and made up but Maya knew her sister had meant everything she'd said, and it was probably all true.

She considered saying something bright and cheery to lift the mood but decided that optimism would go down like a lead balloon. There was nothing she could say to make Beatrice feel any better, so it was probably better not to say anything at all.

She hitched in a little sigh and wished she'd remembered that saying nothing was an option last night. As she drifted away to stretch her legs, she threw the occasional glance over her shoulder at her sister, feeling the heavy weight of her total helplessness on her slender shoulders in the face of Beatrice's overwhelming unhappiness.

It was hard to watch someone you loved hurting.

She loved Beatrice, and no matter how often they squabbled or disagreed she knew that they had an unbreakable bond and that Beatrice would always be there for her.

The connection could not have been stronger if they had been biological sisters instead of Maya having been adopted by Beatrice's parents. Actually, Maya believed that it was stronger because she had a *real* sister out there and she had no connection with her. Her sister— actually, half-sister to be accurate—remained only a name and a face in a photo... *Violetta*. Her half-sister was clearly someone who, like their shared birth mother, apparently did not want to know Maya, did not want to be *embarrassed* by Maya's existence.

Searching out her birth mother was one of the few things she'd done that Maya had never shared with Beatrice or her adoptive mother, her *real* mother. When she had reached out to Olivia Ramsey, she had not been sure what to expect. And when the response had been an invitation to meet up for lunch, Maya had almost confided her very mixed feelings about the prospect of finally putting a face to the name of the stranger who had given her life and then immediately given her away. But she hadn't told Beatrice or their mother, and now eighteen months had passed, and so, she told herself, had the moment for sharing the secret.

Maya eased the vague sense of guilt she still felt for keeping that particular secret by convincing herself that this way there was no risk of Mum or Beatrice thinking that they were not enough of a family for her. Because they were her everything.

If she was being totally honest with herself, her reluctance to confide in them ran side by side with her reluctance to relive in the telling Olivia Ramsey's rejection all over again. Once had been more than enough to have it spelt out that the well-dressed, clearly well-off woman who had given birth to you only wanted to meet up with you years later to tell you, categorically, that there was no place in her life for the daughter she had given away. Showing Maya a photo of the daughter she *had* chosen to keep— Violetta—had been the last nail in the coffin of Maya's hopes of building any kind of relationship with her.

Maya couldn't remember exactly how she'd responded to Olivia's deliberately calm statements of fact…something along the lines of, *No problem, but I'd be grateful for any family medical history that might be relevant to me,* which her birth mother, who had not seemed overburdened with empathy, had accepted at face value.

So she hadn't inherited her own empathy from her biological mother—but what about her father? Well, when she had finally worked herself up to asking the question of his identity the answer hadn't left her any the wiser. Apparently her mother hadn't known his name— but he'd been good-looking, *very* good-looking. Normally, Olivia had drawled, she didn't date men under six feet.

The other woman had volunteered her reason for giving Maya up without any prompting in the same emotionally tone-deaf style: she'd admitted she would almost *definitely* have kept Maya if her married wealthy lover at the time had accepted her story that the baby was his. Only how was she to know he'd had a vasectomy? And surely Maya *had* to agree that saying you are single mother is a total turn-off for a real man?

'Ouch.'

The person wielding the trolley bag like a lethal weapon didn't even acknowledge the collision—of course they didn't, she thought darkly as she took refuge behind a potted palm. It turned out to be a perfect vantage point to watch the progress of an enterprising young artist who was based in the hotel foyer banging out a production line of cartoon portraits of new arrivals.

She rubbed her bruised shin and sighed. This last-minute skiing break had been doomed pretty much from the get-go; it had started badly and gone steadily downhill from there.

They had not even reached the chalet that had held so many good memories of long-ago childhood holidays when Maya had felt a migraine coming on.

It had definitely been a sign of things to come and proved, she reflected grimly, that it was a fatal mistake to try and recapture the past. But when the owner, an old family friend, had offered her and Beatrice the place for a song after a last-minute cancellation it had seemed too good an offer to pass up. So they'd eased their consciences by calling it a working holiday; after all, what better place, Beatrice had said, for Maya to get some inspiration for the winter collection she was trying to put together for the long-delayed launch of their fashion label.

But they had got very little actual work done, not due to Maya's migraine, or the lure of the ski slopes or even the après-ski fun, but solely thanks to the arrival of Beatrice's nearly ex-husband, Dante, who had turned up without the royal fanfare befitting his status as the Crown Prince of San Macizo and thrown her sister's life into chaos yet again.

Maya could forgive him for being the reason that their fashion label had not got off the ground first time around, but she couldn't forgive him for making her sister—who, until she'd fallen in love with Dante, had been the most optimistic and glass-half-full person Maya knew—so damned miserable. These days, even when Beatrice did smile, it was obviously an act; the shadow of misery visibly remained in her eyes.

From her vantage point beside the potted palm, Maya pushed away the thoughts of her sister's doomed marriage and watched in fascination as the young artist's hand moved across the paper managing in a few bold confident lines to pick out the essential features of his victims and magnifying them to comical proportions.

Maya had once thought she had artistic talent, but her youthful confidence in her ability had not withstood the campaign of mockery and humiliation waged by her stepfather.

The man was no longer in their lives and Maya had recovered most of the self-belief he had systematically destroyed, but never regained her uncomplicated joy of expressing herself in charcoal or paint.

In retrospect she could see that the dreadful Edward had probably unintentionally done her a favour—*goodness, but he'd hate to know that*—because there were so many artists far more talented than her who never made the grade and she didn't want to be one of the ranks of *nearly* good enough.

But this guy, she decided, was pretty good. Though to her amusement it was obvious that not everyone was happy with the frequently unflattering though always amusing portraits. But he was doing brisk business and he took the few knockbacks he received in his stride.

'Quantity over quality.' The youthful artist threw the comment towards her over his shoulder, making her start guiltily.

'I think you're very talented,' Maya said with

a smile. She came out from behind the spiky palm fronds and moved in closer as the young man scrunched up his last rejected creation and attacked a fresh sheet.

'It pays the bills, or at least some of them, and beats starving in an attic. That is *so* last century or maybe the one before. God, not again!' He groaned as the hotel lights flickered and went out.

'Is it a power cut?' There had been a moment of total silence but now the place was filled with a jabber of voices, most saying much the same as she just had.

'Who knows? It's been doing it all morning. Ah, and now we have light.'

His clever hand was flying over the paper again, the caricature coming to life like magic. With a few brief strokes a face began to appear along with, and this was the most magical part, a personality.

Head tilted, she studied the face that was taking form. A razor-sharp blade of a masterful nose made for looking down on the rest of humanity bisected a face with impossibly high cheekbones; a mouth with an overtly full, sensual upper lip contrasting with a firm, slightly cruel-looking lower, a deep chin cleft and a squared-off jaw that looked as though it were carved from granite completed the strikingly austere effect.

If the owner of those heavy-lidded eyes with exaggeratedly long curling eyelashes had in the flesh a fraction of the arrogance, self-belief and authority that was looking back at Maya from the paper, he was surely not going to be a potential customer of the artist.

In her private estimation, the subject of the cruel, clever portrait did not look like someone who could laugh at themselves.

Her warm dark brown eyes lifted, sparkling with amused speculative curiosity as she searched the room for the real-life inspiration, but the half-smile curling her lips quickly faded as she recognised the model for the unsolicited portrait.

It wasn't hard to spot him and that wasn't just because he stood inches above most people in the place. An imposingly tall, athletic figure in a long black wool trench coat that moulded to broad shoulders. His jet-black wavy hair was pushed back from a broad brow, nearly touching the snow-crusted collar of the coat as he moved through the press of bodies with a seemingly inbuilt exclusion zone. He was *not*, she mused, someone who could easily fade into the background.

Maya was conscious, not just of the uncomfortable in-your-face aura of alpha-male authority that he projected even from this distance, but the skin-tightening prickle of antagonism it produced in her. She chose to focus on that aspect while trying to ignore the pelvic flutter of awareness she felt as she watched him. He really was the living, breathing definition of compulsive viewing.

Love him or loathe him—there was no in between, she suspected. What was not in dispute was that there was something totally riveting about the man. Maya found herself both repelled and fascinated in equal measure, but then beauty always was fascinating—even if you were only trying to find a flaw in it—and he *was* pretty aesthetically pleasing!

The artist was good, but the closer his subject got, the more the limitations to his technique became apparent, though to be fair no amount of exaggeration could turn this subject into a joke. Everything about him, from the sense of restrained power in his panther-like fluid stride to his perfectly chiselled profile that combined strength and sensuality in equal measures, suggested he was *more* in every sense of the word.

The artist moving forward, sketch pad in hand to waylay his quarry, re-awoke Maya to her surroundings. She blinked and shook her head. The noise of the crowded space gradually filtering back, she was disturbed and embarrassed to realise just *how* hard she must have been staring at the man, as though she were… She lowered her eyes and felt the heat climbing to her cheeks as the mocking term *sex-starved* popped into her head.

It was not a description she could dispute in the literal sense, but the phrase somehow implied that the situation was a bad thing. Maybe it was for some people, but in her own personal situation celibacy was a conscious choice and not bad luck or, as Beatrice suggested, because she was frightened… She closed her eyes briefly, trying not to think about what Beatrice had said. Her sister was hurting badly, and was just lashing out.

Beatrice had passion, and Maya, well, she had…*caution*, and what she suspected was a pretty low sex drive, so she didn't envy poor Bea in the slightest.

She sometimes wondered if her sister had thought she had found with Dante the rare thing their parents had enjoyed before their father had been snatched away from them.

How would you even know if you found it? It seemed to Maya it was much more likely that—always supposing that special someone even existed in the first place—you would walk straight past your soulmate in the street. Maybe it was why most people, or so it seemed to her, either *settled* or, like Beatrice, imagined that they had found their soulmate, only to end up miserable and alone when things went wrong.

Or maybe Bea was right? Perhaps Maya was just scared—scared of offering her love to a man only to have it rejected, or loving and losing him as Bea had… Pushing away the unhelpful thoughts before they could set up home in her head, she allowed herself to be further distracted by the advancing tall, powerful subject of the caricature.

No chance of mistaking him for a soulmate, she mused, rubbing her hands hard against her upper arms to ease the dark prickle she felt under her skin even through the layers, a sensation she had only previously experienced in the prelude to an electric storm.

She decided not to over-analyse this unexpected physical response to a total stranger, because though some people, her sister included, might suggest that *choice* was not involved where attraction was concerned, Maya firmly believed that you always had a choice. So as far as she was concerned, her head would always rule her heart and her hormones, not the other way around.

And there was also the purely practical side to consider. At this point in her life, romance or sex—*what was the difference?*—would have been a complication too far.

She and Bea were trying to start up a fashion business and one of them had to stay focused. Her sister was going through the trauma of a divorce and Maya needed to take up the slack. Her eyes slid briefly to where Bea sat, her death-ray stare glued to her phone, but Maya saw the sheer misery underneath the anger and her tender heart ached. Bea *really* wasn't the best advert for love right now, but, if it ever crept up on her, Maya was determined she was not going to allow her happiness to depend on a man—not *any* man.

She couldn't conceive of feeling that way, *ever*, she was not that person, but if a man made her unhappy there would be no looking back for her. She'd vowed to herself that she wouldn't be weighed down by someone else's baggage.

The heat, the crush of people, in here was un-bearable and Samuele almost turned around and walked straight back through the revolving glass doors and into the street where the snow that was melting on his hair and overcoat had started to fall in earnest. But he had two hours to kill if his cautiously optimistic contact with inside information on the unfolding situation in the airport was to be believed, and suffering from hypothermia was not going to help the situation.

Was anything?

It deepened his sense of grinding frustration to know that there was a private flight ready for him on the runway—*so near and yet so far*—but waiting here remained his best bet of getting back to Rome in time to be with his brother before Cristiano went in for his scheduled surgery.

His fingers curled around the phone in his pocket as he thought about ringing Cristiano again, but on reflection he decided to wait until his revised travel plans were confirmed; he didn't want to make promises to his brother that he could not keep.

His facial muscles tightened in response to an explosion of laughter off to his right, and the sound of happiness grated on his nerve endings. He didn't want to hear it, he didn't want to be here, he wanted, no, he *needed* to be with his brother.

Cristiano was in the worst kind of trouble, trouble not of his making, and he was alone going through this ordeal, because the wife he adored had a *problem* with hospitals. Violetta did not do the *ugly* things in life, or, it seemed, *do* supporting the man she had married while someone cut into his brain to biopsy the reason for the blinding headaches and other assorted symptoms he had suffered in silence for the past six months.

'She cried when I told her,' Cristiano had said.

Female tears did not affect Samuele; well, not all female tears. Even now, after all these years, the memory of his mother's tears, mostly silent, still made his gut tighten in an echo of the remembered helplessness he had felt as a child. But tears that were purely cosmetic or used to manipulate left him cold, and Violetta's were both. Sadly, his brother was not as immune.

Samuele embraced the anger and contempt he felt towards Violetta even as it deepened the frown line that was threatening to become permanent between his thick slanted brows.

His hand came away wet as he dragged it across his dark hair, before clenching it into a fist. *Dio*, what was it with the men in his family and their bad choices in wives?

He supposed that he was just lucky he had never found the so-called *love of his life*. One thing was certain, if he ever saw her coming he'd sprint in the opposite direction. Samuele gave a thin cynical smile that left his dark eyes cold. He was reasonably confident he would not need his running shoes any time soon, because love was a complete work of fiction, and he was not living in the final scene of a Hollywood romantic comedy.

As he made his way over to the bar thoughts of what his brother was going through alone crowded in, dominating his thoughts, so it took a few seconds for the question being directed at him to penetrate.

Samuele glanced at the face of the young man, then looked down at the sketch being held out to him. He flinched inside. It was good, *too good*, for on the paper he saw a man who was clearly too unapproachable for even his own brother to confide in.

The anger he felt at himself, the frustration he felt at being unable first to save Cristiano from a toxic marriage and now from this disease that had sunk its claws into him, surged up inside him. The release after the past hours of enforced calm was volcanic, though it erupted not as fire but ice.

'Is that really the best you can do?' He allowed his blighting stare to rest on the caricature before he trained his hooded gaze back on the artist. 'The future is not looking bright for you, is it? I sincerely hope you have a plan B.' For a split second he felt a surge of satisfaction but then the kick of guilt came fast on its heels.

Talk about finding a soft target, he derided himself, contempt curling his lip, but this time it was aimed purely at himself. The only thing the guy had done was to be in the wrong place at the wrong time and to have a future for him to mock, unlike his brother, who might not.

Bleakness settled over him like a storm cloud, sucking away any form of hope.

'No problem.'

Instead of releasing the sketch to the young man who was backing away, Samuele held onto it, reaching in his pocket for his wallet with his free hand.

Always easier to throw money at a problem than say sorry, Samuele thought cynically, but before any conscience-easing exchange could be quietly made a small figure appeared, her dark hair a riot of flying Pre-Raphaelite curls, her sweater beneath a padded coat a flash of hot orange. She virtually flung herself between him and the young artist, who let go of his sketch and took a step back to avoid a collision.

She had moved so fast that Samuele had no idea where she had come from as she stood there, glaring up at him, her hands on the slim supple curves of her hips.

With a sinuous little spin that rather unexpectedly sent a slither of sexual heat through his body, she directed a warm look at the boy before turning sharply again and continuing to vibrate scorn towards Sam. 'He, *he* has more talent in his little finger than you…*you*…do in your whole body!'

She didn't raise her voice but every scathing syllable reached its intended target—him.

To say Samuele was taken aback by the sudden attack would have been an understatement. On another occasion he would have liked to have listened further to her voice, which, in contrast to her delicate build, was low and husky.

He could imagine it having a rich earthy tone, he could imagine it whispering private things for his ears only…which said a lot for his state of mind, considering that at that moment it shook with the emotions that were rolling off her—emotions that were neither warm nor intimate.

Samuele found his initial shock melting into something else equally intense, as enormous brown eyes flecked with angry golden lights narrowed on his face. The further kick of attraction he felt was suddenly so strong that the pain was actually physical as it settled hot in his groin. There were not many inches involved here—she did not even reach his shoulder—but every single one packed a *perfect* sensual punch.

She was so gorgeous that she couldn't have

faded into the background if she'd tried, but she wasn't trying.

He really liked that.

He took in the details in one swift head-to-toe sweep. Her outfit appeared to be a glorious clash of colours; the only subdued element was her fur-cuffed snow boots, the velvet-looking close-fitting jeans tucked into them a deep rich burgundy, her sweater orange, the padded jacket that hung open turquoise.

She was either colour-blind or making a point; either way it worked, though, having reached her face again, he lost interest in colour coordination because the face occupied by those fire-spitting eyes was beautiful—heart-shaped, surrounded by long dark drifting tendrils of glossy hair that had not been confined in the messy topknot of curls pinned high on her head.

Her delicate bone structure and warm colouring conveyed a sense of both fragility and sensuality. The glowing flawlessness of her skin stretched across smooth, rounded high cheeks projected youth and vitality, the slight tilt of her neat nose gave it character and cuteness. Her mouth, however, was not cute at all; it was full and plump and at that moment pursed as she scowled at him.

He found his eyes lingering overlong on their

pink softness, unaware that the hunger he was feeling was reflected in his hooded stare; he couldn't remember ever having experienced such an instant, intense visceral response to a woman before.

The way this man was looking at her… It was only her angry defiance that stopped Maya turning and running, letting him see that she was only brave on the outside.

If she was really brave it would not have crossed her mind even for a split second to remain a silent observer to this public display of cruel bullying, to pretend she hadn't seen.

The knowledge that she had been tempted to do just that made her almost as mad with herself as she was with the target of her wrath as her eyes were met and held by the piercing stare of the man in front of her, who was towering over her. She embraced her anger as well as the rush of blood to her head, only now she was experiencing another rush of blood, pounding all around her body, because the way he was looking at her made her feel totally exposed and shaky inside.

With a sharp blink of her eyes, she pushed back at the sensation of vulnerability, clenching her jaw as she gathered herself, deliberately focusing on what had triggered such an intense reaction.

As she opened her eyes again and met his stare head-on she was relieved that the *raw* expression she had just seen in his gaze was gone. She lifted her chin; she wasn't the kind of woman who melted into a puddle because a man looked as if he wanted her.

She focused instead on the soul-destroying contempt she had seen in his eyes as he'd spoken to the artist, the dismissive curl of his lips… every contemptuous syllable an eerie echo of ones she had heard so often from her stepfather. The situation had varied but the meaning was always the same: you are useless, worthless, don't even try.

She was no longer a child sitting there with her head bowed taking it, having her self-belief stripped away by her stepfather, and she wasn't about to watch it happen to someone else. She couldn't live with herself if she didn't call out that sort of bullying.

'Everyone's a critic,' she said hotly. 'Especially those who are incapable of understanding artistic talent. You wouldn't recognise quality if it bit you on the—' She felt her focus slipping away like wet rope through her fingers as one of the lights that had lagged behind the others suddenly burst back into life, shining like a stage spotlight directly at the object of her contempt. He was under the spotlight but *she* was the one who dried.

He sighed and stamped the last of the snow off his boots. 'This has not been the best of days for me.'

His voice was deep and edged with gravel, the slightest of accents only upping the fascination factor he held for her.

Her chin jerked upwards. 'Is that a *threat*?'

'How much?' He tossed the question to the youth over her head.

'You think you can buy your way out of anything, I suppose,' she muttered bitterly. Everything about him screamed money and exclusivity, she decided, as her glance lingered on the breadth of his shoulders.

But the realisation that anger was no longer solely responsible for the dizzying adrenaline rush coursing through her body hit her.

He was objectionable and a bully, but she was ashamed to admit she was a long way from being immune to the waves of male magnetism he exuded.

Taking a deep sustaining breath, she broke the spell of those eyes and felt a trickle of moisture snake down her back. She was *not* about to fall in lust with some random stranger. 'You have talent.' She threw the words over her shoulder at the artist. 'And *you*,' she added, killing her smile, 'won't destroy anyone's confidence or fill them with self-doubt.' She lifted her chin a defiant notch and thought, *Not on my watch!*

Samuele had been on the receiving end of a few unfriendly looks in his time, but nothing that came close to the sheer loathing that he was being regarded with by this total stranger.

He found himself wondering what it would take to make her smile at him… *Possibly seeing you lying dead at her feet*, suggested the sarcastic voice in his head.

'And never,' she ground out through clenched pearly teeth to the young man, 'let *anyone* tell you otherwise.'

'I'm fine—' began the artist.

She cut across him unapologetically. 'Never apologise for someone else's rudeness, and don't let *anyone* gaslight you. You have to believe in yourself.'

Samuele was caught between annoyance and amusement. She clearly had issues, but they were none of his business. 'What are you, his girlfriend or his life coach?'

'Just someone who doesn't like bullies,' she sneered. 'What do you do for an encore, show kittens who's boss?' She widened her eyes in mock admiration. 'A big tough man like you, what inadequacy are you compensating for?' she wondered. 'Dumped by the girlfriend?'

'Wondering if there's a vacancy?' he shot back.

He couldn't help his satisfaction as she flushed bright red. 'In your dreams.'

'Oh, I have very interesting dreams,' he drawled in a voice like warm honey.

'I am not interested in your dreams, thank you,' she retorted haughtily. 'Or your suggestive comments.'

The lights went out again with no warning flicker and in the blackness there was the sound of a glass breaking and several giggles and shouts.

In the darkness Maya felt a whisper of sensation on her lips, light as a butterfly's wings. She sighed and shivered, and began to stretch upwards towards the touch, but just as suddenly it was gone, making her wonder if she'd imagined it.

The lights came back on.

He'd disappeared.

She blinked as the young artist handed her the sketch he had done with an admiring look. 'Man, you are fierce!'

'You bet you she is!'

It was Beatrice who'd rushed over and enfolded her in a hug. 'I am so, so sorry what I said before. I know you were only trying to help me and I was a monster.'

'No...no...'

'Utter and total. Really, Maya, I think you have it right; you never want to feel as rotten as this. So, who was that hunk you were just yelling at?'

'I have no idea.'

CHAPTER ONE

Maya put down the phone and eased her bottom on the edge of the table where she had perched for the duration of the call. She pushed a section of hair that had escaped her casual topknot back from her face with her forearm and yawned. If she hadn't been waiting for the call she would have already been in bed, which, given it was a Friday night, she was twenty-six, single and living in London, probably made her what most people would call sad.

She knew she was going to have to do something about her social life, or rather the lack of it, although the irony was she'd actually had an invite tonight: a group from work had been going out for cocktails to celebrate someone's engagement. She had had to refuse, explaining her mum was travelling overseas to stay with her sister and had promised to contact her the moment she arrived.

'A long trip?' someone had asked.

'San Macizo.'

She didn't have to elaborate further. The exotic island had been the location of a recent blockbuster movie and had been very much in the news, as well as the subject of numerous articles. Like the articles the conversation had swiftly moved on from the stunning scenery to Maya's brother-in-law, with his film-star looks, bemoaning the fact that the hot heir to the throne of San Macizo, the delicious Dante, was no longer available; he'd married an English girl, who everyone wanted to be.

If Maya had contributed to this part of the conversation she could have explained that the English girl was her own sister Beatrice, who, after being reconciled with her husband, had now happily taken on the role of Princess and mother, making both roles her own.

Bea was pregnant again and suffering severe morning sickness, so Maya was glad their mum was there to offer support and also fuss over her delicious little granddaughter, Maya's goddaughter.

But Maya had stayed quiet, not because she wasn't proud of her royal connection, but because it was easy to predict the questions they might have asked, like, *If your sister's a princess, how come you're working as a window dresser for a department store?*

The answer, according to her sister, was that Maya was too damned proud, stubborn and stupid to take help when it was freely offered to her. Maya had really appreciated the offers of help, and she knew they were well meant and sincere, but, though it might take longer, when she finally got to where she wanted to be, it would mean so much more to know she had done it herself and not just used her connections and their bank balance.

She yawned, easing one fluffy mule back on her narrow foot, and caught herself thinking about making a mug of cocoa… *Oh, God… cocoa…get a life, Maya!* Would the wine she had opened last weekend still be drinkable?

Cocoa or last week's wine? She had not completely decided when the doorbell rang.

This time of night the only person who rang her doorbell was the pizza delivery service and she had definitely not ordered one.

Puzzled but not alarmed, she went to the door.

She tightened the belt on her robe before she opened the door a crack—one of these days she really would get a safety chain.

It was not a pizza, it was a woman, and she was not alone. Before becoming a proud aunt, Maya wouldn't have been able to guess the age of the dark-haired baby the woman carried, but if asked now she would have estimated him at somewhere between three and four months. But she wasn't in any state to guess; behind the flickering of her silky, sooty dark lashes, the eyes they framed were blank with shock as she stared at her visitors.

She hardly noticed the door swinging wide as she took a tiny step back, but finally she breathed out a shakily incredulous, 'V… Violetta…?'

Because although it really *couldn't* be, the woman standing there—tall, slim, looking as though she had just stepped out of the pages of a fashion magazine, her river-straight waist-length hair with a mirror gloss, her make-up perfectly highlighting her china-blue eyes—was the same woman she had seen in the photo her birth mother had proudly shown her—her half-sister. Maya still had it—it was the only thing her birth mother had ever given her.

'You're Mia?'

'Maya.'

'Of course, Mummy described you perfectly…but I'd have known you anywhere!'

'You would?'

'Absolutely! There's just this *connection* between us; I can feel it, my little sister. Can't you?' As she bent forward to kiss the air either side of Maya's face, Maya instinctively leaned back, not to avoid contact, but to stop the baby being sandwiched between them. 'Although you're older than me, aren't you? But I'm sure you look lovely with some make-up on.'

Maya blinked rapidly, unnerved by Violetta's rather Siamese cat stare and too utterly confused to even register the implication that she clearly did not look lovely without it.

'No…yes, that is, I'm…' Maya shook her head. 'You…here…' She took a deep breath and focused on forming an entire sentence. 'Just what is happening?'

'I needed help—' Maya watched with horror as her half-sister's slender shoulders began to shake, and her lovely face crumpled as tears began to roll in slow motion down her cheeks.

Maya's wary antagonism melted into genuine concern. 'Is there anything I can do?'

'I shouldn't be here, really… I'm so sorry. I should have rung you, I know, but I was afraid you'd say no and I had nowhere else to go. You're our *only* hope, so please don't send us away,' she begged plaintively, hugging the sleepy baby so tight that he gave a little cry of protest.

It jolted Maya free of her shock. 'Oh, no…no, of course not—' She broke off at the sound of heavy breathing a moment before a figure carrying luggage under both arms came into view.

'There's no lift, and you don't travel light.'

Maya, who was feeling as though events were getting way ahead of her, took in the numerous bags now filling the doorway and the panting, sweaty-faced new arrival, who did not look happy, though his frown vanished when Violetta looked at him with tears shimmering in her beautiful eyes.

'Oh, you poor thing! Mia was just about to help you, weren't you?' she assured him, an emotional hitch in her voice as she turned to Maya. 'This man—George, isn't it?—has been a total angel… Now, where is my purse…? Oh, Mia, would you get it for me? And don't forget to give George a healthy tip.'

Mia? Ah, well, she'd been called worse, and she had other priorities, like locating her purse, paying the driver and dragging the luggage wedged in the doorway inside. By the time she had accomplished these tasks Violetta and the baby had transferred themselves to the sofa in her living room, and while the baby dribbled and chewed his fist his mother was giving her attention to the interior decor. It was patently obvious from the flare of her nostrils that shabby chic was not her thing.

Maya waited. There were just so many things to say she didn't know where to start, though it seemed she didn't need to.

Her visitor whispered a tremulous, 'I'm sorry.'

'For what?'

The literal response drew a tiny frown and the intense blue gaze narrowed calculatingly on Maya's face. 'Turning up without warning this way...but I was desperate, although I swear I've wanted to reach out to you for so long...'

'You have? But I thought your mother... *Olivia* said that neither of you wanted anything to do with me...' Maya bit her lip, hating that telltale quivering of her voice.

'When Mummy met you, I was...*vulnerable*. It's a time in my life that I still struggle to talk about. And Mummy always was...*is* very protective of me. Later on, I must admit I was afraid that you'd resent me, even though—' Her lips quivered this time, and her voice cracked. 'Even though Cristiano said that I should... I'm sorry—'

She looked around helplessly until Maya located a box of tissues on the desk behind her. The practical gesture seemed pretty inadequate given the situation, but it was better than nothing.

'Cristiano?'

'My husband.' Violetta took a tissue and dabbed it gently to her miraculously smooth and unblotchy cheek. Maya couldn't believe there wasn't even a smudge to her make-up. 'But he died without ever seeing our dearest Mattio.'

Maya's wide, shocked eyes went to the little baby—her nephew!—and her heart ached for him and his mother. How on earth did some-one recover from a tragedy like that?

'I am so sorry to hear that.'

The baby chose that moment to grab a strand of his mother's dramatically coloured hair in his chubby fist. Violetta let out a squeal, her expression of tragic suffering suddenly mor-phing into annoyance.

'Let me.' Maya leaned forward and unwound the tiny yet tenacious fingers from the glossy strand that started auburn at the root and went through an extraordinary range of shades end-ing in a deep strawberry blonde at the tip. It was hard, given the artistry, to guess what her natural hair colour was.

'And now I... I have nothing!'

Struggling to respond with anything that didn't sound lame and shallow, Maya offered another tissue, which was refused as her half-sister shook back her glossy hair.

'You have this little one and he has you,' Maya finally said hoarsely as she felt her throat thicken with tears. She swallowed hard; if *she* started crying it would not be as pretty as Violetta's efforts. 'All a child needs is to be wanted and loved,' she added, even as she reminded herself that love did not pay the bills. 'I know it must be hard financially being a single parent and—'

'But Mattio is an Agosti!'

Maya shook her head, confused.

Her ignorance appeared to shock the younger woman, whose blue eyes flew wide. 'He is heir to half the Agosti fortune.'

'Oh, right…' Maya nodded vaguely, getting the picture, though to her mind, as useful as silver spoons might be, surely a child would be better off with a living father?

'Of course, the money should have come to me as his widow, but Cristiano changed his will, and I know exactly who to blame for that,' she said darkly. 'Not that I have a problem with the money going to Mattio,' she added hastily, seeing the look on Maya's face.

Maya nodded, feeling uncharitable that she had trouble believing this claim. How could she blame the woman? It must be hard if she had expected to inherit.

'I have a problem with having to go to *Samuele* for every penny. *He* saw to it that Cristiano left financial control of our child's fortune to him.'

'Who is Samuele?' Maya asked, seriously struggling to keep up.

'He is Cristiano's older brother. He's always hated me—he was jealous because Cristiano stopped letting him make all the decisions. Oh, I don't blame my darling Cristiano, he was vulnerable and Samuele dripped poison in his ear and turned my own husband against me... I can tell you don't believe me, but then no one does!' she cried, her voice rising to a shrill hopeless note. 'They don't understand—they think that Samuele is caring of his family, including me.'

Maya pressed her fingers to the throbbing in her temples. With each word a picture appeared that was horribly familiar to her, channelling her anger into a quiet resolve.

'Oh, I understand. I understand *perfectly*,' she said, 'how someone can appear one thing on the surface and be something very different.'

Before he had married her and Beatrice's mother, Maya had believed her stepfather was the person that the world thought he was: caring and considerate and, most importantly, making her grieving mother happy again. Then they had married and the abuse had begun, so subtle, so insidious that her mother hadn't seen that she was being isolated from her friends, her support network, and in the end even her daughters, until it was almost too late. Maya had not known then but she did realise now that Edward had seen her own closeness to her mother as an obstacle to his all-consuming need for total control over his wife.

Golden girl, he had mocked as he'd deliberately set about revealing to the world and her mother that she was not golden at all; she was useless, she was deceitful.

'They call it coercive control,' Maya said grimly. 'But you're not alone.' And neither had she been; Beatrice had been there for her. Now it was Maya's turn to offer support to another woman and she was glad to be able to.

'You understand!' Gratitude shone in her half-sister's eyes that was quickly replaced by despair. 'But there's nothing you can do to help me, because he has everything. Samuele has money and power, and now I think...' She faltered, kissing the top of her baby's head before revealing, 'No, I *know* he's trying to take my baby away from me, but no one will believe me. But maybe they are right?' she cried wildly.

'No, don't believe that, ever! Believe in yourself,' Maya replied fiercely, her voice shaking with emotional emphasis.

'Coming here was a total act of impulse. It all became too much for me and...well, I just need some space to work out what to do next.'

'You can stay here with me. Take all the time you need.'

'Really?'

What are you letting yourself in for?

Immediately ashamed of the momentary flicker of uncertainty, Maya lifted her chin and she smiled. 'Really.'

It had been the early hours of the morning before Maya had finally crawled into bed, but despite being exhausted she slept in fits and starts, repeatedly waking and remembering all over again that Beatrice's room was not empty any more. It was occupied by a half-sister she did not really know, a half-sister whom, given what she was going through, Maya *ought* to feel a connection with, and she was confused by the fact she didn't.

But then maybe it was unrealistic to expect emotions like that to just materialise out of thin air, and it obviously didn't help that she found herself comparing Violetta to Beatrice and finding her blood relative coming out second.

Whatever she did not feel for Violetta was more than compensated for by what she *did* feel for Mattio. She had felt nervous when Violetta, pleading utter exhaustion, had handed over the baby to Maya to feed and change.

Maya had been surprised by the little ache

in her heart when she had eventually handed him back, and it had made her wonder if her own birth mother had felt that way when Olivia had given her up? Had the sound of her crying triggered the same instinct that had Maya leaving her warm duvet cocoon as she heard Mattio wailing in the next room? Dragging both hands in a futile smoothing motion across her wildly tumbled dark curls, she swung her feet to the floor.

Maya closed down the useless speculation over her birth mother and caught sight of herself in the mirror as she grabbed a robe off the hook behind the door, the sleep-deprived face that stared back at her bringing a fleeting grimace to her face.

On the plus side, her disturbed night had not been troubled by the recurrent dream that she half dreaded, half longed for. She never remembered specific details. On waking all that remained was an erotic blur; the sense of deep yearning, the memory of a deep honeyed voice and a strong sense of shame that usually lingered until she'd had her second cup of coffee.

It hardly seemed possible that a chance encounter so many months ago with a tall, arrogant stranger should leave such a strong imprint on her unconscious. She lifted a hand to her suddenly tingling lips. Had he kissed her or had that been a fiction invented by her overactive imagination too?

An extra loud baby cry had her shrugging off the memory of temperature-raising dark eyes. Once outside her room, she thought she could hear the distressed baby cries even more loudly, but then her experience of crying babies was not what anyone would call extensive.

Her niece probably *did* cry, but whenever Maya saw her, which was too infrequently, little Sabina Ella, a deeply contented child, always seemed to be smiling or examining the world around her with big solemn enquiring eyes or giving the deep little belly chuckle that was impossible not to react to.

There was a wistful element to the small smile that played across the fullness of Maya's soft mouth in response to the memories of her last visit to San Macizo. She was really glad her sister had found the happiness she deserved, and that she was finally reconciled with her husband, but she couldn't help wishing that Beatrice had found all those elements a little closer to home.

Approaching the bedroom door, she paused and after a moment knocked, raising her voice to make herself heard above the distressed bawling inside.

'Is there anything I can do or get for you,

Violetta?' she asked, directing her question to the closed door. She paused again and waited, head tipped to one side in a listening attitude, but the only thing she heard was Mattio.

Pitching her voice louder, she repeated her question and was not really surprised when there was still no response; she could barely hear herself above the crying. Tapping on the door again, she called out the other woman's name several times to give her some warning as she pushed it slowly open.

'Violetta?' Maya scanned the room, empty but for the travel cot that held the baby, his wailing subsiding into a series of gulping, heartbreaking breathy sobs as he heard her voice.

Maya walked across to the cot and whispered a tentative, 'Hello there.' The baby's face was red, his eyes puffy with prolonged crying, and when he saw Maya he didn't quiet completely but he did stretch out his chubby little hands towards her.

Maya felt something tighten in her chest, the strangest sensation.

'Oh…' She swallowed, feeling the unexpected heat of tears pressing against her eyelids. That's all we need, more tears, she told herself sternly as she blinked hard. 'So where is your mummy?' she asked, refusing to think about the significance of the undisturbed decorative pillows on the bed until she actually had to. 'Violetta!'

The baby, clearly objecting to her raised voice, started crying in earnest again.

'No…no, don't do that! I'm sorry, don't…oh, God!' Taking a deep breath, she leaned into the cot and lifted out the warm, damp baby. 'Righto!' she said, channelling slightly desperate cheer as she settled him awkwardly against her hip. 'So, let's go find your mummy, shall we?'

The knot of panic in her chest had expanded to the size of a heart-compressing boulder as, jiggling the baby in her arms, she walked through every room in the flat. It didn't take long—there was nowhere a cat could hide, let alone a person—but she retraced her steps anyway.

'This is not happening,' she muttered. But it was, and she had to deal with it. 'Don't worry, it'll be fine,' she said to the baby, and saw that his little head was propped on her shoulder. He had fallen asleep, exhausted by his crying.

There had to be a perfectly logical explanation for this, she thought, and then spotted the note propped behind a framed photo of Beatrice with Dante, who was looking at his wife with an expression of total adoration. There was a name scrawled across the front of the envelope.

Not her own name, but *Mia*.

Well, some people were just bad with names. Weren't they?

She stared at the envelope with a sudden sick feeling of dread in the pit of her stomach. Probably, given the situation, it was totally justified.

Why prolong it, just do it! Better to know the worst.

Or was it, was it really? There were occasions when blissful ignorance had a definite appeal and Maya had always struggled with the 'rip the plaster off and get the pain over with' mindset.

One arm supporting the sleeping baby, she glanced down at his sweet, tear-stained face and wished she could copy him. She blew out a gusty breath and decided to put him back in his cot.

Baby settled, the next thing on her checklist—because this wasn't about delaying, it was prioritising—was the formula sitting in the fridge to inspect. While the letter wasn't going anywhere, when he woke Mattio would need feeding and, of course, changing. Locating the changing mat and nappies and clean clothes took another few minutes, but the letter was still sitting there and now she had run out of more important and less potentially explosive things to do.

With a hiss of exasperation, she snatched at it and ripped it open, but she had barely scanned the contents when the doorbell rang, making her jump.

Samuele lifted his hand off the doorbell and applied his clenched fist to the wooden panel, fighting the urge to batter his way through the last barrier between him and his nephew.

Instead, he took a deep breath and reminded himself that, while Violetta was a piece of work, selfish, cold and manipulative, she would not harm her own child. This small soothing piece of positivity didn't lower his levels of frustration because, though it might be true, Samuele also knew that she would not hesitate to use Mattio to further her own agenda. This particular vengeful widow had never put anyone's needs above her own self-interest and motherhood had not altered that aspect of her one iota.

Samuele's hand lifted to the fading red line that ran down from his cheekbone to his jaw, glad that the one on the other side had already gone. *He* was the target of Violetta's spite, not the baby, but that didn't mean the innocent child could not be collateral damage. His gut tightened with guilt that he had not seen this, or something like it, coming.

He had promised Cristiano so easily that he

would take care of his child. Pulling himself up to his full height, he fixed his steely gaze on the door. He would make good on that promise.

He heard the sound of a key in the lock and took a step back—waiting for...who?

The words of the note still echoing in her head, Maya's unsteady hands were shaking so hard she struggled to get a good grasp on the key in the lock, not realising until a lot of fumbling later that it wasn't locked, it couldn't be locked, because Violetta had left it open when she left.

Just thinking of how *desperate* Violetta must have felt to leave her own baby with a virtual stranger sent a fresh surge of emotion through her body. She'd said in the brief note that she would come back for Mattio...and she *would*, Maya was sure of that. Perhaps she already had?

Relief that Violetta had realised she couldn't desert her baby washed over Maya in a heart-steadying wave. She gave the stiff door an enthusiastic tug, stepping forward as it swung open to reveal, not her half-sister, but a shockingly familiar imposing figure. The welcoming smile of relief vanished from her eyes as reality collided with her dreams.

Her voice shook with the sheer impact of recognition that nailed her to the spot, leaving her feeling as though she had just run full pelt into a wall.

The seconds ticked away as two sets of eyes locked. It was Maya who finally broke the tableau, her chest heaving as she gasped for air before giving voice to her unedited reaction at being faced with the person who had unlocked something inside her so many months ago that she still refused to acknowledge.

'Oh, no... *You!*'

No matter how many times you skydived, there was always that moment of shock in the split second when you actually launched yourself into space. This was the first time Samuele had experienced that same sensation with both his feet still on the ground.

His hooded gaze moved in a slow sweep upwards from her bare feet to the top of her glossy head, taking in everything in between. He clenched his teeth, the twist of lust in his belly that crossed the border into pain all too familiar.

His reaction to this woman was just as visceral as it had been the first time, when her liquid dark eyes had flashed fire at him for being rude to that artist. The same eyes now were glazed with shock. His glance lingered on the soft full outline of her mouth... He had thought about that mouth a lot since that day, wished he had followed through with his instinct and actually kissed her, so he'd know what she tasted like.

A muscle clenched in his jaw. '*You* are the *sister*?' And presumably a part of Violetta's plan to extort money from him.

Not ready to admit to anything just yet, Maya countered this accusation with her own question.

'*You're* the *brother-in-law*?' The man in her dreams, the man she had met for only moments eighteen months ago, and yet who had imprinted himself indelibly inside her head, was Violetta's persecutor!

One dark brow arched upwards as with a contemptuous curl of his lips he announced, 'I am Samuele Agosti, and, as I'm sure you know, I am here to return my nephew home to Italy.'

He had lost none of the arrogance she remembered from Zurich, and, unfortunately for her, none of his rampant maleness. She folded her arms protectively across her chest.

'Well, you've had a wasted journey.'

'Where is she?'

The question was not directed at her but past her, unlike the fleeting scornful glance that she was definitely the intended recipient of.

Her chin went up. 'I'd like you to leave now.' The door only moved a couple of inches before it met the immovable obstacle of his size-twelve foot shod in handmade leather. 'Home for a child is where his mother is—' Maya stopped, unable to prevent the self-conscious dismay from spreading across her face as she realised that even if this were true, Mattio's mother wasn't here.

She was the only thing standing between this man and her baby nephew.

'You don't sound too sure about that,' he remarked.

'You know what I *am* sure of—that I'm going to call the police if you don't leave in the next ten seconds.'

'The thing about threats is that you have to be willing to follow through with them, or at least convince the person they're directed at that you are.'

Maya found her eyes following the motion of his long fingers as they moved from the open-necked collar of his white linen shirt and the vee of olive skin at the base of his throat, up his neck and across the dusting of dark stubble on his firm, square jaw.

There was a challenge in his smile, and the male aura he radiated—his *presence*—could fill an entire arena. This was not an arena, it was a very small, unglamorous hallway, and it made her feel very small and insignificant.

The recognition of the feeling made her square her shoulders. She didn't care who he was, this was *her* space! She drew herself up to her full diminutive height, managing to project a sense of confidence, which was a miracle in itself, considering she was not dressed for dignity—a fact that was just hitting home to her.

Without taking her eyes off his face, she casually reached for the tie on her robe and knotted it around her middle before smoothing down her hair, but it was a pointless exercise, she knew, so she gave it up. Dignity was more than skin-deep.

'I don't bluff.' She tightened her belt another vicious notch and pushed out abruptly, 'Just go away.'

CHAPTER TWO

'Where is she?'

The question flustered her and put her on the defensive.

'She who?'

This drawn-out innocent act tried his temper, but not as much as the unwelcome recognition of his own initial shock reaction to the sight of the woman barring his way. God alone knew how long he had stood there literally in the grip of a hormonal rush worthy of a teenager.

Or a man who had gone too long without?

He found the latter explanation far more palatable and very easily solved. Sex was like any other hunger. It was not at all complicated as long as you didn't start imagining there was anything other than a mutual attraction there. No matter how strong, no lust had a shelf life beyond a few weeks.

'I think we should take this inside, don't you?'

Sam swallowed as an image of her wide

dilated eyes and messy hair floated through his head. Just how responsive would she be in bed…? Frowning in response to the sly voice of his libido, he pushed the images away to focus on the reason he was here.

She panicked. 'No!'

Her response was so unexpected it stopped him and his thought processes dead in their tracks, and it took him a few moments to actually take on board what she was doing.

She stood there stubbornly, a hand braced against either side of the door frame.

'I *don't* think we should take this inside,' she said firmly.

'You've got to be joking,' he said, feeling an unexpected stab of admiration as she tightened her grip on the door frame, blocking his way with, what, an entire seven stone nothing?

Stronger than his admiration was the mental image of placing his hands around her ribcage and bodily removing her from his path. His thought lingered on the image long enough to count as self-indulgent and he frowned slightly.

Maya compressed her lips and maintained her defiant stance even though, truthfully, she was starting to feel a little foolish. As gestures went this one was pretty futile, and she was still suffering from the weird feeling of having entered a conversation midway through.

Forget about the why, and the how, just focus on the now, she told herself, and in the now she physically represented no obstacle to him. He could have lifted her out of the way with one hand tied behind his back… It was far more worrying that the idea of him doing that made her breath come a little too fast as, under the protective cover of her lashes, she made a covert scan of his long lean length. It only revealed what she already knew: he had the physique of a Greek god who worked out a lot—or in this case an Italian god.

So nothing has changed in the twenty seconds since you last drooled over him, Maya!

'Violetta!' He pitched his deep voice to carry and Maya groaned.

'All right,' she sighed out. It was easier to admit the truth, or at least this portion of it, than have him wake Mattio. Dealing with one Agosti male at a time was enough and this one was way too big to rock to sleep. She cleared her throat and pushed away a deeply distracting image of his dark head on her breast. 'She isn't here, but—'

'And Mattio?'

'Well, you can't have him…because he's not here either.'

Sam's brows lifted at her obviously panicky tack-on. 'You are a very bad liar,' he observed, unaccountably disgruntled at the discovery. 'Look, enough.' He brought one long-fingered brown hand down in a slashing motion. 'I really don't care who you have in there, beyond my nephew, who belongs with me.'

'I don't have anyone in there!' she retorted.

But in his mind's eye, Samuele was seeing a lover sleeping in her bed. Grimly, he found he had no problem disturbing this exhausted, sleeping boyfriend.

'You always walk around dressed like that after midday?'

Catching his drift, Maya blushed. 'My sex life is none of your business,' she countered, thinking, *It's just as well he doesn't know I haven't got one.*

Life might be interesting if it were his business.

As he veiled his eyes with his ludicrously long lashes she glimpsed a gleam before he delivered a flat statement that came out sounding a lot like a threat.

'I can stay here all day.'

'No, you *really* can't.'

'I—' He stopped at the unmistakable sound of a baby cry.

'Oh, my God, look what you've done now!' she exclaimed.

On the receiving end of a 'rot in hell' glare, he did not immediately respond to the opening as she stood there, hands pressed together as though she were praying.

A moment later she breathed out. 'I think he's gone back to sleep.'

'I am not going away without Mattio.'

There was no hint of concession in his voice or on his chiselled features. Thinking hard, she considered his beautiful fallen-angel face, her eyes drifting over the angular contours of his lower jaw and hollowed cheeks, which were dusted with dark stubble that emphasised the razor edge of his carved cheekbones and the sensual curve of his upper lip.

'So, I think this is where you invite me in.'

'Or what, you'll barge your way in? I'm warning you, I really will call the police.'

He lifted his eyes from where they had drifted to the gaping neckline of her silky nightshirt, and she couldn't help the shiver of excitement that sizzled down her spine.

'Feel free if Violetta actually isn't here.' He subjected her face to a speculative laser-like scan. 'I'm quite sure this situation will be of interest to them.'

It suddenly occurred to her that this might

well be the case. She weighed her options and discovered she didn't have many.

With a tight-lipped sigh she stepped to one side and without another word he shouldered his way past her.

'Come in, why don't you?' she drawled, sarcasm masking her apprehension as she glared at the man who now dominated her small living room.

Samuele scanned the modest space that had probably been dominated by the stacks of books and a dressmaking dummy draped with fabric, only now they took second place to a baby buggy, a stack of disposable nappies and general baby detritus. But the item his eyes zeroed in on was a stuffed rabbit. He felt his throat thicken, remembering when it had been new, his brother's way of telling him that he was going to be an uncle.

'Don't you mean you're going to be a father?' Samuele had responded.

'Maybe.' His brother had handed him the toy. 'The cancer's back, Sam. I start chemo next week. So, you see, this kid is going to need you to be around.'

'You'll be around for them! You beat it once, you'll beat it again.'

'Sure, I will.'

They had kept up the pretence, dancing around

the truth, right up until the last minute. Sometimes he thought that his little brother had been protecting him, rather than the other way around.

Maya watched a muscle jump in his cheek as he bent forward, pausing before he straightened up with a soft toy in his hand. For a split second she saw something in his face that made him seem almost vulnerable. She experienced a troubling moment of what felt scarily like empathy, but then he looked at her, and his eyes were not those of a man who needed her empathy, they were hard and cold and ruthless.

'So where is Violetta hiding?'

'She's not hiding anywhere...' Unable to sustain eye contact with the darkness in his, she transferred her gaze to the toy trailing from his fingers. 'She's...gone out.'

'Where and when will she be back?' he asked as he arranged himself in the nearest chair.

Maya struggled to contain her panic as she watched him stretch his long legs out in front of him. 'I don't exactly know,' she said, pretty sure she was sounding as lame as she was feeling.

His eyes narrowed. 'Don't know exactly what— where or when?'

'All of those.'

'You know very little,' he observed unpleasantly.

'I know you are sitting in my chair and I

didn't invite you in… I'm sure that's against the law.'

He grinned. 'Only if I'm a vampire.'

Her lips tightened at the flippancy but she couldn't help thinking that it wouldn't actually be such a stretch to see him in the role of a sexy vampire!

'Look, this is ridiculous.' *So was imagining offering him your neck.*

Ridiculous would be him allowing himself to be fobbed off. 'I'll wait for her.'

'No!' She gulped and added, 'I'm expecting some—' She broke off as the sound of a low murmur amplified by the baby monitor on the coffee table filled the room. 'Oh, God, he's woken up again.'

Her eyes widened as her uninvited visitor vaulted to his feet in one smooth stomach-clenching action. Maya was only a heartbeat away from throwing herself physically in his path as he approached the door leading to Beatrice's bedroom. It was crazy; she still thought of it that way, even though her sister had only spent a few nights there before her life had taken a very different direction.

What would Bea do?

She wouldn't have let him in.

Get a grip! Beatrice wasn't here, she was, and she couldn't let Beatrice fight her battles any more. Maya was never going to give in to a bully, not ever again.

She got between him and the bedroom door, and she turned to face the advancing figure, who suddenly seemed about ten feet tall, raising her hands as if she could actually physically stop him. She knew she'd have had more chance of stopping a hurricane! It struck her that the analogy was very apt—there was something truly elemental about him.

'There are rules,' she said, refusing to give ground. 'Ground rules.'

He looked astonished. *Rules...?*

'If Mattio has fallen asleep again, don't wake him up—please.'

She held her breath, once again seeing in her head the image of herself being lifted bodily by two strong hands—which produced another worryingly ambiguous reaction low in her stomach.

She cleared her throat. 'It took a long time for him to settle.'

Sam looked from the door to her pleading face and after a moment he nodded.

Her relief seemed genuine. 'So, what is Violetta playing at? What little scheme have you two been hatching?' he asked.

'I hate to ruin a conspiracy theory with inconvenient things like facts, but there is no scheme or hatching, there is no *us two*.'

'She is your sister, isn't she?' The fact that she looked sexily wholesome on the surface made her far more dangerous than her overtly glamorous but entirely toxic sister.

'Half-sister, actually.'

'She ran to you, left her baby with you, so you two must be close.'

A little laugh escaped Maya's parted lips. 'I hadn't even met her before last night when she turned up with Mattio.'

Unlikely as it sounded, Samuele found he was inclined to believe the ring of truth in her voice.

'So she's using you. Typical.'

'No, she's not… Do not twist everything I say.'

'So when did she leave?'

There seemed very little to gain from not telling him. 'I'm not sure. I woke up, and there was a note…' Maya's hand went to her pocket. 'She seems really desperate.'

He laughed and said something that sounded pretty rude in Italian before he tacked on a polite translation in English. 'She is *really* devious.'

'She's probably suffering from postnatal depression—new mothers need *support*, you know.' As if he'd know the meaning of the word, she thought, throwing a look of seething contempt at him.

'She left her baby and you're *still* defending her. You really don't know your sister very well at all, do you?'

'I know enough, about her and about you too…'

His dark eyes narrowed on her flushed face his expression assessing as his long lashes rested briefly on the cutting angle of his cheekbones. 'Ah, so my reputation precedes me,' he drawled with a slow smile that Maya found almost as disturbing as his apparent ability to read her mind. 'So what has the absent mother been saying? Actually, don't bother, I can guess most of it, but maybe you should allow for a little bit of artistic licence on her part.'

'You probably make her feel inadequate!'

'Projection, much?'

The hot angry colour flew to her cheeks. 'You don't make me feel inadequate.' Her chin lifted to another defiant angle as she claimed boldly, 'Nobody makes me feel inadequate.'

The overreaction hinted at a vulnerability that was none of his business, he told himself, swiftly closing down that line of speculation.

'You don't strike me as an inadequate woman,' he mused, allowing his eyes to move in a slow sweep up her slim body before settling on her vivid heart-shaped face inside the frame of wild silky waves. The delicate features qualified as high on the catch-your-breath index but there was a determination to the round chin and a fierceness in her direct gaze that he seriously admired.

Taken aback by his response, Maya took an involuntary step away from him.

What do I strike you as, then? She pushed away the question as irrelevant and reclaimed the space she had given up. She tightened the sash on her robe another breath-restricting inch while somewhere in the back of her mind a voice reiterated, *It's past midday and you're still in your night clothes.*

'I wasn't talking about me.' Would he have been saying that if he'd seen the person she had been? Her defensive wall wavered and then held against the wave of self-disgust, and she met his dark stare with a semblance of calm.

He arched a dark brow. 'No?' His broad shoulders lifted in a shrug as his gaze moved beyond her to the closed bedroom door. 'If you say so…' He sighed and scrubbed a hand through his hair. 'I am here to see Mattio. Is he in here?' He tipped his head towards the right of the two doors they stood outside.

'That's my bedroom.' *God, Maya, how old*

are you? she thought as she felt the heat rise up her neck. Deciding the best way to deal with the juvenile blush was to pretend it wasn't there, she glared up at him.

'You're not here to *see* him, you're here to take him away and I won't let you,' she asserted, sounding more confident than she felt at her ability to follow through with this claim.

'I haven't made any secret of what I'm here to do and if you're about to threaten me with the law again…' The prospect didn't alarm Samuele overly. 'I'd think that one through if I were you. Bring in the authorities on this one, and, red tape being what it is, I probably won't walk out of here with Mattio, but he *will* leave in the arms of some child protection social worker. And then when my court order granting me temporary guardianship comes through— which it will—I'll be able to take Mattio home.'

'You have a court order…?'

'I will have, soon.' It was not *strictly* a lie, but it would not have bothered Samuele if it had been.

'But,' she quavered out defiantly, 'Violetta is his mother! Don't courts *always* give a child to the mother?'

He gave a hard laugh and slung her a pitying look. 'That's often true—but it does kind of depend on the mother, don't you think?'

'Violetta's not here to defend herself,' Maya argued, knowing that words could be weaponised and a disparaging word here, a scathing comment there, could over time alter people's perception of someone, as she knew to her cost.

'Isn't that the point?' he suggested drily, looking bored with the discussion. 'She dumped a baby on a virtual stranger in a foreign country. That might raise a few legal brows.'

'*Foreign...?*'

'Mattio is Italian, he is an *Agosti*!'

'So is Violetta.'

'Not if Charlie has any say in the matter,' he shot back.

'Charlie?'

'Her next meal ticket,' he outlined with a thin smile.

'I'm not listening to you,' she bit back through clenched teeth.

'Because the truth hurts?'

'You twist everything I say.'

'Twist,' he echoed, raising his hands in a gesture that reinforced the scornful incredulity written on his face.

'For a woman to leave her baby...' Shaking her head, she scanned his face for any sign that he was capable of understanding what a massive thing that was. 'Have you *any* idea of what a terrible place she must have been in?'

'You really are determined to see her as some sort of victim, aren't you? I promise you that is the very last thing Violetta is. Look, Mattio is not your responsibility—'

'It's not about responsibility,' she retorted. 'It's about—' Struggling to put her feelings into words, she clenched her hands and tried to focus.

'It's about what?'

'It's about…' She made herself meet his eyes even though she knew the experience would not be comfortable. 'A child needs to be loved, to be wanted, and you don't really want him.'

'Now you're telling me what I want?'

'You just want to control everything.'

Samuele sketched a thin-lipped smile that he knew didn't reach his eyes. At that moment he'd settle for controlling his own baser urges, which at that moment… He shook his head slightly and thought, *Better not to go there.* The main thing was that he *was* in control.

'You really have swallowed Violetta's fiction hook, line and sinker, haven't you?'

'I haven't swallowed anything!' she fired back. 'I'm not some sort of gullible idiot— though I can see that it would suit you if I were!'

He didn't react immediately to her claim… there seemed little point. As he studied her face it was obvious she believed everything she was saying. His frustration levels threatened to bubble through his enforced calm.

He'd thought that he'd mentally prepared for every scenario he might face to get Mattio back, but in all of those he'd been dealing with Violetta, a known quantity.

This woman was definitely *not* a known quantity; in fact, she was the biggest unknown quantity that he had encountered—ever. A woman who looked as she did but made no conscious effort to use her allure was a mystery to him. She could bewitch a man with a flutter of her eyelashes if she wanted to, but all she did was try and batter him into submission with her totally flawed logic and stubborn arguments.

If he didn't have more important things on his mind, he might have been tempted to find out more about her, against his better judgement, though instinct told him that Maya Monk came with serious complications and possibly not the ones that he was armoured against. All the same, she was intriguing and quite incredibly beautiful.

How was it possible to want to taste a woman and at the same time want to…? He shook his head, despairing that anyone could be so wilfully stupid. This would have been a hell of a lot easier if she *hadn't* believed everything she was saying, and the fact he had not detected the sort of artifice he always expected from a beautiful woman made him uneasy.

His unease deepened when without warning a Eureka smile spread across her face.

'What about Violetta's mother? Could she come and look after Mattio until Violetta gets back?' Maya knew it was a compromise but maybe one that he might accept. 'What…why are you looking at me like that?'

'Your mother too, if I'm understanding your relationship correctly.'

'We're not in contact. Olivia has her own family.' Some of it was in her spare bedroom. 'And I have mine.' What would she not have given for her mum or sister to be in the same time zone right now?

If they had been, they would be here in this room offering her back-up and some much-needed baby advice.

'It's tough being rejected.'

She flinched, really disliking his ability to wander around inside her head. 'I'm not a victim. I was adopted as a baby, and, I told you, I have my own family now.'

'Olivia died six months ago.'

CHAPTER THREE

It was like watching the life story of a flower in time-lapse photography on a natural history programme; blooming, fading and shrivelling in mere seconds.

It was irrational, but he felt as guilty as hell for killing her hope.

'Sorry, I didn't know that.'

She was apologising to *him*? 'There's no need to be sorry, she was nothing to me.' From what Samuele had seen Olivia was a vain, selfish woman who had passed on all those delightful qualities to her daughter.

'Oh…no…me neither, I suppose… I mean, I didn't really know her either. How—?' she began and then stopped.

'She didn't suffer, did she?'

Samuele only knew the bare clinical facts, namely that Olivia had died after complications from a botched cosmetic surgery. He opened his mouth to share these when he met her anxious eyes and paused.

'No, she didn't,' he heard himself say.

Samuele caught a look of relief on her face before she tipped her head in acknowledgement, and her expression was concealed by her wild mass of dark hair as she lowered her head.

So this was what lying to make someone feel better felt like—a novel experience but not one that he was likely to repeat any time soon.

'So this was something your *sister* clearly didn't share with you before she dumped her kid on you.'

Maya sighed. 'She was upset, and she probably assumed I already knew.' Even as she gave voice to the excuse Maya was thinking of the occasions that that there had been for her half-sister to tell her that their mother had died. 'She was desperate.' She felt ashamed of the doubt that she struggled to conceal but could hear in her own voice.

Not desperate, no—Samuele's eyes moved around the room—but the woman he knew would have to be very determined indeed to consider spending a night here.

'She is a widow with a baby, who is being undermined at every move.'

'You don't appear totally naive.' In his view, being idealistic was probably worse. 'So please listen to me when I tell you that this was totally planned, *cara*. She played you, as they say, for a sucker.'

'That's ridiculous!' *Was it?* Little details of the previous evening surfaced in her head that she would not even have thought about if it hadn't been for him planting seeds of doubt. 'I saw her, she was… Why would anyone…?' Her eyes suddenly widened. 'What did you call me?' Not Mia at least, said the catty voice in her head.

He shook his head in a pretty unconvincing attitude of bewildered innocence—she was pretty sure that Samuele Agosti was neither; it was hard to imagine he ever had been.

When she replayed it in her head the casual endearment on his lips sounded like honey, liquid and warm. Just thinking about it ignited another burst of heat low in her belly.

'She isn't coming back, you do know that?'

His expression came as near to sympathy as she'd seen, so she looked over his shoulder, refusing to allow the suspicions he had planted growing room in her head, worried because her hormones could be skewing her judgement. On the other hand, if what he said was true… Despite her determination the thought dropped into her consciousness and the ripples spread.

'I'm not leaving without Mattio,' Samuele stated.

I'm not leaving without Maya.

Maya swallowed past an emotional occlusion in her throat. She could suddenly see her dad so clearly, standing there smiling sunnily in response to being told that there was no parent accommodation available at the hospital—and besides, his little girl would be discharged from the overspill ward attached to the accident department after the cast that encased her broken arm had been checked by a doctor in the morning. She remembered willing him not to go and leave her in this big scary place and being glad he'd stayed even when she had cried that she wanted her mum, not him.

Mum had wanted to be there, he'd told her, but the rail strike meant she and Beatrice couldn't get back from the town where her sister had been competing in an athletics competition until the next day.

Her eyes lifted. There was no resemblance at all between the gangly dad of her memory, with his beard and untidy gingerish hair, and this tall, impossibly handsome man. But nevertheless, they had something in common.

'I need to see him,' he reiterated.

She offered up a suspicious look but couldn't bury the memories rising up in her…seeing the expression in her dad's eyes—the one that had made someone produce a chair for him to sit on.

After a moment she found herself nodding, not, she told herself, because of an expression in *anyone's* eyes, but because there was nothing she actually could do to prevent him.

She stood back and opened the door.

The curtains were drawn in the room; she had never reached the point of opening them. Light seeped between them and there was a lamp on the bedside table that cast more shadow than light.

Hovering uncertainly in the doorway, she watched him move across to the travel cot. He was not a man she would associate with hesitancy, but if he'd been anyone else that was how she would have termed his approach. As he reached it and looked down at the sleeping baby he was half turned to her so she could see his face in profile.

The subdued lighting exaggerated the dramatic bone structure of his face, and maybe it did the same to his expression, but what she saw or *thought* she saw was an almost haunted look of loss that made her feel almost as if she were intruding. Shaking her head at her irrational response as if to loosen the grip of the uncomfortable feelings, she quietly left the room without a word, wishing she could unsee that look. Empathy for him was the last thing she needed to be experiencing; she already felt bad enough for even imagining a fleeting similarity to her dad, who had been her hero. It felt like a betrayal.

She refused to concede that maybe Violetta's monster wasn't a *total* monster, so she focused on the indisputable fact that he quite definitely wasn't a hero, not her definition of one anyhow. She would save her empathy for the baby caught in the middle of a conflict.

Conscience pricking, she walked into her bedroom, musing over her struggle to feel anything sisterly towards baby Mattio's mother, despite her hot defence of the woman. She closed the door behind her, knowing that, as the walls were paper-thin between the two rooms, she'd hear a pin drop let alone someone making off with a baby.

Not that he would do that… On her way across the room she paused as she realised this confidence in him was actually based on nothing more than a very non-evidence-based gut feeling. Her self-reflective line of thought was abruptly terminated when she caught sight of herself in the mirror on the wardrobe door. *Just* when she thought things could not get worse!

She thought longingly of a shower as she left

a trail of clothes in her wake, struggling to open a drawer in the tall heavy chest of drawers of stripped pine to reveal the neatly folded and brightly coloured selection of sweaters inside.

Walking out of the adjoining bedroom, Samuele was struggling to suppress immense waves of sadness, anger and guilt after looking at the child his brother had never met. Life is unfair; live it, he'd been told, except his brother hadn't lived and life wasn't just unfair—it was *bloody* unfair.

He hadn't been able to protect Cristiano, but he was sure as hell going to protect his child no matter what it took. Still lost in his thoughts, he turned his head in response to a sound at the exact moment he was in line with a crack in the slightly open door, delivering an image of a slim, graceful and totally naked figure sitting back on her heels as she pulled open a cavernous drawer.

Smooth, sleek, supple, with perfect curves, she looked like an iconic art deco figure made warm flesh.

He turned his head sharply away, a stab of self-disgust piercing his conscience as his body reacted independently of his brain to the indelible image printed on it.

Flinging the pair of jeans she had grabbed

backwards onto the bed, Maya sifted through the sweaters and hastily selected one.

Still resisting the pull of the shower, she turned the basin taps on full and washed her face. She fought her way into her clothes and cast another despairing glance at her image in the mirror as, brush in hand, she decided to just give up on her hair, choosing instead to secure the wild mass of dark curls at the nape of her neck.

She was halfway through brushing her teeth when she heard a noise from the living-room monitor, followed by a gentle whimper from the adjoining bedroom.

'I think Mattio has woken up again!' Samuele called.

'I'll be right there!' she replied, hastily rinsing her mouth and remembering wryly not taking seriously Beatrice's claim during the early sleep-deprived days of motherhood that she'd struggled to get dressed before midday.

She erupted into the living room like someone reaching the finishing line of a sprint. 'What…why are you looking at me like that?'

He shook his head and crossed the room in a couple of fluid strides. Holding her gaze, he reached out and, before she could react, gently touched the corner of her mouth.

For a breathless moment their eyes clung

as she tried desperately to hide the shuddering skin-tingling awareness that his touch had awoken.

If that was only a touch, imagine what a kiss would do to you, said the wicked voice in her head.

She already knew…the memory of the whisper of an almost-kiss surfaced from the place she had consigned it to and an uncontrollable shiver traced its way down her spine.

'Toothpaste,' he explained, sliding a tissue back into his pocket.

Her hand went to her mouth. Wearing clothes was meant to make her feel more confident and in control but they offered no protection whatsoever from his penetrating stare. 'Oh…right, thank you.' She shook herself and said briskly, 'I need to go and sort out Mattio.'

Samuele watched as she left the room. He could hear the gentle murmurs of her talking to the baby through the monitor and a moment later she returned carrying his nephew.

'Could you put that on the floor?' She nodded to the brightly coloured plastic mat beside the nappy stack. 'Yep, just unfold it for me, thanks.'

He continued to observe as she dropped to her knees and laid the baby on the padded plastic surface and jiggled with one of his feet before she unfastened the all-in-one affair he was wearing. The entire time she chatted unself-consciously to Mattio, discussing what she was doing with the baby boy, who seemed to be listening to everything she was saying.

The change of nappy and clothes completed, she settled back on her heels and gave a little grunt of satisfaction.

'You are really good at that,' he remarked thoughtfully. He knew he was not, and it was not exactly a short trip back to Italy.

'Beginners' luck,' she admitted. 'I do have a niece, although she is a few months older than Mattio. Beatrice, my sister, is already expecting another.'

'So were you both adopted?'

She shook her head as she got to her feet. 'No, Beatrice came along when I was one, a kind of miracle baby. Mum and Dad had been told they couldn't have children.'

'That must have put your nose out of joint.'

She smiled, clearly unoffended by the suggestion, which, he realised, had probably been made to her numerous times. 'No, our parents made absolutely sure we both knew we were special. Beatrice is my best friend.'

A muscle in his jaw clenched. 'Tell her that often,' he heard himself say.

Maya's liquid eyes held the beginning of understanding.

Although one of his rules in life was that he didn't explain himself, he inexplicably felt impelled to add abruptly, 'Because now I can't ever tell my brother that he was my best friend.'

'I should think he knew that, don't you? Sometimes you don't have to say anything.'

The gentle way she was looking at him, as though he was no longer the enemy, unsettled him—or was it the fact that he liked the feeling that they might be coming to a better understanding of each other? No, that was far too dangerous. He didn't appreciate the way his thoughts were going. 'Could be. After all, he knew his wife cheated on him, but we never discussed that.' The closest they'd come was when they'd overheard a group of women in an adjoining restaurant booth discussing the latest rumour concerning Violetta, but Cristiano had cut him off before he could say a word. Subject closed—for ever.

I know you don't understand, but it's my life and I love her.

Her expression immediately froze over at his dig about Violetta. 'You just never give up, do you?'

'I have that reputation,' he responded coolly, accompanying his words with a lethal smile.

Lips tight, she glanced down at the baby, who was happily kicking his legs and blowing bubbles. 'Can you watch him while I go and get his feed?'

She didn't hang around long enough to see his nod of assent.

Samuele got to his feet. He could watch him but he could do very little else. Whenever he had tried to see Mattio, Violetta had always had a reason why it wasn't convenient. Perhaps he hadn't tried hard enough, which was why he was now little more than a stranger to his own nephew.

When Maya returned with the warmed bottle, Samuele was kneeling beside the baby, one large finger in the tight baby grip of a pink chubby hand, but it was the long thin red mark down the side of his face that suddenly caught Maya's attention.

'He has sharp nails,' he mused, standing up and looking slightly self-conscious.

'He isn't the only one,' she said, looking at the scratch on his face and wondering if there were others on his back... The idea of him lost to passion like that left a sour taste in her mouth.

'It's definitely not what you're thinking,' he said drily as she settled with the baby in a chair.

She flashed him a startled look before bending her head over the baby to hide the mortified heat that was stinging her cheeks. 'You have no idea what I'm thinking,' she mumbled, focusing on the baby as he eagerly attached his rosebud mouth to the teat and began to enthusiastically suck.

Samuele knew *exactly* what she was thinking but he didn't say anything until the bottle was empty and she had carefully placed the baby over her shoulder and was patting his back.

'This happened at the will reading.' He touched the mark. 'The others have faded. It was Violetta's reaction to hearing that she would not have control of Cristiano's money, the money that, according to her, she had *earned* as Cristiano's wife, and that apparently *I* am stealing. Running away with Mattio is all part of her vow to make me *regret it.*'

'That's a terrible, wicked thing to accuse someone of!' she exclaimed, horrified. 'You really would say anything to get what you want, wouldn't you? That's slander!'

'Only if it's not true, and there were witnesses there, including the lawyer.'

She shook her head, but Samuele could see, once again, the doubts about Violetta creeping into the edges of her previous certainty. Cuddling the baby in her arms, she got to her feet. 'There are two sides to every story.'

* * *

He sighed out his frustration as she settled Mattio in his little rocking chair. Maya eased her own chair protectively closer.

'I agree. There are always two sides, but it seems to me that you are only willing to hear one. Why are you so determined to believe that I am the one in the wrong? How do you think I knew you existed, knew your name, found this place?'

The groove between her feathery brows deepened as she shook her head.

'I had inside information from Charlie. Believe me or not, but the truth is that Violetta has a new, extremely wealthy boyfriend who very much wants to marry her.' Deluded fool.

'So you don't want another man bringing up your brother's baby?'

'The point is the other man doesn't want to bring up another man's baby or, for that matter, any baby at all.' He spelt out the situation with brutal brevity. 'Charlie wants Violetta but not Mattio. He has no interest in any child restricting his lifestyle.'

'So it was him who told you that Mattio was here?'

He nodded, seeing more cracks appear in her conviction and pushing home his advantage. 'He told me exactly where to find Mattio because it would suit him very well if I claimed the baby.' He held up a hand, the action drawing attention to the thin red line on his face and the tension round his sensual mouth. 'Yes, I know this might be another one of my very wicked lies, so how about you call her and hear the proof from the merry widow's own lips?'

'I can't call her because she left her phone here.'

'That was a nice touch. Let's face it, Maya, you are in no position to negotiate and there is a time limit on being awkward. Not that I'm suggesting you don't do it very well.'

Maya slung him an unamused smile, realising that if he did take the baby, it was going to be harder for his mother to reclaim him. Violetta needed to come back right now, and Maya was sure if she could just talk to her, her half-sister would understand.

'If you know who she's with and have his contact details, then let's call him, but let *me* speak to her. I'm sure by now she'll be feeling…' She petered out. She really wasn't qualified to guess how a woman who had walked away from her child felt. 'Guilty probably, so saying the wrong thing could tip her over the edge.'

'You think I can't be sensitive and tactful?'

Maya pulled a face, which drew a reluctant laugh from him.

To hide the effect the unexpected sound had on her Maya channelled chilly disproval. It was a pity it only went skin-deep; to her shame, just under the surface she was all quivering, melting warmth. 'This isn't a joke.'

The smile in his eyes vanished, snuffing out like a candle. 'No, it isn't,' he said, producing a phone from his pocket. 'How about I put it on speaker? Then if I get too insensitive you can rescue the situation.'

He was being sarcastic, she could see that, but what she didn't understand was what he imagined he could achieve. Did he think he could bully Violetta into telling Maya to hand over her son? Even *imagining* such a situation brought her protective instincts to high-alert level and she'd only known the child existed for hours. Imagine if you'd carried and given birth…being apart from your baby would be like losing a part of yourself. Wouldn't it?

'You must see that the baby *needs* his mother.' She searched his face for any hint of understanding but, after a moment, sighed.

There was more give in a granite rock face.

'It depends on the mother. I don't know how well you knew Olivia, but you were far better off without her, I assure you. Just look how Violetta turned out.'

'We're not talking about me.' And they never would be because she would never invite this man into her head. 'I have no abandonment issues.'

She bit her lip. She was getting familiar with his expressive shrugs; he was able to convey a range of emotions with the slightest movement of his broad shoulders.

'What?' she snapped querulously, because he was staring at her in that unnerving way again.

'You have...' Samuele half lifted a hand and then shoved it safely back into a pocket. The last time he had touched her mouth— No, he wasn't going there again. 'Blood on your lip.'

A man who made a mistake could be forgiven, but if he knowingly repeated that mistake, he was a fool who didn't deserve forgiveness.

Samuele had never had any time for fools. Did it count as foolish, with the very recent memory of the heat that had stung through his body when he'd touched her mouth still fresh in his head, for his eyes to follow the tip of her tongue as it licked the pinprick drop of blood from the plump, pink outline of her bottom lip?

Probably not, but he hadn't followed through with the impulse to replace his finger with his mouth and continue the exploration. He knew his reasoning bore all the classic hallmarks of rationalisation, but there was such a thing as overthinking something.

He accepted that looking at her mouth, or any other part of Maya Monk, wasn't ever going to lead him down a path to inner peace. Luckily, he wasn't looking to take away inner peace from this encounter—just his nephew.

There was a tension in the room that Maya chose to ignore as she nodded pointedly towards the phone he held.

After a moment he punched in a number and laid the phone on the coffee table between them. It was picked up almost immediately and a man replied, sounding distracted, possibly by the owner of the husky female laugh Maya could hear in the background.

'This is Samuele Agosti. Put Violetta on, will you, Charlie?'

There was a silence before the man on the other end began to babble. 'Samuele, it's great to hear your voice, but actually I can't help you—she's not with me...'

'Oh, for God's sake, give me that thing and get out.' There was the sound of rustling and banging and then what sounded like a door closing.

'He's gone. How did you know where I was?'

There was no betraying quiver in the voice;

it was hard and cold and annoyed, but Maya knew without doubt that she was listening to her half-sister.

'Well, you're not with your child so where else would you be?'

'You found him! Damn, that was quick,' she snapped petulantly. 'Clever old you. I really wanted you to sweat.'

The most shocking thing for Maya was that Samuele didn't look even slightly surprised by this vicious, vindictive statement. Instead, he looked…she searched the angles and hollows of his face and the word *dangerous* floated into her head. The ruthless, relentless quality she had been aware of in him was in sharp focus as he allowed the moment to stretch before responding.

'You succeeded.' His glance shifted across to where Maya stood like a frozen statue, her hand pressed to her mouth, horror shining in her eyes.

Breaking eye contact, he shifted his weight from one foot to the other to move her into the periphery of his vision, ignoring the weight of uneasy guilt in his chest.

He had no time to be gentle; she *needed* to hear this. The truth was brutal—everyone learnt that lesson sooner or later. Yes, sometimes having your eyes opened hurt, but walking around with them tightly shut was dangerous, and a woman who'd reached her age should have stopped believing that every person was good and honest.

'I was hoping you'd have to suffer for much longer than this.' The petulance was now laced with viciousness. Maya felt almost numb now as she heard her half-sister hiss, 'Because you deserve it after you turned my own husband against me and stole what's mine. I deserve that money!'

'Would that I could have turned him against you, but he was loyal to you to the end.'

The bone-deep weariness and despair in Samuele's voice finally penetrated Maya's own personal misery. It had all been an act and she had fallen for it.

'You wanted to see me suffer, I get that, but isn't this all a little bizarrely complicated, even for you?'

'If I'd tried to vanish in Italy your contacts would have found me in thirty seconds and I needed to be in London to get my hair done—my colourist here is simply the best.' Her laugh that made Maya think of glass breaking rang out before Violetta added, 'And anyhow London definitely solved the babysitting problem. It was a toss-up, I thought, between that and having someone burn down your bloody castle, but this was more of a "two birds with one stone" thing. I told you that you'd regret cutting me out of the money. Next time I'll get even more inventive, so don't relax just yet, will you, darling?'

'Cristiano left you very well provided for.' Samuele struggled to keep his voice free of the disgust churning in his belly. 'You don't need Mattio's half of the Agosti estate as well.'

'Your brother always did what you told him, but at least your investment advice paid off. I do have a very nice sum, you're right, but half the estate is worth a fortune.'

'It's Mattio's.'

'And Mattio is mine, but maybe now that you've found him I might let you keep him.'

'How much do you want?'

'Oh, darling, you can be so crude. You may hold the purse strings but I hold the baby, so play nice or I might change my mind.'

'I'm listening.'

'So you've met Mother's little mistake, have you? Mummy said she wouldn't be a problem or try and encroach in our lives, but it never occurred to me that she'd actually be useful.'

Samuele was glad that Maya had moved out of his line of vision; he didn't want to see her reaction to that disgusting remark. 'Get to the point,' he bit out.

'I see my future with Charlie.'

'And his millions,' he added contemptuously.

'Well, I wouldn't marry a poor man, would I?' she cooed.

He didn't bother replying.

'It suits me for you to have Mattio right now. Charlie is not really into babies, but there's always the possibility that I might just change his mind about that.' And with that, she hung up.

After any conversation with Violetta, Samuele usually felt as though he needed a shower and this was no exception. He didn't know at what point Maya had left the room or how much she had heard.

She was standing in the kitchen, her head bent. She had dragged her hair across one shoulder and was anchoring it there with her forearm, revealing the sculpted hollows of her collarbones, the delicately defined angle of her jaw and the elegant length of her neck.

She didn't immediately turn when he entered but the added level of quivering tension in her body made it clear she knew he was there.

'I don't know how much of that you heard…?'

Maya's arm fell away and her hair tumbled free as she spun around to face him.

'Enough to know you were right, I was wrong, she was using me and now you've got what you want.' She struggled to keep her voice flat, and struggled harder to push away the overwhelming self-pity, ashamed she was making this personal because the only person who should be considered in this scenario was the baby in the next room. 'I suppose you want me to pack up his things?' Without any warning her dignity was drowned in a rush of blinding anger.

'Is it all about the challenge for you? The winning? I suppose you'll lose interest in him now you've won,' she threw out, not even sure she believed it but wanting to hurt him because—well, she was not about to give him the benefit of the doubt.

Or maybe she just didn't want to be the only one hurting here.

Samuele tensed, every muscle in his face clenching as his face blanked, and anger bit deep at the insult. She had unerringly targeted his pride, questioning his integrity and implying he had no conscience.

He knew many men who were successful because they possessed little or no conscience. When it came to making money a conscience was something of a hindrance so he hid his, which made it doubly ironic that he was insulted now because he'd succeeded.

But when their gazes connected there was no spite in hers, just a mixture of sadness and pain, a pain so deep it took a real effort for him to detach himself from the emotions he saw there. His own anger deflated, leaving a vague sense of utterly irrational guilt in its place.

'This child doesn't have a father, which is not my definition of winning.' He arched a brow. 'What's yours?'

Maya's brow puckered, the muscles on her face quivering as her eyes softened and went liquid. 'I'm so sorry, your brother must have been very young when he died.'

He watched her fighting back tears and struggled to imagine just how uncomfortable that degree of empathy must be to live with as he found himself revealing, 'He tried to hang on to see his son, but he didn't make it. He was the bravest man I have ever known.'

Samuele had never discussed his brother or the battle he had fought with anyone, so why was he suddenly opening up to Maya, of all people? He dodged the answer and swore under his breath. 'You don't have anything to be sorry for.'

'When I lost my dad I bottled up my feelings, but when I actually talked about them—'

In a voice that could have wilted green shoots on a plant, he cut across her. It was for her own sake really; if she started wandering around in his head, she would definitely find more than a few things that she didn't like. 'I appreciate the sharing,' he drawled sardonically, 'but—'

This time it was Maya who shut him down. 'I get the message.'

She did. If he was one of those people who thought admitting to emotions was a sign of weakness, that was his business; it was the baby her heart ached for. Being taught by example that to *suck it up* was what real men did… God, it was so depressing.

As she thought of the baby her eyes softened. She might have been abandoned but there was never a moment in her life after she was adopted that she had doubted she was loved. It was those early years that had made her tough enough to survive Edward's concerted campaign of destruction.

'What will you ever tell him about his mother?' *Oh, God, I said that out loud!*

Bracing herself for another one of his icy put-downs, she maintained a defiant stance as she slowly turned to face him.

'I would write her out of his life if that was possible.'

No ice, just a cool statement of fact, and while she sympathised with his attitude, she still didn't think it was the right one. But then it wasn't her business, was it? she reminded herself.

'Isn't it possible? Isn't she giving you custody of Mattio?' Giving him away as if he were simply a piece of excess baggage. That was when she'd had to leave the room; if she'd stayed there another moment her feelings would have got the better of her and she'd have started yelling down the phone at her half-sister.

'Nothing is ever that simple with Violetta. It suits her now to have me take Mattio back to Italy, but she won't relinquish her maternal control willingly,' he predicted. 'And once she's got Charlie to the altar... Let's just say she can be very persuasive indeed,' he finished grimly, no doubt thinking of the custody battle that lay ahead.

'Oh... I'm sorry.'

He arched a sardonic brow.

'Well, you'd be better for Mattio than she would be. Actually, anyone would,' Maya said honestly.

'Wow, faint praise indeed,' he drawled, the smile in his voice warming his eyes and making her want to smile back.

She fought the urge and dived for the door. 'I'll start packing his things up.'

CHAPTER FOUR

Mattio had dozed off in his little chair. Coming into the living room behind her, Samuele watched as Maya tenderly tucked a light blanket around him and began to pick up the baby items strewn around.

Feeling a stab of self-disgust that even in a time like this he could appreciate, actually more than appreciate, the tightness of her behind under the snugly fitting denim, he cleared his throat.

'I have been thinking.'

One hand on her thigh, the other outstretched to scoop up a soft toy that had found its way under a side table, she lifted her head and looked up at him from under the frame of curling lashes. She was oblivious to the fact the action made her square-necked cobalt-blue sweater gape, giving him a tantalising glimpse of her lacy bra and the suggestive creamy swell of her smooth cleavage. The shadow of her nipples under the lace might have been his imagination which was, to his own annoyance, clearly working overtime.

'Come with us.' The offer was made not because of his recent testosterone rush but *despite* it—it was a purely practical suggestion, he told himself, devoid of any personal feelings.

Purely practical would have been putting an ocean or three between this woman and you, pointed out the voice in his head.

He ignored it and the insulting implication he was not totally in control. For someone who had been born with a hot temper and a tendency to act before his brain was in gear, he was conscious of the need to maintain control at all times. Allowing their emotions and appetites full rein had been the downfall of both his father and brother, so Samuele's life was ruled by his determination to ruthlessly suppress any similar tendencies when and if they ever surfaced in himself.

Maya dropped the toy and came upright with a jerk that made her hair bounce angrily before settling in a silky tumble down her back. 'Is that some sort of joke?'

'No, it's… Have you been crying?' he asked, observing the dampness on her cheeks with a tightening in his chest.

Maya was always alert and very defensive

about anyone assuming that, just because she looked delicate, she *was* delicate. There was something patronising in people thinking she needed to be given special treatment.

So she had zero qualms about lying.

'No, I have not.'

It was crazy! This time yesterday she had not even known this baby boy existed. Maybe it was the fact they had both been abandoned that had brought out these painfully intense protective feelings in her?

'Well, you look—'

'I have *not* been crying—though God knows the way this day is going, it would be small wonder if I had!'

He lifted his hands in an open-palmed pacific gesture. 'Fine, you have not been crying.' He shrugged. 'I have a flight home arranged.'

She had been prepared to hear him out in stony silence, but her curiosity won that battle. 'Where is home?' Where would she imagine Samuele living? She wouldn't be imagining him at all, she reminded herself, but who knew if his voice might continue to seep into her dreams…?

She gave a little shiver. On any measurement scale their first chance encounter had not exactly been a cosmic event and yet it had lingered in her mind. More than lingered, if she was honest, thinking of that voice in her dreams, the touch she woke up remembering, which was an invention of her subconscious, because he had never touched her. Did that merest whisper of a kiss even count?

Now fate, or whatever you liked to call it, had thrown them together once more. Not just a nudge this time, but a full-on red-light collision, and they were connected for ever by Mattio.

He still hadn't touched her.

'Tuscany, outside Florence. The estate has been in our family for generations.' And very briefly large sections temporarily not. The re-alisation that his father had been selling off piecemeal vast tracts of the estate and splitting up the world-renowned Agosti art collection, just to keep his second wife, Samuele's step-mother, in private jets, luxury yachts and jewels to wear when she lost yet another fortune at the gaming tables, had caused Samuele to abandon his medical degree course midway through.

Medicine might provide status, respect and job satisfaction, but if he wanted to succeed in his determination to restore his family's heritage he needed money, the sort of money that the financial services sector could provide for someone who was successful. And Samuele was hugely successful, his rise had been meteoric and he had never regretted his decision, not once.

Before his father's death he had discreetly, through a series of anonymous holding companies, managed to reacquire seventy per cent of the estate that his father had sold. After his death there had been no need for discretion and the restoration of the Agosti villa in Florence had been completed the previous year.

He had expected success to feel more...*victorious*? He pushed the thought away. The truth was, it was hard to be enthused about anything since Cristiano's death. And now he had someone to hand the reclaimed heritage on to. He had Mattio.

He would always put Mattio's needs ahead of every other consideration, including his own conscience.

'I have a private plane waiting.' He said it in the casual way that, in Maya's experience, only people with a lot of money spoke about such things. 'I'll need a nanny for Mattio.'

'I'm not a nanny!'

'*Dio*, I wasn't offering you the job.'

He was secure in his self-control, but inviting this woman to live under the same roof as him on any sort of permanent basis, given the chemistry that existed between them, would break too many of his self-imposed boundaries when it came to allowing women into his life. And if ever he'd met a woman who was incapable of recognising a boundary, let alone staying the right side of one, Maya Monk was it.

He didn't need a woman like her in his life—actually he didn't need any woman. Of course, there were women he had sex with occasionally—he needed sex, the same as any man—but they never threatened his inner peace.

Another word for loneliness, mocked his inner voice, but he didn't care if it was true. Isolation was preferable to the option both his father and brother had embraced: marrying wives who'd taken them for every penny and made them smile while they did it.

Embarrassed heat stung Maya's cheeks. There was nothing like refusing a job you hadn't been offered to make a girl feel stupid. 'Oh, well…my mistake.' Her firm little chin lifted, defiance exuding from every pore as she added mutinously, 'But it sounded to me like you were.'

His gaze drifted from her narrowed eyes to her sensuous mouth that couldn't look thin and mean, even though she was clearly trying. When it came to a live-in nanny, he would definitely not choose one that looked like Maya Monk. A world where she was a permanent feature in his life without her sharing his bed was an absolute non-starter… No, the person he had in mind was sturdy and no-nonsense, radiating a comforting, calm, kind vibe. Would it be sexist to put any of those things in the ad?

'I travel light, and I have no experience of babies,' he admitted, thinking he had even less experience of women who made him laugh. 'Let alone travelling with one.' Logic told him there had to be more to that endeavour than there appeared. 'And it's going to take me a little time to find a suitable nanny. In the interim, I was thinking that you could…help out with Mattio. I've watched you with him—you're good with him, he knows you and you seem like a…safe pair of hands.' With a soft heart, which of course was what he was counting on.

'So you don't want a nanny, you just want an unqualified, unpaid dogsbody!'

'Are there qualifications for doing someone a favour?' he asked with a shrug. 'And payment isn't an issue—name your price.'

She reacted huffily to the suggestion that she could be bought. 'I can't be bought.'

He fought the impulse to share his cynical view that that fact alone made her unusual, if not unique.

'Not a very practical response, but fine, if that's what you want, I won't pay you.'

She threw him a narrow-eyed look of dislike. 'I suppose you assume that just because I'm female I know about babies.'

Female... Yes, she was... The provocative blood-heating image of her slim, smooth, naked body, *very* female naked body, floated into his head, making it hard to stick to his point. 'You really could do with some lessons in selling yourself.'

'I'm not trying to sell myself,' she said, her voice barely audible beyond the sound of her low shallow breaths, which made the subsequent decibel rise all the more apparent as she suddenly added, 'And I really don't care what *you* or anyone else thinks about me. I care what *I* think about me.' To his ears it had all the hallmarks of a classic *she protests way too much* denial.

She was too busy trying to inject some much-needed neutrality into her voice to notice the thoughtful expression that slid across his face. 'And I've already said no.'

'Yes, you did.'

You didn't have to do much reading between the lines to work out that once she *had* cared about what someone thought, and that someone had done some serious damage to her self-confidence.

She had recovered because she was obviously a strong woman, but there were always scars…even if they weren't visible. He'd come across men like that; ones who made themselves feel big to disguise the fact they were hollow and weak. He would have liked to get his hands on—

He forced himself to de-escalate his growing antagonism towards this faceless creation of his imagination, the man who'd probably tapped into the passion he sensed in Maya, who had maybe made it harder for her to enjoy it with the next man who came along.

But he was not that man.

'You wouldn't be doing it for me,' he emphasised. 'You'd be doing it for Mattio. What's a few weeks out of your life? The poor kid hasn't had much continuity in his so far.'

Even a compulsive liar had to speak the truth occasionally, Maya thought sardonically as her half-sister's words floated through her head. *You don't know what Samuele is capable of.*

Well, she now knew one thing he was capable of after this breathtakingly blatant attempt to play on her feelings for Mattio.

'For future reference,' she told him crisply, 'I don't respond well to moral blackmail. Not that there will be—a future, I mean,' she tacked on, wincing, because the only thing she'd managed to do was make it sound as though they had a past.

They didn't have a past, present or future. She had spent more time in the company of the woman at the checkout till at her local supermarket than this man, and she actually knew more about her!

It was just the entire off-the-scale hothouse weirdness of everything about the last few hours that had fed this strange feeling of intimacy between them, utterly misplaced intimacy, she told herself.

'Sorry, that was below the belt.'

She suddenly caught an expression in his face and wondered if he felt guilty. If he did, it couldn't be *that* guilty. It wasn't in his nature to give up, and when one tactic failed you tried an alternative one. He didn't disappoint her.

'I need your help and if you can put aside your dislike of me… I mean, you don't have to like me or trust me, and any practical inconvenience I will sort out with your employer or whatever. Will you promise to think about it?'

She struggled not to feel disarmed by his sincerity, but knew she was losing the battle as she felt her antagonism melting away. 'How long before you need to know?'

He glanced at the thin metal banded watch on his wrist. 'Five…no, make that four minutes.' He looked at her, one dark brow arched, and produced a white grin that would have given the devil a run for his money—a very attractive devil.

She gave a small laugh of disbelief.

'And I would really appreciate your input into the recruitment of the nanny too,' he said, dangling the suggestion like a carrot of temptation.

She breathed out heavily. 'I just can't…' Her voice trailed away as the exhaustion she'd been holding at bay with sheer willpower suddenly hit her, like walking into a wall, and bone-deep weariness came flooding in.

'Are you all right?' He stood braced, looking as though he was fully prepared to catch her if she fell, which was a good thing because she really felt as if she might go down.

She pulled herself to her full height, but she still had to tip her head back a long way to look him in the face.

'I'm fine,' she grouched irritably, wishing she could throw something more than his concern back in his face, then sighed as she felt impelled to add, 'Thank you.'

'You need to sit down. You're having a vasovagal attack.'

'A what?'

'You're going to faint.' Taking matters into his own hands, he took her by the shoulders and manoeuvred her onto the nearest sofa. One finger pressed into the middle of her chest sent her backwards while he lifted her legs onto the cushions.

'I don't faint.' In her head it was a firm, calm statement, but sadly it emerged as a weak little whisper. Maybe she would just lie there until the world stopped spinning. Things were a bit vague and hazy, and she couldn't even work up the enthusiasm to react when she felt cool fingers taking the pulse on her wrist. 'Who made you the expert on fainting anyhow?'

Eyes closed, she missed the look that crossed his face.

'I suppose you've been making girls swoon all your life,' she observed waspishly as she experimentally opened her eyes to discover the world had stopped spinning.

'Take it slowly,' he cautioned as she lifted herself up onto an elbow.

A massive surprise when she ignored him and sat up, swinging her legs to the floor. 'Did you get much sleep last night?'

It seemed like a century ago since she had opened her door to her half-sister, and the memories were already meshed into a kaleidoscope of intertwined images.

It had been one hit on top of another. The exhaustion she was feeling was not just about sleep deprivation; it was emotional.

'Take this.' She curled her fingers around the warm teacup. 'You can sleep on the plane.'

She flung him a look and grimaced as, cradling the cup between her two hands, she lifted it to her lips and drank. 'I don't take sugar.' She took another sip anyway. 'I can't just drop everything…my job…' Her voice trailed away. She was expecting her redundancy notice to arrive any day now, not that that made any difference.

'Where do you work?'

She named the department store. 'I'm a window dresser.'

'But I saw the sketches…'

Her glance went to the folders stacked behind the folded architect's table, which she'd intended to put away in the spare room. 'My sister and I had plans to start a small fashion label, but she got back together with her husband, and start-up businesses need some serious capital and time investing in them… In the meantime, I do actually like my job.'

'Don't married women work?'

'It would be a long commute. Beatrice lives in San Macizo.'

His mobile black brows lifted. 'Yes, I can see that would be pushing it…' He paused, a frown corrugating his brow. *Beatrice?* As in the—'

She cut him off. 'Yeah, I have royal connections.'

'Who could surely give you the capital you need to start up your business?'

At the hint of criticism in his voice she fired back angrily, 'They have offered and I refused.'

'Interesting.' She didn't ask what was so interesting and he didn't elaborate. 'So you have a niece, and now you have a nephew too.' He watched closely as the shock of recognition flickered in her eyes.

'Yes.'

'I imagine that you'd do anything for your niece?'

'Obviously,' she responded, indignant that there could be any doubt about that before she saw the point he was making.

It was true she would do anything for little Sabina, who had an adoring mother and father, who would never ever be abandoned or made to feel she was not worthy of love. She looked up at Samuele over the rim of her teacup, feeling lighter as she shrugged off the invisible but very real weight of indecision.

Why would she do any less for her nephew, who was so much worse off than her niece?

'I'll do it.'

It would be fine, she told herself. All she had to do was remember that she could not fall too deeply in love with her nephew because, in reality, parting was inevitable.

The uncle...well, there was no danger of love being involved there, but she would have to keep some sort of check on the surges of attraction that might put her in danger of doing something stupid.

Like flying off to Italy with a man you barely know where your lack of childcare skills is going to be outed very quickly.

CHAPTER FIVE

She struggled to shake the feeling that she was there under false pretences as Samuele's staff deferred to her on every matter to do with the baby on board.

Apart from an interval when he became fretful, which, according to one sympathetic steward who seemed knowledgeable about such things, meant that he was probably teething, he'd been no trouble at all.

'Look at those hot little cheeks, bless him. We didn't sleep for a week when our eldest was teething,' she said, setting out the bottle of formula Maya had not needed to request, but had magically appeared.

As Maya jogged up and down later, Mattio in her arms, she could appreciate how much harder this might have been if there were more than the one other passenger on board. Samuele was certainly not going to complain about the noise of a grizzling baby, but even he had spent most of the flight locked in a private cabin where she presumed he was working, only appearing when they were about to land to ask, in what she felt was a critical way, if she'd had any sleep.

Did she look that bad?

'He's teething,' she said stiffly, nodding to the baby, who had just nodded off himself.

'Oh.'

Maya quite enjoyed seeing him look out of his depth. She could imagine that it was probably a once-in-a-decade thing, so she didn't let on that she was too.

Once they disembarked a well-oiled machine seemed to spring into action, making the transfer into a luxury four-wheel-drive painless and swift.

The only blip in this process was when the passenger door was opened by one of the team whose sole purpose in life appeared to be saying *'si'* to Samuele. Though to be fair his attitude did not suggest he required deference. He was relaxed with all his staff, who seemed pretty at ease with him too. Maya, whose nervous system was on permanent red-alert mode around him, felt quite envious. She hesitated at the car door. She had intended to sit next to the baby in the back seat, though perhaps there was no such safe distance when it came to Samuele.

'Is there a problem?' Samuele sounded impatient. She noticed he had got changed on the flight and the black jeans that greedily clung to his muscular thighs seemed a very valid reason not to sit beside him. God knew when he'd found the time to swap clothes, but then it seemed to Maya that he did everything at a million miles an hour. He was not, she decided, the sort of person to take time out to appreciate a sunset or a view. Did he ever actually relax?

'I was wondering if we'd see much of Florence. I've never been there but I understand it's very beautiful.'

'Another day I'll give you a guided tour.'

'Oh, I didn't mean—'

'Get in, Maya.'

She got in rather than make a fuss and any concerns she had about making stilted conversation were unnecessary because they were barely outside the city limits when she fell asleep.

When she woke, confused, her head propped against the padded headrest, a blanket from the back seat thrown over her, she was too muzzy-headed to think about how it had got there. Samuele wasn't in the car.

She rubbed her eyes, knowing that it was a given that her hair would look as though there were small animals living somewhere in the wild mass of curls. She took in her surroundings. The car was stationary and they were parked at the side of a narrow empty road where the trees lining the road ahead and behind had thinned to reveal what was the most incredible panoramic view she had ever seen in her life. She'd clearly been wrong: Samuele did stop to look at the view.

She gave the peacefully dozing baby in the back seat a quick glance before she unfastened her belt and exited the car. Her nostrils flaring at the pungent scent of pine and the wild thyme that released its sweet scent into the air, she picked a path across to where Samuele stood, his tall figure dark against the backdrop of a deep cerulean-blue sky.

'Sorry I fell asleep...oh, my, it's so beautiful.' She sighed, her eyes drawn to the view that stretched out before them. Against the distant backdrop of the purple hills the undulating fields were a patchwork of colours, gold with wheat and green grazed by animals impossible to identify at this distance. The separate areas were defined by rows of statuesque pine and dotted with sculptural cypresses, and ribbons of water gleamed as they wound their way down the sloping hills that, to her uneducated eyes, seemed to be covered with the regimented neatness of vineyards.

For a long time she said nothing. 'It's almost...*spiritual*.' The words emerged without any conscious thought and a moment later she gave an embarrassed little laugh and angled a look up at him. Samuele was no longer staring at the landscape, but looking at her, the expression on his face making her insides quiver.

'That probably sounds stupid.'

'Not at all. It's taken some people a lifetime to see that, and some,' he added heavily, 'never do.'

He redirected his stare to the vista but there was a brooding quality to his stare now that hadn't been there before.

'When do we reach...your home?'

'We have.' He opened his hands wide to encompass the land that stretched out before them. 'We have actually been on the estate for the past twenty minutes, and the village is about five minutes back there. You'll be able to see the house once we come out on the other side of that copse.'

'I had no idea that it was so...vast,' she admitted, making some serious adjustments to her preconceptions of the Agosti heritage. 'You own an entire village?'

'My family has cared for this land for years and it has cared for us...and many others in return. Until recently.'

'Recently?' she probed warily, wondering if he was alluding to his brother's death.

'My father stripped everything of value he could and sold off the rest to keep his wife in private jets and fuel her main hobby which was—and presumably still is—gambling,' Samuele said heavily. 'She went into rehab after my father's death, where she met her new husband; in a twist of irony, he owns a string of hotel casinos.'

'When you said his wife, was she not your mother?'

'My mother is dead. My father's second wife was Cristiano's mother. I remember that she adored him as a baby but as soon as he passed the cute baby stage she treated him pretty much like an out-of-date handbag.'

The calming effect of the beauty of the land he loved so much, the land that would never hurt him, evaporated as he dwelt on the destructive emotion his father had called love. Even at the end, when he'd known that the woman he'd worshipped was having affair after affair, he'd still defended her to his eldest son. And then, to Samuele's despair, exactly the same fate had befallen Cristiano.

'She didn't consider she had an addiction problem so my father didn't either. His duty to the land, his tenants, his family…he sacrificed them all for this insanity of selfishness, which went disguised as love.'

The delivery was flat and even but despite, or maybe because of, his measured neutrality Maya could feel the emotions throbbing in every syllable.

'But the land—you said this is yours now…?'

'I started buying it back anonymously as soon as I could afford to, and now it is almost back to what it once was.' He still had hopes of tracking down the last few elusive classical sculptures that would complete the art collection that had rivalled many museums.

'Wow, that couldn't have been cheap…' She flushed as his eyes swivelled her way. 'Sorry, I didn't mean to sound nosy.'

'Yes, it wasn't…er…*cheap*, *cara*.'

To her relief he seemed amused, not offended.

'I am an investment banker, so raising capital is what I specialise in, and the finance industry pays extremely well.' He had not drifted into finance, he had deliberately plotted a course, and the rewards, not the job satisfaction, had been his motivation for doing so.

He inhaled, drawing in the sweet clean air as he scanned the horizon. To Maya, it seemed as though he was letting the peace, the sense of continuity over the ages, visibly seep into him.

'So the estate is a hobby?'

He continued to look into the distance. 'No, finance is my hobby. The estate is my life.' He turned to face her. 'So, are you ready?'

Caught staring at him, she shifted guiltily and began to move towards the four-wheel-drive. 'I'm sorry I fell asleep...' she said again, skipping to fall into step beside him.

It was a subject he did not particularly want to think about. He closed it down with a light teasing reply. 'Relax, you don't drool.' But he couldn't close down the images that stubbornly remained inside his head or the memory of the scent of her hair as it tickled his neck.

After the second time of nudging her head back onto the headrest, he had finally let it stay where it kept falling against his shoulder.

'Sorry, I wasn't much company.'

'A woman who doesn't talk while I'm driving is my kind of perfect.'

Maya huffed a little as she tried to keep pace with his long-legged stride. 'Did you take classes in sexist chauvinism?'

He flashed her a look, all white teeth and testosterone.

'No, I am totally self-taught.'

The exchange had brought them level with the luxury off-roader that stood in the sculpted shade of a cypress tree. 'Your mother must be so proud of you,' she muttered, raising herself on tiptoe to look through the back window she had cracked open before she'd left the car. Mattio had not moved an inch.

'She's dead, remember.'

She shot him a contrite look. 'That was a stupid thing for me to say!'

'Oh, I don't know, it was quite funny. Relax,' he said matter-of-factly, opening the passenger door for her. 'I barely remember her.' Sometimes a memory would surface, triggered by a scent or a familiar object. 'And my life did not lack female influence for long,' he added in a tone hard enough to cut through diamond. 'She was barely cold in her grave before I had a stepmother and, four months later, a half-brother.'

Her eyes, widened in comprehension, flew to his face. 'Four months?'

His fingers curved around her elbow to give her a steadying boost into the seat of the high-level vehicle, which brought her face level with his.

'A married man having an affair…' he mocked. 'Who'd have thought?' Not Maya, clearly, and her naivety made him perversely want to shock her more. 'When I was going through my father's papers I found some of my mother's things.' Untouched and gathering metaphorical dust, since they'd been consigned to a filing cabinet with the other *unimportant* items.

'There were some legal documents dated the day before her death. It turns out he had served her with divorce papers, something that was not revealed in the inquest, I would imagine, seeing as I think they might have had a bearing on their verdict of accidental overdose. Maybe if there had been a suicide note…?'

The way he relayed the details, with a total absence of any emotion, was somehow almost *more* shocking than the story itself.

It made her wonder just how deep he'd buried the trauma. She never doubted there *was* trauma because Maya knew from experience that it never, ever went away, not until you faced it.

'I suppose there are some things you can never know.' Given the story, his attitude to marriage and women was hardly surprising.

He met her sympathetic gaze with a look that was dark, hard and unforgiving. 'Oh, I know, I know full well that my mother killed herself because she was being traded in, because she didn't give a damn about what or who she left behind—namely me.'

He'd thought the words plenty of times, but he'd never actually said them out loud before.

The pity he could see shining in her luminous eyes was the reason why.

Samuele looked away from those eyes, asking himself yet again what it was about Maya Monk that made him open himself up this way. He had revealed more about himself in the space of the last few hours than he had told anyone—ever.

'I don't need your pity.'

'Good, because you haven't got it. There's a difference between pity and compassion, you know! You're angry with a parent for leaving you—believe you me, that doesn't make you unique around here, Samuele. Your mother found it impossible to carry on living but that doesn't mean she stopped loving you.'

He climbed into the vehicle after her, staring stonily ahead as he reversed out of the clearing at speed.

'Sorry,' he said as they hit a particularly bad pothole that almost jolted Maya out of her seat. 'Resurfacing this road is due to start next month. If we were approaching from the other way, the road is almost civilised.' He was watching her as he turned the corner; he liked to see people's reactions as they got their first glimpse of the castello.

Maya's jaw dropped as she took in the square towers in each corner of the massive sandstone edifice and the teethlike projections high up along the walls between them. It seemed to ramble, if you could use such a word for such a formidable-looking building. 'You live in a palace!'

'Castello di Agosti is classified as a castle. My family have lived here since the thirteenth century, apart from a short period when it was used as a hospital during the Second World War.'

'It's...'

'I have never seen a ghost.'

'I wasn't going to ask that.' But, of course, now she was thinking it. 'Are there many suits of armour?'

'A few, hopefully not dusty. Relax, the place has been totally renovated with all mod cons. You look more apprehensive than the tenants did when I introduced some new eco-farming methods. We have a long-term strategy here.'

They were driving along a wide, smoothly surfaced driveway now that wound its way through lush parkland. As the road divided she saw a field with horses in.

'Years ago our stud was world-renowned. We've just started building up a breeding programme again in a small way.'

It seemed to Maya that nothing here was built on a small scale.

'Oh, my!' She twisted her head to see the gardens that they were passing, stone terrace after stone terrace spilling flowers above a formal walled garden with a series of classical looking fountains.

She settled back into her seat as they drove away from the castle and through an archway into a gravelled area surrounded by low stone buildings.

The car stopped and a small welcoming party appeared: two young men in white shirts and dark trousers, who began to unload their luggage; a woman with no visible waist and a lovely smile and another young man, who were introduced by Samuele as the housekeeper, Gabriella, and his private secretary.

While the housekeeper got tearful over Mattio, Maya watched Samuele and his secretary talking quietly. A few moments later she could almost see him shrugging off his city persona; here he was king of the castle, though a very chilled-out king. In fact, he looked more relaxed than she had imagined possible.

'I have some things to attend to, so I will see you at dinner. Gabriella will look after you,' Samuele said, turning to her.

'I don't expect you to look after me,' she blurted.

He tipped his head. 'You are our guest.' There

was nothing in his words, but the light in his eyes made her stomach muscles quiver.

'*Our*…is there a…do you have a…? Are you married or anything?' She paused awkwardly, the idea he wasn't single sending panic that was quite out of proportion with the possibility through her body as she stood there kicking herself for not asking earlier.

'Not even *anything* at this present moment. It was just a figure of speech.'

At the outset Maya had no idea what her role was classified as being while she was here, and she had half expected to be accommodated in the servants' quarters. Although if what she had seen was any indication the servants' quarters would be pretty five star.

There were several gasp-out-loud moments as she was led by the housekeeper, who'd offered to carry the travel seat that Mattio was snuggled in, an offer Maya declined, through the vaulted hallway with its stone walls and up a grand staircase that divided into a gallery at the top.

'The frescoes are in the west wing,' Gabriella explained as she led the way along a long corridor that could have easily accommodated a couple of football pitches.

Maya nodded, as though she knew about wings or frescoes.

When they finally reached the suite of rooms she had been allocated it was clear that she was not expected to slum it. She was given the tour of the additional nursery first, which was decorated in lemon and blue and was utterly charming, as was the well-equipped mini kitchen stocked with enough baby formula to feed ten babies.

'It's all wired for sound,' the housekeeper explained as she led her through to her own private sitting room, which was palatial in size and charmingly furnished with antique furniture, but nothing heavy or dark.

The bedroom, with its balcony, was dreamy with a four-poster and the same delightful feminine furniture, but it was her bathroom that stopped her in her tracks. Massive enough to dwarf the double-ended copper tub built for sharing, it boasted a stone fireplace complete with a wood burner, and a walk-in shower that had more touch buttons than a space module and a shower head the size of two dinner plates!

Setting Mattio's seat down on the marble floor, she sniffed a couple of the oils in the crystal flagons set along the matching marble shelf and turned on a tap in one of the twin sinks.

She could, she decided, picking up a fluffy

towel from the top of one of the stacks, quite happily just live in here.

In the meantime, it was time to check out the kitchen for Mattio's feed.

'So, kiddo, what do you think of your place… not bad, hey?'

CHAPTER SIX

The knock on the door pulled Maya away from the mirror. Did people actually dress for dinner outside movies and royal palaces? Where did castles fit into the scheme of things? Maya did have some experience of palaces and, though her sister had instigated a more casual approach since she'd taken up residence, when it came to family dinners at least, her life still involved a number of tiara occasions.

Luckily here Maya was not the hostess, family or a guest, in any proper sense of the word, so it was just as well she didn't possess a tiara or even a formal dress, at least not one she'd packed. She was normally a meticulous minimal packer and had not adapted well to the 'throw everything into a case in five minutes flat' approach.

But you worked with what you had, and her choice tonight had been between a good pair of jeans—aubergine velvet—an orange minidress she had worn once for a christening and a mid-length silk slip dress in a jewel-bright turquoise that could be dressed up or down.

The lack of jewellery to accessorise equated with dress-down, but the spiky-heeled ankle boots in a leopard print, which had involved the death of no leopards or, for that matter, any animals whatsoever, were definitely dress-up. They also made her appear quite tall, which although an illusion still felt quite nice.

She had worried when she'd first paraded in front of the massive ormolu framed mirror. True, the high neck of her dress revealed her collarbones, but nothing else. It was only when she turned around that you got the *wow* factor or, depending on your viewpoint, the *too much* factor. The back of the dress dipped dramatically almost to her waist and, while she *normally* didn't flinch from being slightly in your face clothes-wise, tonight she had to admit to having some doubts.

Twisting around to look at her rear view, she frowned, then caught herself thinking, *What am I doing?*

Self-doubt was something she had left far behind her, and it had not been easy to do. She was no longer that person, the one who had felt as if she were fading into the background. It was no figure of speech—there had a point in her adolescence when she had *literally* felt almost invisible, thanks to evil Edward. Rediscovering her love of colour had been a visible reflection of how she felt inside—and how well she'd recovered from the abuse he'd heaped on her.

But there was bold and then there was all that flesh… She solved this problem by leaving her hair loose so her exposed shoulder blades and all but the lowest section of the small of her back, just before the dip to her waist, were concealed beneath a curtain of curls ruthlessly tamed—with her hair there was no other way—by the brilliant product she had dragged through it with her fingers.

She took a deep breath, and pasted on a smile. She *could* do this, she'd just think of it as having a solo takeaway in front of the telly, except of course it wasn't either. It was the solo thing that bothered her most, which was insane. This categorically *wasn't* a dinner date, or for that matter any sort of date at all!

The woman on the other side of the door was young, more a girl, really, and was wearing the sort of informal uniform adopted by most staff that involved a white shirt and dark trousers.

Maya struggled to keep her smile in place as the girl's eyes widened in shock, doing a face-to-floor-and-back-again sweep. Her response was not *quite* a jaw-drop, but it came very close.

'Hello,' Maya said.

At the gentle prompt she flushed and rushed out, 'I am Rosa and I am here to sit with the little one.'

'Of course.' Maya stood back to allow the girl to enter the room. 'He's asleep.' She paused; it seemed ironic, considering the number of times she had been asked for ID to confirm her age, but this girl did look *very* young. 'Are you sure...?'

Rosa seemed to correctly interpret the hesitation to hand over the care of the baby that Maya didn't totally understand herself.

'After school I worked in a pre-school nursery for a year. I begin my pre-nurse training at the university next month and I'm the eldest of seven.'

Which makes her much better qualified than me to take care of a baby, Maya mused wryly.

'Wow, that's, well... I've made a few notes for you if he wakes up.' She handed over the sheets she had jotted down some notes on.

'Thank you. Would you like me perhaps to get someone to show you down to the dining room...?'

It was an offer that Maya would have definitely appreciated had she not decided during the last ten seconds not to go down to the dining room at all.

'Actually, no, would it be possible for me to have a sandwich here?'

The girl looked confused.

'I'm feeling just a little tired and not so very hungry after all, so a sandwich in my room… that would be just fine.'

The girl tipped her head in compliance, very obviously struggling to hide the fact that she thought Maya was insane as she backed out of the room.

When the door closed, some of the tension left Maya's shoulders. She was, she told herself, totally comfortable with her choice.

It was important for her to believe it was a decision that had nothing to do with backing away from a challenge. It had been one of the things she had promised herself that she would never do once she had rebuilt her confidence one painful brick at a time after her stepfather had destroyed it with his insidious campaign— a person got told they were worth nothing on a daily basis and eventually they began to believe it.

She told herself that she had recovered fully from what had happened, but the questions Samuele had asked about her business hopes had shaken loose some uncomfortable possibilities she had been unconsciously avoiding. She did not regret refusing Beatrice and Dante's offers of assistance, but there were alternatives she could have taken. There were business loans available for new start-ups; she had done all the research into them, but at the last minute she had always backed away, telling herself that she didn't want to start out weighed down with debt. But she could see now the truth was that she was scared. Somewhere in the back of her mind she could still hear her stepfather telling her she was hopeless, useless.

It wasn't about pride or practicality; she was just scared, even if she hid it well.

And tonight? The strong reluctance to leave Mattio was totally genuine, and it had taken her by surprise, but wasn't there an element of her using it as an excuse not to spend the next couple of hours with Samuele?

In her defence, even if there was, she couldn't really be blamed; being around him was very exhausting because she couldn't lower her guard. She wasn't quite sure what she was guarding against, but she knew it was essential that she do so.

There were times when she decided to be brave and this wasn't one of them. Despite being more relaxed now she had made a decision—admittedly her jaw was still aching, but her teeth had unclenched—the static buzz of panic in her head had not gone away but it was less deafening.

Samuele would probably be relieved by her no-show. If he hadn't actually said that small talk wasn't really his thing, she felt it was a safe assumption to make, and she wasn't here to socialise anyway so starting as she meant to go on seemed a logical choice. In retrospect the entire 'what am I going to wear?', 'do I look good in this?', butterflies-in-the-stomach fizz of mingled excitement and anxiety was rather embarrassing, more suited to a date than what this was.

What was this?

She quickly gave up on finding a definition. It was far easier to say what it was not, and that was a date in any sense of the word.

She was just hoping that they were generous with the sandwiches because she had lied to Rosa—she was starving.

She wasn't really sure how long she'd been standing there lost in thought, but when the polite knock on the door came she still hadn't got around to kicking off her heels. Opening it wide ready to receive the tray—probably silver—she felt her smile fade and her hand drop to her side as she found herself facing not someone bearing a tray, but someone pushing a trolley, and another someone swiftly bringing up the rear.

'Oh, that is…' She gave a shrug, thinking it might not be a bad thing that there was wine when she spotted the cooler. She wasn't really much of a drinker but something to take some of the tension out of her shoulders would be good. 'Lovely,' she tacked on, stepping back to let them enter. It was easier than arguing and she wasn't about to send back good food when she was this hungry!

Hovering to helpfully close the door behind the waiters, who had their hands full, she found herself being pushed backwards as the door opened even wider to admit a tall figure. Her heart jolted.

Oh, dear, this wasn't going as planned!

Samuele had chosen to dress down but in a 'not as we know it' way, in black jeans that clung to his narrow hips and a pale blue linen shirt. Only a strong sense of self-preservation stopped her giving a little whimper of appreciation. It was the artist in her, she told herself. *The woman in her,* countered the voice in her head.

Samuele paused, registering her presence— how could a man not?—but resisting the very strong impulse to turn and stare. He conversed casually with the two staff members, delaying the moment just to prove to himself that he could. He was attracted to her, absolutely, but nothing had essentially changed; he was in perfect control of himself.

Maya was playing catch-up. Caught off guard by the sudden turn of events, her brain had lagged behind. The door was still open and she caught herself actually considering in a half-hearted joking way if anyone would notice if she just slipped away.

Man up, Maya, she told herself sternly. *You're the one who always says face your fears*—but her internal pep talk came to an abrupt halt when she realised she didn't want to know what she was afraid of.

Her eyes went to where Samuele stood looking impossibly handsome. He was smiling in response to something one of the waiters was saying, responding a moment later with a comment that made them both laugh. The informality she had noted since they'd arrived continued to surprise her; she had assumed that he'd be a remote authoritarian employer who demanded deference.

But then he didn't have anything to prove, did he? He had already their respect, so he didn't have to *demand* deference, it was just there. Watching the exchange made her think of the times when her stepfather would get huffy when people didn't use his full academic title.

She could remember squirming with embarrassment when he would speak over someone with a corrective *Professor* Edward Tyler.

In the time it took for her thoughts to slide through her head the small table beneath the window had been covered in a pristine white creaseless cloth, the finishing touches of crystal wine glasses and silver cutlery laid with geometric precision.

All impressive, but she barely noticed the crystal or silver; the thing that was registering with Maya was the fact they had laid two places. On one level she was aware that the light-headed fizz of excitement she was feeling at the thought of dining alone with Samuele in her suite was not an appropriate response.

She planted a hand against her throat, feeling the frantic pulse leap and twirl, and wondered if this was what a panic attack felt like, soothing herself with the reflection that even if it was it wasn't fatal—at least she didn't think so…

He turned, acknowledging her presence for the first time as the door closed behind his staff. 'I said we'd serve ourselves.' He offered the translation even though during her ridiculous panicking she had barely registered they were talking Italian.

'This is all…' she paused, clearing her throat as he reached for the bottle in the ice bucket. Popping the cork with a practised twist, he raised an interrogative brow and she hastily added faux-calmly, 'Very kind of you, but it's totally not… It isn't necessary.' She tried channelling a cool she was a million miles from feeling. 'I would have been fine with a sandwich,' she said, allowing her eyes to touch his but not making the mistake of maintaining eye contact.

'What? And leave you all dressed up and nowhere to go?'

He smiled slowly, and his eyes, as they swept up her body from her toes to her head, left a tingling trail of heat across her skin. 'You look lovely.'

She pulled in a tense breath and smiled nervously. 'I feel a bit overdressed.' *That* embarrassment she could shrug off; less easy was coping with the suffocating thud of her heartbeat, and the tingling sensation under her skin, as though a million butterflies were beating madly to get out.

Samuele was pretty sure he could have dealt with her overdressed problem in no time at all, but that would be playing with fire, so he closed down the visuals that went with the thought.

And you're not playing with fire already?

He closed down the inner voice too and dragged out a chair for her. He watched her hesitate before moving forward gracefully on those crazy heels, her slim thighs pushing against the silky jewel-bright fabric with each stride, forcing his pulse rate even higher. She looked sleek, sexy and exotic with her dark hair streaming like a glossy cloud down her back, just allowing him a peek of her naked lower back. The painful effort of not allowing the desire he felt to show on his face sent a trickle of sweat down his back.

What the hell are you doing here, Sam?

If his life was a roadmap, he felt that right at this moment he was standing at a crossroads. There were two paths ahead. He could see them perfectly clearly: one led to a business-like short-term arrangement involving looking after Mattio for a few weeks, the other led straight to the bedroom.

One involved the short-term pain of self-denial, the other led to short-term, incredible pleasure... Ironically it was the degree of desire he felt to pursue the second option that made him hesitate. He'd already accepted that Maya was not the same as any other woman he had ever met.

Or was it just his own reactions to her that were different?

It wasn't just the utterly ridiculous level of attraction he was experiencing, it was *her… She* was different. When she was around he could not rely on the neat compartments that made his life run smoothly; nothing was contained.

He was so, so tempted to ignore the red warning signs in his head. If alcoholism ran in his family, he would have avoided alcohol; with his particular family history there were certain situations and women he avoided…and he certainly didn't need distractions in his life at the moment, as he focused on putting the last few pieces of the Agnosti estate back together. True, his work ethic had never stopped him having sex before, the difference being— he knew full well—that he had never had sex that touched his emotions.

And she already had, without them even kissing properly…but the admission came reluctantly. It had to be the same reason it had been almost *too* easy for him to open up and tell her such intimate, long-held secrets.

He was confident he *could* stay in control and have her at the same time, he would not admit to a weakness that suggested otherwise, but he didn't want to look at a woman when he left her, and see the shadows under her eyes and worry.

Who was he kidding? She had long-term relationship written all over her beautiful face! She would need things he didn't have to give because he had chosen his path in life. Loneliness was an infinitely preferable option to living his life being manipulated—and humiliated—by the woman he loved.

'I didn't expect this.' Maya paused, trying not to breathe in the clean masculine scent of him as she felt the warmth of his breath on her cheek. 'I just didn't want to be too far away from Mattio the first night we were here.' It was at least part of the truth; actually, it continued to amaze her every time she realised how deep the baby had burrowed his way into her heart so quickly.

Logic told her that it would be foolish to grow too fond of Mattio when very soon she would be walking away from him.

He wouldn't remember her, he was only a baby, but that didn't matter; she would still feel guilty when she left him, and she would always remember him.

Sadness filtered into her dark eyes as they lifted just as Samuele extended the wine bottle towards her glass. Unfortunately logic did not really play a part when it came to genuine emotions.

'No…yes,' she stuttered, struggling to keep the sudden rush of desperation from her voice as she removed her hand from the top of the crystal glass and pressed it close to her chest instead to hide the fact it was shaking; *she* was shaking.

Anyone would think you'd just made some sort of profound discovery, she mocked herself. *But you just fancy the man—it's hardly a shocking newsflash.*

Having never before felt a physical attraction this strong to any man, she could now see how some people mistook lust for something much more profound. But it was not a mistake she was about to make.

'Sorry to invade your space.' He looked around the room. 'Are you happy with your suite?'

'Absolutely.'

'And apologies again for the candles.' He cast an amused glance towards the lights flickering in the candelabra and gave a light laugh. 'I think my request to have dinner here with you was misinterpreted.'

Maya gave a laugh that she hoped sent the message that she had not for one moment misunderstood what this was. Absolutely *not* a date.

'I was thinking that dinner might be a good time to debrief one another each evening— would that work for you? Though obviously, should a problem arise re Mattio, I am available at any time. His well-being is my top priority.'

It was utterly irrational, given the circumstances, to feel chagrin. 'Of course, it is, and I have to eat,' she said, discovering her appetite had pretty much vanished despite the mouthwatering smells wafting towards her. 'So here's to the evening version of a working breakfast,' she said, raising the glass to her lips and taking a large mouthful.

She regretted now not taking the option of eating in more formal surroundings, not that the private lavish sitting room was exactly an intimate space. It was the company not the location that was the problem, she realised gloomily.

'My reputation would not survive if you leave here a shadow of your former self.'

'It all looks delicious,' she said brightly. 'But I'm afraid that there isn't much to report as yet. Mattio took his feed and he settled into his nursery pretty well. Do you want me to sleep in his room?' She had noticed the divan in the corner of the nursery.

No, I want you to sleep in my room. 'Of course not!' he snapped.

'Fine, I was only wondering—'

She stopped as his phone began to shrill, a look of annoyance crossing his face. 'Sorry, I meant to turn it off.'

'No problem.'

He glanced at the screen and grimaced. 'I have to take this.'

She shrugged and nodded.

His English was so syllable perfect, his accent barely there, that she had almost forgotten that it wasn't his first language. So when after listening for a few moments he launched into a heated diatribe in his native tongue she was jolted back to the reality of the situation.

Which was that he was Italian to his fingertips. Yes, he probably could make a shopping list sound sexy, but his sudden urgent passion as he spoke was utterly transfixing…in a stomach-quivering sort of way.

A few moments later he slid the phone back into his pocket and, with a face like thunder, hammered out staccato fast what was presumably a shortened version of the conversation. In Italian.

She waited until he had finished, or at least paused to draw breath, to remind him quietly, 'You know I didn't understand a word you just said?'

He swore then in several languages and dragged a hand through his hair, ruffling the dark strands into toe-curlingly sexy spikes.

'Sorry, it's just that there are problems with one of our tenants. By the time my father died the place had been starved of resources for years, not to mention that there were entire areas where the trees had been razed... Ancient woodland raped for a quick profit.' The disgust in his voice was also etched in the bleak lines of his face, and his jaw was clenched so tight she could almost hear it grinding.

'Nothing replanted, land over-fertilised and the village was depopulated. There was nothing left for young people any more. A small investment meant ecotourism produced some almost immediate profit, but it's a long-term game. We'll start to see the benefits of the green approach soon, and in two years we might start to see some profit. Most of the tenants are on board with the plans but...' His expression darkened. 'There is a tenant who is not on board, for reasons I don't quite understand. He's not one of the old school, he is young and ambitious—exactly the sort of person I thought would be behind us.'

'But he isn't.'

'No, he isn't. There's an area of marshland which is important ecologically, as it's home to...' He paused and looked at her, suddenly seeming to remember who he was talking to. 'I'm so sorry, this must be boring you.'

'No, it isn't.' She was fascinated by this evidence of his connection to the land. 'It sounds like a difficult situation.'

'You could say that. I have been informed that some heavy machinery has arrived and his intention is to drain fifty acres of the marshland and put cattle on to graze. Apparently the concrete foundations for a barn arrives in the morning. Everything I'm working for will be destroyed for a quick profit. I have to go.' He got to his feet. 'I must stop this.'

Maya laid down her napkin and got to her feet and walked with him to the door. 'Well, goodnight.' She held out her hand. 'And good luck.'

He angled a sardonic dark brow. 'I'll probably need it—' The lights suddenly dimmed and went out completely, leaving the flickering candles as the only illumination in the room, highlighting the angles and planes of his face. 'Does this remind you of anything?' he murmured huskily.

Mesmerised by his dark stare, she nodded. 'The airport hotel. I wondered…'

'What did you wonder, *cara*?'

The words, uttered in a low gravelled tone, were almost like a physical caress. She swallowed. 'Did you kiss me?' she whispered.

He shook his head. In the semi-light his teeth were very white as he produced a slow smile, even while his eyes stayed dark and intent. Maya was too mortified to notice. Why, oh, why had she aired her fantasies out loud? Of course, he hadn't kissed her!

'No,' he confirmed. 'That was not a kiss.'

'Oh…?' she said, glad of the shadows to hide her embarrassed blushes.

He moved in a step and looked down into her face, murmuring something in Italian under his breath as his hand went behind her head. 'But this *is* a kiss.'

In the private theatre of Maya's thoughts and dreams he had already kissed her a thousand times, but this was different; it was so much better, it was *real*. Her initial pliant shock as she melted bonelessly into his arms suddenly gave way to a hunger that matched his own. One muscular arm banding her ribs, he lifted her feet off the floor as the kiss became more combative, more urgent.

Maya focused on not sliding to the floor as he placed her back on her feet and took a step back. She stared straight ahead, her eyes level with the middle of his heaving chest.

Yes, she had imagined what a kiss from him would be like, but it was nothing at all like that. She gave a wild little laugh. 'Yes, that was definitely a kiss. Oh, God!'

'Exactly.' His chest lifted in one last soundless jagged sigh before he turned and walked away with the sweet taste of Maya in his mouth.

CHAPTER SEVEN

She tensed at the tentative tap on the door, but only slightly. She didn't associate Samuele with tentative, so it was unlikely to be him. She had thought this morning might be awkward after their kiss, actually she had thought of spending the day in her bathroom, but it wasn't, because he didn't put in an appearance, and she ate her breakfast alone.

It had been a solitary sort of day. Maya had spent most of it in the nursery suite, although she had walked around a section of garden with Mattio in a pushchair, longingly eyeing up the extensive parkland and the oak woods beyond. She knew they were oak trees because she'd asked a gardener who was working outside. Their conversation had involved a lot of hand gestures, his English being only slightly better than her Italian, but she thought he'd understood her when she'd said she'd like to walk in the woods. There had been a moment when the communication had broken down and he had been particularly emphatic, saying *cinghiale*, and getting quite agitated, repeating it until in the end she'd nodded simply to soothe him.

Her visitor was Rosa, who would have been the babysitter of choice last night. Her English was excellent and Maya would have quite enjoyed a chat, but the girl was here to relieve her from baby duties. It was not presented as an option and the instructions had come directly from Samuele.

'Rafael will show you to the leisure suite. Do you swim?' Rosa asked.

'I don't have a costume.'

The girl gave a little giggle. 'There will be no one else there, but of course there are costumes available for when there are…guests, you understand.'

Maya did understand, of course she did, and she was instantly determined not to wear a swimsuit that had previously been worn by one of Samuele's female *guests*.

'You are not like them. I mean…'

Maya took pity on her confusion. 'I wouldn't mind an hour or so's break,' she admitted. 'But Mattio hasn't had a nap yet or—'

The girl dropped down beside the chair where the baby kicked his legs and continued to chew on a teething ring. 'Me and the bambino will be fine, you go, or I will be in trouble.'

Maya nodded and Rosa beamed. 'Shall I call Rafael?'

'No, it's fine, I'll find my own way.'

The girl looked doubtful. 'It is in the below part of the castello, in the cellar. There are lifts, which are quite well hidden.'

'I'll be fine,' Maya promised.

Had she actually intended to take advantage of the pool she would have accepted the services of a guide. The castello was a warren of rooms and corridors and even making her way to the dining room for breakfast she had got turned around twice, but she intended to head outside to explore the oak woods and maybe even the vineyards beyond.

As she made her way through the parkland heading towards the wooded area she saw the elderly gardener in the distance and waved cheerily at him as he waved back enthusiastically.

It was good to be outside. She might have escaped the luxury of the castello, but the thoughts in her head were less easy to escape. She speeded up, ignoring the jeering voice in her head that was playing on a loop… *You can run but you can't hide.*

She didn't slow until she reached the trees.

To her relief there was a definite pathway and she felt confident that she wouldn't get lost. The confidence began to ebb as the trees got denser and began to close in on her, but the path was still clear even though it was darker here, so she pushed on, breathing in the pungent scent of warm earth underfoot. Several times she imagined she heard rustling, and once a flicker of movement in the periphery of her vision but, peering through the branches, she saw nothing.

She was actually on the point of turning back when the trees began to thin and the path opened up into a small clearing. She let out a small cry of delight, and had crouched down to examine the tiny flowers that carpeted the floor when she heard a snap of twigs and a snuffling sound.

She froze, this time knowing it was definitely not her imagination. She wasn't alone.

'Is somebody there?' *What are you going to do if someone says yes?* that voice jeered again. *Run!*

She huffed out a laugh of sheer relief when out of the undergrowth a little pig appeared, furry and ginger with stripes down its back. Utterly charmed, she rose to her feet and approached it slowly so as not to frighten it. 'Hello there, little one, are you lost? Ooh, hello there as well,' she added, moving forward, her hand outstretched as three more of the cute creatures appeared, making little whining noises.

She reached into her pocket to find her phone, as she had to have a photo of these, when a loud grunting and squealing behind her made her jump. She almost dropped the phone as she spun around expecting to see more piglets.

She froze. This was not a cute creature, though it might once have been. She knew she was looking at the adult version, and a prickle of fear made the hairs on the nape of her neck stand on end. The tiny eyes gave it a mean look as it stared at her past its long, hard snout, and the piglets started squealing even louder. The parent—mother?—started forward, letting out another angry snorting noise.

Samuele was petrified. 'Do not run, Maya,' he said as quietly as he could, struggling with the image in his head of her being run down within seconds.

Maya was frozen to the spot.

'I can't.'

'Oh, *cara*, you can,' he insisted softly, cold sweat slicking his skin as he watched her poised like a gazelle about to run. 'Now, don't make any sudden noise but start to back away from her very slowly.'

She began to turn her head to look at him. 'No!' His voice dropped back to a low, soft, soothing monotone as he emphasised, 'Do not turn around or look at me, just keep moving backwards, perfect, perfect…very slowly…'

She clung to his voice like a lifeline, each calm yet emphatic syllable stopping her succumbing to total panic.

'Samuele…'

'You will be fine, I promise. I won't let anything happen to you, but be careful and do *not* fall over.' He had seen the damage a female wild boar could do in defence of her young; she might lack the tusks of the male, but she was fast and those teeth could inflict some wicked wounds. The idea of them tearing into Maya's flesh filled him with a fear that was visceral in its intensity.

One of the piglets rushed towards Maya and he clenched his teeth against a groan as the mother's angry squeals intensified—she was going to charge.

Without taking his eyes from the animal he reached down for the fallen branch his boot was balanced on.

'Maya.'

She was shaking, her chalk-white pale face dotted with beads of cold sweat. Being paralyzed with fear had taken on an entirely new meaning.

'Can you hear me?'

'Yes,' she whispered.

'You are going to do what I tell you, when I tell you and not before…do you understand?'

She nodded. 'Yes.'

'Good girl. There is a track behind you and to the left—it goes uphill. I want you to run, but not until I say. Run and don't look back, don't stop until you reach the observatory.'

'The what?'

'You will know when you're there.'

'What about you?'

'I will be fine if you do what I ask you to.' The rustle as he tightened his hand over the branch turned the boar's mean red eyes his way, and she began to move away from Maya. 'That's it, come over here, Mama Boar. Now get ready, Maya.' He lifted the branch and banged the ground, yelling like a banshee, the infuriated animal charged and he shouted, 'Now, Maya! Run, *cara*, run!' He waited just long enough to see that she had taken off before he hit the ground running, still yelling as he did so.

There was no way he could outrun an enraged boar who, despite her bulk, could really move, and he knew that his only chance was getting high enough up…once he was sure that Maya was far enough away from those teeth.

Maya ran, her heart pumping, self-preservation giving her feet wings as she ran, instinct rather than a recollection of his instructions putting her on the right path. Panting tears sliding down her cheeks, she ran on uphill, stumbling over roots but knowing that she could not fall… She barely noticed when a stray overhanging branch delivered a glancing blow to her cheek. More tears blurred her vision as she refused to look back—*don't look back, and don't fall.*

Her lungs felt as though they would burst when the trees cleared quite abruptly and she saw her goal. The small, square stone building with the domed roof of glass was an incongruous sight, but she wasn't asking why it was there. She was only focused on the sanctuary offered by the metal-banded doors, thinking… *Not locked, please, not locked!*

It wasn't.

One side of the double doors opened without any effort on her part as she slipped inside the sanctuary and closed it fast behind her. She leaned against it, eyes closed and shaking with reaction, her laboured breathing gradually slowing.

Oh, God… Samuele!

Her eyes flew wide and she turned and pushed the doors she had just closed open again. She was sobbing again, loudly, but she didn't hear as she was seeing him banging the ground with his stick, deliberately drawing the vicious animal to him... She had left him, deserted him, *abandoned* him; she was *that* person, the person she despised.

If he was harmed she would never forgive herself.

Self-disgust settled over her like a black cloud as she waited, her eyes trained on the woods, alert to any sign of sound or movement. If he was hurt or worse it was on her.

He could be lying out there slashed and bleeding, needing help. She became so convinced by the lurid images in her head that she had just made the decision to go out and find him when he appeared.

She didn't immediately see him, just a movement in the periphery of her vision. She had been willing him to appear, but he came from a totally different direction.

The relief was so intense she thought she was going to faint, then she realised the faintness was probably associated with the fact she was hyperventilating.

Consciously slowing her breathing, she took a step towards him.

'You're not dead!' Even as she spoke it crossed her mind that she had never seen anyone look more alive. His eyes were burning bright, the glitter in them almost incandescent, though one leg of his trousers was ripped from the ankle almost to the thigh, revealing olive-tanned hair-roughened skin and long slabs of muscle.

There were scratches on his face, some oozing blood, but he looked totally relaxed as he drew level with her and he wasn't even breathing hard. It struck her that he looked more dangerous than the boar.

A danger that anyone with a pinch of sense would run away from, but his hands lay heavy on her shoulders and she couldn't have run even if she had wanted to, which she didn't.

'Dead?' He laughed and shook his head. 'The *cinghiale* rarely kill but they can cause some serious damage and ugly scars. Some hunters say boars are more dangerous than bears, though we don't have any of those here.' His white grin appeared. 'Just wolves.'

He was giving her a natural history lesson! She had been half out of her mind and he was telling her it wasn't so very bad...*cinghiale*... why was that Italian word ringing bells?

Sam's eyes moved swiftly across her face, noting the bruise developing on her cheek, his jaw quivering as he felt a twisting sensation in his chest, a tenderness that he was reluctant to name.

'You did good,' he said roughly, releasing her.

'I did,' she agreed breathlessly.

Her eyes widened, and she stood there visibly trembling as he reached out again. She stayed statue-still, her eyes connected with his, swaying slightly as his fingers pushed into her hair, lightly grazing her scalp.

He felt her shiver and watched the pupils of her eyes dilate, the longing in her eyes… It was hard to not see danger when it was literally staring you in the face.

It was just seeing her here safe and sound, the relief, the elation after the not knowing, the nightmare scenarios that had been going through his head while, *Madre di Dios*, he'd been trapped up a tree until that damned boar had finally given up the hunt.

They were all good reasons for the way he was feeling but not excuses… Control…he needed control.

'Got it! Did you leave any forest out there?' he asked, opening his hand to reveal the twig he'd gently pulled out of her hair before he dropped it and ground it underfoot, his eyelashes lowering to hide the burning desire in his eyes.

The anticlimax was as shocking as a slap, and the subsequent mood change as dramatic as it was intense. She wanted to cry again, and she could actually feel the tears pressing at the backs of her eyes. You're in shock, she told herself, glad to put a name to the roller coaster of emotions and her heightened mood.

'You found it, then.'

He was looking past her, and she turned her head, not even pretending an interest as her glance moved through the open doors of the observatory to the interior. She was seeing the cedar-lined walls within for the first time, hung round with bookcases and with a sumptuous day bed just to the right of the spiral staircase. From where they stood, she could see just make out the glass dome above the telescope set in a mezzanine observation platform.

'My grandfather was a stargazer. Actually, he was quite a well-respected amateur astronomer, so he restored the observatory and—'

'You enjoyed it, didn't you?' Maya interrupted ruthlessly. She could feel the emotions building up inside her, feel the pounding in her temples like a hammer hitting a crumbling wall…each thud destroying more of the mortar and her self-control.

He recognised the antagonism shining in her eyes, but he didn't really understand it. He hadn't exactly enjoyed the heart-pumping run here, seeing as every step had been burdened by the *not knowing*, the fear eating away at him that she might have been hurt. Every second he'd had to spend up that damn tree not knowing if she was all right had felt like a century, so when he'd seen her standing there unharmed it had felt like... He actually had nothing to compare the feeling to, it was way more complex than anything he could imagine, but perhaps akin to the sheer elation you felt when you emerged from the icy water after wild swimming.

'Well, it's always good to get the better of a boar,' he responded calmly, sticking to facts, not feelings. 'The thing to remember is you can't outrun them, so don't try. Your best bet is to climb a tree. I did,' he admitted, working on the theory that while he was talking he couldn't be kissing her, and he wanted to, he really wanted to... He needed to taste her, and the greedy need was hampering his ability to frame coherent sentences. 'They are incredibly destructive beasts. They cause total havoc. Last year they took over a thousand gallons of grapes and it's virtually impossible to keep them out. We put down miles of electric fences around the vineyards but they just jump them, and I'd take the tusks of a male over the protective instincts of a female any day.'

'You think I want a natural history lesson?'

He bent in, struggling to catch her quiet words, but a second later he was leaning back out again, because he had no problem hearing the next thing she said—they probably heard her in the village five miles away.

'You were enjoying yourself beating the piglets in some macho game while I,' she shouted, stabbing a straight finger hard into his chest, 'I,' she repeated with another stab into his muscular chest, 'I thought you were dead!' she shrieked. 'And it was my fault.'

The fight left her without warning; her legs sagged and she would have slid to the floor had the arm wrapped around her ribs not taken the weight. She looked up at him through the overflow of luminous tears that started to seep out from the corners of her eyes.

'You're crying…' Samuele really didn't know how to deal with the protective surge he felt as he watched the tears silently slide down her cheeks.

'No, I'm not,' she denied fiercely, as though he had insulted her by caring.

Fine, he thought, adopting a heart-of-stone expression, although it was incredibly hard when she looked so fragile...so sexy. 'You're in shock.'

Maya wanted to lash back and tell him he had no idea what she was feeling, only neither did she.

The beginnings of a bewildered frown froze in place as he reached out and cupped her face, his fingers cool on her skin. His expression was fierce his concentration total as he followed the path of his thumb as he slid it across the red mark that stood out against the smooth skin of her cheek.

'Sorry,' he said, clearly misinterpreting her shiver. 'You were very stupid—'

She could not in all honesty deny this.

'And very, very brave...' He brought his face in close, his nose grazing hers, his breath warm on her cheek. 'You are driving me totally crazy, you know,' he rasped, ignoring the voice in his head that told him he was finally losing control of the situation, losing control of himself.

Why bother fighting? said that wicked voice of temptation in his head. *Just relax, enjoy it while you can...*

His face was so close Maya couldn't focus, so she closed her eyes and felt his lips against her eyelids.

'Look at me!'

She responded to the fierce command at the

same moment he settled his mouth on hers, the sensuous pressure drawing a whimper from her throat, then, when his tongue slid across the outline of her lips, she grabbed hold of his shirt in handfuls just to stop from sliding to the ground. His lips were cool but she could feel the primal heat coming off him in waves, smell the musky scent of arousal.

Shocked by the fist of need in her belly and the surge of desire that was tangled in with a mess of emotions, she reached up instinctively, her arms curling around his neck, pulling him down to her while arching upwards, wanting... wanting more... Reacting with a fierce little gasp of shock to the very explicit proof of his arousal as she felt the imprint of his erection grinding into her belly.

She was plastered against him, but then with no warning at all the sensual connection was broken and the heat was gone as he physically put her away from him, the only warmth his big hands that still spanned her waist.

'You understand that this is just sex, right, Maya?' He'd never slept with a woman where the warning had been needed, because they'd always understood the game; he'd never needed to hear the words to give himself permission to continue, either. It was just sex, he reiterated to himself, panic bolting through him as he imagined her saying no to his question, because she wanted more from him. Because he couldn't give her more.

The more she totally deserves, taunted the voice of guilt pricking at his conscience.

His eyes were dark and smoky, his skin when she placed a hand flat on his chest was hot too… This was not a rejection, she understood that; it was just him laying out the rules before they started.

As she had never had sex before, she doubted she would notice the difference between that and…anything more. *Just sex,* he'd called it. But it wasn't as though she'd asked him for more, was it?

Not as if she deserved more!

Not as if she deserved love.

No wonder your biological mother rejected you…

'What is it?' he asked, watching the expressions flicker across her lovely face and feeling a rush of protective emotion that was so intense he felt as though someone had reached inside his chest and squeezed his heart.

She shook her head and smiled, feeling suddenly liberated. She would *not* allow Edward to spoil this moment or any other moment for her. She was not a child any longer with no self-esteem and Samuele was not trying to diminish her, he was only being honest.

'I was just remembering something someone used to say to me.'

Her stepfather had been so clever at locating a weak spot and exploiting it. He'd clawed at the one tiny shadow inside her heart that still grieved because she'd been abandoned by her own mother, and by the time he'd finished with her, she had carried an echo of that fear into adulthood. It had prevented her having any intimate relationships because she was afraid of being rejected, for being made to feel like that little girl who didn't deserve love.

'I will make you forget him, *cara*.'

She smiled. 'I've already forgotten. I want you, Samuele, you are exactly what I need right now.'

A low growl was released from his throat as the last shreds of control he had placed himself under snapped.

It felt as though she were being swept away by a fast-flowing river as his mouth came crashing down on hers; his grip on her waist tightened as he lifted her up against his tense, hard length. Not thinking through her actions, because she was deep in instinct territory now, she wound her arms around his neck, sinking her fingers into the hair on his nape and kissing him back hard as her legs wrapped tightly around his waist to hold herself there.

He broke off the kiss long enough to give a fierce grin as he slid his hands beneath her bottom and they stumbled the few steps to the stone building.

On the receiving end of Samuele's deep, drugging, sense-shredding kisses, she barely registered him kicking the door closed behind them, but she knew that they were alone and common sense, along with the rest of the world, was locked outside.

Samuele pushed aside all the plump scatter cushions on the day bed with one sweep of his hand. He sat down on the upholstered edge and Maya, with her legs still around his waist, landed sitting on his lap.

Her head had slid to his shoulder and he hooked a thumb beneath her chin and tilted her face up to his. He could see that her eyes were big and unfocused, the velvety pansy-brown glazed with passion.

With an almost feral groan he kissed her hard, lowering her back onto the day bed, which was wide enough to accommodate them both side by side, but he fell on top of her, a knee braced either side of her body. He pulled himself up just far enough to free his shirt from his jeans and fumbled with the belt. Clenching his teeth with frustration at the delay, he tore at the buttons on his shirt, before tugging at his zip, giving only partial relief from the painful constriction.

Maya placed her hand flat against the ridges of his belly. Simultaneously shocked and excited by the hardness and heat of his skin, she grabbed the loose ends of his belt and tugged. He resisted, drawing a cry of protest from her aching throat that faded into a whimper as he took the edges of the long-sleeved T-shirt she wore and pulled it over her head.

She didn't have the strength or the will to move her hands, so they still lay splayed above her head in an attitude of submission. Her breath, coming as a series of uneven shallow gasps, snagged on a moan as he slid the straps of her bra over her shoulders, massaging and kissing the skin stretched across the angle of her collarbones before he traced a moist path down the valley between her breasts with his tongue.

He lifted himself off her just enough to fight his way clear of his shirt, and she came up on her knees to help him, kissing his chest as it was revealed, tasting the salt in his sweat as she slid her hands over his golden skin.

Her bra of tartan satin followed his abandoned shirt, sailing somewhere over her head as he threw it away.

'*Dio!*'

The peaks of her breasts hardened and tingled under his scrutiny. She arched at the first touch of his hand and fell back onto the day bed, gasping, at this, their first intimate, skin-to-skin contact. She twisted and squirmed against him as her small hands went to the half-open zip of his jeans. She struggled with it until he rolled away and, lifting his hips off the bed, peeled the jeans off along with his boxers. He snatched his wallet from his jeans pocket, before kicking his clothes away until they fell with a thud and clatter on the other side of the room.

Maya swung her legs over the side of the bed and unfastened her cotton pedal pushers. She stood up for a moment to pull them down over her hips and step out of them.

Turning, she reached up to find Samuele's hands curling around her upper arms, knowing as he found his eyes on her, devouring the abandoned look of her, that it was an image that would stay with him for ever. Her skin was like silk, her body as beautiful as her face, and he knew she was a perfect fit for him.

She *was* perfect and utterly oblivious to the fact, too. There was nothing feigned about her natural sensuality that made her every move provoking and exciting to Samuele.

She made him feel utterly insatiable… He drew her to him, greedy to touch her everywhere, feel her, explore the smooth softness of her slender, toned body, unable to imagine ever having enough of her.

Lying on top of him, Maya could feel the deep ripples of his muscles as she touched him, exploring the hard counters of his body. Surrendering to the urgency that was burning her up from the inside out, she revelled in the freedom he was giving her to express herself, the lack of any boundaries, as his hands and mouth were everywhere, drawing gasps and moans from her.

When he asked her what she liked she told him with breathless honesty.

'Everything…every part of you.'

His control broke and then she was beneath him, her legs parted, as he teased her with the pressure of his erection against her damp mound until finally he couldn't hold out any longer. Grabbing a packet from his wallet, he sheathed himself quickly and surged smoothly into her.

The pleasure that rushed through her as he entered her drew a deep moan of ecstasy from her lips. Gasping and trembling with an overload of feeling, she reached up and kissed him on his mouth before trailing her tongue along the damp corded skin of his throat.

Then it began in earnest, the slow delicious torment of his fluid, sensuous advance and retreat. The intimacy of being joined with him was like nothing she had imagined it could be; she could literally *feel* the thudding of his heart against her own. Having him inside her felt so incredibly *right*, and with each thrust he touched a part of her that no one had ever touched before, winding her tighter and tighter until she felt as if she were going to explode into a million stars.

She opened her eyes and saw the raw naked need in his eyes; it was like looking into a mirror and seeing exactly what she felt on someone else's face.

The sudden intensity of her release was shocking, like free falling without a parachute but with no impact, just waves and waves of bone-deep drowning pleasure that was better than even the most vivid of her dreams...

CHAPTER EIGHT

Maya slowly floated back down to earth. There was sound and light, and she could see an expanse of blue through the incredible domed glass ceiling.

What would it be like to just lie here with your lover and do nothing except make love under this roof of stars? Well, she didn't have a lover and she hadn't made love either. She'd just had sex, and now it was over.

He rolled away from her and as she looked at his sweat-slicked face through the veil of her lashes she could see that the distancing was not just physical.

Was it wrong to want to prolong the moment, hold on to the image of delicious warm intimacy for a little while longer, even if it wasn't real? Well, it was what she wanted, even though she knew a clean break would be less painful, so she closed her eyes and went for the masochistic option.

Not that she had any room for complaint. This was exactly what she had signed up for and she'd do it again in the blink of an eye.

As her breathing gradually slowed, she knew there was probably a *'You should have told me'* coming, but she wanted to both delay the moment…and stretch out this moment at the same time.

It said something about her day when discovering an observatory in the middle of a forest was the least surprising thing that had happened to her!

She turned her head and looked into the eyes of the most surprising thing. His expression was veiled, and it didn't alter even when she reached out and laid her hand on his chest, feeling the thud of his heart through her fingertips, still wanting to keep a connection, any connection, between them.

'I keep thinking, what if you hadn't been in the woods at exactly the moment that I stumbled across the boar?'

He looked at her sharply and gave a harsh laugh that faded quickly. 'Stumbled,' he echoed. 'You think it was a lucky coincidence or fate maybe?'

'Wasn't it?'

'No, it was not. It was because old Santino nearly gave himself a heart attack running to get help,' he said grimly. 'The only coincidence involved was him bumping into me first. He was totally desperate. He said you were going into the woods even though he had warned you about the boars, and explained how dangerous the females were when they had litters in this season, and how one boar had killed his dog last year.'

The gruesome details made her flinch. 'The *gardener*, Santino?'

'Yes, the gardener, Santino. How could you be so foolish, so arrogant, as to ignore his warning and put yourself in danger like that?' He'd been so angry, he'd intended to shake her when he found her; instead he'd made passionate love to her.

'But he doesn't speak much English and I... oh, God...*cinghiale*. He was warning me. I didn't understand. I just pretended to because he seemed so upset.' There was a slightly hysterical sound to her laughter, and she had to literally bite her tongue to stop it.

Beside her Samuele had gone very quiet; he had rolled onto his side, and now he lay propped on one elbow looking down at her. She refused to meet his eyes, because she knew exactly what was coming.

And it came, although his voice was not as

cold as she'd expected; it was totally neutral, which was somehow worse.

Samuele had to force himself to unclench the muscles in his jaw so he could speak. 'You know that can't happen again, Maya,' he said. Inside his head, he was thinking, *You knew it shouldn't have happened even once, Sam! Virgin, she'd been a virgin!* God, this was utter madness. He'd used the *'This is just sex'* line on her as though it were some sort of magic talisman that let him break his self-imposed rule about sleeping with her, and now look what had happened!

'Why didn't you tell me I was your first?'

Maya sighed, retracting the hand that had still been touching his hair-roughened thigh, and finally met his penetrating gaze. 'It wasn't relevant.' She felt him stiffen and saw the outrage flare in his eyes...which jolted her temper into life.

'It was *my* choice who I slept with first, Samuele. Mine. When, where and with whom, and I made my choice. I don't think I owe you any explanations, do I? Because, like you said, it was just sex and that happens to suit me perfectly.'

'I don't believe you,' he said flatly.

She saw no reason at all to give him the psychological advantage of being the one looking down on her, so she sat up in one fluid motion, with only her tangled dark curls to hide behind.

If things had been different she might have felt self-conscious about being naked, but ironically lovemaking with the patently enthusiastic Samuele had made her even more confident about her body, and anger, which she had fully embraced by now, was a very good antidote to shyness.

'Fine. So you were present for the most important moment of my life. Is that what you want me to say?' She rolled her eyes but didn't quite meet his—that would have required better acting skills than she possessed. She even delivered a laugh, hiding the truth inside a joke and a series of increasingly desperate lies. 'Look, maybe you think every woman you meet is looking for love, but me, I'm not. I'm actively avoiding it. I mean, why should you be the only one?'

Through the veil of her lashes she could see the jibe had found its mark, and she felt a stab of bleak satisfaction. 'Virtually everyone I have ever cared for, and even those I didn't, have abandoned me at some point in my life. Why would I set myself up for even more pain by falling in love?' she pointed out, embracing what she had never admitted to herself before and feeling weirdly liberated because of it. 'My own mother rejected me—*twice*, actually, when you think about it. She clearly never loved me, and neither did Violetta.' Sadness filled her face as she admitted quietly, 'My dad died when I was only a child and I was devastated because I loved him so much. My mum remarried and—well, let's just say you're certainly not the only person who's seen a parent make a terrible second marriage. What did love do for her? And while my sister Beatrice is happy now, she went through absolute hell to get there.

'*She* thinks love is a price worth paying, but *I* don't. My mum and dad were blissfully happy for a few short years but when he died, I think a part of her did too, and she ended up marrying a man on the rebound who was a total control freak. He tried and almost succeeded in isolating her from everyone who cared for her, and he practically ripped our family apart doing it.

'The truth is, I owe you a sincere debt of gratitude, Samuele.' She saw surprise move at the backs of his eyes and felt a stab of triumph. 'I thought that I couldn't have sex without a relationship, that it would feel cold and wrong. But it didn't, and it was incredible. So you have opened up a whole new world of possibilities for me.'

He isn't rejecting me—I'm rejecting him...

She repeated the confidence-enhancing mantra inside her head over and over. It didn't matter if it was true, because it was always about how it *looked* rather than how it actually *was*, and she looked totally confident as she surged gracefully to her feet. Displaying an almost balletic poise, she moved around the room, unhurriedly gathering her clothes.

It was hard to project dignity while you were untangling your bra from a lampshade, especially when you could feel a pair of jet-dark eyes following your every move, but Maya thought she pulled it off. Cool and businesslike might have been preferable, and she might well have said more than she'd intended to about her past, though the details of her big speech were already a bit of a blur. But what she *had* done was establish that she was *not* crushed by his declaration that he wouldn't sleep with her again. Because she was his equal. Actually, she decided, she was *better* than him.

Sam watched as she turned her back to him and he had a last flash of her small, high, coral-tipped breasts that had fitted so perfectly into his hands before she covered them with the tartan silk bra. Then she pushed her hair out of the way, drawing it over her shoulder to gain access to the fastening.

The Pre-Raphaelite mass of curls always

made him think of an old film… He remembered it being themed rather appropriately around a young woman with incredible hair who discovered her sexuality, a view and the Italian scenery all at the same time.

Well, Maya had certainly discovered her sexuality, he thought grimly, and now she was going to be exploring it with someone else. The image of these faceless recipients of her loving sensuality sent a knife thrust of something acidic that he *refused* to admit was pure, undiluted jealousy.

Recognising the source of the feeling in his gut when he imagined someone else pushing his face into her hair, breathing in the scent of her, of that someone feeling the brush of the silky cascade against his chest and belly, exciting nerve-endings into painful life, would be to admit to a vulnerability that he was unwilling to own.

Pushing away the images, he rose to his feet, watching the flexing of her shoulder blades cause a little ripple of delicately sculpted muscle under the surface of her creamy skin.

'I need to get back to Mattio now.' Maya tossed the information over her shoulder, feeling a stab of shame that he was her only reason for being here, and yet she'd so easily forgotten her responsibilities.

As the fastener clicked home and she was able to drop her arms, she turned to see him standing there stark naked. Her mood of defiant confidence slipped away as she stared, literally transfixed by the sight of him. There was not an ounce of surplus fat beneath his olive-toned skin to disguise the delineation of his athletic frame, the deep muscles on his long thighs, the powerful muscles of his broad shoulders and chest, and the washboard corrugation of his belly.

Things newly awoken inside her tightened and clenched. Who was she kidding? Samuele had not opened her up to a world of sensual possibility, he had just *spoilt* her for any other man! She couldn't even bear to contemplate the idea of another man touching her as intimately as he had…

'Mattio will be fine,' he said quietly. 'And you will be a celebrity once everyone knows what happened.'

The colour slid from her face. 'You're going to tell them?'

'You will, I would imagine.'

She stared at him. Why would she tell everyone she'd slept with Samuele?

'The bruise on your face is going to take some explaining if you don't tell them about the boar.'

She reached for her shirt then, crushing it to her front as she felt the wash of embarrassed colour rise up her neck. She would have died rather than admit the misunderstanding.

He watched her from under his lashes as he pulled his jeans up over his narrow hips, knowing the conclusion she'd just jumped to. Boast about sleeping with a virgin? Ignorance, in his mind, was no defence; he certainly wasn't going to expose his shame. It didn't matter which way you looked at it, he had the experience, and he'd made a move on her when she'd been at her most vulnerable, shocked and upset after almost being badly injured.

The terrible truth was that he would do it again in a heartbeat…and now he knew that Maya Monk could very quickly become his drug of choice, the only option was to go cold turkey. It disturbed him that for the first time in his life his contempt for his father, his despair for his brother, both locked into marriages that amounted to contractual humiliation, was now leavened with the smallest kernel of understanding. Not that Maya bore any resemblance to his toxic stepmother…but that only made her more dangerous to him, not less.

Having her under the same roof as him for several weeks might be a challenge, but maybe he deserved to suffer after what he'd done?

Keeping an emotional distance from her wasn't going to be painless either.

'I'll go first,' he said as she walked through the door ahead of him.

'Because you're big and male and I'm a weak little woman?' she jibed.

No, because I can't take looking at your delicious rear all the way back without wanting to have you up against the nearest tree. He shrugged. 'If you like.'

Even though he didn't turn around he must have sensed her hesitation as they approached the trees again. 'Don't worry, that family of boars have probably moved on,' he lied. In actuality he didn't have a clue if they had or not. He'd protect Maya even if he had to pick her up and run all the way back to the castello with her.

'No, it's not that. It's just…you saved my life and I didn't say thank you.'

He paused and looked back over his shoulder. 'I think you said thank you very nicely indeed. In fact, it was one of the nicest thank-yous I have ever received, *cara*.'

He winked at her, then watched the angry colour stain her cheeks. He turned away thinking, *Job done.* Having her angry with him was no bad thing. He resolutely ignored the hollow feeling in his stomach.

CHAPTER NINE

It was two weeks and the bruise on her cheek had almost faded. She had woken the next day to find she had a black eye and her face had gone through some lurid colour changes since then; now a light touch of concealer and you wouldn't know it was there.

If only other things that had happened that day had faded so easily...though a part of her didn't actually want them to. Samuele had been right: her encounter with the wild boars had made her a bit of a local celebrity.

She had a lot of sympathy and was repeatedly told how lucky she was. It seemed everyone had a story of someone who hadn't been as lucky: the hiker who had nearly lost an eye and had been massively disfigured; the farmhand who had fallen and been trampled coming out of his encounter with several broken ribs and a smashed leg...he still walked with a limp, she was told darkly.

Maya had made a point of going out to the gardens to search out the gardener and offer her thanks and apologies. She took Rosa with her to translate and showed Santino the app on her phone she would use to translate for herself in future.

She stayed and won a friend by asking about the gardens that he and his team kept so beautifully, and he was eager to tell her about the years when he had been the only one left to tend them and how it had simply broken his heart to see the historically important landscapes being taken over by Mother Nature.

'Now,' he proudly explained, 'I have every resource I ask for and a team.' He spoke at length about last summer and the massive party with famous people and the filmmaker who had wanted to make a documentary about the gardens. 'The son,' he finished, cryptically tapping his nose. 'He is nothing like the father...'

It was the first time she'd heard this opinion actually voiced, but it was implied in so many other conversations she had had. Samuele was more than simply well regarded; he was flatout adored by the people of the estate.

She wondered what the high-flying financiers in their smart suits—not that any of them filled out a suit like Samuele—would make of the man she had seen last week?

Her thoughts drifted back to her solo walk she'd fitted into her daily routine, which no longer involved intimate dinners with Samuele. Sometimes Rosa, who had become her official helper with Mattio, stayed to eat with her, which involved far less tension.

Maya's walk that particular morning last week had taken her past the stables. She was a bit nervous of horses, or at least the height they were from the ground, so she had been far enough away to stay unseen, or at least that was what she had thought until that final moment when Samuele had turned and looked directly at her. To her eternal shame she had ducked down behind a hedge, a bit like a child who covered his eyes and thought no one could see him.

Only she wasn't a child and she had sat there and sworn under her breath, waiting for her humiliation to be complete when he came over—but he hadn't.

While it had lasted, the show she'd seen had been quite a masterclass in horsemanship; if anyone had filmed it on their phone it would have gone viral in hours!

How could it not? It had everything: a tall, gorgeously handsome man radiating authority standing there, seemingly oblivious to the

slashing hooves of the young horse he was trying to tame.

Maya's initial gut-chilling fear had given way
to fascination as she'd watched him. It had been
like a ballet really, the horse advancing and re-
treating and Samuele standing there completely
unfazed, radiating the sort of confidence that
you couldn't learn or fake or buy, and gradually, almost by osmosis, it had seemed to infil-
trate the animal's panic.

She hadn't been the only one watching the
show, the fence had been lined with stable
hands who had seemed as fascinated as she'd
been.

Samuele hadn't appeared to *do* anything except talk softly. Nothing had happened fast but
by imperceptible inches he'd won the horse's
trust until he was able to stroke his silky face,
after which he'd trotted around the exercise ring
quite happily.

That was when he'd turned and looked at
her; that was when she should have walked
calmly over to him and said something bland,
talked about the weather, anything but what
she'd done.

She still cringed when she thought about
what she must have looked like.

Would he comment on it this morning? she
wondered, gathering up the folder containing

the nannies' CVs and sticking it into her shoulder bag. She assumed that that was why he had requested her presence this morning, via email, which had been the form of communication he had favoured since they'd had their...sexual collision. It was how she'd decided to think of it, like a traffic accident that had happened because you hadn't been paying attention to the road, or because you'd allowed yourself to think about something else instead, like him, standing naked in front of you... Which wasn't going to happen today, she told herself firmly.

It would be their first meeting that wasn't accidental in two weeks. They'd occasionally passed one another in one or other of the maze of corridors and once she had been going into the magnificent leisure suite when he'd been coming out, his hair wet... She'd felt dizzy for quite a while after that. A few minutes earlier and she would have seen him sleek and semi-naked in the pool, maybe even joined him there...? Then who knew what might have happened? Her vivid imagination had supplied several possibilities in glorious Technicolor.

She had not ventured back there since.

Their paths had almost crossed a few times when he'd come to see Mattio, but each time he had she'd been taking her walk and Rosa had been in charge. The girl had given her chapter and verse of how good he was with the baby and how interested he was in Mattio's progress.

Maya couldn't decide what was worse: the possibility he was avoiding her, or he'd forgotten she existed and moved on.

Another one of his personal secretaries, the woman, appeared as Maya approached the office door. Maya suspected that being psychic was probably a required qualification for working closely for Samuele—that and an inbuilt immunity to his intellect-dampening aura of raw masculinity.

That disqualified her on both counts. She was almost as miscast as an employee as she was a lover, even though technically she wasn't either. She'd just been a steamy one-afternoon stand for him, and, far from feeling as if she worked for him, she was actually treated more like a guest by everyone she encountered here. Everyone except the boss, who acted as though she were invisible. Yes, it suited her too, but she didn't have to be happy about it, did she?

'Just give him a minute and then go right in.'

She probably hadn't meant it literally, but Maya got her phone out to time it anyway, and saw she had a missed call from Beatrice. She felt a pang of guilt.

Beatrice and her mum knew she was in Italy but not where or why. When she'd initially told her sister her destination, Bea had immediately concluded that Maya was there in connection with the embryonic design business that had once been their joint project.

'Oh, so that supplier you were talking about, they lowered the costs, did they? That's marvellous! The samples you sent me, the colours of that wool are just perfect. The offer of the start-up money still stands, you know, it's not charity. Dante and I, we believe in you.'

The opportunity had been there for Maya to put her right, but she'd been afraid that if she started talking about Samuele and Mattio and Violetta, it would all spill out, and then the moment had passed. She had allowed the misunderstanding to go on, and the longer it had lasted the more difficult the idea of coming clean had become, and now it weighed heavily on her conscience. She would tell Bea and Mum soon, but it seemed easiest to wait until she could explain the situation in person.

Then perhaps they could explain it to me, she thought. Because when she lay awake at night wondering how she'd got herself into this situation, the answer was no more clear-cut than her feelings for Samuele were.

She was sitting with her back to him and the doorway, unaware of his presence as she slid her phone back into the big leather bag with a file sticking out that she wore slung over her shoulder.

Samuele couldn't see her face, but he'd spotted the tension in her narrow back and he found himself wondering about the person on the other end of the line who had put it there.

'Good morning, Maya.'

She got to her feet as though shot and spun around, her colour-clash statement relatively sedate today. She had on an acid-green shirt tucked into a pair of black pedal pushers, and she wore flat black pumps embellished with embroidery on her narrow feet. Her glorious hair was confined at the nape of her slender neck by a leather lace.

Samuele could almost see the boundaries that he had spent the last two weeks constructing dissolve. In his mind he was immediately unfastening the tie and spreading out her hair down her back—which in this fantasy was naked.

She was naked quite a lot in his mind. Actually, she was in his mind far too much, full stop.

'H-hello,' she stammered out. 'She said to come in but I…wasn't sure.'

He had not been sure either, but he was now.

You did not need to have second sight to see what was coming down the line. Violetta was already hinting—*taunting* might be more accurate—the fact that she felt she held the winning card. But her inability to resist turning the knife in his back had actually worked in his favour this time.

He had given himself time to stall by paying her latest thinly disguised blackmail demand, but he had no illusions that it would be the last one. And when she got bored with taking money off him, she would move in for the kill.

It was not really about money or maternal feelings for Violetta; it was all about revenge and power plays.

The money didn't matter to him, but Mattio did, and he was prepared to go to any length to fulfill his promise to his brother—including marriage.

He'd sworn to Cristiano that he would always do what was best for Mattio, and he was ashamed that he'd been willing to deprive the baby of the sort of mother he deserved just because Samuele hadn't looked beyond his own fears of becoming like his father or brother.

But he wasn't either of them, and he could see now that it had been ridiculous to compare his situation with theirs. For starters, poor Cristiano had not been able to see a single fault in his toxic bride and his deluded father's obsession had made him similarly blinkered. While *he* was perfectly aware of Maya's flaws—it was hard not to be when she was the most challenging female he had ever met!—he was certain she would make the best mother to Mattio, and the fact that there was already a blood tie between the two could be an important factor in securing her agreement to his plan.

'Do you want to come through…?'

Maya's heart flipped at the sound of his voice, but before she could respond he was already moving towards the door, taking her agreement as a given. And who could blame him? She hadn't been resisting much of late; maybe once a people-pleaser, always a people-pleaser.

Taking a deep breath, and hating the idea she might be a pushover, she clutched her bag containing the folder and followed him through to his inner sanctum.

As with three quarters of the sprawling castle, this was a room she had never entered—it was probably the first and last time.

She hadn't been sure what to expect, but it was actually pretty modern and utilitarian, dominated by a massive desk with several computer screens. One wall was book-lined, and there was a stack of free weights on a purpose-built stand. She pushed away the mental picture of a sweaty Samuele taking a break from the stress of moving around billions by stretching his muscles to the limit, and focused on the only decorative touch, which was a black and white framed drawing of the castello.

He saw her looking at it. 'The artist is disputed but it shows the place before the more contemporary additions, as in sixteenth-century contemporary.'

'It's very striking.'

He had moved to stand in front of the full-length window, and she tried hard not to sigh wistfully. He was wearing a beautifully tailored dark suit, making him looking formal, exclusive, distant and quite incredibly gorgeous.

'Th… This is a very nice room…'

He cut across her stuttering opening and nodded to one of the leather chairs set on the opposite side of the desk from him. 'Have a seat.' He took his own seat behind the massive desk, which occupied a large section of the pretty large room.

Right…so far, so formal—very formal, Maya thought uncertainly, feeling as though she had been sent to the headmaster's office, though the analogy had some major flaws.

She had never felt this sexually wound up in her school days or for that matter her adult days until the day she'd met Samuele. In her head, her life was pretty much divided into the pre- and post-Samuele days, and now his presence and the knock-on effects seemed to have altered every aspect of herself.

She kept pushing away the intense feelings he aroused in her, but they just kept pushing right back. It felt like an emotional tug of war and, as much as she might call for a referee's intervention, she had already been pulled well and truly over that red line, she thought with a despairing surge of self-realisation.

Well, it was done now; she had finally allowed herself to care enough for someone and had been rejected...and she'd survived the experience. Well, for an entire fortnight she had... She took a deep, steadying breath. See, she was still breathing so it wasn't terminal! So long as he *never* discovered that she lay in bed every night *longing* for him, she could cope.

At a distance he'd sent her nervous system into meltdown; this close to him there was no possibility she could pretend, to herself at least. But although she might have lost the ability to lie to herself, she could still fake it with the best of them in front of him.

'Would you like coffee?'

'No.' She took out the file and put it on his desk. 'I've made some notes,' she offered.

He looked at her blankly.

'The applications for the nanny,' she said,

all business. 'Your message didn't say, but I assumed this was what we were going to discuss?'

'Ah, yes… I thought I might go and see Mattio later, take him for walk maybe?'

'It's Rosa's afternoon off, I'm afraid,' she said, unable to resist the dig.

Did he get it or had she been too subtle? It was hard to tell. The planes and angles of his face were designed to be inscrutable, though on anyone else she would have called the dark bands along the slashing angles of his cheekbones a blush.

'You could come too.'

'Come where?' She regarded him warily, thinking that this encounter was all as tense and awkward as she'd imagined. Maybe he was working up to some sarcastic remark about her ducking out of sight at the stables the other week?

'You like the rose gardens, I understand.'

Understand…understand from who? 'What, have you got a spy network watching my every move?' She was only half joking. 'Fine, you really don't have to ask my permission to take Mattio for a walk. Tomorrow?' She raised a cool brow. The significance of his suit, beside the fact it made him look even more exclusive and unattainable, had not been lost on her.

'I've obviously caught you on your way to…'

It could have been just about any place; he seemed to commute to many of the world's capitals the way some people took a bus to the next town, only for him it was a private jet.

'I just got back actually.' Samuele reached for his tie, loosening the constriction at his neck. 'I'd like to know how you think Mattio is getting on. If there are any changes you think should be made…any improvements…?'

He was delaying bringing up the real reason he wanted to talk to her, and he knew it. Finding the right words was not something that he normally struggled with but, in his defence, these particular words were of the life-changing variety. 'Is there anything you need?'

'Wouldn't that be something better discussed with the new nanny? There are some very good candidates here, several with rave reviews.' She was glad, of course, she told herself fiercely, that Mattio would be in the care of someone who came highly recommended by satisfied previous parents, who knew a lot more about child development than she did. She'd always known she had been a brief stopgap in a desperate situation, but the knowledge that her time left with Mattio was coming to a swift end felt like a heavy weight pressing on her chest.

'I have…a…' He paused and dragged a hand

down his cleanly shaven cheek before clenching his long fingers into a fist. It was so unlike his normal cool, articulate self that she stared. Perhaps his thoughts were still on whatever high-powered business had taken him away from home this time.

The tension in the room was almost a physical presence; suddenly she couldn't stand it any more and surged to her feet.

'Look, shall I come back if you're...busy,' she hastily substituted, thinking *distracted* was nearer the mark.

He watched silently as she turned and moved towards the door, offering no opinion on what she'd just said... She stopped and swung back, the feelings that she had been suppressing suddenly bubbling to the surface and spilling out into hasty speech.

'Look, I *know* it was just meaningless sex and I *know* that it's not going to happen again, so treating me with simple basic *civility* is not going to raise my expectations for a repeat performance.' Her dark angry eyes raked his face. 'Are you *punishing* me for sleeping with you by ignoring me? I wasn't stalking you the other morning, you know—I was just passing by. How was I to know you were some sort of horse whisperer? Oh, God!' She finally ran out of breath but not nearly soon enough.

Her horror-filled eyes met his momentarily before she squeezed them closed, and with nothing to duck down behind this time, she covered her face with her hands instead.

She kept them there as his hands on her shoulders guided her back to the chair and then pushed her into it again.

'It was the best meaningless sex I have ever had—*you* were the best meaningless sex I have ever had.' Maybe meaningless sex was all he was capable of, Samuele thought bleakly. Not that he envied his father or his brother, but at least they had been capable of feeling a deep unselfish love for someone else, even if it had been based on lies.

Her hands fell away. 'Am I meant to be flattered—?' She broke off when she registered the expression on his face.

His eyes were filled with emotions too intense and complex for her to even begin to guess the cause and his grin lacked its normal voltage.

'I could have phrased that better,' he admitted, but that was clearly as much as he was prepared to admit.

'It's always nice to be good at something. I could put it on my next CV. Good with children and great at meaningless sex...'

He didn't smile, but then she didn't smile either; it had been a very bad joke.

The look in his eyes was really worrying her—he'd probably reject her concern, but what the hell? 'What's wrong?'

She didn't really expect a response to her blunt question, not one so unambiguous, or immediate, or sad.

'It would have been my brother's twenty-ninth birthday today.'

The last vestiges of her animosity and resentment shrivelled away and her tender heart ached with empathy for the pain etched on his face.

'Hearing people here talk about him, he sounded as if he was a good person.'

He nodded. 'He would have been a wonderful father and I think he would think you are acting like a wonderful mother—'

Was this his subtle way of saying she had overstepped her authority?

'I know I'm not Mattio's mother.'

'You're more of a mother to him than the one he's had,' he pushed out in a bitter voice. 'I've never previously thought that a mother figure was essential for a child's well-being and development, but I think I was wrong.'

'You're not going to give him back to Violetta!' she cried in horror. 'I know that legally she is his mother but—'

'No, I'm not letting him go back to Violetta,' he promised, the metallic glint in his eyes as hard as his voice.

Some of the tension left her shoulders but Maya, who had surged to her feet, stayed standing. Samuele moved around the desk and sat on the edge facing her, now at eye level, his long legs stretched out in front of him.

'And apparently, we are to expect a wedding invitation from her soon.'

'So what does that mean? Do you think that she'll try to take Mattio back?'

'I would say that's inevitable.'

'But she doesn't love him!'

'You know how convincing she can be, Maya.'

Her eyes fell as she remembered how easily her half-sister had fooled her. 'Oh, God! But this Charlie she's marrying…didn't you say he doesn't want children?' she cried, clinging to this straw of hope, not wanting to contemplate Mattio being caught up in a toxic tug of war.

'I have no doubt that before long Charlie will do anything she asks just to keep her happy. It's what Cristiano did.'

'But she'll abandon Mattio again! And this time, you might not find him.' Her face creased in anguish at the thought. 'You *can't* let her do that to him,' she declared fiercely.

'I have no intention of allowing her to do that. I intend to make a full custody claim. In the meantime I will keep paying up just to keep her quiet. It's better for now if she thinks she is winning.'

'Paying up?' Comprehension hit her. 'She is *blackmailing* you?'

He shrugged and gave a dry smile. 'Very carefully worded blackmail, but essentially yes.'

'But isn't her Charlie disgustingly rich…?'

'It's not about the money for Violetta—this is about her wreaking revenge on me for thwarting her claim to half the Agosti estate. And it's about power. Remember, she does hold a trump card, actually more than one. You said it to me yourself back at your flat, didn't you? Any court will initially favour a mother over other family members, and Mattio needs a mother in his life at least for the early years.'

She fixed him with an unwavering gaze and wondered at what age he imagined that you *stopped* needing your mother.

'The obvious solution is for me to marry.'

'So have you changed your mind about marriage?' she asked, taken aback.

'Not about marriage as an institution, no, but about being married, yes.'

'Is there a difference?'

'I think if *true love*,' he drawled contemptuously, '*really* existed, then marriage would be redundant. Two people wouldn't need a legal framework to trap them together.'

'Trap…?'

'Oh, I know divorce is relatively simple nowadays, but so many hang on in there when it's obvious it's beyond hope of saving. Marriage is just a contract, not some sort of magical spell that grants eternal happiness and joy. If it's drawn up with both parties' interests in mind, the duration of the contract is flexible and there are no unreasonable expectations like monogamy, then I see no reason why it couldn't be successful.'

'Successful maybe, but it's not really marriage, is it?' This cold-blooded description horrified her.

'An open marriage.'

'So not really marriage at all, then! Because marriage is about faith, trust…' She couldn't bring herself to say *love* or even think the word while she was in the same room as Samuele.

'Marriage in this case is about securing the future security and happiness of my brother's child.'

'Of course, but—' Her thoughts skidded to an abrupt stop and she had to try and conceal a gasp of shock. She had been hanging onto a rock wall of denial by her fingernails for weeks and she'd finally lost her grip.

Not being able to say the word in a man's presence wasn't exactly one of the most recognised symptoms of being in love, but, nevertheless, she was.

She had fallen in love with a man who was capable of giving his love and loyalty to a child that carried the bloodline he was so proud of, and to the land that was his heritage. A man who thought marriage *might* work, but only if you took love out of the equation. There was no room in his life for a woman, no room for her.

She wasn't sure if it was a bitter laugh or a despairing sob that was locked in her throat, but it hurt as she remembered that she'd always believed *not* falling in love with the wrong man was a matter of choice. She marvelled now at her own arrogance and was suddenly deeply fearful for her future.

'So you see that I didn't ask you here to talk about nannies, because I am very much hoping that there will be no need for one.'

She had started shaking her head. 'You want me to stay on here until you've found a suitable wife?'

'I want you to stay on here—but as my wife.'

He watched her drop down into the chair she had recently vacated. Luckily it was still there, though he doubted she would have noticed if she'd landed on the floor.

'That is *insane*!' Her laugh was edged with hysteria. 'The only thing we have in common is Mattio.'

'Isn't that enough?' His shoulders lifted as his dark eyes moved over her face, lingering on the plump curve of her lips. 'But actually it's not true. We also have a similar sexual appetite, don't we? What we have, between us—that kind of chemistry is rare, *cara*, and exceptional sex is even rarer.' Two years of enjoying the pleasures of Maya's body and exhausting his hunger for her would surely compensate for any temporary loss of freedom.

Breathing hard by the time he finished speaking, Maya shook her head in an effort to free her mind from the spell of his smoky voice and the erotic images his words had evoked.

'Yes, we *do* have Mattio.' His delivery was now flat and cool. 'And he deserves the very best. You are the best for him, and there is the blood connection between you, which, given the circumstances, could be a significant factor.' He paused, his crazily long lashes veiling his eyes momentarily.

'I know he's the last bit of your brother you have left and the heir to—'

'He is the heir to the Agosti name,' Samuele cut in. 'And the responsibility that goes with it. But he is not Cristiano's child.'

The blood left her face and her heart went into high gear. She could hardly hear past the dull thud in her own chest; whatever she had expected to hear, this was definitely not it. 'What are you saying?' she whispered, her eyes trained on his face.

'That, unlike you, I have no blood connection with Mattio,' he said roughly, in a voice that cracked with the effort to keep it free of emotion.

'This is the thing that Violetta is blackmailing you about.'

He shrugged. 'It's her trump card.'

'How long have you known?'

'Cristiano told me before he died, when he asked me to keep Mattio safe, to take care of him.'

'Your brother knew that the baby wasn't his?' Her thoughts raced to process the flow of information.

'Violetta couldn't hide it—the dates made it utterly impossible. Cristiano told me he was out of the country for a significant amount of time when Mattio was conceived. If my brother had lived he would have been the child's father and that is all that mattered to him…'

Would he have been as big a man as his brother? It was a question Samuele had asked himself many times. How could any man know the answer until he was faced with the situation himself?

'Mattio *is* an Agosti, he *is* my heir and I will do anything it takes to keep him safe and keep my promise to my brother.'

Including marrying me.

'Who else knows about this?' she asked.

'I have told no one but you.'

His trust and giving her joint responsibility for the secret he had shared with her changed things in a way she could not put words to—it altered the dynamic between them.

Samuele trained his gaze on her face. 'I'm asking for two years of your life… You would still be young enough later to go on and have a family of your own,' he pointed out, conscious of an odd ache in his chest at the thought of her holding children she'd created with another man. 'There would, of course, be the option to extend that period should both parties be agreeable, and the golden handshake you'll receive at the termination of the marriage would obviously mean that you'd be able to maintain the living standards you'd have become accustomed to.'

'I don't give a damn about money!' she snapped. She wanted his love and he was offering her a soulless marriage.

He watched as she covered her face with her hands again and felt a tug of guilt.

'We have nothing in common... Look at this place,' she said, spreading her hands wide to encompass the room and everything beyond.

'We do. We both love Mattio.'

The response cut right through her defences and directly into her weakness. *Love...* She did love Mattio, but she loved Samuele too. Only what the heart wants the heart can't always have... *But isn't it better to enjoy what the heart can have while it lasts?* that insidious voice tempted.

Halfway through the internal dialogue she realised that she was actually considering it. Maybe he read the self-revelation on her face because he put his hand in his pocket and pulled out a small box.

He opened the box, flicking the catch up with his finger to reveal a velvet lining that was old and worn. Maya wasn't looking at the box, but the prize it contained, a prize that would be a great big fat lie on her finger.

'This was my grandmother's, with a few

greats added, who was Russian originally. I repurchased it quite recently.' Along with several other items with a similar Russian royal family provenance. He could already see in his mind's eye the emerald necklace in the stunning enamelled setting sitting comfortably between Maya's lovely breasts… The image came with a distracting rush of that mix of painful yet pleasurable heat.

With a tiny gasp she put her hand to her mouth, her big eyes going from the ring to his face and back again. Even he could see that the square-cut emerald surrounded with clusters of brilliant diamonds, set on a wide gold band etched with a scroll pattern and inlaid with yet more precious stones, was stunningly beautiful.

She shook her head.

'People often marry because there is a baby,' he pressed. 'The baby might not be ours, but is this situation so very different? The principle is the same, securing the welfare of a vulnerable child.'

Maya looked up at him, loving every line, every carved angle and patrician hollow of his face… She also loved Mattio and she knew her heart would break if she left him. She had so much love to give, so wasn't it genuinely better to give it even knowing that, in this case, it would never be returned?

It was as if all her secret dreams of love and her worst nightmares about abandonment had collided. She couldn't possibly see how this would end well for her, but Samuele was right about one thing: Mattio had to be protected.

Her hand shook as he slid the ring on her finger. It was a perfect fit.

'I have one stipulation. *I* don't think that monogamy is an unrealistic expectation.' She could stand many things, but that was the one betrayal that she knew would totally crush her.

There was a pause, then he said slowly, 'I think I can accommodate that.'

She immediately started tugging the ring off her finger. 'What are you doing?' he asked sharply.

'Taking it off. I can't walk round with a fortune on my finger. We can wait until things are official and I've told my family.' *Oh, God, my family!* she groaned inside.

'Things are already official, so I see no reason to wait. It is the formal opening of the Villa Agosti gallery in Florence in two weeks, so your first official role as my bride-to-be will be to act as hostess.'

'I'm not really a front-of-house sort of girl, Samuele. I am more backstage, prop moving, that sort of thing. I thought I'd just be doing nursery things.'

'You will be doing all the things that would be expected of my fiancée,' he said flatly.

The emphasis on *all* made her sensitive tummy muscles quiver. 'What,' she asked, her alarm shifting up a gear as he framed her face with his hands, 'are you doing?' Silly question—it was pretty obvious what he was doing.

The kiss was long and hard and depleted her of any final remnants of resistance. 'I am making it official,' he rasped throatily, before picking her up and sitting her on the desk, then slowly pushing her back until she lay there watching through half-closed eyes as he threw his tie across the room.

'What if someone comes in?' As resistance went it was pretty half-hearted.

'If you even notice, *cara*, I will be deeply insulted.'

Her breath quickened. 'You make a lot of assumptions...'

He gave a wolfish grin, oozing arrogance from every perfect pore as he planted a hand flat on the wooden surface either side of her face. 'I don't think it is an *assumption*—' she whimpered low in her throat as his scorching lips moved up the column of her neck '—to say that we definitely do not need a rule book in our bedroom.'

CHAPTER TEN

Maya smiled, and a low husky laugh vibrated in her throat as her fingers tangled in the dark hair of the man whose head lay nestled between her breasts in the bed she had shared with him for the last two weeks.

'What are you laughing at?'

'You… No, not really,' she added quickly. It was just she had never imagined that sex could involve humour.

The depth of the sharp soul-piercing tenderness she felt for Samuele was something she had never dreamt of either. As for the desperate raw passion he could awaken in her, she sometimes didn't even recognise herself in the woman she became in his arms.

His head lifted, his dark heavy-lidded eyes still slumbrous from their recent lovemaking.

'I just remembered you saying we didn't need a rule book in the bedroom.' She gave a languid sigh as he slid his way up her body until their faces were level.

'I remember that too.'

Samuele could count on one hand the times he had spent more than one night with the same woman, because the next night would have been much the same and, put quite simply, he had a low boredom threshold.

He had heard it suggested that he was attracted by the thrill of the hunt but in reality there rarely had been a hunt. He didn't make the mistake of putting that down to his own irresistibility; he believed women were attracted by what he represented to them, which was money, power and his supposedly glamorous lifestyle.

He looked at the lovely face inches from his own, no make-up, hair wild, flushed cheeks. No two nights were the same with Maya; her glorious lack of inhibition, her innate sensuality and the fact she gave everything of herself every single time they made love made her the sexiest woman he could ever have imagined.

He quite simply could not get enough of her. His idea of heaven was being stranded on a desert island and having her five times a day, but even that wouldn't be enough; where Maya was concerned, he'd discovered he was insatiable.

'You taste of me,' he said, dipping his tongue into the warmth of her mouth.

'You taste so good too,' she husked against his lips, meeting his tongue with her own.

Sometimes during moments like this Maya could hardly believe the level of intimacy between them, and how natural, how *right* it all felt.

'I should get up,' she said, not moving.

'You're still worried about tonight?'

Samuele felt a by now familiar surge of tenderness as she grimaced and gave a little shrug. Maya never went for the sympathy vote.

'Don't be, *cara*,' he said, pulling himself into a sitting position and dragging a hand through his tousled hair.

'Easy for you to say—you're used to being stared at.' *And lusted after,* she added silently as her eyes followed the liquid glide of perfectly formed muscles under golden skin as he stretched hugely.

'And you're not?' There was a lack of vanity and then there was blindness. 'You must know that you are an incredibly beautiful woman and you certainly don't dress to be invisible.' He sensed her stiffening and tagged on quickly, 'Which is good—I really like your sense of style.'

'I don't want my self-worth to be based on the way I look, Samuele, because looks fade.'

'I think you have a few years left yet,' he

teased, taking pleasure just from studying the delicate lines of her face. It was young and smooth now but, gifted with a bone structure like hers, experience and time would only enhance what she had.

She flashed him a quick glance from under her lashes before looking away and muttering, 'I was invisible once.'

His fingers, moving in a sensual sweep down her spine, stilled. 'Your stepfather?'

Astonished eyes flew to his face. 'How on earth did you know it was him?'

'A couple of things you've said.'

And he'd remembered? *Do not go there, Maya, do not start seeing what you want to see.* He's observant, that's all. A skill that had helped make him a respected name in the world of finance. Her Internet research had revealed that about him, also that the respect came tinged with a healthy dose of fear; he had a reputation for total ruthlessness.

He was certainly a ruthlessly efficient lover.

'Edward seemed nice, kind, caring before they were married, but afterwards he changed, at least when Mum wasn't around, towards me and Beatrice. I was so afraid of him—'

Beside her she could feel Samuele stiffen, and he swore and said something harsh in his mother tongue.

'No…no…' she said, laying a pacific hand against his heaving chest. 'There was nothing physical and it was only little things at first. Everything I did he mocked, like a birthday card I made for Mum once. He looked at it and laughed and threw it in the bin saying that I couldn't give her that sort of rubbish.'

Samuele's big strong hand came to cover hers, his fingers sliding in between hers. She smiled her gratitude; the warm pressure was comforting.

'He chipped away at my self-esteem until in the end I didn't have any, no confidence at all. He used to say the only thing I had going for me was a pretty face and when I started getting teenage acne he had an absolute field day!' She felt Samuele's fingers tighten around her own. 'I would dread him coming in and finding something about me to laugh at. I wanted so badly to be invisible and I eventually became a grey little mouse scared of her own shadow.

'I don't know what would have happened if it wasn't for Beatrice. She was tougher than me, and she gave as good as she got, so he didn't pick on her as much. Mum had it bad too. He wanted a child that was *his* child, and she went through cycle after cycle of IVF to try and please him. It affected her health terribly but he acted as if he was the injured party.

'Maybe that was when she started to see what he really was, and she began actually listening to what Bea and I told her, and believing us. I will always remember the expression on his face when he arrived home and she'd packed his bags.

'I saw a therapist.' She glanced at him to see how he took this. There were still some very outdated views out there about mental health.

'That's really good,' Samuele said, struggling to keep the burning anger that was consuming him from his voice at the picture she'd painted that he knew only hinted at the true extent of all she had suffered. The need to reach out and comfort her was alien to him and he wasn't quite sure what to do. 'Did it help?'

'It did help, yes, but Mum still tries to compensate. She feels guilty that she didn't see what he was doing. I hate that she and Bea still feel like that, as though I'm weak or fragile and they have to protect me.'

'So you became the unbreakable Maya Monk.' In her bold, bright colours and her hit-the-world-head-on attitude. But underneath all that armour, she was the little girl who had been the victim of a coercive, controlling bully.

She was, he decided, the strongest person he had ever met.

Maya blinked, realising with a sense of shock

just how much she had told him, more than she had ever admitted outside the therapist's office, probably more than she had admitted inside it too!

'I suppose I should get up,' she said, suddenly feeling shy and exposed…although *exposed* was a funny word to use when he had seen every little bit of her, loved every little bit of her.

It was moments like this, when everything felt perfect, that she often heard Edward's voice telling her she wasn't good enough, that she didn't deserve to be loved by anyone.

She listened and there was nothing.

She rolled back to Samuele and took his face between her hands. 'Thank you!' she said fiercely.

'For what?'

You made me believe that I'm worth loving.

There was a quizzical furrow in his brow as he studied her face and tried to interpret her silence. 'The gallery opening will be hard for you, won't it?'

'I'll be fine.'

He recognised her factory-setting response for what it was—a cover for the fact that she was not all right at all. He felt guilty for the times he had taken it at face value because it had suited him to do so.

'You'll be fine, I know, and I'll be there for you tonight. You won't be alone because I will be with you every step of the way. Oh, and if you *really* want to say thank you, I can think of several ways…'

She gave a sultry smile. 'So can I.'

'I haven't seen anyone older than nine years old literally press their nose to the window like that before.'

She sniffed and rubbed the fading mist from the window before settling back into her seat. 'I'm sure it's very *uncool* to be excited, but you know what?'

'You don't care,' he completed seamlessly.

'Not even a little bit. Florence may be your backyard but to me it's…' She mimicked one of his shrugs when words failed her.

'I don't take it for granted, though. Actually I *like* seeing the world through your eyes, though only occasionally. Otherwise I'd have given away all my possessions by now to a charity for donkeys.'

'It was a worthy cause and you shouldn't have been looking at my bank statement!'

'You left your laptop open on my desk.'

She gave a little snort and looked out of the window again. They had left the river and the cathedral behind when the car in front slowed. As they approached a building with a classical facade set back from the road behind an elaborate wall, Mattio stirred slightly, his sleepy brown eyes opening briefly before they closed again. They took a sharp right and drove through the archway into the private internal courtyard, and Maya straightened in her seat, bracing herself for the inevitable meet and greet.

'You'll be fine, *cara*, you have nothing to prove.'

Only she did, and he had to know it. He couldn't be that naive, could he? She was about to marry Samuele Agosti, not only the most handsome man on the planet, but also a legend in his own lifetime. The interest in their engagement wasn't just trending on social media, there were several column inches devoted to the upcoming marriage in all the serious financial journals.

She tried to focus on the pluses, which included the fact that Beatrice wouldn't be here tonight. She loved her sister dearly, but not the awkward questions she would inevitably ask.

Poor Beatrice's morning sickness had got worse, necessitating bed rest and an intravenous drip, so she had been admitted to hospital for a while. Back home now, she was being fiercely guarded by Dante and their mum.

Maya's mother was set to meet Samuele next week when she would fly out to spend a couple of weeks at the castello.

So all she had to do tonight was cope with the world's press, half of whom seemed to want to know up front *who* she would be wearing tonight.

The only thing that was stopping her running for the hills was the security of knowing that Samuele would be at her side. His support made all the difference to her.

As she slid out of the air-conditioned car into the fragrant afternoon warmth she knew her mind should have been on higher things than wondering which of the outfits she had brought with her to wear tonight. But first impressions counted, and photos that were taken tonight would be images the whole world would look at tomorrow and in the days and weeks to come.

Also her choice of dress was one of the few things she felt she had some control over. She tucked her finger, weighted down by the beautiful heirloom ring, into her pocket and emptied her mind of worries. She was determined to take pleasure from the beauty of the cloistered space with the rows of fountains, their spray catching and reflecting the light as it fell into a long central pool.

As she tilted her head to examine the seemingly endless number of windows that looked down from the wrought-iron balconies on three sides of the space, the sun dazzled her and made her blink as she brushed stray strands of hair off her face.

'Good journey?'

Maya smiled as she identified the familiar lanky figure of Samuele's male private secretary, Diego, a nice, friendly reception committee of one. A combination of his youth and his ready smile made Diego, who had travelled ahead with all the bags and baggage—one small child and a white tie event meant they were not travelling light—someone she could relax around.

'And you?'

'Fine—' His glance drifted to where Samuele stood, a phone pressed to his ear, a daunting frown pleating his brow visible for a moment before he turned, presenting his broad shoulders to them.

Maya tried not to register the obvious tension in his back and widened her smile to include Rosa, who had stayed the night with relatives in the city and volunteered to help out tonight. 'Hi, Rosa, I hope your family are well.' She glanced towards the open door of the car and the sleeping child. 'He slept all the way here. I probably should have woken him but he looked so peaceful.'

On cue Mattio opened his eyes and started squirming in his seat. Maya moved to unclip his belt but Rosa, neat in a practical pair of chinos and blue shirt, beat her to it. 'I've already scoped out the nursery. Shall I give him his feed?'

'Would you?'

Rosa opened the stroller that had been unloaded with a practised flick of her wrist. 'We'll be in the nursery when you're ready,' she said as she snapped open the safety harness, ignoring the wail of protest from her passenger.

Maya, who saw that Samuele had finally pocketed his phone, pressed a kiss to the top of the increasingly tetchy child's head. She felt secure in the knowledge that he was safe with Rosa. She was so good with him, to the point when there were times she made Maya feel like an amateur.

Maya began to weave her way through the fountains towards the spot where Samuele stood, conscious as she did so that Diego had hung back discreetly.

As she got closer she sensed a tension in Samuele's stance, but also an excitement, which made sense. Tonight was important for Samuele, she knew that, it was the culmination of the years of rebuilding the lost family heritage that meant so much to him, not just to preserve it, but to make it relevant to the twenty-first century. Could it be that despite his seemingly laid-back attitude he was more worried about tonight than he'd let on?

'Good news, they have finally located the missing Agosti statues.'

'Oh, that's terrific!' She knew how much this news meant to Samuele, in a symbolic, end-of-the-journey sort of way.

Locating and acquiring the entire Agosti collection had been the singular most difficult element of his self-imposed task and one that many doubted was achievable.

Officially tonight was all about the Agosti collection, the largest number of ancient Roman and Greek statues in private hands in the world, now housed in the newly restored Villa Agosti, and to finally be shared with the world.

The fact that there were only half a dozen missing pieces was considered a miracle by many, but for Samuele, who did not cut himself any slack, it had constituted a failure.

'The thing is I have to go right now, because there's a Russian collector after them too...'

She pulled in a tense breath and brought her lashes down in a self-protective sweep. 'Now?

But…couldn't you send Diego? Why do you have to go in person?'

Impatient to be gone, Samuele shook his head. 'I'll be back in plenty of time before it starts tonight,' he soothed. 'It's an hour there and an hour back tops. The vendor is a pretty eccentric character, who doesn't seem so much interested in an advantageous offer as she does my star sign. She insists on meeting me in person, something to do with a *planet alignment*…?'

Maya swallowed, struggling to inject a suitably amused note into her response and failing miserably.

'She sounds pretty *interesting*. Obviously you must… It's fine, I understand. Obviously you must go,' she said. But as she spoke she was aware that her response implied he was asking her permission; the fact was he was going whether she liked it or not.

'So you're fine with this?'

She could see from the look in his eyes that he was already not here—*she* wasn't here. She clamped her teeth over the words he wanted to hear and flung out a cold and resentful response instead. 'And if I'm not would it make any difference to you?'

His lips tightened with annoyance and he sighed. 'You're making this into a big thing and it really isn't. I'll be back before you know it, certainly in time for the speech-giving later on. Diego will look after you. I'm sure I'll even make it back for the photoshoot. They want some footage of us in the gallery. Look, here's Diego now.'

The young man punched the air in triumph when Samuele outlined the developments.

'Sure…sure…' he said when Samuele told him the plan. 'Anything,' he said, turning to Maya. 'And I'm your man.'

No, she wanted to say, *you're not my man… and my man isn't really my man.* Letting herself believe otherwise was the road to madness. She was probably going to have a lot of moments like this one, so she'd better get used to it.

Moments filled with suppressed resentment. Moments when she felt very alone.

'So it's all good, then?' Samuele said distractedly.

Without replying she turned with a brilliantly insincere smile to Diego so that she wouldn't have to watch Samuele turn and walk away from her. Which of course he did.

After a prompt from her Diego was only too happy to launch into an explanation of what a feat the restoration of the villa had been.

'Restoration is a delicate balancing act, too much and you lose the authenticity. I can never get over the fact that standing here you're literally yards from the most famous historic sights of Florence.'

Maya walked alongside him as he displayed his knowledge, only hearing one word in three. She knew that the restoration of the collection was important to Samuele so she had hidden the extent of her nerves about tonight.

They kicked in hard now.

CHAPTER ELEVEN

There was no *us* involved in the gallery photoshoot. Just Maya, dwarfed, despite the high heels, by the pale statues around her, a flash of colour in a monochrome backdrop in the cerise silk shirt dress that was one of the new additions to her wardrobe, as were the dramatic thirties-style drop earrings.

To complete her transformation into a sophisticated stranger her hair had been tamed, with the help of Rosa, into a smooth ponytail. Perhaps sensing the importance of the occasion every curl stayed in dutiful submission during the mercifully short photoshoot.

Back in their private suite on the top floor of the villa, Maya reviewed her performance. While she had not said anything witty or wildly interesting, settling instead for polite, she had not said anything too stupid either, and she had neatly sidestepped the couple of questions that were invitations into controversial subjects.

Diego had said that Samuele would be proud of her.

She had wanted to retort that she didn't want his pride, she required his presence.

He had promised her he'd be there, and he had let her down. She didn't even rate a call or text to say he was running late.

'Any luck?' Maya stood up, the tulle layers of the dress she'd changed into for the speech-giving flaring around her as Rosa returned to the room.

The girl shook her head. 'No, I'm sorry, Diego can't get through to him either…it keeps going to voicemail.'

Maya compressed her lips. Five minutes ago the news had come that everyone had arrived and, with it, the gentle suggestion that it was not done to keep royalty waiting was left hanging in the air. She had felt a clenched fingernail away from total panic.

Fortunately, her mood had moved on. She no longer felt like hiding in a cupboard, she felt like hitting someone—all right, not someone, just the one person who had let her down, abandoned her to her fate, after he had *promised* to be there with her.

Just as her dad had promised he'd be back to watch her in the Christmas nativity play, but he hadn't come back, had he? They'd told her that he wouldn't be coming back, ever, but she had refused to believe them. She'd sat on the window seat looking down into the street, sure that his car would appear, totally sure because he had promised… Finally she'd fallen asleep and someone had put her to bed.

She'd waited the next day and the next but he'd never come.

She'd never forgotten the feeling, and all her life she'd been guided by a determination never to experience it again, until Samuele!

Even as she embraced her anger she knew it would eventually ebb and she'd just be left alone again.

There was a tentative tap on the door and the person who appeared in response to her *come in* revealed breathlessly, 'The royal party has arrived.'

'I'll be right there.' She knew etiquette meant she as hostess should have been there to greet them…but, thanks to her experience on San Macizo, ironically royalty was one of the few things that didn't spook her about tonight. The same could not be said for everything else.

'Right then, Rosa, he's a no-show so let's do this.' She glanced at herself in the mirror, and decided she looked like a cross between an old-fashioned Southern belle and a lampshade.

'But no, not in this meringue of a dress. Help me out of it, will you, Rosa?'

A wide-eyed Rosa obliged, helping Maya to slip into her second choice for tonight, which had actually been her first choice before she'd doubted herself.

Five minutes later she looked at her reflection in the same mirror and a very different Maya looked back, a much more edgy, sexy Maya.

The pretty froth of pale lemon tulle was gone, and in its place was a scarlet full-length silk slip dress; simple and dramatic, it clung lovingly to the curves of her body.

She had added a dash of old red lipstick on top of the frosted gloss she had previously applied and it didn't take much to intensify the grey eyeshadow she wore to give it a smoky effect.

If she'd had time she would have put her hair down again, but while she had pretended an indifference to the waiting royalty, she was aware that she really didn't have time to hang around, so her hair would have to stay in the classic chignon that it had been tamed into, emphasising the length of her slender neck.

She stood poised at the top of the stairs underneath the spotlight of a chandelier, conscious of a sea of eyes looking up at her, her heart thudding frantically. There was a split second when she wanted to pick up her skirts and run away as fast as she could.

Then she focused on one face, she had no idea who it was, but blanking out the rest worked. She got down the stairs, and the rest was a blur. She parried the obvious questions about Samuele's absence without actually giving a straight answer, but luckily most people didn't seem to realise it until she had moved on.

Every lie and prevarication had only built the resentful head of steam that was choking her. Perhaps he was making a blatant point that her importance in his life came way below a bunch of statues?

Her homework on the collection paid off; she was able to give intelligent responses to several questions. There were a few speeches, people said complimentary things about the evening and her...and then she was told it was her turn.

'What?' she whispered frantically to Diego, who had pretty much been her shadow all evening.

'Well, officially it is—'

'Samuele's turn,' she bit out.

Diego gave her an understanding look. 'There is no need for you to do it. I could make a small speech apologising—'

She was tempted—oh, my, but she was *so*

tempted to let him do that—but she shook her head. 'No, that's fine, I can do this.'

'I'll introduce you, shall I?'

'That would be good, thank you, Diego.'

She actually had no idea in the world what she was going to say until she started.

'I'm sure you're all wondering where Samuele is—well, so am I!'

She paused for the ripple of laughter, which came satisfyingly on cue. Sometimes the truth worked better than a lie. Samuele didn't ever explain himself to anyone, so why should she do so in his absence?

'The fact we are here tonight is a testament to one man's determination and single-minded vision, not to preserve this collection, but to celebrate it. Because the past is an organic living thing, which has shaped all our presents and our futures...'

She sensed Diego, who up until that point had looked ready to stage a face-saving intervention, relax. And she continued to speak.

The adrenaline was already fading before she reached the privacy of her room, having checked on Mattio and been assured by Rosa, who had an adjoining room to the nursery, that she would get up in the night if needed.

By the time Maya had closed the door it had

gone completely. She could barely stand and she was shaking with anger.

She looked at the champagne in the silver bucket, the two glasses clearly ordered earlier before Samuele had got a better offer. Presumably he was somewhere celebrating his latest acquisition with someone else. A female someone else.

She walked across and picked up the bottle.

During the evening she had imagined, numerous times, the pleasure of throwing his ring in his face and walking away.

But the moment she had looked at the sleeping baby she'd known that was not an option open to her. The trouble was she'd made the mistake of equating great sex with caring, possibly even love. She shook her head at the extent of her own wilful stupidity.

She had allowed herself to believe that Samuele had started to care for her, that his tenderness in the bedroom and the closeness they enjoyed there had translated to them as a couple outside the bedroom too.

Well, tonight her self-deception had been revealed in all its horrific glory, and she only had herself to blame. She was convenient in bed; outside it, she was only there for Mattio. In fact, she was little more than a nanny with a ring.

* * *

Samuele fought his instinct to go straight to his room, but fortunately he almost immediately bumped into Diego.

The other man's jaw dropped in shock. 'What happened to you?'

Samuele dragged a hand across his hair to remove some of the excess moisture. 'I fell into a river. Could you get me some dry clothes? I'll get changed before I—'

'Of course, of course…did you get the statues?'

'Never actually got there,' Samuele admitted, not adding that he'd got halfway there and turned back. With every mile he had driven the image of the expression on Maya's face that had said she was far from fine hadn't faded; it had got clearer, as had the excuses he had used to assuage his guilt.

Yes, the acquisition of those statues would finally give him closure over what his father had done, but at what cost? People broke promises every day, and yet he'd convinced himself he would be back in time, and that, even if he wasn't, it would be good for Maya to face her fears.

Like you're facing yours, had mocked his inner critic as the small pokes attacking his conscience had become a sharp knife blade.

Cursing, he had taken the return exit at the last moment and, ignoring the recalculations of the onboard satnav, he'd headed back to the city.

He'd almost made it too. He would have done, if he hadn't glanced across at the exact moment that guy had climbed onto the railings of the bridge.

By the time he'd reached the foot of the bridge there had been quite an audience gathered. Several had been taking videos on their phones yet no one had been going near him.

'Has someone called the police?'

'An ambulance more like…'

'Yes, I called them—and an ambulance.'

There was a communal gasp as the man tottered.

Samuele swore and began to climb the bank towards the pedestrian path across the bridge.

'Keep back!' the guy yelled hoarsely.

Hell, he looked so young! What could lead someone with their whole life ahead of them to a place like this? 'Fine, I'm not coming nearer to you, but I'm afraid I can't hear very well, so I'm just going to climb a bit higher.' He put a hand up and vaulted onto the guard rail where the man stood, though still a good twenty feet away.

'I'm not going to come any closer… My name is Samuele…and yours is…?'

'Go away! I know what you're trying to do!'

Which is more, Samuele thought wryly, *than I do.* It wasn't really a matter of doing the right thing; it was more a matter of doing something. Something that hopefully didn't make a bad situation even worse…

The thing was, he really thought that he was talking the man down, or at the very least injecting some level of calm into the situation, but it was the sound of a police siren that did it. One moment he was listening to Samuele tell him that he too had lost someone he loved very much and the next he had just launched himself off the bridge into the river below.

Samuele's response had been less down to finely honed logic and more to a split-second instinct. He'd jumped in after him.

'Sorry I left you in the lurch like that. Did you have my notes for the speech?' he asked Diego, stripping off his wet shirt and fighting his way into the clean one that had been provided.

'I did. But actually, your fiancée, she gave the whole speech herself.'

In the act of zipping himself into dry trousers Samuele froze and ground out a curse.

'Actually she—'

Samuele silenced him with a hand. 'No, it's all right.' Although it really wasn't. 'It's not your fault. I'll get this—'

'But—'

'It's fine, Diego, leave it to me.'

Maya had kicked off her shoes but she was still wearing the red dress and she was still raging high on her second wind of fatigue-defying fury when the door opened.

She knew exactly who was standing there but she didn't turn her head as she crammed the last item into the case and forced the lid closed before she straightened up.

'I am so, so sorry, *cara*.'

'Oh, well, then, that makes everything all right, doesn't it?'

She moved towards him with a sexy glide of red silk that sent a surge of heat through Samuele's body. 'I'm sure,' he rasped, 'that it's not as bad as you think. I'll phone around and do a bit of damage control.' He took in the significance of the cases and his expression altered, his eyes hardening. 'You're not going anywhere.'

'No, I'm not—you are.'

'What?'

'Don't look so worried, it's not as if you'll have to resort to sofa surfing, but the thing is

I just didn't want to sleep in the same room as you!'

'*Dio*, Maya, I know it must have been bad tonight but—'

'You think I made a fool of myself, don't you?' she said. 'Well, it's always good to know what a wonderful opinion you have of me, but sorry, I don't require your efforts in damage limitation, because I smashed it—I was a success, brilliant.'

'That's fantastic! I knew you could do it—'

She folded her arms across her heaving chest and directed a narrow-eyed glare up at his face. 'Not two minutes ago, you didn't! You thought I'd fall flat on my face and you let me do it because you're a selfish bastard who really doesn't give a damn about me.'

'Look, I'm sorry but tonight—I shouldn't have left in the first place. I should have refused to jump through hoops for the sake of the statues.'

'Easy to be wise in hindsight,' she sneered. 'Tonight you did me a favour—it really brought a few thing into focus. I would walk away from you right now if it weren't for Mattio, but *he* needs me, so *I* won't abandon him. I will marry you, and I will do this sort of nonsense tonight, but I will *not* continue to share my bed with a man who cares more about a few lumps of old marble than he does about keeping p…promises he has m…made to people.' She scrunched her eyes closed and stood there, her hands clenched into fists. 'I will not cry over you.'

'Oh, *cara*…'

Her eyes flew open again, wide, dark and stormy. 'Don't *"cara"* me! I am making the rules now. I was a very good deal for you, Samuele, and you blew it!'

'My God, you're so gorgeous.' With a hunger approaching desperation, his eyes moved over the soft, delicate contours of her face.

'Do you really think that a few compliments will make me melt into your arms? Oh, yes,' she added, in full flow now, 'and I have decided I want to alter the terms of our *contract*. That open-marriage deal you suggested? I've started to think it's a damned great idea!'

It took a while for his brain to decipher the words she'd just spoken, but when it did he went pale and literally swayed where he stood.

'Open marriage?' His woman seeing another man? *His* Maya, his *wife*, being touched, made love to by someone else? The reaction to the images in his head rippled through him like an electrical charge and his body went rigid with rejection. He scowled fiercely. 'I don't think so.'

A sudden need to reach out to her made him take a step forward but then she snapped out, 'It was your idea to begin with, *remember*? And unlike most of your ideas, I think it's a good one. Very *civilised*!' she hissed.

'This is all just a misunderstanding,' he protested.

'No, it's not. Have you even heard a word I've said? I hate you!'

'Let me explain…' He stopped as his voice was drowned out by a loud wail.

'Now look what you've done!' she accused, pushing open the door into the living room that separated the bedroom from the nursery wing.

Samuele, a step behind her, stopped short when they entered the nursery, where the wail was now almost deafening. Rosa was standing there with the crying baby in her arms.

She gave Maya a look of gratitude as the baby was transferred to her.

Samuele heaved a sigh of frustration. 'We'll speak again in the morning.'

The first thing Maya did the next morning, after she had applied the cold compresses to her eyes to help the puffiness that was the cost of crying herself to sleep, was scroll down her phone to see if she had been as much of a success as she had boasted to Samuele.

She typed in the word Agosti and waited for the results. The news of the gala was there but preceding it was the headline: *Italian Banker in Dramatic River Rescue!*

She swung her legs over the side of the bed and clicked the viral video attached to the headline.

The video was still playing when she ran into the sitting room where Samuele was sitting on one of the sofas, looking as though he hadn't slept a wink.

She looked wildly from the phone in her hand to him. 'Why didn't you tell me?'

'I was waiting for you to wake up.'

'You jumped off a bridge!' She was shaking the phone at him, the video still playing.

'There weren't many other options, *cara*.'

'Maybe *not* jumping off a bridge?' Her brain had been frozen with panic, but as it started working she felt dizzy with fright. *She could have lost him!* 'That's why you didn't arrive back on time, isn't it?' When she thought of all the things she'd said to him, she could have wept if she'd had any more tears left inside her. 'Why didn't you send me a message?'

'My phone was at the bottom of a river and it took me some time to convince the hospital staff that I wasn't suicidal myself.'

'Did he…the man…did he…?'

'The jumper survived.' One day he might be grateful he was alive, but not last night—a fact he'd managed to communicate to Samuele as he had dragged him onto the shore before collapsing himself.

The things she'd said last night, the emotions she'd revealed, would be impossible to back-pedal from. The only real option that Maya could see going forward was to explain that she'd reacted that way because she was so very much in love with him. In fact, she thought almost numbly, it would be a kind of relief to have it out in the open at last.

It would also be the kiss of death to any sort of ongoing relationship other than as Mattio's parents. But that wouldn't change anything either, just speed up the inevitable, because there was no way she could hide her true feelings for him for very much longer anyway. It wasn't in her nature.

He had moved to stand beside her and she could already feel her resolve slipping as the warmth of him, the well-known scent of his body, reached out and enveloped her. She clenched her hands to hide the fact she was shaking and studied her bare feet.

'Were you on your way to get the statues or…?' She despised herself for delaying the moment of truth.

'I was on my way back, but I never actually got there,' he admitted huskily.

She looked up to see that he was right there and looking into his dark eyes made her tremble. 'I don't understand,' she whispered.

'I didn't get there because I thought you needed me. As it turned out I was wrong, and you were right—you did smash it. I am so proud of you.' He took her face between his hands. 'I am such a fool, *cara*. Even as I was turning the car around to come back to you, I wouldn't admit to myself why. I was too weak, too scared to admit that I loved you with all my heart.

'Last night when you said you wanted an open marriage I was devastated. After you sent me away I could see my whole empty *safe* life stretching out in front of me without you, and all of the things I worked so hard for, they would mean nothing if you are not in my life, by my side. I know that you wear my ring already, *cara*, but I never asked you to marry me, not really. So, Maya, will you please be my wife and I promise I will try every day of our lives together to be the husband you deserve? But only if you stop crying, *cara*, because it is killing me!' he groaned out. 'I need you to love me back, but if you can't I'll spend my life trying to persuade you!' he vowed fiercely.

Maya dashed away the tears that were running down her cheeks. 'Samuele, I love you so much it hurts—'

She didn't get any further than that because he was kissing her and she was kissing him back.

'I love you,' he murmured against her hair when they finally came up for air. 'Have I said that already?'

She pulled back and caught his hand, lifting it to her lips, loving the way his eyes immediately darkened. 'Some things can never be said too often. You have shadows under your eyes, my darling…'

'I spent a very long night realising what a fool I'd been and it was only the fact that I knew you'd hardly had any sleep either that stopped me waking you up… How is Mattio? He sounded pretty upset last night.'

'I think it was just a touch of colic.'

'You're going to make a wonderful mother. Oh, God, Cristiano would have been such a great father. I don't know what I'm doing half the time.'

'You're a great father too, Samuele. There's nobody who will love Mattio more than you. Speaking of which, if I could love you more than I already do, I would,' she whispered huskily as she gazed at him with eyes shining with the strength of her feelings. 'If only Violetta—'

'I have already disposed of that problem—oh, not literally.' He laughed when he saw her face. 'Not that the idea is not tempting,' he added drily. 'But when she heard we were getting married and were applying for full custody, she knew she'd lost because she'd already abandoned Mattio once, so she settled for a final payment instead. Everyone, it turns out, has a price.'

'That must have cost you a lot of money.'

'Money is not important. What is the most important thing is that she has agreed to allow us to formally adopt Mattio so he will officially be our child, and he and our other children will inherit equally.'

'Are we going to have more children?'

'You like the idea?'

She nodded. 'And I will love them all equally,' she promised with damp eyes. 'If they grow up to be like their father, how could I not?'

EPILOGUE

Maya lay on her back on the day bed in the observatory and squirmed languidly, digging her bottom into the soft layer of sheepskins she lay on. 'I wondered what it would be like to make love under the stars.'

'And now you know,' Samuele said smugly. 'I arranged the meteor shower especially for you.'

'Do you think your grandfather ever did this?'

'What, make love under the stars the night before he got married?'

'Well, I quite like the idea of the continuity,' she teased.

'Then I can think of a more pleasant form of continuity. That we spend each of our anniversaries here under the stars making love, though I might not be able to pull off the meteor shower every time.'

She emerged from the long languid kiss with

a smile on her lips. 'In six hours and twenty-four minutes, I will be your wife.'

Samuele had wanted it to happen immediately but Maya had insisted she wanted to get married with her family there, which had meant that they'd had to wait a few months until Beatrice's morning sickness had improved enough for her to travel. The timing was perfect: in a dual celebration that morning they had signed the final papers that made them Mattio's adoptive parents.

'Are you all right about it?' she asked.

'Having the woman I love more than life by my side for the rest of our lives? I am *very* all right, *cara*. Come here and I will show you how all right I really am.'

'You've only got six hours and twenty-three minutes left…'

He grinned. 'Six hours will do me just fine.'

* * * * *

Captivated by The Italian's Bride on Paper?
Read Beatrice and Dante's story in
Waking Up in His Royal Bed.

*And why not lose yourself in these other
Kim Lawrence stories?*

A Wedding at the Italian's Demand
A Passionate Night with the Greek
The Spaniard's Surprise Love-Child
Claiming His Unknown Son
Waking Up in His Royal Bed

Available now!

What Wade had done for her had cracked her heart open—not all the way wide, just the smallest possible bit. But it was still enough to let the light in, and now there was no turning back. Joy filled her like sunshine.

"I'll do it," she blurted before she could stop herself. "If the social worker says we can move in to your house temporarily and if you agree to help, I'll take care of the baby."

Wade's mouth curved into a tentative smile that seemed to build by the second, as did the sudden swirl of panic in Felicity's chest. "Seriously?"

Her heart felt like it had lodged at the base of her throat. Everything was going to be fine, though. This was only temporary. He realized that, right?

She held up her hands. "Just until the holidays have passed, or until someone steps up and applies for adoption. Can you live with that, Smokey?"

Wade's grin widened until it seemed to take up his entire handsome face. Good gravy, what was she getting herself into?

"I can live with that," he said.

But could she?

Dear Reader,

Welcome back to Lovestruck, Vermont! *A Firehouse Christmas Baby* is the second book in my new series for Harlequin Special Edition. The Lovestruck, Vermont series is a group of four interconnected books about newcomers to a charming small town where love comes in packages. I hope Wade and Felicity's Christmas love story gives you a heaping dose of holiday feels!

Like the last book in this series, the hero of *A Firehouse Christmas Baby* is a firefighter. Shortly before I began working on this book, I took a tour of a local fire station here in my hometown for research purposes. What a fun day that was! The firefighters of San Antonio Fire Station 34 spent half a day answering questions and showing me around. They even posed for selfies with me. We also talked for quite a while about the Safe Haven law, which provides safe places for parents of newborn infants to take their children if they feel unable to care for them. Firehouses are designated Safe Haven locations, and to date, more than four thousand infants in the United States have been surrendered under this law.

I was immediately drawn to the idea of writing about a Safe Haven baby during the holidays, because the concept seemed like a wonderful way to explore the spirit of Christmas. When I mentioned this to the firefighters at SAFD Station 34, one of them—Captain Jeremy Huntsman—suggested a special twist to the story. It was a brilliant idea, and I've indeed used it in this book.

I hope you enjoy this poignant trip to Christmas in Vermont. As always, thank you so much for reading. And please look for the next book in the Lovestruck series, coming April 2021.

Happy reading!

Teri Wilson

A Firehouse
Christmas Baby

TERI WILSON

HARLEQUIN
SPECIAL
EDITION

Recycling programs
for this product may
not exist in your area.

ISBN-13: 978-1-335-89498-4

A Firehouse Christmas Baby

Copyright © 2020 by Teri Wilson

This edition published by arrangement with Harlequin Books S.A.

For questions and comments about the quality of this book,
please contact us at CustomerService@Harlequin.com.

Harlequin Enterprises ULC
22 Adelaide St. West, 40th Floor
Toronto, Ontario M5H 4E3, Canada
www.Harlequin.com

Printed in U.S.A.

Teri Wilson is a *Publishers Weekly* bestselling author of romance and romantic comedy. Several of Teri's books have been adapted into Hallmark Channel Original Movies, most notably *Unleashing Mr. Darcy*. She is also a recipient of the prestigious RITA® Award for excellence in romance fiction for her novel *The Bachelor's Baby Surprise*. Teri has a major weakness for cute animals and pretty dresses, and she loves following the British royal family. Visit her at www.teriwilson.net.

For anyone who has ever needed a safe haven.

Chapter One

Here's the juicy secret no one tells you about firemen: pretty much of all them, Wade Ericson included, are deathly afraid of one thing. And it's probably the thing you'd least expect.

Scratch that. It's definitely the thing you'd least expect. Burning buildings? No problem. Smoke inhalation? Not a picnic, but firefighters have equipment to deal with that sort of danger. Fires that burn hotter than the surface of the sun? Again, just an ordinary day at the office.

A tiny, newborn baby, on the other hand, will leave most firefighters quaking in their flame-resistant boots. That's right—a baby.

Technically, it's the *imminent arrival* of said baby that's terrifying. If a woman in labor is relying on a firefighter to deliver her child, something unexpected has likely already happened. The number of things that can go wrong seems endless. Firefighters are in the business of saving lives, and no life seems quite as pure or precious as an innocent newborn. No one wants to screw that up.

No one, including Wade Ericson.

Wade would've quite literally rather walked through fire than respond to the call a few weeks ago for an expectant mom in distress in a stalled car on the state highway on the outskirts of Lovestruck, Vermont. Lovestruck was a quiet, sleepy little town—the sort of place where firefighters actually rescued kittens in trees. Just a month ago, Wade had shown up at a call for a house fire that turned out to be a *dog*house. Muffin, the resident of the doghouse, was tucked safely inside her owner's arms and watched as Wade valiantly sprayed the animal's tiny three-foot-by-three-foot structure with his fire extinguisher. Mission accomplished, day saved.

Which is all to say that no one in the history of the LFD had ever been called upon to deliver a baby before—not even Cap, Wade's long-time supervisor and overall father figure of the guys at Engine Co. 24, Lovestruck's lone fire station.

There's a first time for everything, though, and in the wee hours of the morning on Thanksgiving Day, Wade delivered his very first baby. *With any luck*, he thought hours later as he stood at the window of the labor and delivery unit at the big hospital in Burlington and watched the newborn sleep, *it will also be my last. One and done.*

He returned to a hero's welcome at the firehouse. The guys all clapped him on the back, and Cap hugged him so hard that he thought his bones might break. Jack Cole, LFD's lieutenant and Wade's closest friend, even baked him a cake—devil's food with rich chocolate icing and a plastic baby rattle perched jauntily on top. Jack himself was a dad to twin baby girls, which probably explained why he had easy access to a baby rattle, but even his response to the news of Wade's heroics was "Better you than me."

Wade ate his cake, and even though he'd been awake for probably thirty-six hours straight at that point, he posed for a picture for the front page of the local paper, the *Lovestruck Bee*. The mayor called to thank him for his service and then sent half a dozen pizzas to the firehouse. But when the celebration was finally over and, at long last, Wade stretched out on his bunk to close his weary eyes, he cried like a (yep, you guessed it) baby.

He was so damned relieved. The baby was healthy and happy, and the mother—though at fifteen or sixteen, practically a child herself—was resting comfortably up in Burlington. He'd managed to deliver a happy ending, all wrapped up with a neat little bow. It was over.

Except it wasn't. Not really.

"Are you going to this thing?" Jack asked two weeks later as he and Wade were perched atop the LFD's ladder truck, stretching a banner across Main Street advertising the upcoming Lovestruck Christmas festival.

Two weeks, one day and six hours after the birth of the baby, if Wade was keeping track. Which he wasn't—not intentionally, anyway. He just couldn't seem to shake the memory of the infant boy's delicate little fingers and toes. Or the way the newborn child had looked at him when he'd stopped crying and opened his eyes for the very first time, as if he'd been nothing short of awestruck by the circumstances surrounding his birth. *Join the club*, Wade had thought.

"The Christmas festival? I don't have much of a choice." Wade squinted at the banner through a swirl of snowflakes. It looked a little high on the right. "I'm in it."

"You're in it?" Jack nudged the banner higher and then frowned as Wade tugged it down a few inches. "What does that mean?"

"It means I'm in it. I'm playing the part of

one of the Christmas characters," he said without quite meeting Jack's gaze.

Wade had been avoiding this conversation for the past few days, for multiple reasons. If it had been up to him, he wouldn't have been forced to have it to begin with. But when the mayor of Lovestruck specifically asks a firefighter to do something, the firefighter does it, even if that something involves dressing in a ridiculous costume for the entire town to gaze upon. Wade didn't make the rules. The mayor didn't just send congratulatory pizzas—she signed his paycheck, as well. He had no choice in the matter.

Jack let out a bark of laughter. "You're going to be Santa Claus?"

"What? No." Wade started making his way down the ladder so he could check the banner from the street. Santa? How old did Jack think he looked? Normally that role went to one of the retirees from the library's rocking chair crowd. Delivering the baby might have aged him a bit, but he was pretty sure he had a few decades to go before climbing into a plush red Santa suit.

"An elf? Please tell me it's an elf. You'd look great in green hosiery." Jack snorted. "Eat your heart out, Will Ferrell."

He was practically yelling from the top of the ladder. Wade glared at him from the cobblestone street. Now he'd get to share his news with Jack at full volume in front of the greater population of Lovestruck, most of whom were lingering outside the entrance to the Bean with peppermint mochas in hand as they watched the banner go up. Super.

"I'm going to be Joseph, you idiot," he said tersely.

Jack's brow furrowed. "Seriously?"

Was it really that hard to believe? Granted, Wade didn't exactly have a reputation as a Biblical-type figure, but Jack had apparently forgotten that Wade had recently become the town poster boy for anything and everything baby-related. If anyone in Lovestruck was suited to play Joseph in the living nativity display, it was Wade. The mayor and the entire town council thought so, anyway.

"Yes. You know the drill—the living nativity runs every night leading up to Christmas, so laugh it up. Starting tonight, I'll be freezing my butt off in a pile of brown robes next to a live donkey and some cantankerous sheep from Old Bob's farm."

And a plastic baby. Can't forget the baby.

An ache burned deep in Wade's chest, which he pretended to believe was a product of the frigid December air.

Banner securely in place, Jack climbed down the ladder to stand next to him. They both gave it another once-over, making sure it looked decent before lowering the ladder.

"I'm not laughing," Jack finally said, crossing his arms. "I think it's nice, actually. In a way it will make the Christmas festival's living nativity scene a little more meaningful this year."

Wade took a deep inhale of frosty air. Instinct told him to argue. He'd only been doing his job—he'd delivered a baby, which in no way compared to being the father figure to the infant Jesus. And the experience had left him more rattled than he cared to admit.

But he understood Jack's point. He also understood his hometown, and there was no doubt at all in Wade's mind—Lovestruck was going to eat it up.

From the looks of things, they already were. The crowd outside the Bean was beaming at him from a distance. Clearly the moms pushing strollers and holding the hands of their bundled-up, mittened preschoolers had overheard. Word would surely spread far and wide by the end of his shift.

He averted his gaze. Weeks ago, if anyone had told him that he'd suddenly become Lovestruck's unofficial bachelor of the year, he would have been thrilled. It was weird, though. Mothers stopped him in the Village Market and wanted to snap photos of him kissing their babies' foreheads. Someone had started an online crowdfunding site for an LFD beefcake calendar, starring Wade as the cover boy. Women were dropping by the station, bringing him casseroles.

Be careful what you wish for. "It's Christmas, and we're talking about the birth of Jesus. Expecting me to improve upon it might be asking a bit much, don't you think?"

"Point taken." Jack shrugged one shoulder. "I just have one question—if you're playing Joseph, who's Mary?"

"Good gravy, Felicity. You look downright angelic."

Felicity Hart glanced down at the huge swathe of silky blue fabric that her friend Madison Jules had just artistically draped over her body. Instinct told her to check her reflection in the huge mirrored wall of her brand-new yoga studio, but she knew it wasn't necessary. Like Felicity, Madison had once worked on New York's Fifth Avenue, at one of the most respected fashion magazines in the country. She could probably drape a Virgin Mary costume better than Coco Chanel, may she rest in fashionable peace.

Coco, not Madison, obviously. Madison was perfectly fine, living her best life with her new firefighter husband and his precious twin babies in Lovestruck, Vermont, the most adorable Vermont town that Felicity had ever seen. In fact, Lovestruck was so adorable that, after she'd served as Madison's maid of honor, Felicity had impulsively quit her job, packed up every last Louis Vuitton handbag she owned and opened a yoga studio smack in the middle of Main Street.

Felicity and her Vuittons lived above the studio in a tiny attic apartment with a pitched ceiling, knotty pine walls and a pile of handmade quilts that she'd found in an old trunk in the studio's storage room. It was all very sweet, very wholesome. Very Hallmark movie–esque. And honestly, that's what she needed now, more than anything. Because the move from New York to Vermont hadn't quite been as impulsive and whimsical as she'd let everyone believe.

But Felicity was trying her best not to think about that right now. There were more pressing matters to contend with, like the fact that her yoga studio hadn't exactly gotten off to a rip-roaring start. Perhaps she'd overestimated the appeal of bendy fitness practices in a place where people used idioms like "good gravy" on a regular basis.

She arched a brow at Madison. "You're really leaning into the whole small-town thing, aren't you?"

"What do you mean?" Madison blinked back at her, seemingly bewildered.

"Never mind." Felicity made a mental note to start using similar, cutesy expressions. Maybe if she did, she'd finally start fitting in, and Madison would no longer be her sole yoga student. "Are you sure I look Christmassy enough? You know, in a nativity-scene-appropriate sort of way?"

"Absolutely." Madison looked her up and down again before adjusting a fold in the white gown Felicity wore beneath the silky blue cape. "You make a gorgeous Mary. Joseph won't be able to keep his eyes off you."

Felicity's face went warm. "That's not what I meant and you know it."

She wanted to look *Christmassy*, not gorgeous. If she'd learned one thing about Lovestruck so far, it was that people really got into Christmas around here. It was one of the main reasons she'd let Madison talk her into playing Mary in the living nativity scene to begin with.

The fact that local firefighter Wade Ericson— Lovestruck's honorary patron saint of newborns— would be stepping into the part of Joseph was nowhere on her list of reasons to say yes. If anything, it was a deterrent.

Madison sighed. "You know every woman in a fifty-mile radius without a ring on her finger would kill to play Mary to Wade's Joseph this year, don't you?"

"With one notable exception," Felicity said.

She loved her best friend. She really did, but this wasn't the first time Madison had ventured dangerously close to matchmaking territory. Plus, she knew good and well that dozens of women, if not hundreds, would probably kill for the chance to dress up like Mary and spend a silent night, holy night with Wade Ericson and a handful of live farm animals in the town square. It reminded Felicity of that line from her favorite movie, *The Devil Wears Prada*—"A million girls would kill for this job."

Well, guess what. Anne Hathaway wasn't one of those girls, and neither was Felicity.

"Fine, I know you have a lot on your plate right now." Madison held up her hands. "I just don't get it. Jack and I were both sure we noticed serious sparks between the two of you at the wedding."

"That was then." Felicity swallowed around the lump in her throat that sprang out of nowhere every time the topic of conversation veered anywhere close to the vicinity of babies. Ugh, when was that going to stop? It had been six months already. Madison didn't even know—no one in Lovestruck did. "And this is now."

"I'm just going to nod like that makes sense," Madison said.

"And that's precisely what makes you a good friend." Felicity spun around in her Mary robes and struck a ridiculous catwalk pose. Anything to change the subject. "Plus the fact that you're a fashion genius."

Madison laughed, and then her gaze snagged

on something outside the front window of the empty yoga studio. "Speaking of Joseph-slash-Wade, he just pulled up to the curb. Are you two riding together?"

"Yes. The mayor didn't want us walking the full length of Main Street in our costumes because she thought it would spoil the surprise of who got the Joseph and Mary roles, so she asked us to drive. But the parking lot is sure to be packed, so we're carpooling."

"Carpooling," Madison echoed. "Kind of like sharing a donkey in Biblical times. You have to admit it's sort of romantic."

"You have got to stop," Felicity said, even though her heartbeat kicked into high gear at the sight of Wade's masculine profile behind the wheel of the LFD's small utility vehicle.

Good gravy, he was handsome.

She swallowed hard. *Listen to yourself. You're actually starting to sound like a Vermonter.*

On any other day, Felicity would have considered that a good thing. Alas, today wasn't any other day. Today was the opening night of the Lovestruck living nativity scene, and she was about to spend hours pretending that she, Wade and their fake baby in a manger were a family. She was just about ready to call an Uber to take her back to Manhattan.

Why on earth did I agree to this?

"I should probably go before your Aunt Alice sends out a search party," Felicity said.

Madison's aunt owned the yarn store next door to the yoga studio and was as plugged in to Lovestruck's social scene as she could be. She'd apparently been the city's volunteer coordinator for the living nativity display for decades, which was the other major reason Felicity had agreed to participate. No one wanted to disappoint Aunt Alice.

"Jack and I are bringing the girls later, so keep an eye out for us!" Madison gave her a quick one-armed hug so as not to crush her costume and waved at Wade while Felicity locked up the yoga studio.

"Have fun." Madison grinned and headed toward Main Street Yarn while Felicity's face went warm again.

The awkward truth of the matter was that Madison and her husband were 100 percent correct. There had definitely been sparks between Felicity and Wade at the wedding last month—so many sparks that Felicity had been grateful for the dozen or so firefighters in attendance. In the back of her mind, she'd almost hoped that once she moved to Lovestruck, something would come of those sparks.

But moving day happened to fall on the morning after Wade delivered the baby and, well…

She couldn't go there. Felicity's new life in Lovestruck came with a strict anti-baby policy, even if those babies were on the periphery. It was a matter of self-preservation. The only exceptions were Emma and Ella, Jack and Madison's twins, because she couldn't exactly avoid her best friend's stepdaughters. She could, however, avoid Wade Ericson and his baby-saving aura.

Except for now.

"Hey, Felicity." Wade's mouth curved into a lazy grin she felt down to the tips of her toes.

"Wade," she said primly, and then frowned once she managed to drag her gaze away from his chiseled features and flirty dimples long enough to realize he wasn't dressed in anything remotely resembling Biblical garb.

He was dressed in his regulation dark blue LFD T-shirt and cargo pants, which had the annoying effect of reminding Felicity that he was a bona fide hero. Equally annoying—the apparent firefighter fashion code that required the sleeves of his T-shirt to intimately hug every bulge of his rock-hard biceps. It was snowing, for heaven's sake. Shouldn't he be wearing a coat? Or better yet, a drab brown robe?

"Where's your costume?" she blurted, feeling ridiculous all of a sudden in her virginal attire.

"It's at the station. I got stuck on a call for a

medical assist and came straight from the hospital."

Of course you did, thought Felicity. She wondered if the medical assist involved an infant, but she didn't dare ask.

"I didn't want to be late picking you up." He strode to the passenger's side of the car in three easy strides and held the door open for her. "Do you mind if we swing by and get my costume on the way?"

"Sounds great." She aimed for a beatific smile, but it quickly turned awkward as she tried to scoop miles and miles of blue silk into her arms so she could climb into the car.

So much for looking angelic.

Wade laughed, deliciously low. "Here, let me help."

He gathered an armful of fabric trailing the ground behind her, and Felicity did her best not to stare. Why did a vision of herself as a bride and Wade helping her with the train of her Vera Wang suddenly flash in her mind? Good gravy, indeed.

"Here you go," he said, gently placing the blue silk onto the seat of the car beside her. "All tucked in."

Then he reached across her to fasten her seat belt, and Felicity didn't dare breathe.

But it was too late. She could *feel* his warmth, and his swoony firefighter scent—reminiscent of a campfire under a snowy starlit sky—was already making her head spin.

Too close. Way too close.

She muttered a thank-you and closed her eyes until she heard the car door shut.

"Thank you, by the way," Wade said as he climbed behind the wheel.

Felicity felt herself frown. "For what, exactly?"

"For not asking if my medical assist involved delivering another baby."

At first Felicity thought it was a joke, but the serious set of his jaw told her otherwise. "Is all the attention getting to be too much?"

"Not exactly, it's just…" Wade shook his head as they headed toward the firehouse at the far end of Main. "I don't know. It's not something I want to keep dwelling on, that's all."

"I understand," she said, a little too quickly. "No baby talk tonight, I promise."

He turned to smile at her, but it didn't quite reach his eyes.

Interesting. Wade seemed different, for lack of a better word. Ordinarily, he was all easy charm and flirty banter. But, if he didn't want to dwell on baby-related conversation, she was all for it.

"Here we are." He shifted the vehicle into Park in front of the firehouse and glanced at Felicity's costume filling up most of the space in the floorboard. Then his mouth hitched into a half grin that made him look much more like the old Wade who'd lowered her into an over-the-top dip on the dance floor at Jack and Madison's reception. "Given your billowy robes, do you want to just stay here while I run in and change real quick?"

She nodded. "That would be a definite yes."

"I'll be Bethlehem-ready and back in a flash." He winked, and it seemed to float deliciously through her.

How was she going to do this for the entire festival? Thank goodness there would soon be a number of live sheep between them to serve as a buffer.

She took a deep breath and toyed with the gold locket she always wore on a chain around her neck. Everything was going to be fine. The Joseph costume would probably work wonders in helping her forget about Wade's biceps. But, just as she was beginning to feel the tiniest bit confident about the coming hours, a sharp rap on the car window caught her off guard.

She gasped, heart hammering. And when she swiveled her head to see who'd knocked on her window, her surprise crystalized into panic.

A young girl stood on the other side of the glass—she couldn't have been more than fifteen or sixteen years old. She wore a long puffer coat that gave the impression of being part winter attire and part security blanket, and the pink knit hat on her head had a fuzzy pompon on top. It fluttered in the icy Vermont wind. But Felicity couldn't seem to focus on anything but the bundle in the girl's arms.

A baby.

The infant was so tiny, so delicate. It looked like a newborn. What was a baby this fragile doing out in the cold?

Felicity fumbled with the controls but couldn't get the window open, so she opened the car door and tumbled outside in a pile of blue silk. Only then did she notice the tears streaming down the teenager's face.

"Are you okay?" Felicity asked, and a terrible fear began to swirl low in her belly.

Please don't let this be what I think it is.

The girl sniffed. "I need you to take my baby."

Felicity swallowed hard, panic beating its frantic wings against her rib cage. She'd heard of this kind of thing before—the Safe Haven law, which allowed parents who were unable to care for their children to anonymously leave them at a designated place like a hospital or police station.

Or firehouse, she thought, glancing at the building where Wade had just vanished inside. Her gaze darted to the apparatus bay, hoping against hope that another firefighter would notice what was happening and come rushing to her aid. But the bay was empty, and then she remembered that the fire department was always a big part of the Christmas festival. They were probably all already down at the town square, passing out candy canes from atop fire engines wrapped in twinkle lights.

"Um, why don't you let me go get someone to help you?" Felicity said, trying her best to calm the tremor in her voice. The girl seemed frightened to death. "There's a fireman right inside. I'm sure he'll know what to do."

"No! No way. He might recognize me. Google said I could leave the baby here and someone could adopt him and give him a real home. I don't even have to leave my name." The girl waved a hand at Felicity's costume. "And look at you. You're the Virgin Mary, right? It's like a sign."

It wasn't. It couldn't be, but the girl seemed so desperate, and Felicity was beginning to worry about what might happen if she didn't take the baby. "I want to help you. I do. Please just let me get a firefighter…"

The girl thrust the whimpering infant toward Felicity. "*Please*. I would've just dropped the baby off at the doorstep, but I didn't want to leave him alone in the cold. Please just take him and give him to the fireman."

Leave the baby out in the cold?

Just the mention of that dangerous possibility had Felicity reaching for the child and holding him tight against her chest. He mewed like a kitten, so tiny, so fragile, and at that very first contact with his soft little body, time seemed to stop. The snowflakes drifting down from above danced in aching slow motion. The sounds of the Christmas festival down the street faded into background noise. All Felicity seemed to hear was the infant's tiny puffs of breath and the beat of his sad little heart, crashing wildly against hers. She felt herself start to shiver, and she knew without a doubt it had nothing to do with the cold.

Felicity took a deep breath as her mothering instincts came back in full force. Muscle memory was a wondrous thing—as much as she wanted to resist the sweet, unfortunate child, she knew just how to hold him to warm his chilled little body. He stopped whimpering and burrowed into her embrace. She bit down hard on her bottom lip to keep herself from crying.

Hold it together.

"Are you sure you don't want to leave your name, in case you change your…" Felicity looked up, and her voice fell away.

The girl was already gone. She'd left nothing behind with her newborn child except a trail of scattered footprints in the snow.

"It's okay," Felicity whispered against the baby's downy head. "Everything is going to be okay."

But she wasn't altogether sure if she was talking to the baby or to herself. She rocked back and forth in an effort to soothe them both, and when Wade called her name, the sound was like music to her ears—the sweetest Christmas carol she'd ever heard.

"Felicity?" He stopped dead in his tracks, his brown robes whipping in the wind as every last bit of color drained from his face. "Is that..."

She nodded, and hot tears spilled down her cheeks. "A baby."

A Christmas child.

Chapter Two

Wade was from Lovestruck, born and bred.

He'd grown up on pancakes with real maple syrup and bright autumn leaves bursting with colors as vivid and bright as those lined up in his crayon box. He'd taken his first steps at the library on Main Street, where his mom had been the head librarian until she'd gotten sick. In high school, his first job had been tending sheep on the weekends at a small, family-owned farm on the Vermont Cheese Trail.

Wade loved Vermont's harsh winters and messy mud season just as much he loved its picturesque covered bridges. His childhood hadn't exactly been idyllic—until his father finally left for good—but he'd never wanted to live anyplace else. Never even considered it. Applying to the Lovestruck Fire Department straight out of the Fire Academy had been a foregone conclusion.

Being a firefighter in a town like Lovestruck was different than working for a big-city department, though. When Wade was a rookie, he'd had to wait nearly three months to work his first actual fire.

He'd been so prepared. So ready. And as the days turned into weeks, week into months, his readiness had seemed to smolder into something less bright, less intense—anxiety. The more time he'd had to think about it, the more worried he became that when he finally saw his first fire, he might do something wrong. Make some fatal mistake. He had needed to get it over with, just to prove to himself that he had what it took to run into a burning building. He'd heard about rookie firefighters freezing up on their first hot run, and his deepest fear had been that it might happen to him. Especially since he'd had months to worry about it.

Cap had tried to quell his anxiety by reminding him to never wish for a fire. Ever. If he spent his entire career doing safety equipment checks and rescuing cats in trees, it meant his community was safe and sound. Wade agreed, of course.

But when he had finally gotten his first code red call, the rush of adrenaline he'd felt as he'd entered an apartment building marbled with smoke and heat had been a relief.

He'd done it. At last. He hadn't panicked at the sight of out-of-control flames, nor had he gotten claustrophobic from the oppressive weight of his gear. Once the fire had been safely put out, Cap had snapped a photo of Wade's ash-covered face and his bright white smile. The picture still hung in his locker—a reminder that he had what it took to be a first responder. He would always choose to run toward danger when others were running away from it. *Always*.

Wade never worried about freezing up again.

But that's exactly what happened when he exited the fire station dressed in his Joseph robes and saw the baby in Felicity's arms. He just couldn't seem to make himself move. He could only stare at the infant's upturned nose and plump cheeks, nipped pink from the cold. This wasn't just any baby—it was *the* baby. *His* baby.

No, he tried to tell himself as his heart pumped so hard and fast that he couldn't seem to take a full breath. *Not yours. Not really.*

He'd helped deliver the child, that's all. He certainly wasn't the baby's father.

But for some nonsensical reason, the thump of Wade's heart and the rush of blood in his ears sounded eerily like one word, repeating itself over and over again.

Mine. Mine. Mine.

He'd know that child anywhere. The baby in Felicity's arms was the same infant he'd helped to deliver two weeks ago. He knew it as surely as he knew his own name. What he couldn't seem to figure out was what the baby was doing here, at the firehouse without his mother. Nor could he figure out why he was gripped by a sudden urge to wrap the child in his arms and never let go. The instinct to protect the tiny, innocent baby was crippling.

Still, all he could seem to do was stare at Felicity as if she'd somehow morphed into the actual Virgin Mary in the few minutes he'd been gone.

What the heck is happening?

His throat went bone-dry as all his worst rookie fears suddenly seemed to be coming true. Probably because when it came to babies, he was still very much a rookie, regardless of what everyone else in Lovestruck might think.

"Wade?" Felicity blinked up at him with eyes as bright as the bluebells that grew wild behind the firehouse every spring. "I…"

She shook her head as her bottom lip began to wobble, and tears streamed down her face, the fear in her expression seemed to mirror his own. If he didn't get ahold of himself and do something, he was going to have a crying woman and a potentially abandoned infant on his hands.

The baby began to cry. And the sound of his lonely, plaintive wail, coupled with his tiny, scrunched-up face snapped Wade into immediate action. He bolted toward Felicity, brown robes dragging behind him along the snowy ground.

"What happened?" he said, reaching for the child as if it was the most natural thing in the world.

The relief in Felicity's eyes as she handed the baby over to him was palpable, but her empty arms told another story. She suddenly didn't seem to know what to do with her hands, as if she longed for two very opposing things at the same time.

Or maybe Wade was just projecting.

"You were inside." Felicity pointed toward the firehouse with a shaky hand. "And a girl knocked on the window of the truck. She looked panicked, so I climbed out and, the next thing I knew, she shoved her baby into my arms."

Wade nodded, encouraging her to continue as he tried to remember everything he'd ever heard about how to properly hold a newborn.

Support the baby's head and neck. Be mindful of the soft spot. Make sure the baby's face is turned out to allow him to breathe.

He must have done something right, because

the infant stopped crying, and Wade's heart stopped aching quite as badly as it had just moments before.

"I'm sorry." Felicity pressed her fingertips to her lips and shook her head. "I tried to get her to stay until I could get help. I told her you'd be out in just a minute, but she said you might recognize her."

And that's when Wade knew for certain that his mind wasn't playing tricks on him. The child in his arms was indeed the famous baby he'd helped deliver two weeks ago. Deep down in his gut, he'd known all along. But he'd been holding on to a sliver of hope that he was wrong.

He glanced down at the baby, marveling at how light the child felt in his arms. As dainty as a snowflake. "Did the mother say anything else?"

Felicity nodded. "She said, 'I need you to take my baby.' She said she'd read on the internet that she could bring the baby here and someone would adopt him. I tried to get her name, but she said she didn't have to."

"She's right," Wade said. "Vermont's Safe Haven law means she can give up the baby anonymously."

Such a thing had never happened in Lovestruck before, though. According to what the mother had told him when she'd given birth on Thanksgiving Day, she didn't even live in the Lovestruck town limits. She lived in a rural community two counties away, closer to Burlington. Under the Safe Haven law, she could have taken the baby to any police or fire station, a hospital or house of worship. There had to be at least half a dozen of those closer to the young woman's home.

Which meant she'd specifically wanted to leave her baby with him.

"Okay." Wade swallowed hard. "Everything's going to be fine. There are procedures for this sort of thing."

"Good." Felicity blew out an exhale, as if she'd finally remembered how to breathe.

Wade wished he could hug her, but he had an armful of baby and was far too rattled to attempt multitasking. He also wished—very much so— that Felicity wasn't dressed like the Virgin Mary. She looked so pretty draped in Biblical blue silk, and coupled with the live infant cooing against his chest, it was just too much. Like this moment was predestined somehow. Fated.

"What are those procedures, exactly?" Felicity glanced down at the baby and then back up at him. "What do we do now?"

We.

Thank God. If she left him to deal with the child alone, he wasn't sure he could handle it. Some hero.

Wade took a deep breath. He'd been trained for instances exactly like this one. He knew precisely what he was supposed to do—examine the baby to make sure the child was unharmed and then transport him immediately to a hospital. From there, the Department of Child and Family Services would take over. They were used to this sort of thing. They did it every day. They'd most likely place the child in a foster home, and Wade would be free to go.

And he'd never see the baby again.

His throat burned. He looked down at the tiny bundle resting in his arms and breathed in the newborn's soft, baby powder scent. He couldn't drive to Burlington and hand the child over to a government agency. Just the thought of it made him sick to his stomach.

"We're calling Cap," Wade said.

Cap would help him. He'd understand Wade's dilemma—at least Wade hoped he would.

But whatever happened, Wade didn't want to go through it alone. Maybe it was the fact that he and Felicity were both standing there on a cold December night, dressed as Mary and Joseph. Or maybe it was the way her eyes seemed haunted every time she looked at the baby, but it felt like they were in this thing together. And he wanted, *needed*, it to stay that way. At least for now.

"Don't go," he said, and his voice sounded rusty all of a sudden, like it hadn't been used in a very long time. Then again, Wade wasn't accustomed to asking for help. He was unflappable. Like most firemen, he was always composed, always in control.

Until now, it seemed.

"Please," he said, as evenly as he could manage. "Please, don't go."

Back when Felicity worked at *Fashionista* in New York, the magazine did a glamorous photography spread based on the scientific principle of the flight-versus-fight response. Sometimes called the acute stress response, fight or flight refers to the human body's physiological reaction to anything extreme or terrifying. Triggered by the nervous system, a rush of hormones flood the body, propelling a person to either stay and fight or run away as fast as they can.

The photo spread, shot on location in the hall of dinosaurs at the Museum of Natural History on the Upper West Side, was somewhat ridiculous. Reed-thin models in sky-high Jimmy Choo stilettos ran away from T. rex skeletons, while others pretended to box a Brontosaurus with diamond-encrusted boxing gloves from Tiffany and Co. Absurdity aside, seeing the pictures on the glossy pages of the magazine where she worked made Felicity wonder what she might do when faced with imminent danger.

Flee? Or stay and fight for her life?

Now that she was inside the warm firehouse, settled into one of the soft leather recliners with the LFD logo embroidered on its back, she still wasn't sure. There was an infant on her lap, staring up at her with baby blue eyes and a tiny little mouth as perfect as a pert little bow. Felicity's heart was pounding so hard and fast, she knew she was definitely having some sort of major physiological response, but she couldn't decide which one it was.

Was it possible to want desperately to flee and somehow also long to stay and cuddle the innocent baby cooing away on her lap, all at once?

"Well." Cap sighed and sat back in the recliner beside her.

He'd arrived at the station within minutes of Wade's call and, for the past half hour, had been listening intently to Felicity's recap of the encounter with the desperate young mother. She'd told the story at least ten times by now, but it never seemed to get any easier. The lump in her throat was a hard rock, and it was beginning to feel like it might be permanent.

"Well," Cap said again, clearly at a loss for words.

Felicity understood why he felt so unsettled, but it seemed like such a strange word to keep repeating.

Well…well.

Things weren't well at all. In fact, she hadn't felt so unwell in quite a while. Six months, to be exact.

"It definitely sounds like the mother has chosen to engage a safe haven." Cap sighed again and stood. "We've never had a safe haven baby here in Lovestruck, but I suppose there's a first time for everything. Wade?"

Wade's gaze shifted from the baby to Cap. "Yes?"

He'd been strangely quiet since they'd moved into the firehouse, and once Cap arrived, he hadn't added a single word to Felicity's statement. He'd just leaned against a nearby wall with his arms crossed and his brow furrowed. The only time he seemed to relax was when he looked at the baby.

"Since you were the one on duty when the child was brought in, you need to be the one to take the baby up to the hospital in Burlington." Cap raked a hand through his salt-and-pepper hair. "A social worker will want to talk to you and have you fill out some forms. Felicity, I hate to ask you to make the trek up there, but it would be great if you went along."

Felicity's pulse beat so fast that she felt like she was choking on it.

"No," Wade said quietly.

Thank goodness. The more involved she got

with this mess, the worse she'd feel when it ended. She couldn't accompany Wade all the way to the city just to drop the baby off like an unwanted animal at the pound. Just the thought of it made her stomach turn.

"I'm afraid they'll want to talk to her, too," Cap said. "She was the only person who had any direct contact with the mother."

"No," Wade said again—louder this time, with an edge that made Felicity go still. "I don't mean that I don't want Felicity to come along. What I'm trying to say is that we can't turn that baby over to the state."

Cap's gaze narrowed as uncomfortable silence fell over the room. If the baby hadn't just closed his eyes and fallen asleep, Felicity would have gotten up and gone someplace else. Anyplace, really. From what she knew of Cap, he was a perfectly nice man. Madison's husband, Jack, almost seemed to think of him as a father figure, and up until now, she'd only seen Wade treat him with the utmost respect.

But Wade had just refused an order from his captain, and it didn't seem to be going over well. An angry-looking vein had just appeared in Cap's temple, a definite cue for Felicity to leave and let these two alpha males battle it out for themselves.

She wasn't about to disturb the sleeping newborn, though. There wasn't an ounce of formula on hand. Or a baby bottle. Or diapers. Or anything that infants needed. If this child started fussing, she'd have no way to make him stop, and he'd already been through more than any tiny baby should.

"Disobeying an order isn't like you, son," Cap finally said.

Wade seemed to soften at the endearment. The tense set of his shoulders relaxed, ever so slightly. But his eyes grew shiny, and Felicity definitely knew she was witnessing something she shouldn't.

"I know, and I'm sorry," he said. His gaze flitted briefly toward Felicity and she looked away.

The set of Cap's jaw went as hard as granite. "What aren't you telling me?"

A silence fell over the room, so tense and thick it was almost palpable. The infant's soft sleep noises seemed deafening all of a sudden.

"It's the same baby," Wade finally said.

Cap's mouth fell open. At first Felicity didn't know what Wade meant, but then she remembered what he'd said in the SUV on the way to the firehouse and the way his smile hadn't quite met his eyes.

No baby talk tonight, I promise.

She'd given him her word, because he didn't want to dwell on the baby he'd helped deliver—

the baby everyone in town couldn't stop talking about.

Could the infant in her lap be the very same baby?

A cold chill swept over Felicity as the young mother's panic suddenly made more sense.

He might recognize me.

Cap studied the baby through narrowed eyes. "Are you sure?"

Wade nodded. "One thousand percent."

The two of them looked at one another for a prolonged moment, and something unspoken seemed to pass between them.

Cap sighed. "I understand why you might feel attached, but—"

"But nothing. I'm not turning that baby over to the state. I can't do it, not now. It's almost Christmas. What if the mother comes back? What if…" The hint of desperation in Wade's tone seemed to scrape Felicity's insides, reopening wounds that had scarcely begun to mend.

What if?

Felicity allowed herself a brief moment to look at the baby's face—*really* look, as opposed to just sneaking glances at him as if she were terrified of his fragile vulnerability. Which she sort of was. Although truthfully, her own vulnerability was equally terrifying.

Everything about him was so tiny and precious. His delicate eyelashes rested against pale skin, so fair it was almost translucent. And his mouth was as pink and perfect as a rosebud. Of course Wade didn't want to turn him over to the state. Felicity completely understood his hesitancy. She understood more than he or Cap could possibly know.

Cap's eyebrows rose. "You're telling me you want to keep the baby."

"What? No, of course not." Wade went pale again. "I don't think so, anyway."

Good. A million things could go wrong if he tried to adopt this child. He'd have no idea what sort of pain he was opening himself up to. As much as Felicity hated to admit it, Wade was better off following Cap's orders and taking the baby straight to the hospital.

But there was no way she was going with him. Wild horses couldn't drag her there.

"You don't think so?" Cap said.

Wade shook his head and dragged a hand through his hair. He looked impossibly weary all of a sudden, as if he'd been carrying the weight of the world on his back these past few weeks, instead of a mere six pounds and thirteen ounces. "I just need some time with him, okay? I feel responsible for him, and in my head, I know that the responsible thing to do is to take him straight to Burlington. But in my heart…"

His voice cracked, and Felicity's eyes filled with unshed tears. Everything went blurry, like a watercolor painting. She really needed to leave—the sooner, the better.

"Please, Cap? Isn't there anything you can do? It's the holidays. Just give me until after Christmas." Wade's hands flexed and unflexed, like he was preparing for some sort of battle.

Cap must have finally gotten the message that he wasn't going to back down, because the older man glanced at the infant sleeping in Felicity's lap again, and this time, his expression turned tender. "I could probably give the social worker up in Burlington a call and see if we could place the baby with someone here in town. But I'm warning you, it's a long shot."

"But it's possible?" A smile crept its way to Wade's lips, and a rebellious little flutter traveled through Felicity's belly.

She hadn't been sure anything could make Wade Ericson more attractive, but his sudden attachment to an abandoned baby definitely did the trick. Ugh, why did she have to be so weak?

"Only if there's someone here in Lovestruck who's undergone official foster care training. If not, you're out of luck," Cap said. "And that's assuming the social worker will even agree to try to find placement for the child here in town."

Felicity coughed. "I'm sorry to interrupt, but I just remembered there's someplace I need to be."

Both men frowned in her direction.

"You mean the living nativity?" Wade said.

"Don't worry about that." Cap shook his head. "I spoke to the mayor and told her it would need to be postponed because Wade had to go out on an emergency."

"No, I don't mean that. It's something else." Felicity gathered the baby in her arms. He squeezed his little hands into fists, as if in protest, and hot tears stung her eyes again, clouding her vision. "I just need to go. Right now."

She offered Wade the tiny bundle, begging silently for him to take it.

He did, peering intently at her, face etched with concern. "Is everything okay? Do you need me to come with you?"

She shook her head. The absolute last thing she needed was baby-loving hero Wade Ericson to escort her home.

Anything but that.

"I'm fine. Really. I just—" She waved a hand toward the exit. A chill wracked her body, she felt cold and hot at the same time, and panic clawed at her from the inside out.

This is it, she thought. *Fight or flight.*

Wade took a step closer. If she didn't get out of here right now she'd get caught up in the foster parent discussion, and she couldn't let that happen. No way.

So in the end, Felicity chose flight. And without another word, she turned around and ran right out the door.

Chapter Three

The door banging shut behind Felicity felt like a punch to Wade's gut. He wasn't sure why, but he got the distinct feeling he'd just done something wrong.

Very, very wrong.

But he had no clue what it could possibly have been. He'd been on the receiving end of plenty of door slams in his bachelor life, and usually he had a good idea what he'd done to deserve them. No such luck this time.

"That was an oddly abrupt departure." Cap frowned in the direction of the closed door. "Did I miss something?"

"I think we both did," Wade said. But he couldn't begin to unpack the myriad of social cues he'd apparently missed where Felicity was concerned, because the tiny baby boy in his arms was beginning to wake up.

He blinked big blue eyes up at Wade, and even though Wade was fairly certain two-week-old infants weren't capable of focusing at such a young age, an immense vulnerability swept over him. He felt raw. Seen. Seen in a way he'd never quite felt before.

And then the baby's tiny face turned pink and he began to wail.

Crap. What had possessed him to think he needed to be involved in this situation in any way? He had no clue what he was doing.

It's going to be fine. You're not keeping the baby. You just want to see for yourself that he's properly taken care of.

Wade shifted the baby from one arm to the other and did his best to emulate the rocking motion Felicity had used earlier while he'd been busy calling Cap. Despite the hesitancy in her expression, she'd been a natural with the infant. And, in the moments when Wade had been pretty sure she thought he wasn't looking, she'd seemed downright entranced by the child. Serene. Beatific, even.

Or maybe that had just been the Virgin Mary costume talking.

Somehow, he doubted it. In any event, she was gone now, which was perfectly fine. She didn't owe him a thing. They barely knew each other, and after all, he was the one who'd suddenly decided he couldn't bear to send the baby off to strangers in Burlington.

"Wade." Cap arched a brow as Wade continued trying the shoosh-bounce thing Felicity had done.

As best he could remember, it had involved a lot of rocking, combined with soft shushing sounds. Clearly, he was doing it wrong.

"Yes?" he said, just loud enough for Cap to hear him over the baby's cries.

Cap massaged the back of his neck. The lines in his forehead seemed to be growing deeper by the second. "You're making a valiant effort, but I don't think bouncing around and whispering *hush* are going to cut it."

"Oh." Wade's heart sank a little. He'd realized his little baby dance wasn't making much of a difference, but having those suspicions confirmed by an outside party didn't feel great. He needed some sort of manual. Or better yet, a miracle. "Should I sing instead?"

He couldn't think of a proper lullaby off the top of his head, so he launched into an admittedly off-key version of "The Wheels on the Bus Go

Round and Round," replacing the word *bus* with *fire truck*. As one does.

Cap covered his face, shoulders shaking with quiet laughter. Which made exactly one person in the room who was entertained. The baby was still decidedly unimpressed.

Cap shook his head. "Good grief, please stop."

Wade clamped his mouth shut. The infant kept on fussing. Other than being worried about the child's well-being, Wade didn't really mind the crying. It was more of a loud mewing than an outright roar, sort of like a lion cub testing out his lungs.

He arched a brow at Cap. "What's wrong with my singing?"

"In a word?" Cap snorted. "Everything."

Wade rolled his eyes. "That's really helpful."

"The child needs more than off-key nursery rhymes. He probably needs baby formula." Cap pulled a face. "And he definitely needs a clean diaper."

Diapers. *Of course.* Wade probably should have thought of that first thing. And formula, too, obviously. "I know you think I'm terrible at this, but it's just until you get in touch with the social worker and a local foster home is secured. It's temporary."

"Very *very* temporary. I'm probably breaking a law or two as we speak." Cap heaved another huge sigh. "Why don't you run out to the Village Market and get some baby supplies? I need to get that social worker on the phone ASAP."

"Sure, no problem," Wade said, feeling a bit more confident now that he had an actual plan of action. Like most firefighters, he was a big fan of organized preparation. All it took to master an emergency situation was a calm demeanor and a clear-cut plan.

As if the baby had a point to prove, he curled his hands into tiny fists and let out a piercing cry.

Make no mistake, mister. You're not in control. I am.

Wade offered the screaming bundle of joy to Cap. "He's all yours. I'll be right back."

Cap let out a sardonic laugh and held up his hands. "Whoa there, Mary Poppins. I'm not looking after him. He's your responsibility now."

Wade just stood there, not knowing quite what to do.

"Temporarily," Cap added. Then he jerked his head in the direction of the apparatus bay. "Take the SUV. There should be a car seat out in the supply closet. You remember how to use one of those, don't you?"

Of course, he did. The station offered free car seat checks every other weekend. Wade knew more about child safety devices than most of the actual parents in Lovestruck. He'd just never had the need for one before, nor had he ever had to drive anywhere with a fragile two-week-old tucked into the back seat behind him.

"Sure." He shrugged one shoulder. Village Market was just down the street. How hard could it be to run a quick errand?

"Good luck. I've got calls to make." Cap dug the keys out of his pocket and dropped them into Wade's outstretched hand. Then he stalked toward his office, leaving Wade and the baby alone together.

Wade's gut tangled in a knot as he looked down at the unhappy infant. He could do this. He just needed to follow the plan. Step one: car seat. Step two: diapers and formula.

And probably baby bottles. And maybe a pacifier. Did babies this small even use those? He had no idea, but he sort of wished he had one on him at the moment. Was it bad that he wished for one? Probably...

Definitely.

Good grief, what was he doing?

"We're off," he called. Cap was probably just bluffing, trying to rattle some sense into him so he'd back down and agree to take the infant to Burlington—to follow procedure, as he'd been trained to do his entire career.

But if Cap was bluffing, he didn't let on. Wade's only answer was a resounding silence.

"Okay, kiddo, it's just you and me," he murmured, shifting the baby boy into a cradle hold. He felt like he was trying juggle some precious piece of artwork, crafted from spun glass. "But don't get used to it."

At least the car seat went in smoothly, other than the fact that it took Wade three times longer than usual to get it fastened with a living, breathing baby strapped inside. During the short drive to Village Market, he probably maxed out at fifteen miles per hour. Every tiny pothole felt like a crater, but they made it. And, by some miracle, the baby was sound asleep upon their arrival.

Wade almost hated to get him out of the car seat at that point, so he sat inside the LFD utility vehicle for a second, listening to the infant's snuggly sleep sounds. For a tiny thing, he sure made a lot of noise. It reminded him of his mom's ten-year-old Cavalier King Charles spaniel, Duchess. Duchess snored loud enough to peel the paint off the walls.

Wade would know—he'd become Duchess's doggy dad when his mom lost her battle with breast cancer last year. Not *caretaker*, not *owner*. Not even the somewhat-tolerable *pet parent*. In her will, his mom had declared him Duchess's *doggy dad*. He liked to think she'd chosen the phrasing because she'd wanted to make him laugh. It had…and then once he'd gotten home from that first meeting with her estate attorney, he'd buried his face into the dog's soft fur and wept.

The aptly named Duchess was a royal pain in the backside. The snoring was just the tip of the iceberg. She chewed things and she liked to bark. A lot. She was also partially deaf, which supposedly explained all the barking. According to the vet, she couldn't hear herself bark, so just kept at it in an effort to make certain she was expressing herself. Wade wasn't sure he bought that explanation. Either way, he loved that dog simply because she'd meant the world to his mom. She liked to call Duchess the grandchild she'd never had.

Wade's gaze remained glued to the rearview mirror, which he'd angled to afford himself a clear, unobstructed view of the sleeping baby. A lump formed in his throat as he took in the infant's tiny little fists and the delicate furrow in his brow, as if the child felt as confused and angry about his current set of circumstances as Wade did. As if he *knew*.

Wade cleared his throat, to no avail. The lump remained, and somewhere in the back of his head, he heard his mom's voice—the teasing tone she'd always used when she talked to the dog but was really trying to pass along a message to Wade.

The grandchild I never had…

Did his recent preoccupation with the baby in the back seat have something to do with losing his mom, knowing he'd never given her the one thing she wanted so badly near the end? Undoubtedly. He just wasn't sure what to do about it.

The only thing he knew for certain was that he wanted to do right by the child, especially since fate or some other unseen force kept throwing them together. At the moment, doing the right thing meant food and diapers—sticking to the plan, not indulging in introspection. While he was at the market, he should probably pick up some dog food, as well—the special, poultry-free kind that cost a significant portion of his paycheck. Duchess was allergic to chicken and turkey, because of course she was.

"Come on, little one," he said as he climbed out of the driver's seat and unfastened the buckle holding the small baby in place.

Wade moved as slowly as he could, doing his best not to wake the infant. The snoring bundle felt warm, heavy with sleep. Wade was hoping to make the market run as speedy as possible, for several reasons. First, he needed to get back to the station and attend to the infant's needs. Second, he really didn't want to be spotted shopping in the baby section of Village Market. If he did, the Lovestruck rumor mill would never let it go.

Never ever.

Fortunately, the small mom-and-pop grocery store was virtually empty, thanks to opening night of the Christmas festival. It was probably winding down for the night by now, but Wade was able to move stealthily through the store, even while having to push his grocery cart one-handed so he could keep a firm grip on the baby. He tossed a few cans of Duchess's high-end dog food into the basket and then hauled his cart toward the diaper aisle as fast as he could.

And that's where he was busted—spotted at once by a cluster of the moms who liked to gather outside the Bean, balancing hot maple lattes in the cup holders of the strollers they pushed up and down Main Street every morning. Only instead of yoga pants and puffy coats, they were all dressed in the official holiday-themed Lovestruck mom uniform of gaudy Christmas sweaters, skinny jeans and chunky snow boots with fur trim. And every one of them lit up like a Christmas tree as their gazes strayed from Wade's flushed face to the baby in his arms.

Wade froze, a reindeer in headlights.

"Wade?" one of them said. It was Diane Foster, the redhead who called the fire department every autumn to ignite her heater's pilot light, even though all it took was a simple flip of a switch. "Wade Ericson, is that you? With another *baby*?"

"Um, no." He shook his head as if the blanket-wrapped child in his arms was imaginary. The women exchanged curious glances with one another. "I mean, yes. But it's not what—"

His words were immediately drowned out by a chorus of squeals.

"Oh. Em. Gee!"

"Aren't you just the *cutest*?"

"Wade Ericson, you are the sweetest man in Lovestruck. Sweeter than pure Vermont maple syrup."

But it's not what you think.

Who was he kidding? This situation was precisely the sort of thing his baby-centric fan club would swoon over for days. He didn't even want to think about how they would react if they knew the little boy in his arms wasn't just any baby, but was in fact *the* baby—the very infant that the entire town had been obsessed with for weeks.

Wade's jaw clenched. They couldn't find out. No way, no how. The poor kid had been through enough already.

"Ladies, please." He held the pointer finger of his free hand to his lips. "You'll wake the baby."

"Oh, right. Silly us." Diane Foster pressed a perfectly manicured hand to her chest. "So sorry."

"It's just that you look beyond adorable holding that baby," one of the other moms said.

Everyone nodded.

"Just precious," Diane added, and then her left eyebrow arched ever so slightly. "Who did you say the sweet little tot belongs to again?"

He hadn't. And he wouldn't. Wade wouldn't know how to answer that question even if he wanted to, which he most certainly did not.

"I'm babysitting for a friend." He flashed the moms a wink, because he figured the only way to get out of this encounter without divulging any factual information would be to flirt his way through it.

Predictably, it worked like a charm. Copious amounts of eyelash fluttering followed. A woman holding a jumbo-sized box of Pampers and wearing a sweater with a sequined Grinch face on it sighed.

"Your friend is one lucky lady," she said.

Wade needed to get out of here. Things were getting weird. He glanced up and down the aisle. He'd never seen so much baby paraphernalia in his life. It was going to take him an eternity to figure out the barest baby necessities, and now he was going to have to do it with an audience. Unless...

"I don't suppose you ladies could help me figure out what this little tyke needs? I'm kind of in a hurry." He flashed the moms a smile.

Bingo. Ten minutes later, his cart was overflowing with diapers, formula, bottles, baby wipes and a few other items that he'd never heard of before but were absolutely essential, according to the moms. He'd figure everything out once he got back to the station.

He blinked hard when he saw the total on the little machine at the checkout and then swiped his credit card as fast as he could. His fan club was lined up behind him at the register, but he was nearly home free. So long as the baby kept snoring, he could make a clean getaway without having to answer any more questions.

See, he thought to himself. *This isn't so hard.* He gave the moms a parting wave for good measure.

And then his cell phone rang.

The baby began to stir as Wade steered his cartful of bags out of the way. When he dug his phone out of his pocket, Cap's name lit up the illuminated screen. He had no choice but to take the call.

"Hello. Sorry, Cap. I know it's taken a while, but I'm leaving Village Market and I'll be back in just a few minutes."

"That's not why I'm calling," Cap said. "I have news."

Wade's heart began to ricochet around in his chest. He also couldn't help noticing that his left arm was getting sore from cradling the infant. How was that possible? He worked out every day at the firehouse. Maybe he was on the verge of some sort of cardiac episode.

Or maybe you're afraid of saying goodbye to the child you're holding.

No. He refused to believe it. There had to be a certified foster home someplace nearby with a family willing to look after a baby for the holidays. Who would say no to a newborn at Christmas?

"What's the news, Cap?" Wade inhaled a ragged breath. *Please don't say there's no room at the inn.*

"You're not going to believe this. We've got one registered foster home here in Lovestruck."

"That's fantastic." Wade felt himself smiling like a kid on Christmas morning.

"It is…and it isn't," Cap said. "Believe it or not, the foster parent is Felicity Hart."

Wade went still. Felicity had gone through foster parent certification? That certainly explained why she'd been so great with the baby. But why hadn't she said anything when they'd been discussing trying to place the infant with a foster family in Lovestruck? She'd been so quiet.

Wade's gut churned.

And then she ran.

"I'm sorry, Wade." Cap cleared his throat, and when he spoke again, his tone was less business-like and gentler. "The social worker gave her a call, and she said no. She said she just can't do it."

"That can't possibly be right." Wade closed his eyes. The moms were staring at him again, and he couldn't take it. Not now. "Are you sure?"

"I'm sure, son."

It was the *son* that broke him. No one had called Wade that since his mother passed, and now here he was with a homeless baby in his arms. A baby he was suddenly powerless to help. A baby who deserved to be called son...by someone, somewhere.

And then, as if he knew, the little boy in Wade's arms began to cry.

Chapter Four

What have I done?

Felicity burrowed deeper into her bathrobe as she sat on her sage green velvet sofa and stared blankly at the Hallmark Christmas movie rerun currently playing on her television screen. She'd opened a bottle of dry cabernet and crawled into the bathrobe—from an insanely expensive luxury brand favored by Chrissy Teigen, which Felicity had received as part of her Christmas bonus from *Fashionista*—the minute she'd hung up the phone a little over an hour ago.

She should have never answered the call to begin with. The words *State of Vermont* flashing across the top of her cell phone screen should have been enough to run for cover. But instead of declining the call and activating her do-not-disturb setting, she'd gone ahead and answered it. She just hadn't been able to help it. Her heart hadn't let her.

At least she'd managed to say no. She couldn't take on a foster child. There was simply no way. Her emotional state was far too fragile to let another baby into her life, and even if she wanted to care for the tiny infant, her living situation in Lovestruck was hardly ideal.

She glanced around her tiny efficiency apartment and winced. She'd done her best, but no amount of lavender paint and repurposed French country-style bookshelves could make the cramped space look like anything other than what it was— the converted attic space perched above her yoga studio. As it turned out, the Realtor had been using the term *converted* awfully loosely.

The sloped ceiling meant that Felicity could only stand fully erect at one end of the room, and the kitchen area was comprised of a single-burner stove, a decrepit microwave and a sink with about half as much room as her Hermès Birkin bag. She couldn't possibly care for a baby in this environment. She could hardly care for herself.

Looking back, she should have probably saved some of the money she had paid her contractor to finish out the yoga studio and gotten a proper apartment before draining every last drop of her savings account. But the studio was beautifully serene, with blond bamboo floors and soothing periwinkle walls. The surround sound system was so realistic that when she played her birdsong playlist, it legitimately seemed as if songbirds flitted around the room. Felicity just knew every yogi in town would love the space as much as she did.

Spoiler alert: there *were* no yogis in Lovestruck. Not a single one, if her dwindling bank account was any indication. Namaste.

Still, saying no to the social worker had been a struggle. Every time she closed her eyes, she saw the baby boy's sweet, innocent face. His delicate fingers. The wisps of soft blond hair on his perfect little head. Every time she took a breath, she imagined his baby powder scent.

She was losing it.

She reached for the wine bottle for another pour, but just as the deep red wine began to spill into her glass, the buzzer rang downstairs.

Well, this is a first. Felicity frowned into her cabernet. Who would possibly be dropping by the yoga studio at eleven p.m.?

Or ever, actually. Her last three classes had attracted zero participants. Even Madison hadn't been in class for almost a week. Between her job at the local paper and doting on her new family, she just didn't have the time.

For a hot second, Felicity thought about not answering the bell. The odds of finding someone down there in need of a late-night emergency one-on-one yoga session were slim to none. But she couldn't afford to turn away even a sliver of business. Sheer desperation, coupled with another ring of the bell, propelled her to her feet.

"I'll be right down," she called, ducking to avoid the exposed beam that ran the length of her ceiling.

The narrow stairway that led down to the studio never failed to freak her out just a little bit in the evenings, mainly because Lovestruck was so quiet this time of night. It was such a stark contrast to Manhattan, which always did its best to live up to its reputation as the city that never sleeps. Lovestruck, on the other hand, seemed to roll up the sidewalks and turn out all the lights right after dinner. And dinner was typically served at five-thirty, not nine p.m.

Felicity had been a Vermonter for two whole weeks, and she'd yet to grow accustomed to it. So she wrapped her robe more tightly around her frame and padded across the smooth floor of the yoga studio, mildly alarmed at the sight of a distinctly male silhouette standing on the other side of the frosted glass door.

You're fine. There are no serial killers in Vermont. Were there?

She squared her shoulders and reminded herself that she'd once almost been forced to pepper spray Elmo in Times Square after he'd gotten a little too aggressively friendly. She'd walked away from that incident just fine. Surely she could handle Lovestruck after hours.

But when she swung the door open and took in the tortured expression on Wade Ericson's chiseled face, her confidence took a major hit.

"Wade." She gave him wobbly smile. Why did she feel like crying all of a sudden? "What are you doing here?"

"I'm sorry. I know it's late." He raked a hand through his dark hair. Bits of snow glittered in his close-cropped beard, and the ivory cable-knit fisherman's sweater he was wearing was frayed around the edges. His coat was unbuttoned, exposing a tiny hole that had formed near his left shoulder where the yarn had begun unraveling.

Felicity couldn't take her eyes off the spot. *That's exactly how I feel*, she thought. *Like I'm unraveling.* The strange sensation had started the moment the panicked teen had placed the baby in her arms, and she couldn't shake it, no matter how hard she tried. If anything, it was growing worse.

"Can we talk?" Wade said, and then he cleared

his throat in what seemed like an attempt to disguise the ache in his tone.

He's unraveling, too.

Felicity was desperate to say no. Opening the door any wider would be just like opening her heart, and she just wasn't ready for that. She wasn't sure she ever would be.

But there was no way she could say no—not after what they'd been through together tonight. "Come in. It's freezing out."

A flurry of snowflakes and crisp winter air ushered him inside, and Felicity pulled the door closed behind him, locking the dead bolt with a click that echoed throughout the empty studio. Once a New Yorker, always a New Yorker.

She turned around, and Wade was right there, close enough for her to breathe in his campfire scent. She had a sudden craving for roasted marshmallows.

"Um." Felicity took a small backward step and averted her gaze, but Wade was everywhere—reflected in the studio mirrors on all sides. "Why don't we go upstairs?"

Seconds later, they were inside her tiny apartment, which wasn't much better. Wade seemed to take up every bit of available space.

"Can I get you something? Wine, maybe?" She waved a hand toward the opened bottle of red sitting on a tray on top of the tufted ottoman that pulled double duty as her footrest and coffee table. A tiny Christmas tree sat beside it, decorated with a string of white twinkle lights and smooth round satin ornaments.

Wade's gaze settled on the green glass bottle with a vacant stare, and Felicity gnawed on her bottom lip. This was worse than she'd thought. The poor guy was too shell-shocked to form a response.

"I'll just grab you a glass. Sit," she said.

She gave his chest a gentle, wholly ineffectual shove. Despite its uselessness against his brick wall of a torso, Wade took the hint and lowered himself onto her velvet sofa.

"I didn't realize you lived above your yoga studio," he said quietly as she poured his wine.

"It's supposed to be temporary," she said, cheeks going warm.

Why was she apologizing for where she lived? The same apartment in the most desirable parts of Manhattan would rent for a small fortune.

But they weren't in New York. They were in Lovestruck, where white picket fences and farm houses with gabled roofs were all the rage. And as much as Felicity hated to admit it, she wanted those things. She was tired of the chaos and noise of the city. She felt like she'd been running on a hamster wheel for the entirety of her adult life, and she wanted off. Becoming a foster mother had changed her in so many ways, all for the better.

The irony of it all was that she'd never wanted a baby. She'd been perfectly happy living her best life as the beauty editor at *Fashionista*, single girl about town. Growing up on a steady diet of *The Devil Wears Prada* and *Sex and the City* reruns had led her to the Big Apple, where she'd made each and every one of her dreams come true.

And then her sixteen-year-old cousin had gotten pregnant and begged Felicity for help. What was she supposed to do? Lori's parents had tossed her out of the house, so Felicity let her move in for a while. After all, she was just a kid—a kid who'd always hero-worshipped Felicity. Somehow, as the weeks and months passed, Felicity became more and more invested in Lori's pregnancy. She was all Lori had, and on the foggy, gray morning when her baby had been born, it had been like the clouds parted for Felicity. She'd fallen in love with the baby girl on sight. When Lori had told the hospital she wanted to give her up for adoption, Felicity didn't have to think twice about signing up for foster care training. The baby was family—*her* family. And she had been ready to claim her as her own and take care of her after Lori moved back home.

Raising a baby in Manhattan wasn't easy, but Felicity had figured it out. She'd done her very best for six precious months, and right when she'd thought her life had changed for good, everything had come to a screeching halt. At the eleventh hour, Lori had changed her mind. Even though she'd never so much as changed a diaper or even visited Felicity since the baby was born, she hadn't wanted to sign the adoption papers. She'd wanted to raise the baby on her own. Overnight, Felicity had gone back to being alone. She hadn't known how to go back to the person she'd been before. She'd tried, but she just couldn't do it.

And then Felicity had met Madison, and every time her new friend had mentioned Lovestruck, Vermont, the reverence in her tone spoke to something deep inside Felicity. In her darkest moments, the idea that someplace like Lovestruck could even exist had been the one thing that kept her going.

If only she could go there someday...

If only she could wipe the slate clean and leave the past behind...

If only.

Vermont was supposed to be her fresh start, her new beginning. And her fresh start was *not* supposed to involve falling in love with another baby. She couldn't go through that again. It would break her this time.

Felicity sat down beside Wade and folded her hands in her lap to keep them from shaking. "Listen, I know why you're here. You obviously found out that I'm on the list of regional foster parents, and you want me to reconsider taking care of—" she paused before she blurted out the words that were on the tip of her tongue. *Our baby boy.* The sweet abandoned infant wasn't hers, no matter how natural it felt to hold him in her arms. And he certainly wasn't *theirs*. She and Wade were practically strangers. "—the baby boy."

"You're not just on the list. You *are* the list." Wade turned a tender, almost apologetic, smile in her direction.

Oh. She took a sharp inhale. *Oh, wow.*

The social worker hadn't shared that information with her. Still, what was she supposed to do? Set up a crib in her semi-converted attic space and promise herself not to get attached this time?

Too late.

She stared down at her trembling hands. "I, um…I didn't know that. And now you're here to try to change my mind."

He gave her chin a gentle tap with his fingertips until she met his gaze. "You can relax, Felicity. That's not why I'm here."

Wait. *What?*

She blinked. "Seriously?"

"Seriously." He withdrew his hand to reach for his wineglass, and the reflection from the lights on the Christmas tree seemed to dance and swirl in the ruby-red liquid as he brought it to his lips.

Felicity was suddenly overly aware of the press of his warm thigh against hers. She and Wade had never touched each other so casually before, and now in the span of five minutes, she'd given him a playful shove and he'd cupped her face with his fingertips, leaving a trail of goose bumps in their wake. It felt…nice.

Nicer than it should have.

Her brain told her scoot away—even just an inch or so—but she couldn't seem to make herself budge. They'd shared something today. Something intimate, in its own special way. Maybe that explained her sudden urge to rest her head on his broad shoulder, close her eyes and bury her hands in that cozy cable-knit sweater of his, as if it were a security blanket.

"Why are you here, then?" she finally asked, fiddling with the sash of her bathrobe in a pathetic attempt to occupy her wandering thoughts.

"I just wanted to thank you for everything you did today. I didn't mean for you to get dragged into all of this, I promise I didn't."

So he truly wasn't going to try to convince her to take care of the baby, at least short-term. A quick stab of something that felt too much like disappointment hit her square in the heart.

"It's not your fault. It just—" she shrugged "—happened."

Right. Except they'd been dressed as Mary and Joseph, and the baby was the very same one Wade had delivered a few weeks ago. Those were two awfully gigantic coincidences. No wonder she couldn't shake the nagging feeling that destiny had played a part in placing that baby into their hands.

She took a deep breath. "I can't be his foster mom."

Wade slid his gaze toward her. "I know. You said no, and I respect that."

"I mean, look around." She threw up her hands. "This place isn't fit for a family."

"No argument there," Wade said, and the corner of his mouth twitched into a tiny, almost imperceptible grin. "It's rather cozy, though."

Felicity stood, crossed her arms and frowned down at him. "Stop it. I know what you're doing."

Wade dragged himself to his feet, obliterating her fleeting sense of superiority. Then he angled his head toward her. His gorgeous, gorgeous head. "And what would that be, exactly?"

"You're trying to use some sort of reverse psychology on me." She lifted her chin, putting her mouth dangerously close to his. Within kissing distance, almost.

Focus. No one is thinking about kissing.

She cleared her throat. "It's not going to work."

Liar, liar. Pants on fire. It was sort of working, and one of them was definitely thinking about kissing—maybe even both of them.

Wade arched a brow.

Ugh. He might be beautiful and gallant and heroic, but he was also infuriating. "Truly, it's not. I'm probably not even going to end up staying here in Lovestruck."

She hadn't intended to blurt that out. She hadn't even allowed herself to consciously think about a future anyplace else. But if her yoga studio didn't start attracting clients soon—even just a handful of them—she might not be able to pay her rent on the studio. So much for the old adage that if you could make it in New York, you could make it anywhere.

"But you practically just got here," Wade said.

"I know, and it was a stupid whim. Apparently Lovestruck isn't exactly a yoga hotspot. I should have done more research before I packed up and moved here." Fled was more like. Felicity had been running away from New York as much as she'd been running toward Lovestruck. She should have known Vermont wouldn't be the utopia she'd thought it was after visiting for Madison and Jack's wedding. No place was perfect.

"You need clients?" Wade's forehead crinkled. "That's why you might leave?"

"Yes, I need clients. I'm pretty desperate, actually." Felicity would have thought such an admission would have been more painful to articulate, but not after today. Her problems didn't seem quite as important anymore. Nothing had changed, and somehow everything had, all in one day. "I'm just not really desirable foster parent material at the moment."

"Understood." Wade nodded, and his gaze flitted around the apartment before settling on the small Christmas tree in the center of the room. There was only a sliver of space between his head and the ceiling, and they weren't even anywhere near the sloped section of the attic. "Although, if it's your apartment you're worried about, you and the baby could always stay with me."

Felicity stared at him as if he'd just sprouted another head. Stay with him…as in *live together*? He couldn't be serious.

Wade shrugged one muscular shoulder, as if he'd just suggested they go out for a casual coffee or hot chocolate date instead of sharing a home and raising a child together. "But I guess that's off the table, because you've already made up your mind."

Had she?

Oh, right. She had.

Everything was starting to feel a lot less cut-

and-dried than she'd thought it was since Wade's earlier bombshell.

You're not just on the list. You are the list.

She'd told the social worker no, and now the baby would be turned over to the state and Wade would probably never see him again.

Felicity nodded, but she wasn't altogether sure what she was agreeing with anymore.

"Thanks for the wine. I should probably get going. I know it's late, but I just wanted to say thanks, and I guess I also wanted to make sure you were okay." He smiled at her, and it felt like her heart was being squeezed in a vise. "It's been quite a day."

"It sure has." She tried her best to smile back at him, but she couldn't quite manage it. Tears filled her eyes, and she bit down hard on her bottom lip.

She couldn't let Wade Ericson see her break down. He didn't want to know how she was doing—not really. Her emotional baggage was far heavier than he could possibly imagine.

"Bye, Felicity." He took one of her hands and squeezed it tight.

For an instant, Felicity could picture the two of them in one of Lovestruck's fairy-tale cottages, complete with a white picket fence and a glittering Christmas tree by the window—a real one, with strings of popcorn and cranberries hanging from its branches. And next to the tree, bathed in the golden glow of the twinkle lights, stood a bassinet.

Wade released Felicity's hand, and the crazy daydream disappeared as quickly as it had come to her. She clutched the front of her bathrobe for dear life and thanked her lucky stars he was leaving. She needed to get her bearings. Wade had been right—they'd had quite a day.

But it wasn't all bad. In fact, at times, it had been rather nice.

"Wait," she said as he started to make his way down the stairs.

Wade glanced over his shoulder, and his eyes seemed a little less blue than they had before. The touch of green in his irises shone bright, like a spark of Christmas hope. "Yes?"

"I'll think about it. If the social worker will let me sleep on it, I'll give her my answer tomorrow." What was she saying? She couldn't do this. Somewhere deep down, though, she had a feeling she might *want* to. Maybe, just maybe, she needed that sweet baby boy as badly as he needed her. "But I'm not making any promises."

Not yet, anyway.

Chapter Five

Wade stared into his coffee early the following morning, thinking about Felicity in her oversize bathrobe and wondering if she was tucked into her little attic apartment thinking about him.

Probably not. She seemed more like the chai tea type, not that her morning choice of beverage was any of his business. He just couldn't seem to stop thinking about her. And the baby, of course. Felicity and the baby. The baby and Felicity. His mind was a jumbled mess. It didn't help matters that he couldn't seem to picture one of them without the other. Every time he closed his eyes, he saw Felicity standing outside the firehouse in her blue silk robe, cradling the baby in her arms as snow fell around them—gentle and ethereal, like feathers shaken loose from a pillow.

For Wade, Felicity and that sweet child were now forever intertwined. He needed to get past that, somehow. He *wanted* to get past it. He just wasn't sure how.

He took a gulp of hot coffee, relishing its bitter burn. Like everyone else in Lovestruck, he preferred a splash of maple syrup in his coffee— sometimes, he even liked a dollop of that surgery sweet flavored creamer that the other firefighters all pretended not to drink, even though they went through gallons of it down at the station. But this morning he was punishing himself. Vermont's favorite baby-saving hero didn't deserve maple syrup, and he *definitely* didn't deserve fancy creamer.

Duchess knew. Wade wasn't sure how, but the dog seemed very aware that he'd done something despicable. The furry little Cavalier King Charles spaniel usually sat right at his feet when he stood at the kitchen counter and drank his first cup of coffee in the morning. On a typical day, she'd paw at his feet and gaze up at him with her melting brown eyes until he gave her a nibble of bacon. Or three. Because yes, Wade was a total softy.

Not today, though. Once Duchess finished her bowl of premium poultry-free, gluten-free, genuine Angus beef filet mignon dog food, she padded right past him to steal his spot in his favorite recliner. Currently, her chin was propped up on the arm of the chair while she watched snowflakes dance against the windowpane, refusing to look at him.

"You've proven your point," he muttered. "I shouldn't have done it."

Contrary to what he'd told Felicity, he'd absolutely shown up on her doorstep last night to try to convince her to take in the baby. He'd wanted to check on her, too, because she'd definitely seemed rattled when she'd left the firehouse. But he'd also had an agenda, and now he felt like a grade-A jerk.

All it had taken was one look at her tearstained face for him to see that she hadn't made her decision lightly. Clearly there was more to her story than he knew, and he needed to step back and respect her choice. Which he was doing now. One hundred percent.

Wade wasn't sure where the offer to let her and the baby move in with him had come from. He'd been exhausted on every possible level—emotionally, mentally, physically. Otherwise, he'd never have made such an absurd suggestion. Bachelor life suited him. He wasn't made for commitment. Most of the single women in Lovestruck knew this about him. Although, it had been a while since he'd felt like dating. Heck, he still hadn't quite adjusted to caring for a silly dog. What sort of rational person asked a stranger to live with him, anyway?

A desperate one.

He took another gulp of black coffee and winced. Gross. Duchess's gaze finally swiveled toward him as he reached for the maple syrup.

"Stop looking at me like that, dog." He poured a splash of pure Vermont glory into his cup. "I'm going to make it up to her. I'm going to do something nice for Felicity. Just wait and see."

Wade had never felt like the hero everyone in Lovestruck seemed to think he was, but he was a decent guy. Mostly, anyway. He shouldn't have tried to meddle in the foster home situation, just like he shouldn't have felt a jolt of pure joy shoot through his chest when Felicity told him she'd reconsider. Only a few months had passed since he'd been bugging Jack about not being totally honest with Madison when he'd found out the truth about their weird pen pal situation. Of course, that arrangement had worked itself out. Eventually.

Wade simply needed to take his own advice and fix things with Felicity. She wasn't his secret pen pal or his girlfriend, but after yesterday's events, he felt connected to her somehow—more connected than he'd felt to anyone in a long time.

He didn't want to ruin the strange, newfound intimacy between them. She'd seemed so rattled last night, so vulnerable. He felt utterly helpless where the baby was concerned, but he could make things better for Felicity.

And he knew just how to start.

It took multiple cups of chai tea and a dash of superhuman effort for Felicity to drag herself downstairs in time for her early-morning gentle yoga class. She hadn't slept much at all after Wade's late-night visit. Mostly, she'd just stared at the ceiling, wondering why on earth she was thinking about moving in with a near-stranger and caring for an abandoned infant.

She blamed Christmas. After all, what kind of monster refused to take in a helpless baby during the holidays?

She did, apparently. Felicity herself was the monster.

But she couldn't dwell on that right now. She had a class to teach…maybe. So far, the early-morning gentle yoga session had been the only class on the schedule to attract a regular following—*if* Madison's Aunt Alice and the two or three ladies from her knitting circle that she sometimes managed to drag along could be considered a following, per se.

Felicity loved those women. They definitely counted, and not just because they liked to bring her homemade cobblers and pies. Failing to show up for them wasn't an option, no matter how emotionally and physically exhausted Felicity was, so fifteen minutes before class started, she padded downstairs and flipped on the studio lights. A nice, quiet, gentle yoga class was probably just what she needed to give herself a little perspective, anyway. She was pretty sure she wasn't a monster. She was just heartbroken. Opening her home to a baby was one thing, but opening up her heart again was another matter entirely. And Felicity wasn't sure how to do one of those things without the other. She wasn't sure it was possible.

Should it be possible?

Breathe. She turned on the sound system and a soothing lullaby accompanied by gentle ocean waves filled the air. *Just breathe.*

Felicity took a deep inhale. She couldn't teach class if she was a jumbled-up mess inside. For the next hour or so, she just needed to concentrate on mindfulness and put all thoughts of babies and a certain charming firefighter out of her head.

No problem. She could totally do that. She could do anything for sixty minutes, right?

Wrong!

When Felicity unlocked the frosted glass door and pushed it open, the face she saw on the opposite side didn't belong to Alice at all. It belonged to the ridiculously handsome, baby-saving fireman himself, Wade Ericson.

"Um." Felicity shook her head, convinced she was having some strange hallucination—a result of sleep deprivation, no doubt. Then she blinked hard, but he was still there, grinning his trademark flirty grin.

Where was Alice and her cobbler? Felicity would have traded her Birkin bag for a glimpse of Madison's aunt holding a pie then, instead of Lovestruck's favorite firefighter.

Okay, maybe not the Birkin. She hadn't *completely* lost her mind.

"What are you doing here, Wade?" Honestly, was he going to keep showing up on her doorstep at odd hours? It was awfully…unsettling. "I have class in a few minutes."

"I know. That's why I'm here." A smile tugged at his lips, and Felicity's stomach did a rebellious little tumble. "That's why *all of us* are here."

He jerked his head toward the right, and Felicity managed to drag her attention away from him long enough to see three burly men standing a few feet away. Madison's husband, Jack, gave her a reluctant wave and the other two men shifted awkwardly from foot to foot, looking as if they'd rather run into a burning building than attempt a single downward dog.

Felicity bit back a smile. Was this really happening? "This is quite a surprise. Since when do Lovestruck's bravest have a sudden passion for yoga?"

The firefighter standing closest to Jack—Brody, if Felicity was remembering correctly—shrugged. "Since Wade woke us all up this morning when he called and promised to volunteer for every Fancy rescue for the next six months if we signed up for your sunrise class."

Jack jabbed him with his elbow.

"What?" Brody frowned. "Was it supposed to be a secret?"

Wade's face turned a nice, Christmassy shade of red. "Anyway, do you have room for four new students this morning?"

Felicity probably should have turned them away. This was charity, plain and simple.

But it was also undeniably sweet. Wade had actually listened to her last night, and he was doing what he could to help. She doubted his motives were pure. After all, she was supposed to give him her final answer today about the baby.

Still, her heart felt full to bursting all of a sudden. And she definitely couldn't afford the luxury of turning away students. So Felicity swallowed what little pride she had left and pushed the door open wide. "I think I can squeeze you in."

The men made their way inside, and as they

filed past her, Felicity snagged Wade by the elbow. "Not so fast there, Smokey."

He let out a low chuckle that she somehow felt deep in the pit of her stomach. "Smokey, huh? As in Smokey the Bear, right? I like it."

Of course he did. Felicity's cheeks grew warm. "There's something I need to know."

Wade winked. "I'm an open book."

She wholeheartedly doubted that was the case. In the past twenty-four hours alone, he'd already surprised her in myriad ways. It was happening again, even now. There were tiny flecks of gold in his eyes that she'd never noticed before, shimmering like starlight against the deep blue-green of his irises.

She swallowed hard. Why had she pulled him aside, again?

Wade leaned closer. He smelled like a snowy Vermont morning, all frosted air and evergreens. "What is it you need to know?"

Why are you doing this?

Why does that baby mean so much to you?

Are you really as heroic as you seem?

She couldn't force the words out, so she smiled and asked something else. "Brody said you promised to volunteer for every Fancy rescue for the next six months. What does that mean, exactly? Rescuing people James Bond–style, in tuxedos?"

Her question was far less probing, but still

something she was curious about. And honestly, as far as things she wanted to know about Wade Erickson, it was only the tip of the iceberg.

"Tuxedos? Hardly." Wade laughed and raked a hand through his hair, still glittering with tiny bits of snow. "Fancy is the name of cat."

Surprised, yet again. "Oh, wow."

"Unfortunately, Fancy has a bad habit of getting stuck in trees," Wade said.

"And the fire department has to get her down?" Felicity had never seen such a thing in Manhattan. Ever.

Wade shrugged. "It's not a requirement, but we like to help out the community."

Felicity felt herself smile. "By rescuing kittens in trees."

"Hey, it's not as easy as it sounds. Fancy is— how should I put this?—rather rotund. Not to mention, cranky. The last time we sent one of our guys out to rescue her, Jack ended up in the hospital."

And Wade had just volunteered to keep that cat safe for the next six months. All for her.

Felicity could have kissed him, right then and there.

"Any more questions?" Wade reached to tuck a stray lock of hair behind her ear, and as if he could read her mind, his gaze drifted slowly downward, until it landed on her mouth.

So many.

Felicity licked her lips, then took a giant backward step when she realized what she was doing.

"Nope. We're good, Smokey," she said, and then made a beeline for her yoga mat at the front of the room.

So many questions.

Alice showed up just minutes after the firefighters did, along with a nutmeg maple cream pie and two of the ladies from her knitting circle. Felicity wasn't sure which group seemed more enthusiastic about class—the grandmotherly knitting enthusiasts, now that they'd been joined by some rather valiant surprise guests; or the firemen, once they realized their sixty minutes of gentle stretching would be followed by Alice Jules's homemade baked goods.

Either way, Felicity could have wept with delight. Her little yoga studio was filled with warmth and laughter. Finally, *finally*, things at Nama-Stay Awhile were like she'd imagined they would be when she'd yanked all the money out of her savings account and invested everything she had in her new life in Vermont.

Okay, so maybe they weren't *exactly* how she'd pictured them. Never in her wildest dreams had she thought that her sunrise gentle yoga class would be such a hit with first responders and senior citizens, nor had she thought she'd ever be sitting cross-legged on her yoga mat while she ate maple cream pie after class. Her yoga teacher training class had in no way prepared her for Lovestruck. But maybe she could make a go of it here, after all.

"Here." She tiptoed toward Wade's mat at the back of the class and offered him the near-empty pie pan. "You deserve the last slice."

He shook his head. "No, I don't. All this camaraderie is your doing. Your class was just what I needed. I feel more relaxed than I have in weeks. All I did was coerce a few guys into coming along."

She glanced toward the front of the room where the firefighters were offering up suggestions for whatever Alice baked for the next class. They were planning on coming back for the next sunrise class—all of them, fireman and knitters alike.

"How crazy is this?" Felicity couldn't stop smiling. "Seriously, eat the last piece of pie. You deserve it."

"Share it with me?" He sat down cross-legged on his mat and patted the empty space beside him.

She nearly said no, out of habit. She hadn't come here looking for a relationship…with anyone. No babies, no men. Her heart already felt like it had been put through a paper shredder.

All she wanted was to teach class during the day and dart back up to her little attic apartment at night. Alone.

Small towns didn't operate that way, apparently. In Manhattan, she could have easily planned such an existence. In a city of millions, it was so easy to get lost in a crowd. Not here, though. Here there were Christmas festivals, pies and cats in trees. She couldn't get lost in Lovestruck if she tried.

Wade gave his yoga mat another pat, and she finally acquiesced, handing him one of the plastic spoons Alice had brought in a little silver bucket tied with red gingham ribbon. She grabbed a fork for herself, and they speared into the single slice of pie at the same time.

Felicity laughed and met Wade's gaze in one of the mirrored studio walls. Why did this feel like a picnic date instead of just two people eating pie straight from the tin after an exercise class? She didn't want to think about the answer to that question any more than she wanted to meet his gaze full-on. Looking at his reflection was much easier. It felt less vulnerable, somehow. But the longer they sat there, watching one another in the mirror, the more exposed she began to feel.

Felicity looked away, concentrating intently on the empty pie pan. "Thank you for this morning. It really meant a lot to me, even though I *still* know what you're doing."

"I don't think you do," he said softly.

She turned and accidentally looked right at him, drawn like a magnet toward the earnestness in his tone. Then she swallowed hard. "Come on, Wade. We both know this was for the baby. You're still—"

"No," he said, cutting her off. "This wasn't for the baby. It was for you. No strings. You have my word."

Well, then. Just what was she supposed to do with that information?

Nothing at all. No strings means no strings.

The decision was hers and hers alone. She could stick to her guns and protect herself, or she could open herself up to more pain and heartbreak. More goodbyes that tore her to pieces.

Across the room, Alice's knitting ladies laughed at something Jack said. In Manhattan, the second a yoga class was over, everyone bolted for the door, Felicity included. So far, none of her new students had even rolled up their yoga mats.

More moments like this one.

What Wade had done for her had cracked her heart open—not all the way wide, just the smallest possible bit. But it was still enough to let the light in, and now there was no turning back. Joy filled her like sunshine.

"I'll do it," she blurted before she could stop herself. "*If* the social worker says we can move into your house temporarily and *if* you agree to help, I'll take care of the baby."

Wade's mouth curved into a tentative smile that seemed to build by the second, as did the sudden swirl of panic in Felicity's chest. "Seriously?"

Her heart felt like it had lodged at the base of her throat. Everything was going to be fine, though. This was only temporary. He realized that, right?

She held up her hands. "Just until the holidays have passed, or until someone steps up and applies for adoption. Can you live with that, Smokey?"

Wade's grin widened until it seemed to take up his entire, handsome face. Good gravy, what was she getting herself into?

"I can live with that," he said.

But could she?

Chapter Six

"You're late," Cap said without tearing his gaze from the computer at the dispatch desk when Wade and Felicity walked into the firehouse.

They'd come straight from yoga, and yes, Wade was technically late for his shift—by a minute and a half. He'd promised Cap he'd leave promptly at eight in the morning to drive the baby to the hospital in Burlington.

But Wade was never late. Ever. He prided himself on his punctuality, just as he tried his best to be the best possible firefighter he could be. It kept him from feeling like an imposter on the occasions when he was awarded medals for bravery. Or congratulatory pizzas from the mayor. Or casseroles…

Wade glanced down at the 13x9 plastic-covered dish on the farm table. A Post-it Note with his name scrawled on it in loopy, feminine handwriting was stuck to the Saran Wrap. He didn't know the handwriting, but he recognized the aroma. Chicken and wild rice—the third such casserole he'd been gifted since he'd delivered the baby.

Wade wondered if Felicity liked chicken-and-wild-rice casserole. He supposed he was about to find out. They would probably be finding out a lot about each other in the coming days.

He cleared his throat. "Sorry, Cap. But we've got some news."

We. As if they were a unit. A couple. A family.

Slow your roll, Smokey. It's only temporary. Super. Now he was calling himself by Felicity's silly nickname.

"What?" Cap spun his wheeled chair around, doing a double take as his gaze landed on Felicity, standing quietly beside Wade. He stood. "Felicity, hello. This is a surprise."

"I'm sure it is. I'm sorry I left in such a hurry yesterday. I've had a chance to think things over, and I…" Her voice drifted off as her attention snagged on the casserole.

"Don't mind that. Just another drop-off from

one of Wade's devoted fans." Cap picked it up and shoved it at a rookie firefighter nearby. "Go put that in the fridge, will you?"

"Wade's fan club?" Felicity frowned in the direction of the passing rookie and then swiveled her attention back to Wade. "Does that happen often?"

"It does not," Wade said decisively.

Simultaneously, Cap said, "All the time."

"Wow." Felicity's frown deepened.

Was it Wade's imagination, or did she take a tiny side step farther away from him?

"We're not here to talk about casseroles. We're here to talk about the baby," Wade said. "Actually, where is he?"

Wade glanced around the firehouse's common area. The box of diapers he'd purchased the night before was sitting open in one of the recliners. Several rinsed bottles were lined up in a drying rack on the kitchen counter, and a puff of baby powder hung in the air. The infant himself, however, was nowhere to be seen.

"The little rascal is napping in my office." Cap jerked his head toward a closed door decorated with a plaque shaped like a fireman's badge that read *Captain Jason McBride, Engine Co. 24.* "Jack brought over a portable crib late last night, and we set it up in there."

That made perfect sense. Since the twins had

been born, Jack had accumulated enough baby supplies to open his own Baby Depot.

Felicity crossed and uncrossed her arms as if she'd been prepared to hold the child and suddenly didn't know what to do with herself. "I've had a change in heart. I'd like to take care of him during the holidays."

She nodded, voice shaking ever so slightly. "Or until someone steps up to adopt him, if that happens sooner. But I know this time of year can be difficult for the foster care system, and Wade and I have discussed things. I think we've come up with a good solution."

Cap headed toward the farm table. "Let's sit down and talk this out."

Wade let Felicity explain things to Cap. As the only certified foster parent in the room, she was the one running the show here. He wanted Cap to understand that he knew he was only playing a supporting role. He still didn't quite understand why it meant so much to him to have the baby stay in Lovestruck until he found a permanent home, but he was willing to roll with it. He had to. Fate had somehow seemed to cast him into the role of the kid's guardian angel. Apparently, fate had a twisted sense of humor.

Wade was no angel, but he managed to keep his mouth shut long enough for Felicity to convince Cap that moving into Wade's home temporarily and caring for the child was a good idea. Cap didn't ask Wade how he felt about the arrangement. He supposed he'd made his feelings clear enough already. So half an hour later, Cap stepped into his office and closed the door behind him to make the call to the social worker.

Felicity fidgeted in her chair beside Wade while they waited.

"Are you as nervous as I am right now?" she whispered.

Wade laughed under his breath. "Here I thought it was just me."

He glanced at her hands, clasped loosely together and resting on the surface of the table, and his fingertips twitched. Instinct told him to reach for one of her hands and cradle it in his, but something stopped him—something that seemed casserole-related somehow. She hadn't really looked directly at him since the mention of his fan club.

"There's something else we should probably talk about while we wait," she said, focusing intently on the rough-hewn surface of the table.

The spot where they were seated was the heart and soul of Engine Co. 24. It boasted as many scorched marks from family-style meals as it did scuffs and dents from ash-covered fire helmets. This was the place where Wade had interviewed for his spot as a rookie. It's where he'd spent the past five Christmas Eves and Easter Sundays. It's where Cap sat him down last and told him his mother had passed away.

Wade had been out on a call—a traffic accident twenty miles outside the Lovestruck town limits. It had been a long, exhausting night, and he'd had nothing left in him when Cap had given him the news. He'd known it was coming. After months of chemo and radiation treatments, he should have been prepared. He'd thought he was, but on that hot summer night when Cap had sat across from him and told him how sorry he was, Wade had broken down.

He wasn't sure why that particular memory had made its way to forefront of his consciousness, now of all times. But it had, leaving Wade with the uncomfortable realization that the firehouse table was the place where he'd become a man, in so many ways. And now it was the place where Felicity was telling him they shouldn't become romantically involved.

Wade tensed. Apparently, he'd let his mind wander and missed something terribly important.

He regarded Felicity, studying the graceful curve of her neck and the subtle, downward tilt of her bow-shaped lips until she met his gaze. "I'm sorry. What did you just say?"

She blinked at him, eyes shining bright. "We should have some ground rules, don't you think?

Just to ensure everything goes as smoothly as possible."

"And you think these ground rules should include a ban on any sort of…"

"Interpersonal relationship." She nodded, and a faint blush made its way up her neck and settled in two bright spots of pink on her cheeks.

Wade couldn't help but grin. Felicity Hart was quite lovely when she was flustered.

"I'm sure you agree," she said primly.

Wade most decisively did *not* agree. Not that he planned on wining and dining Felicity in between late-night feedings and diaper changes, but he liked her. A lot. More than all of the casserole queens put together.

Still, she was so far out of his league that he would have been crazy to think about actually pursuing her. She'd undergone foster care training. Wade figured there had to be a story there, but he wasn't about to push. He knew enough to understand the basics—Felicity was a good person. Too good for the likes of him.

Just smile, say yes and go with it.

"What if I don't agree?" he heard himself say instead.

Felicity's gaze drifted toward his mouth until her lips parted ever so slightly. Then she cleared her throat and sat up in her chair, spine going ramrod straight. Picture-perfect yoga posture.

"We can't get involved if we're taking care of an infant."

"Obviously. Whoever heard of romantic partners raising a baby together?" He knew he shouldn't have said it, but the temptation was just too great.

Felicity's eyes narrowed, but the corner of her lips quirked up into a smile. "It's settled then." She nodded. "No dating."

Before Wade could respond, she pointed at him and glared. "And none of that."

"I'm sorry, none of what?"

She waved a hand in front of him in an all-encompassing gesture. "*That*. You're flirting."

He shook his head. "This is just my face."

Was he flirting? Not intentionally, but there was an undeniably pleasant zing zipping through him. It happened every time he and Felicity were alone together.

"My point exactly." She rolled her eyes, but her gaze flitted to his mouth once again.

Then the door to Cap's office flew open and Felicity jumped, scooting her chair farther away as if they were two teenagers who'd been caught kissing outside the principal's office at school.

"Congratulations," Cap said, oblivious for once in his life. "You two are parents."

Felicity's appointment as the child's foster parent was temporary—just until after the Christmas holidays, when Vermont's social services offices would be back up and running at full capacity. The social worker saw no problem with Felicity living with Wade, so long as he began the process of getting certified as a foster parent on his own. Cap had obviously pulled some strings in this regard, although the social worker had apparently been more than accommodating since he'd been asking on behalf of the great and mighty baby-saving hero Wade Ericson, famous throughout Vermont and beyond.

I'm in so much trouble, Felicity thought as she held the baby close to her chest and got her first glimpse of Wade's home.

She'd apparently forgotten where they were, because she'd assumed he lived in a sleek, urban bachelor pad, complete with a giant flat-screen television and a talking, high-tech stainless steel refrigerator bursting at the seams with casseroles. Did such places even exist in Lovestruck? Apparently not, because she was currently standing on the sidewalk in front of a charming little cottage with whimsical gingerbread trim, a shady wraparound porch and, *of course*, the requisite Lovestruck white picket fence.

The man was too good to be true. Seriously, was he actually real? No wonder women were showering him with homemade dishes.

"Home sweet home." Wade winked.

She sighed.

"It's my face again, isn't it? My bad," he said. Then he winked *again*.

Why on earth had she mentioned the no-flirting, no-dating, no-relationship ground rules? Now it was all she could think about. Wade, too, if his secret little smirk was any indication.

Felicity took a deep breath and headed up the walkway toward the front porch. Wade followed, jingling his keys. As he slid one of them inside the lock, Cap pulled up to the curb in an official LFD vehicle with the social worker—Patti Martin—seated beside him. A second SUV with the fire department's crest emblazoned on the passenger-side door slowed to a stop next in line.

Great. It's a party.

The baby squirmed and cooed, and Felicity rocked him gently in her arms. Wade ran his hand over the infant's soft little head with one hand and waved at Cap and Patti Martin with the other. His LFD shirt rode up ever so slightly, exposing a quick glimpse of the heroic abdominal muscles Felicity had tried oh-so-hard not to notice during yoga class. Her breath clogged in her throat.

Maybe a party was a good thing. She wasn't sure she was ready to play house with Wade quite yet.

He pushed the door open and held it open wide for her. "Come on in."

Felicity's mind immediately conjured up an image of a groom carrying a bride over the threshold. What was *wrong* with her?

Luckily, her absurd train of thought was quickly interrupted by yapping and the scramble of paws on the cottage's hardwood flooring.

Her gaze flew toward Wade. "You have a dog?"

"Yes." His brow furrowed, but of course it didn't make him look any less handsome whatsoever. He just looked charmingly crinkled all of a sudden, sort of like George Clooney. "Is that a problem?"

"I don't know. Possibly?"

What if the dog wasn't gentle with the baby? It was probably some big, boisterous, manly breed like a golden retriever or a Labrador. Maybe even a dalmatian. Wade really should have told her about the dog instead of springing it on her like this.

She braced herself, tightening her hold on the baby, but the dog that came barreling into view didn't look a thing like she expected. It wasn't so much a dog as it was a prancing ball of silky copper-and-white fur with the biggest brown eyes Felicity had ever seen on such a tiny animal.

"Oh, my. It's a lap dog." Felicity let out a laugh before she could stop herself. Wade Ericson, burly firefighter hero, had a fluffy little *lap dog*.

"She's not a lap dog." Wade grunted as the

sweet little dog pawed at his shins. "She's a Cavalier King Charles spaniel."

"My mistake. That doesn't sound lap dog–ish at all," she said. Seriously? The dog had a fancy royal-sounding breed name, and were those *pink bows* on her ears?

Wade followed Felicity's gaze to the satin bows. "She just had her grooming appointment. It's a regular thing they do there."

"Naturally." Felicity nodded. "Somehow I suspect this particular dog won't be a problem at all."

"I wouldn't count on it. She has a naughty streak a mile wide. But don't worry about the baby. She's great with kids. All people, really. She's a love bug."

Felicity relaxed, ever so slightly. If the dog was great with people, where did the naughty streak come in?

"Hi there, Duchess," Cap said as he and Patti Martin climbed up the porch steps.

"Her name's Duchess? That's adorable." Felicity glanced up at Wade, and a muscle in his jaw ticked. She was goading him and she knew it— playing with fire.

But he deserved it after the way he'd responded when she brought up the no-dating rules. The teasing glint in his eyes couldn't have been accidental. Or maybe he was right—maybe he was physically incapable of flirting and he just had a serious case of RBF. Resting bachelor face.

Either way, it was a relief to finally have the shoe on the other foot.

"She's just precious," the social worker gushed. From the minute she'd set foot in the firehouse after driving down from Burlington with the necessary paperwork, it had been clear that Patti Martin was ready to sign up for Wade's fan club.

Felicity kept reminding herself that was a good thing, lest she end up taking care of the infant in her tiny attic apartment. Still, she and Wade hadn't even survived their first day together and all the female attention aimed his way was already driving her nuts. She wasn't sure why it rubbed her the wrong way like it did. If she didn't know better, she might have thought she was jealous. Which she wasn't. *Clearly.* She'd been telling the truth when she'd said she thought getting romantically involved in any way would be a terrible idea. Agreeing to be the baby's foster mom was already making her feel ten times more vulnerable than she'd imagined it would. Falling for Wade was out of the question.

But that didn't mean she'd enjoy choking down his casseroles.

"I'll have this set up in no time," Jack said as he brushed past her, heaving the disassembled crib he and Brody had brought over from the station.

Brody was two steps behind him, hauling an industrial-sized box of Pampers. "We've also got your diapers, bottles and formula, and I'll run out and get anything you might need while you and Wade sit down and sign the papers."

"Thank you," Felicity said, swallowing hard.

Wade studied her as Cap and the social worker moved toward a smooth pine dining room table that looked more like something out of *House Beautiful* than anything she would have ever associated with Lovestruck's favorite firefighter.

"Hey, are you okay?" he said, just audible enough for Felicity to hear him.

A shiver coursed through her. "Just peachy."

When she'd agreed to this, she'd known that in many ways, she would be stepping into the great unknown. Babies were anything but predictable. But so far, nothing about today had gone as she'd expected—the charming home, the sweet little dog, the way the other firemen had suddenly started treating her like a kid sister.

Her ridiculous fury over the casserole.

"Okay, then. Let's do this." Wade placed his hand on the small of her back and began escorting her and their baby—their *temporary* baby—toward the pretty dining table.

Felicity didn't have the heart to tell him that

casual touches like this were exactly the sort of thing she wanted—*needed*—to avoid, probably because she liked it so much. It felt nice…natural.

Which is precisely the problem.

She needn't have worried, though, because halfway across the room, he seemed to realize what he was doing and snatched his hand away and shoved it in the pocket of his LFD cargo pants. Her rebelliously misguided heart sank all the way down to her faux fur–trimmed Gucci ankle boots.

The next half hour was a blur of paperwork and instructions. Cap bounced the baby in his arms while Felicity and Wade signed one document after another.

Finally, Patti Martin smiled at them from across the table. "One last thing. What's the baby's name?"

Felicity and Wade looked at each other.

"Do you know?" he asked.

Felicity shook her head. "No. Everything happened so fast when the mother brought the baby to the firehouse. She never mentioned it."

"The hospital might have a record of it," Wade said.

The social worker shook her head. "We'd want to choose something new in order to protect the privacy of both mother and child. The Safe Haven law promises anonymity at every stage of the process. I just thought maybe you'd already begun calling him something?"

"Not yet," Felicity said. She hadn't dared.

"The state can assign him a first name, unless there's something particular you'd prefer to call him?" Patti glanced back and forth between Felicity and Wade, pen poised midair above her stack of documents.

Felicity cast a hopeful glance at Wade. He had the longest history with the child. He should definitely be the one to choose a name. The thought of a baby being named by a governmental entity was too sad to even contemplate, especially at Christmas.

"Don't look at me." Wade shook his head. "I have no idea how to name a baby."

Sure you do, Felicity started to say, but something about Wade's bottomless blue-green eyes stopped her. There was a hint of sadness in his gaze, so subtle it was barely noticeable, but very much there.

"Don't overthink it. You can't really go wrong with a name," Cap said, shifting the baby so he rested against his shoulder. He moved one of his big palms in soothing circles over the baby's tiny back.

"Is there a family name you're fond of?" Patti eyed him over the top of her reading glasses. "Your father's name, perhaps?"

"Not my father's." Wade's lovely mouth—the

very same one that always seemed to be curved into a crooked smile—flattened into a straight line. Beneath the table, out of view from everyone but Felicity, his hands curled into fists.

Felicity swallowed hard.

Do something. Say *something. Anything.*

"How about Nicholas?" she blurted. "Like Santa? Since it's Christmas and all? We could call him Nick. Or Nicky."

Cap pointed a finger-gun at her with his free hand. "I like it."

"How about you, Wade? Can you live with Nicholas?" the social worker asked.

"It's perfect." Wade nodded, and his trademark smile reappeared as quickly as it had gone away.

Felicity was almost convinced she'd only imagined his fleeting moment of angst. Almost, but not quite.

"Nicholas it is, then," the social worker said.

Duchess slipped under the table, sat down on Felicity's foot and let out a contented sigh.

Felicity smiled, and then in flagrant violation of her own rule, she reached for Wade's hand under the table and covered it with hers. She squeezed it hard and didn't dare look at him, because her eyes were on the verge of filling with tears. But there was gratitude in the way he squeezed her hand back—and something else, too. Something that stole the breath from her lungs and sparkled inside her, like snow on Christmas morning.

She wasn't even sure why she felt like crying all of sudden. She wasn't sure of anything at all, except the bone-deep realization that there was far more to Wade Ericson than met the eye.

Chapter Seven

Jack glanced up from the stove when Wade walked into the firehouse kitchen the following morning, looked him up and down and smirked. "So how did the first night go?"

Wade scrubbed his face with one of his hands, mildly surprised when his fingertips came in contact with two days' worth of scruff. He'd forgotten to shave this morning. Yesterday, too. Was it possible that a tiny, seven-pound baby could completely disrupt a person's life in a mere thirty-six hours?

Yes, apparently. It was indeed possible. Wade was living, walking proof.

"Does the sleep deprivation show?" he asked, dropping down onto a bar stool to watch Jack flip pancakes.

Jack loved kitchen duty. He probably should have been a chef instead of a firefighter, but no one at Engine Co. 24 wanted to tell him that, lest he pursue a new occupation and leave the others to fend for themselves.

Actually, now that Wade thought about it, Jack's kitchen prowess was probably the result of being a single dad to twin girls. Before Madison had come along, Jack had been a bit of a mess, but his culinary dad-skills had always been on point. Case in point—Engine Co. 24 had a regularly scheduled fish sticks night.

Jack's smirk grew smirkier, if such a thing was possible. "Oh, how the tables have turned. I remember when you were the one lecturing me about getting sleep. It's been a single day and look at you."

Yeah, look at me. Wade eyed his distorted reflection in the nearby toaster. He had a serious case of bedhead and something that looked suspiciously like spit-up on the shoulder of his navy LFD shirt. But he also had a glorious, goofy smile on his face. He couldn't seem to rid himself of it, no matter how hard he tried.

"Here." Jack slid a plate in front of him. "Applejack pancakes."

Wade took a bite. His breakfast both sounded and tasted like something a four-year-old might eat, but he was too tired to care. Plus it was delicious.

I could get used to this. He shoveled another forkful into his mouth, and when the voice in his head piped up again, it sounded an awful lot like Felicity. *It's only temporary, Smokey.*

"These are great. Thanks, man," Wade said. He felt his goofy grin fade ever so slightly.

"Seriously, though. How did the first night go? Are you and Felicity taking turns getting up with the baby?"

"Nick." Wade gestured with his fork. "That's what we're calling him."

Jack nodded. "Nick—I like it. Who came up with it?"

"Felicity did." Wade dropped his gaze to his pancakes. "She thought it might be cute to call him something Christmassy."

And Wade had been all too happy to agree. He would have probably voted for *Ebenezer* or *Clark Griswold* if it had meant getting off the topic of his father. Wade didn't like to talk about his dad. He didn't much like to think about him, either, and he most certainly didn't want to name an innocent baby after him.

"To answer your question, yes. We agreed to take turns for the late-night feedings. We're supposed to be on an every-other-night schedule," Wade said.

Jack arched a brow. "But you're not?"

"Last night was Felicity's turn, and she did her part. But I'd hear her tiptoeing past my room, and then I'd hear her getting the bottle ready…singing a lullaby." A surge of warmth filled Wade's chest just thinking about it. "I couldn't just lie there and let her do everything by herself. You know how it is."

Jack squinted at him. "Not really. Have you lost your mind? When someone volunteers to take the late-night shift, you let them."

"Right." Wade rolled his eyes. "Because that's what you did when Madison was working as your night nanny? You shut yourself in your room, conked out and didn't interact with her at all."

"That was different," Jack said flatly.

"How so?"

Jack smirked the smirkiest smirk of all. "Because I was falling in love."

Wade cleared his throat. "That's not what's happening here."

Obviously not. Wade's life had taken a bizarre tailspin on the night Nick was born, and he was still trying to make sense of things. Felicity was like the calm in the middle of a storm, but that didn't mean he was developing feelings for her.

He wasn't allowed to do that, anyway—which

was probably why he couldn't seem to stop thinking about her tumbling blond hair or her perfect pink lips. So lush, so kissable.

"I believe you," Jack said, but they'd been friends and coworkers long enough for Wade to know when he was lying.

"Stop it," Wade said through gritted teeth.

Jack poured another ladle full of batter into his frying pan. "I will not stop it. First you drag me out of bed and force me to sign up for six weeks of sunrise yoga classes, and now you two are living together and raising a baby. What exactly is going on between you and Felicity?"

Wade took a deep inhale. He had no idea how to answer that question with any sort of honesty. Nor did he know how to put a label on feelings he'd never experienced before. Until now.

When Felicity had reached for his hand under the table as they'd been discussing baby names, he'd felt centered in a way he didn't know was possible. Like they were a unit. A team.

A family.

I don't have the first clue what's happening between us, but it feels important. It feels like everything.

He swallowed hard. The applejack pancakes felt like rocks in the pit of his stomach all of a sudden. "Nothing is going on. She stepped up to give Nick a home until Christmas. It really doesn't have anything to do with me."

"Except that the home she's giving him is yours." Jack pointed a spatula at him. "Your house. And your baby. Sort of."

Wade pushed his plate away. "No, definitely not my baby. I was just doing my job the day he was born, that's all. It could have been any one of us."

Jack shrugged one shoulder. "But it wasn't any one of us. It was you."

Wade glared at him. He much preferred the heart-to-hearts they'd had back when Jack was the one in the hot seat.

"I'm just saying I can understand why you'd feel a certain connection with Nick. I get it. I'm a dad..." Jack let his voice drift off, but Wade heard the unspoken word at the end of his sentence—*too.*

I'm a dad, too.

Except Wade wasn't a father, and he never would be. He wasn't like Jack. Jack was born to be a dad. It came as naturally to him as breathing. Not so for Wade. Until he'd met Cap and Jack, he didn't even know what a good father looked like.

"I'm not adopting him, if that's what you're getting at. Neither is Felicity. We're just giving Nick a home for the holidays," Wade said, pretending that it didn't sound like he was speaking for the both of them, as if they were a real couple.

"Besides, Felicity and I barely know each other. You're making it sound like we're playing house or something, and that's just not the case."

"I believe you," Jack said again.

Wade wanted to shove his dumb spatula down his know-it-all throat. "I mean, you should see our bathroom. The countertop is barely visible anymore. I've never seen so many lotions, potions and powders in my life."

Wade was beginning to think that buying a home with three bedrooms and only one bathroom had been a mistake. How was that even possible? He was a *bachelor*.

"She used to be a beauty editor. Potions and powders are sort of her thing." Jack shrugged. He would know, since Felicity and Madison had worked for the same Manhattan magazine before Jack's grand gesture brought Madison back to Lovestruck.

And Wade supposed he had a valid point. Still, the potions were only the tip of the iceberg. "Are shoes her thing, too? And purses? Because she's got them lined up in rows along the wall of the spare bedroom, like a fancy designer army."

It was astonishing, really. When he'd driven his truck over to her yoga studio so she could gather her things together, she'd just kept bringing one handbag after another out of her tiny attic apartment. That place was like a clown car full of Chanel.

"Sounds like a complete and total nightmare. No wonder you're not interested in her," Jack said.

Wade knew good and well what Jack was doing, but he wasn't going to fall for it. He wasn't about to sit there and admit how much he liked watching Felicity with the baby—the tender way she touched him and the ache he got deep in his chest when she sang to Nick in soft, dulcet tones. She liked to entertain him with Christmas carols, especially The Beach Boys' "Little Saint Nick." Just thinking about it made Wade feel warm all over.

Jack scooped up the last batch of pancakes from the skillet and added them to the pile he'd created during their conversation. Knowing the rest of the guys in the station, it would be gone in five minutes flat.

Wade snagged another one with his fork before word got out. "I can see that smug look on your face, dude. You're not hiding it very well."

"I wasn't trying to hide it." Jack shrugged. "I was just thinking."

Wade stopped chewing. "About?"

Did he really want to know? Probably not, but he had to ask.

"For someone who insists he's not in a relationship, you sound…"

Wade glared at his friend again. "I sound what, exactly?"

Baffled? Intrigued? More fascinated by Felicity that he wanted to admit?

"Married." Jack snorted. "You sound married, my friend."

Madison greeted Felicity at the studio first thing in the morning with a yoga mat tucked under one arm and a baby bouncy seat tucked under the other. She then tried to tell Felicity that she could skip teaching class and they could simply ooh and aah over the baby instead. Felicity wasn't having it, though. She felt guilty enough about taking her friend's money for studio membership, not to mention the hand-me-down baby items that she and Jack kept tossing their way. Felicity wasn't about to shortchange her on downward dogs.

Baby Nick bounced gently in the seat while they went through a few flows. Felicity kept sneaking glances at him as she moved through her poses, telling herself she was simply being a conscientious caregiver as opposed to being completely besotted by the child.

Boundaries, she repeated over and over in her head as she wobbled in tree pose. Then Nick made a snuffling sound, and Felicity all but fell over as she scrambled to check and make sure he didn't need something, like a bottle or a cuddle. *Or a caregiver who isn't trying her best not to get attached.*

"Look at him," Madison said, running a thumb in tiny circles over Nick's adorable little fist. "He's fine. Nothing to worry about. I think he's as blissed-out and relaxed by the bouncy seat as I am by all the sun salutations we just did."

Felicity arched a brow. "Are you trying to tell me you've had enough? Because we technically have ten more minutes until class is over."

Madison glanced around the empty studio. "I don't think the rest of the class would mind if we cut out and went to the Bean for coffee instead. What do you think?"

What did Felicity think? Just the idea of a hot maple latte nearly made her weep, that's what she thought. "I didn't get much sleep last night, so that actually sounds amazing."

Madison rolled up her yoga mat. "Super. Let's get Nick bundled up and head over there."

Felicity checked, double-checked and triple-checked the diaper bag to make sure she had everything, which seemed silly since the Bean was just at the end of the block. But she didn't want to mess anything up. Poor Nick had been through enough already. Just the fact that she'd been the one to choose his name broke her heart. For now, he didn't even *have* a last name. The social worker had left that spot blank on his paperwork until someone applied to adopt him.

She didn't like to think about that empty line on the forms any more than she liked to think about the panicked look in Wade's eyes when Patti had suggested naming Nick after his father. It had been so contrary to his typical devil-may-care grin. Then again, she'd gotten a glimpse of Wade's more serious side back when they'd been on their way to the living nativity and he'd thanked her for not asking about his infamous baby rescue.

What was it she'd said in response?

No baby talk tonight, I promise.

My, how things had changed.

"Do you know anything about Wade's father?" Felicity blew gently at her steaming cup of coffee as the scents of nutmeg and warm maple rose up from her mug. She never drank flavored coffee back in New York—just plain black. Who was she anymore?

She glanced at Nick, nestled snugly in his bouncy seat in their booth in the far corner of the Bean. Best not to ask that question, she supposed.

"Hmm." Madison glanced up from her own steaming mug. "I don't think so. His mom passed away last year. They were pretty close, apparently. As far as I know, his dad hasn't in the picture for years. Why?"

"Just wondering." Felicity nibbled on her bottom lip. She shouldn't be asking questions about Wade and his family. She shouldn't be thinking about him at all, actually.

Still, there were a few things that were far too surprising—and hilarious—not to share.

"He wears the most hideous socks around the house. You would die if you could see them." She smiled into her coffee cup, remembering how adorably rumpled he'd looked when he'd staggered out of his bedroom at three in the morning to keep her company while she'd fed Nick a bottle. She'd never seen anything quite like the socks—saggy, multicolored, misshapen and somehow not quite mismatched but not identical, either.

This morning, after he'd left for the fire station, Felicity had done a load of baby laundry and when she'd opened the dryer, she'd found four more pairs of the silly things.

If news of Wade's ugly socks could make an impression on anyone in Lovestruck, it was Madison. She was, after all, the resident fashion columnist at the *Bee*. She leaned closer, eyes wide. "How hideous are we talking about?"

"Awful beyond all description," Felicity said flatly, and both women collapsed into giggles. "Honestly, the casserole queens have no idea."

Madison cocked her head. "The casserole queens?"

"You don't know about Wade's fan club? Apparently, he's quite the ladies' man. And he's got a freezer full of casseroles to prove it. Last night, we had chicken and wild rice, courtesy of Barbara of the swirly handwriting and pink Post-it Notes." To Felicity's great dismay, it had been delicious.

Madison's eyes danced as she sipped her latte.

"What's that look?" Felicity plunked her mug down on the table.

Madison shrugged. "I don't know. I guess the thought of you snuggling up to Wade in his ugly socks and sharing a casserole seems really sweet."

Felicity snorted. "Hardly."

It hadn't been altogether terrible, though, hideous socks notwithstanding. Felicity was doing her best to chalk it up to three-in-the-morning grogginess.

She narrowed her gaze at her friend. "Why are you so intent on trying to throw us together, anyway?"

"You two seriously flirted with each other at the wedding. Don't try to deny it." Madison arched a brow.

"That wasn't Wade flirting. That's apparently his default personality," Felicity said, not liking the sudden crispness that crept into her tone. If she kept this up, Madison was going to think she was jealous.

Oh, no. Felicity swallowed hard. *Was* she jealous?

"Come on," she said, trying her best to sound breezy and light. Wade Ericson and his terrible socks were none of her concern. They just happened to be sharing a roof. *And a casserole. And a baby. And a life.* "Wade is Jack's best friend. Surely you're aware of his reputation as a ladies' man."

Madison nodded. "Oh, I've heard the rumors. But I've lived in Lovestruck for a while now, and I've never actually known him to wine and dine anyone. I think it's just a matter of the entire town having a crush on him, including a good portion of the married women."

Interesting. "In any case, there's nothing going on between us. Wade and I have both agreed that it would be a bad idea. I also think we should probably keep the fact that we're living together under wraps."

"Does Wade agree to that, too?" Madison's eyes bored into her. It was quite unnerving.

Felicity squirmed in her seat. "Not yet, but I'm sure he will. You know how this town is. If anyone found out that I was living with Wade and we were taking care of Nick together, we'd never hear the end of it. People would have us married off within minutes. It would be a disaster."

A *complete and total* disaster—far worse that Wade's socks or his trio of video game consoles. Three? Really? Wasn't one enough?

"There's no way you're going to be able to keep it secret." Madison shook her head. "Trust me, secrets don't last long in this town."

"I'm not talking about a lifetime. Christmas is in less than two weeks. Surely we can keep things under wraps until then," Felicity said.

But no sooner had the words left her mouth than a nearby squeal pierced the air, just as a cluster of women descended on Felicity and Madison's booth.

"Oh. My. Goodness," one of them said, hand fluttering to her throat as her gaze homed in on Nick, still sleeping peacefully in his bouncy chair. "Is that Wade Ericson's baby?"

Felicity's heart nearly thudded to a stop. "Um."

Who were these women? There had to be at least three or four of them. Maybe more. It was hard to tell because all of them either had babies strapped to their fronts in brightly colored sling-type contraptions or their mittened hands were attached to fancy ergonomic strollers.

"Hi, Diane." Madison waved, but no one seemed to be paying attention to her. Every single one of the moms clustered around the table was too busy fawning over Nick to give her the time of day.

"It's not Wade's. Remember, he said he was babysitting for a friend," one of the moms said.

"You must be Wade's friend." A woman with striking red hair pointed a slender finger at Felicity and grinned.

"Told you," Madison muttered.

The entire coffeehouse went silent as every set of eyes in the Bean turned toward Felicity and Nick. Only two sounds managed to work their way into Felicity's consciousness—the frantic rush of blood in her head and the cheery Christmas carol playing over the Bean's sound system.

He sees you when you're sleeping.

He knows when you're awake...

So did every last person in Lovestruck, apparently.

Good gravy, what now?

Chapter Eight

Later that night, Wade and Felicity made their postponed debut as Joseph and Mary in the living nativity scene at the Lovestruck Christmas festival. Given his new, near-constant state of exhaustion, Wade would have preferred finding a substitute couple. Also, he wasn't crazy about leaving Nick with a sitter. Neither was Felicity, even though Madison and Jack hardly counted as babysitters. They were more like an honorary aunt and uncle, with the added bonus of being official parenting "experts."

Sort of. The *Bee* seemed to think so, at least.

In any event, the living nativity was only

scheduled to run for two hours. Nick would be fine. Besides, the mayor wouldn't hear of finding a substitute couple. She wanted Wade to fill Joseph's sandals, period.

He did his best not to stare at Felicity standing beside him, once again dressed in her Virgin Mary costume. Keeping his gaze fixed forward was difficult, though.

For starters, a camel stood just to his right, and the beast had been gradually inching forward all night, pretty much obstructing Wade's view of the crowd, and vice versa. He'd tried to nudge the animal back in place a few times, but his gentle prods had been mostly ineffective. Plus, Wade had heard a rumor from the previous year's Joseph that sometimes camels spit. So far, this year's camel seemed perfectly pleasant, but Wade wasn't keen on taking unnecessary chances since being spat upon by a camel didn't sound the least bit enjoyable.

Oh, the things he did for his hometown.

In all honesty, though, the camel had little to do with why his attention kept straying toward Felicity. Every time he saw her in her pretty blue costume, his throat grew thick. She took his breath away, even when she vibrated with nervous energy—which she'd been doing since the start of the Christmas festival two hours ago.

Wade chalked it up to stage fright. After all,

Joseph and Mary were the biggest stars in the living nativity, behind baby Jesus, obviously. But the Christ child was played by a plastic doll instead of a person, which left Wade and Felicity as the center of the town's attention. Other than the camel and a handful of farm animals, that is.

"How are you holding up?" he asked under his breath. Every fifteen minutes or so, the spotlight above the crèche went dark while the soundtrack to the nativity scene started over again at the beginning, focusing on the angel appearing to the shepherds and their trek to Bethlehem.

Felicity blinked up at him in the darkness, snowflakes swirling around her heart-shaped face. "I'm okay. A little cold, I guess."

"I thought you might say that." Wade winked at her. "I arranged a little surprise to warm us up."

He opened the box that the wise men had just presented them for the fourth time in a row. Two paper cups from the Bean sat inside, alongside a generous chunk of warm, fragrant gingerbread.

Felicity gasped. "Is that…?"

"Hot chocolate?" Wade plucked one of the cups from the box and offered it to her. "Yes, ma'am, it certainly is."

"This hardly seems Biblical, but at the same time, it feels like a miracle." She took a sip, closed her eyes and let out a contented sigh that warmed

Wade's heart more than any amount of hot cocoa ever could. "Thank you, Joseph."

"You're welcome, Mary." He broke off a piece of the gingerbread. "Try this. Alice made it, so it's sure to be delicious."

"Wow, you really are full of surprises."

He shrugged. "I figured it might be a bit chilly, even with a space heater disguised as a bale of hay. Vermont winters are no joke."

"I'm beginning to realize that," she whispered. "I suppose we should probably hurry, though."

"Why? Are the shepherds already headed this way again?"

"Not yet, but the camel is eycing the gingerbread." She grinned at him over the top of her steaming cup of cocoa.

"It's good to hear you laugh," he said before he could stop himself. "You've seemed a little nervous."

"Really? I was going for beatific. Or at the very least, somewhat angelic."

He ran a fingertip gently down the side of her cheek. "You always look like an angel. I don't think you can help it."

Her cheeks flared pink, and then her gaze dropped slowly to his mouth. Wade stopped breathing for a second as he reminded himself they had rules about this sort of thing—rules he desperately wanted to break in a thousand different ways.

Then the camel let out an ill-timed snort, and they both jumped. Hot chocolate sloshed out of the tiny hole in the lid of Wade's cup and splashed on his hand.

"You're doing it again," Felicity said flatly.

"What?"

"*Flirting.* In a Biblical setting, no less." She gestured toward the plastic baby in the manger and the surrounding farm animals, who all seemed bored out of their minds. Only the camel remained bright-eyed and bushy-tailed. "It's like you can't help it."

Maybe I can't. Not when it came to Felicity, anyway.

He cleared his throat. "I'll have to watch that."

"You definitely should." She gave him a firm nod and brushed gingerbread crumbs from the front of her blue silk robes. She couldn't seem to look him in the eye all of a sudden.

Interesting. Wade felt himself grin as he popped the last of the gingerbread in his mouth.

"I'm serious," Felicity said, casting a nervous glance in his general direction. Although she was still looking more at the camel than she was at him. "Haven't you noticed that everyone is looking at us? And I *do* mean everyone."

Wade squinted into the distance, where the majority of the town strolled from tent to tent, enjoying the Christmas festival. A crush of people watched the shepherds head their way.

"That's sort of the point." He gestured toward the sheep, the manger and the ridiculous camel. "It's literally the entire reason we're standing here."

"Right, except they're not looking at us in a Biblical way. They think we're together." She waved a hand back and forth between them. "As in, *together*. Like a couple. You should have seen the moms at the Bean today. They all acted like I was your baby mama or something."

A muscle tensed somewhere in his jaw. Was he grinding his teeth all of a sudden? "Would that be so terrible?"

Felicity arched a brow. "Think about it. You probably wouldn't be on the receiving end of any more casseroles."

He didn't care about the casseroles. He cared about *her*—and Nick—even though he wasn't technically supposed to.

"We can't have that, can we?" He slammed the wise mens' box shut and tucked it out of sight.

A coldness had crept its way into his tone—a bite he didn't like and was by no means proud of. He could have sworn he saw the camel flinch.

Listen to you. You sound like your so-called father.

Maybe he was just imagining things. After all, he'd spent the better part of his life avoiding emulating his dad. Plus, Wade hadn't even seen the man since he was nine years old. It was strange how vivid the memories still were—the terrible way his father used to speak to his mother, the tears she always did her best to hide. The Saturday morning Wade had woken up to his favorite chocolate-chip pancakes topped with pure Vermont maple syrup and the news that his dad had walked out and wasn't coming back had been the best day of his life.

Until recently, anyway. The last couple days had been awfully nice. So nice that he didn't want to think about them too hard, because he knew they hadn't been altogether real.

"I'm sorry," he said quietly. "I just…"

I just hate these silly rules. I want to know you, really know you. And I think you want that, too. But I can't seem to figure out what's holding you back.

Felicity turned soft eyes on him, and for a brief, breathtaking moment, he knew—he just *knew*—she didn't care about rules or casseroles, either. Somewhere deep down, she had to know he wasn't just flirting with her. The hot chocolate, the firemen he'd dragged to her yoga studio, the fact that he got up at night to help her with Nick, even though it wasn't his turn…he wasn't flirting. He was courting her.

Except he couldn't do that, could he? They had an agreement. And they had a baby…

A baby who was depending on them. He could *not* screw this up.

"Smokey," she whispered, and a tiny smile made its way to her lips—a smile that seemed as if she didn't know whether to break his heart or to break every rule that had ever existed.

Wade had never wanted to kiss a woman so badly in his life. "Yes?"

The spotlight overhead flicked back on, flooding them with blinding light. The gold locket Felicity always wore glimmered in the brightness. Time was up. The shepherds had arrived, along with a few wise men, a donkey and all the prying eyes of Lovestruck—the ones Felicity seemed so keen on avoiding.

Wade turned toward the light and tried his best to act like Joseph, a man who'd loved a woman and her baby so much that he'd raised the child as his own. A family man in the truest sense of the word.

Playing the part wasn't quite as hard as he'd imagined it would be.

The rest of the night sped by in a dizzying whirl of wise men, angel wings and assorted livestock. Felicity wasn't sure why the living nativity included a pair of alpacas, as that didn't exactly seem Biblically accurate, but they appeared to be a Lovestruck necessity. She just went with it. If the nativity scene in *Love Actually*, her favorite Christmas movie of all time, could boast an octopus and three lobsters, then she could get on board with a couple of curly-haired alpacas.

Her favorite moment of the night had been when Wade surprised her with the secret hot chocolate and gingerbread, of course. She'd practically been frozen solid up until then, and the gingerbread had been the best she'd ever tasted— warm, sweet and rich with the flavors of cloves, nutmeg and cinnamon. If she thought too much about sipping cocoa beside Wade and the way she couldn't stop looking at the charming crinkles near the corners of his eyes or the insanely appealing squareness of his jaw, she might have to admit that the warm gingerbread and hot chocolate hadn't actually been the cause of the woozy, pleasant warmth that coursed through her. So she very purposefully *didn't* think about it. She did her best, anyway.

She glanced at Wade sitting beside her in the front seat of his SUV as they made their way back to his cottage. He hadn't said much since she'd complained about the Lovestruck moms thinking they were a couple. His initial response had been a lighthearted question.

Would that be so terrible?

Still, somewhere beneath his lopsided grin and those devil-may-care eyes of his, she'd seen something else—something that made her want to throw caution to the wind and put an end to the casseroles once and for all.

And then the lights came back on, and Felicity had come to her senses. Nothing about this crazy Christmas holiday was real. She and Wade weren't a real couple any more than they were the actual Mary and Joseph.

Nick babbled in the back seat, drawing a smile from Wade. He glanced at her and sighed. "He seems happy. I guess getting a babysitter for a few hours might not make us terrible parents, after all."

Parents. Gosh, that's what they were, wasn't it? For the time being, at least.

She nibbled on her lip. "I guess not."

Wade looked back toward the windshield, but Felicity noticed a small furrow form between his eyebrows.

"Can I ask you something?" he finally said.

"Sure, so long as I get to ask you something in return." It was only fair, right? There were certain things she didn't want to discuss—with anyone— but her head was full of questions about Wade.

She wasn't about to pass up the chance to get to the bottom of his ugly-sock mystery.

He nodded. "It's a deal."

"Fine. What do you want to know?"

He drew in a long breath and released it. "How do you know so much about babies?"

"Oh." Felicity hadn't been sure what to expect, but it hadn't been this. "Well…"

There were a million different ways she could have answered his question. She could have said something smart and safe, like that she'd babysat a lot as a kid or that she came from a large extended family with babies galore. Both of things had been true.

But Wade knew she'd been certified as a foster parent, and she had a feeling such a general question was his way of asking to know more about that, without overstepping. She hadn't exactly been an open book.

Wade had opened his *home* to her. Plus his generous, casserole-laden freezer. And more, really. He'd brought the firemen to her yoga studio and snuck her hot chocolate and gingerbread in a box that was supposed to be filled with gold, frankincense and myrrh. She could trust him with at least the less painful parts of her story.

"I went through foster training, and then I became the foster parent to a newborn." Felicity's hand automatically went to her locket, and she wound the chain around her fingertips. "She was with me for six months, so I guess you could say I had a lot of on-the-job training."

"Six months?" Wade glanced at her, and she did her absolute best to remain poised. Stoic. "It must have been hard to say goodbye."

The hardest moment of my life. "It was. Very." She flashed him as bright a smile as she could manage. "Okay, my turn now."

He eyed her with concern. "How long ago was this?"

Felicity's heart beat hard beneath her blue silk robes. "That's two questions."

"Indulge me, just this once?"

She made the mistake of glancing at him, just long enough to go all swoony at the sight of his lopsided smile. Ugh, why did that happen every single time?

"It was about six months ago," she said.

"That's not very much time." He pulled the car to a stop, and Felicity realized they'd reached his driveway. Still, neither of them made a move to leave the car, and Felicity's neck grew hot while he studied her. "I understand why you initially said no to taking care of Nick. What made you change your mind?"

She shook her head. *Not going there, Smokey. Not unless you want a sobbing Virgin Mary on your hands.* "That's definitely another question."

"Fair enough." He winked at her, but as familiar as the gesture might be, he didn't have his usual, flirty expression. There was something more honest about the way he looked at her—honest enough that she knew she wasn't going to confine her one and only question to his fondness for nutty socks. "Ask me anything?"

"Why didn't you want to name Nick after your father?"

His smile died on his lips, and she immediately regretted asking the question.

"Never mind. I shouldn't have—"

He held up a hand and grinned again, but it didn't quite reach his eyes. "No, it's okay. You answered me, and now it's my turn."

Felicity nodded. The air inside the car seemed impossibly thick all of a sudden.

"My dad wasn't…isn't…a very nice person. I actually don't know if he's alive or dead, because I don't have a relationship with him anymore. He verbally abused my mom when I was a kid. One minute, he'd be talking to her like a rational person, and the next, he'd be calling her horrible names. My mother didn't have an unkind bone in her body." Wade's voice dipped low, quiet. Felicity could barely hear it above the muffled patter of snow on the car windows. "Until I was nine years old, all I wanted to do was protect her."

"What happened when you were nine?"

"That's two questions," Wade said, a half-hearted smile tugging his lips. He shrugged one shoulder. "My dad up and left. Sometimes I wonder if he realized that the way he treated my mom just ended up bringing the two of us closer together in the end. She meant the world to me. She passed away last year, and Cap has sort of stepped in as a father figure. Not that I should need one, considering I'm a fully grown man."

He certainly was, and he had the broad shoulders and rock-solid biceps to prove it. Neither of which Felicity should have been thinking about right then. "Everyone needs a family, Wade. No matter how old they are."

Wasn't that why they were sitting here, side by side, with a baby tucked into the back seat? Nick needed a family, and somehow, some way, she and Wade had stepped up. Only now was she beginning to understand why.

Wade needs this. He needs this just as much as Nick does. Her throat went tight. *As much as I do.*

Wade's expression softened, and when his lips parted, ever so gently, Felicity had the feeling he was going to say something else—something important. But Nick started whimpering in his car seat before Wade could get it out.

"Duty calls," he said, and then he slid out of the car, leaving Felicity with a lump in her throat that she wasn't sure would ever go away.

Chapter Nine

The following morning, Wade shed his Joseph persona and resumed his regular role as an LFD firefighter.

Switching personas was more disorienting than he would have thought, probably because his "normal life" was becoming less and less normal by the day. He'd been up three times in the night with Nick, and his home no longer resembled a bachelor pad in the slightest. In the wee, pre-dawn hours, an empty baby bottle sat atop his video game console in the living room. A baby blue knitted blanket from Main Street Yarn covered his leather sofa, and a pair of Felicity's girlie high heels were in a heap in the corner of the room.

He squinted at the shoes. They were mismatched, which seemed odd. Why would Felicity wear shoes that didn't match?

The mystery was solved upon closer inspection. The stilettos weren't a coordinating pair, but they both bore a matching set of small, canine bite marks.

Duchess. Wade sighed. The dog was going to make him look bad, just when he and Felicity started getting closer. Then again, hadn't he warned Felicity that the little spaniel could get into trouble?

He picked up one of the shoes and saw the words *Kate Spade* etched into the soft leather. Hoo boy. This couldn't be good.

He backtracked to his bedroom where Duchess lolled at the foot of the bed like Marie Antoinette. She cocked her head at him, pink bows askew.

"See this?" He held up the shoe. "No. Bad dog."

Duchess whined and rolled over onto her back in a picture-perfect display of surrender. The dog had an uncanny ability to tug on the heartstrings, he'd give her that.

"Do you think you could stay out of trouble while I'm at work?" He crossed his arms and glared down at her, but her tail wagged as if he'd just promised her a doghouse made of bacon. "Please?"

She flopped over, crawled to his pillow and then yawned and promptly went back to sleep. Wade's lecture had fallen on deaf ears in every sense of the word. He thought that using the chewed-up designer shoe as a visual aid would have helped, but who knew?

As a precaution, he picked up Felicity's pink purse from the sofa in the living room and placed it safely out of canine reach on the kitchen counter before he left. One fashion disaster was enough for the day.

"Rough morning?" Jack asked when he walked into the kitchen at the firehouse. As usual, he stood at the stove poking at something with a spatula.

"Sort of, I guess. Duchess has developed a fondness for Felicity's shoes." Wade reached for a coffee cup. "And I didn't get much sleep, but I'm starting to get used to that."

Especially if it meant seeing Felicity walk around in the semi-darkness in her ruffly pink robe and girlie velvet slippers—so long as Duchess didn't get to the slippers first. In any case, there were certain benefits to getting up for the middle-of-the-night feedings.

"I can't do anything about your first problem, but I got you something that might help you out with the second." Jack waved his spatula at a shiny reindeer bag sitting on the kitchen table.

Wade examined the bag. The reindeer stared back at him with comical googly eyes, and he got the definite feeling it had originally been purchased with Emma and Ella in mind. "Is this a Christmas present? For me?"

Jack shrugged. "Just something I picked up. It's more of a baby gift, but Madison thought I should wrap it properly. We've got Christmas gift bags and wrapping paper coming out of our ears."

Wade peered into the gift bag. Two white, handheld radios were nestled among piles of glittery tissue paper. "Walkie-talkies?"

He still didn't qualify as a baby expert, but he was fairly certain Nick was too young for those.

"Wow. You really are new at this, aren't you?" Jack rolled his eyes. "They're not walkie-talkies. It's a baby monitor. You put one in the baby's room and the other wherever you are. That way when Nick wakes up, you'll know. You might actually get some rest at night instead of trying to sleep while staying on high alert."

"That's genius." Wade picked up one of the baby monitor consoles for a closer look and ignored Jack's amused expression. Yes, he was a beginner at the dad thing, but he was learning.

You're not actually *a dad, remember?*

He placed the baby monitor back inside the wrapping. "Thanks, man."

"Sure thing. Just trying to help." Jack shrugged and slid his skillet full of sizzling breakfast sausage onto a platter. "I know you and Felicity haven't had much of a chance to go shopping for baby supplies, and I figured you could use them."

Wade plucked a piece of sausage off the counter and wondered if it was a bad thing or a good thing that he was getting used to hearing Jack talk about Felicity and him as if they were a unit. A couple. Everyone in town seemed to be doing it, according to Felicity. Come to think of it, no one had dropped off a casserole for him in days.

He laughed quietly to himself and then looked up to find Jack watching him with a smirk.

"What?" Wade said.

"You just look happy."

I am...for now. But Wade knew just how fleeting happiness could be. And nothing about his new normal was permanent. He wasn't even sure if he wanted it to be.

Liar.

All at once, Wade couldn't seem to look at his friend. And when Cap strolled into the kitchen and asked who wanted to do the inspections at the Christmas-tree lot that had been set up on the sidewalk near Village Market, Wade was the first volunteer. Being stuck inside with his thoughts was beginning to feel far more dangerous than anything related to fighting fires.

"She ate your shoes?" Madison's hand flew to her heart, and she gasped. "Oh, my gosh, were they designer?"

Felicity nodded as she rocked Nick in her arms and paced the floor of the empty yoga studio. "Kate Spade—from the *Fashionista* closet."

One of the perks of working for a fashion magazine had been access to *Fashionista's* legendary "closet," which contained all the clothes, shoes and accessories used for photo shoots and video content for the magazine's social media. Nearly everything Felicity wore had come straight from the closet, including her coveted Birkin bag, which would've been impossible to purchase on her editor salary. As it was, the bag had been in such high demand that the fashion editor organized a drawing for the purse, and Felicity had been the lucky winner.

Of course, if Nama-Stay Awhile continued at its current dismal pace, she might have to sell it on Poshmark to continue feeding herself once she was no longer living with Wade.

The very idea of it made her ill, although she wasn't entirely sure which was worse—the potential loss of her Birkin or Wade Ericson. The more she got to know him, the more she realized that walking away from him was going to be a lot harder than she'd anticipated. Even her rules couldn't seem to protect her anymore.

He's not actually yours. You can't lose someone who never belonged to you to begin with. Right. She wasn't Mary, and Wade wasn't Joseph. The baby in her arms certainly hadn't come into their lives in a manger. Once Christmas was over, everything would go back to normal.

"The dog sounds terrible. Truly awful," Madison said as she rolled up her yoga mat. She'd popped in for the half-hour lunch-break class that Felicity had thought would be a huge success.

Wrong.

Again.

Maybe it was for the best, though. Nick wanted to be held, and since Madison was her only student, they'd decided to just chat and take turns rocking him until Madison had to get back to work at the *Bee*.

"She's not so bad. She's an awfully cute dog, and she worships the ground Wade walks on. Me, not so much."

Madison's eyes narrowed. "You mean there's a pattern to this behavior?"

"Sometimes I think so. She either sleeps on Wade's bed at night or on the floor beneath Nick's crib in the nursery, but she won't set foot in my room." Or technically, set *paw*.

"Except to steal your shoes," Madison said flatly.

Felicity stopped pacing and rubbed her hand in gentle circles on Nick's little back. "Good point."

Wade had warned her the dog could be a handful, but maybe her behavior was personal. Was that even possible?

"Hey, look! Someone's coming." Madison pointed to the frosted glass door of the studio, where a shadow loomed, followed by a knock. "Maybe you have a new client."

Felicity handed over the baby. "Let's hope so. Can you watch Nick real quick while I get that?"

"Sure."

Maybe appearing in the living nativity had actually been good for business, just like she'd hoped when she'd originally let Alice talk her into it. That had been Felicity's plan all along, before she'd upped and moved in with Joseph. Oh, what a difference a few days had made.

Her hopes dashed when she opened the door and found Diane Foster standing on the threshold in street clothes and nary a yoga mat in sight. "Hi, Diane."

Diane grinned. "Oh, hi, Felicity. Good. I was hoping you wouldn't be too busy to come to the door."

Too busy? Ha.

Diane bent to pull a small, foil-wrapped pan

from the storage department of the baby stroller at her side. "Here."

Felicity glanced down at the baking dish and then back at Diane. "Is that a casserole?"

Unbelievable. Now Wade's fan club was dropping off meals at her yoga studio? A hot spike of something that felt far too much like jealousy hit her in the center of her chest.

"It's brownies, actually. Peppermint dark chocolate swirl." Diane pushed the pan closer. "You do like chocolate, don't you?"

Felicity took the brownies. What else was she supposed to do? Plus, they smelled heavenly— like Christmas decadence on steroids. Maybe she'd polish them off herself and "forget" to tell Wade they'd ever existed.

Whoa, there. Her inner green-eyed monster was showing, and not the Grinch.

Oh, God. I am jealous.

She plastered on a smile. "I do like chocolate, and I'm sure Wade does, too. I'll be sure and tell him you brought them by for him." It would be humiliating, but she'd manage.

Diane waved a hand. "The brownies aren't for Wade, silly. They're for you."

"For me," Felicity echoed. What was happening? No one had ever presented her with home-made baked goods in her life.

Except, now that she thought about it, Alice

was always baking things and bringing them to class. And now the queen of the Lovestruck moms was giving her brownies—*peppermint dark chocolate* brownies that in no way resembled the boxed variety that Felicity usually whipped up on a whim on Friday nights to enjoy with a glass of wine and a chick flick.

Was this what people did in small towns? It seemed almost too good to be true, and something that would never, ever happen in Manhattan. The thought was almost laughable. If a near-stranger had ever presented Felicity with a pan of homemade brownies in New York, she wouldn't have gone anywhere near it.

"Yes, for you. Just a little welcome to Lovestruck. We're all so happy about you, Wade and the little one." Diane's gaze drifted over Felicity's shoulder toward Madison, cooing at Nick.

"Well, thank you. It's a lovely surprise." Felicity really didn't want to invite her inside. What would she possibly say if Diane pressed for details about the baby? It seemed rude not to, though. "Would you, um, like to come in for a bit?"

"So sorry, I can't. We're actually on our way to knitting class next door at the yarn shop."

Felicity exhaled in relief, despite the realization that Main Street Yarn apparently managed to attract students to a midday class. What was she doing wrong?

"Another time, maybe," she said.

"Oh, I almost forgot!" Diane picked up a small stack of envelopes that were resting on the canopy of her baby stroller. "The mail carrier came by just before I knocked. He left these for you."

"Mail *and* brownies. Thank you." Felicity reached for the envelopes, and when she caught a glimpse of the item at the top of the stack, she froze in place.

Diane must have said goodbye, because in what seemed like a split second, she was gone. Felicity couldn't be certain, though, because there was a terrible roar in her ears. She couldn't tear her attention from the Christmas card in her hands. It was a photo card—one of those postcard-style Christmas greetings, boasting a sweet picture of a young mother and her baby, dressed in matching Christmas dresses.

Lori and Ariel.

Felicity was spellbound by the image. Ariel had gotten so big, and Lori looked so natural holding her. So happy.

Like a real mother.

Felicity's legs went wobbly. She needed to sit down—now—and then possibly eat the entire pan full of brownies. She knew from experience that chocolate wasn't an actual remedy for heartbreak, but it couldn't hurt.

"Felicity, is everything okay?" Madison said.

Felicity looked up, and the sight of Nick's angelic face managed to pull her back to the here and now.

"Sorry, I just spaced out there for a second." She shoved the mail into the pocket of the fuzzy Angora sweater she liked to wear to and from the studio. Then she held the brownie pan aloft. "Look, we have brownies."

"Nice." Madison waggled her eyebrows and lifted a corner of the foil to take a peek.

"Is it? Why would Diane Foster cook for me? I thought she only did that for Wade," Felicity said. Under her breath, she couldn't help but add, "Like every other woman in Lovestruck."

Madison snorted with laughter, prompting a giggle from Nick. "That's just what people do here, and Wade is a local hero. You didn't think it really meant anything, did you? Diane is married."

"You haven't seen the casserole collection in his freezer. It's a thing to behold."

Madison let out another snort and looked Felicity up and down. "Oh, my gosh, look at you. You're jealous."

"No, I'm not," Felicity said in the most jealous-sounding tone imaginable.

"You *are*. I knew there was something going on between you two." Madison bounced Nick in her arms with renewed vigor. "But honestly, don't give the casseroles a second thought. The town has a collective crush on your man, that's all. It's perfectly innocent. Kind of sweet, actually."

"He's not my man," Felicity countered. "I know it might look that way, but…"

Her voice trailed off as a thought occurred to her—an idea she'd never considered before, even though it was as obvious as the nose on her face.

"What?" Madison's brow furrowed.

Felicity shot her a triumphant grin. "I think I just figured out why Duchess is eating my shoes."

"We need to have a chat," Felicity said.

Duchess peered up at her from beneath Nick's crib and wagged just the tip of her tail. Felicity had tried her best to lure her out into the open. She'd offered up every variety of edible incentive, from boxed gourmet dog treats to sliced deli meat from Village Market. But the stubborn little dog wouldn't be swayed.

Fine.

Felicity wasn't backing down. "I know what's going on here. You're jealous."

Duchess blinked her wide eyes, then looked away and started licking one of her paws.

Felicity sighed. "Ignore me if you like, but I'm not going away."

And neither were her shoes. They were all simply going to have to find a way to peacefully coexist.

"Look, I get it. Wade is yours. It's only natural to feel slightly threatened by a new female in his life. He's special, and of course you want to protect him."

Felicity's soul ached every time she thought about what he'd told her about his father. If anyone deserved to be part of a happy family, it was Wade. "He's a good man—caring, thoughtful… heroic."

Her tummy fluttered. "Not to mention charming. And handsome—can't forget that. You're a dog, so maybe you haven't noticed. But let me assure you, by human standards, he's quite the specimen."

Duchess looked up and cocked her head.

"Right. You knew that. How could you not?" Felicity took a deep breath. "But what I'm trying to say is that you don't have to worry. He's yours, and nothing will ever change that. I'm not going to fall in love with him. I promise I'm not. *Ever.*"

The dog rested her head on her paws and sighed.

"No matter how bad I want to," Felicity added, and to her great mortification, tears pooled in her eyes.

She'd reached a new low, apparently—crying to Wade's dog over how irresistible he was. This wasn't how her little lecture was supposed to go. RIP her closet. She probably wouldn't have a single designer shoe left after Christmas.

But then she heard someone make a tsk-tsk

noise behind her. A very male, very heroic some-one. "Never, ever? Are you sure?"

She turned around, even though what she wanted most of all was to dive under Nick's crib and hide alongside Duchess.

Wade stood in the doorway to the nursery, grinning from ear to ear. His feet were clad in his hideous socks, and he was dressed in an old, faded LFD shirt and sweatpants. Felicity wanted nothing more than to crawl into his lap, sit by a cozy fire and feed each other Diane Foster's brownies. If a few pair of Kate Spade shoes had to sacrifice themselves to make it happen, so be it.

Her mouth went dry. "You're home."

Thank goodness the man couldn't see inside her head. Although, who was she kidding? He'd evidently just heard an earful.

"Yep."

"I was just having a chat with Duchess about my shoes, and…um…other things."

His eyes twinkled. "So I heard."

"*Private* things," she added as her face prick-led with heat.

"Sorry. I got home a few minutes ago and I couldn't help overhearing." He nodded in the direction of the changing table, where a brand-spanking-new baby monitor sat with a little blue light blinking in the corner.

Super. He'd heard everything.

Felicity's mortification magnified tenfold. She crossed her arms, but it only made her more aware of the panicked beating of her heart. "Since when do we have a baby monitor?"

"Since today. It was a gift from Jack. I came by at lunch to drop it off. I thought I'd surprise you and Nick, but you weren't here." A dimple flashed in his left cheek.

Ugh, did he have to look so thoroughly pleased with himself?

"That was really thoughtful." Her lips curved into a tight smile. "It just would have been really nice to know it was here."

"No worries. Your secrets are safe with me," he said.

But was her heart? That was the million-dollar question.

"Come into the living room. I've got another surprise for you two."

"Is it more surveillance equipment?" she said flatly.

Wade laughed as he turned and walked away.

Focus on his socks. If anything can make him seem less attractive, they should do the trick.

But she couldn't seem to keep her gaze from straying to the way his T-shirt stretched across his broad back as he moved. Or how charmingly rumpled he looked.

Wait. Was that a pine needle poking out from his thick brown hair?

"Ta-da," he said, gesturing toward a blue spruce tree standing in the corner of the room. The evergreen was tucked by the window, so tall and elegant that it nearly scraped the ceiling.

Felicity gasped. "It's gorgeous."

"I had to inspect the Christmas-tree lot today for work. They passed with flying colors, by the way. While I was there, I kept thinking about the tiny tree back at your apartment. I thought you might like to have one here, too." His expression turned slightly sheepish, and Felicity thought this might be the side of Wade she liked best of all— not the flirty, confident firefighter everyone in Lovestruck knew and loved, but the tender side of him. The vulnerable side. The side no one got to see but her.

"What do you think?" he asked.

"I think it's perfect." *I think* you're *perfect.*

Her head swirled with a lovely combination of Christmas-tree scented air and longing. What was it that she'd just promised Duchess?

I'm not going to fall in love with him. I promise I'm not. Ever.

She took a step toward him. Duchess would forgive her if she kissed him, right? Just this once.

But as she drew closer to him, she caught sight of a flash of pink over his shoulder. It was a bubblegum-hued lump on the floor, tucked halfway beneath the sofa, as if someone had tried their best to hide it but couldn't completely banish it from view.

No. Felicity's heart sank. Duchess had struck again.

"My Birkin!"

"What's a Birkin?"

Wade wasn't sure what was happening, but it definitely wasn't good. For a second, Felicity had been looking at him like he was as magical as Santa and all nine of his flying reindeer, and the next, she'd run across the living room in a panic.

"What's a Birkin?" She stared at him, agog, as she clutched her big pink handbag to her chest. Images of Linus and his blanket from *A Charlie Brown Christmas* flashed through Wade's head. "You cannot be serious right now."

He held up his hands. "You've got to help me out here, babe."

Whatever a Birkin was, Wade wasn't a fan, seeing as it had just interrupted the most intimate moment he and Felicity had ever shared. Still, he hated to see her so upset. Surely there was something he could do to get this evening back on track. They had a tree to decorate, popcorn strings to make, maybe even a little slow dancing in the soft glow of the tree lights. Somewhere around here, he had his mom's old collection of Christmas albums. Was there any sort of chaos that couldn't be calmed by The Carpenters' "Merry Christmas, Darling"?

Wade's body tensed at the memory of Felicity's aching promise that he'd overheard on the baby monitor. *I'm not going to fall in love with him. I promise I'm not. Ever.*

Right, so he probably shouldn't be thinking about slow dancing—especially since he had no intention of falling in love, either. He and Felicity were just two people who happened to be raising a baby together. Temporarily. He wasn't sure why he was going around buying Christmas trees and doing yoga in his spare time.

"Does this make things clear for you?" Felicity thrust her bag toward him.

Uh oh. Duchess had evidently acquired a taste for bubblegum-pink leather.

"So a Birkin is a purse," he said calmly.

She glared at him so hard that Santa was probably writing his name on the naughty list in permanent black ink. And then she stormed past him toward the guest room and slammed her door with enough force to rattle the windows.

It looked like Wade would be decorating the tree solo. Merry freaking Christmas.

Chapter Ten

Later that week, with her uniquely embellished—thanks to Duchess—Birkin bag slung over her shoulder, Felicity took a deep inhale of coffee-scented air. The interior of the Bean smelled fantastic, even though commingled somewhere with the rich holiday aromas of espresso beans, gingerbread and peppermint mocha, there was still an underlying base note of maple. She was still in Vermont, after all. Maple syrup was pretty much what glued Lovestruck together.

Not technically true, Felicity admitted to herself. Her time in Vermont had certainly been adventurous, but in addition to giving her a crash course in small-town life, the past couple weeks also made Felicity realize that the glue holding the Lovestruck community together was its people. As intrusive as it could be, it was also sort of…nice.

Wade was the hometown hero, and now everyone else in Lovestruck seemed to be falling in love with Felicity by association. Every night, crowds swarmed to the living nativity scene at the Christmas festival. Lovestruck moms kept popping by the yoga studio to drop off holiday baked goods and tell Felicity what a perfect Mary and Joseph they were. It would have been just lovely if she and Wade were a real couple. A family.

But they weren't, and now all the attention was making it harder and harder for Felicity to remember why she'd insisted on the no-romance rule. Since the baby-monitor incident and the near-kiss by the Christmas tree, she'd renewed her commitment to not let herself fall for him. The damaged Birkin had saved her. Every now and then, though, she couldn't seem to remember why.

To protect your heart, remember?

Right. Her heart. She glanced at Nick, tucked in his puffy little snowsuit beneath a soft flannel blanket in his new stroller—the most recent hand-me-down from one of Wade's fellow first responders. Lately it sort of seemed that her heart no longer resided deep inside her chest, nor did it reside in her pink Birkin. She felt more like it lived in tiny onesies and the hand-knitted baby bootees that Madison's aunt Alice kept bringing to gentle yoga class.

Would it be so bad if she agreed to keep caring for Nick after the holidays? Not at all, which was precisely the problem. The longer this arrangement lasted, the harder it would be on her when it ended.

Felicity placed her order and pushed Nick's stroller to her favorite corner booth, all the while glancing over her shoulder in case the Lovestruck moms happened to be around. She hadn't allowed herself to set foot inside the Bean since the last awkward encounter. But a girl could only go so long without proper coffee, especially when she was getting up every other night to take care of a baby.

Don't you mean every *night?* Her face went warm as she thought about how she and Wade had continued handling the late-night shifts together instead of taking turns. That probably needed to stop. And it would…soon.

Maybe.

"Excuse me." A throat cleared nearby as a shadow fell over Felicity's table.

She nearly jumped a mile in her seat. Ugh, she was supposed to be looking out for the moms so she could hide instead of daydreaming about Wade and his irresistibly broad shoulders.

"I'm sorry. I didn't mean to startle you," the owner of the shadow said. Not one of the moms, as it turned out, but an unfamiliar man in a finely tailored suit with a camel-colored scarf wrapped around his neck.

Felicity blinked, stunned into silence by the sight of exquisite wool cashmere. She hadn't caught a glimpse of Armani menswear since the day she'd left Manhattan. Oh, how she'd missed fashion.

"You're Felicity Hart, right?" He offered her his hand for a shake. "Brad Walker from Lovestruck Real Estate."

"Oh, right. We've talked on the phone, and your assistant, Betty, has been really helpful since I moved to town. It's nice to finally meet you in person." She stood to take his hand.

"Please sit." He smiled down at Nick, sleeping soundly in his baby carrier. "If this is a bad time, we can chat later. I didn't realize your son was asleep."

Felicity's heart gave a little squeeze. *Her son.* "It's fine, really. Was there something you wanted to talk to me about?"

He nodded. "Yes, actually."

"Have a seat." Felicity waved toward the leather bench opposite the table from her. It wasn't as if she was in a hurry. Mornings at the studio had finally picked up, thanks to Alice's knitting group and the guys from the fire department. But from about ten a.m. onward, her days were free and clear.

Caring for Nick had provided a nice distraction, as had spending time with Wade. Neither of those situations would last forever, though. At some point, she was going to have to stop living in a holiday fantasy world and deal with her very real, very complicated life.

The barista called her name and Brad volunteered to fetch her coffee. He returned with two steaming cups, slid across from her and handed her the one topped with whipped cream and nutmeg.

"Thanks." She took a sip of her gingerbread latte and braced herself for whatever Brad wanted to discuss with her.

She'd paid her rent on the studio, hadn't she? Had she gotten so wrapped up in her temporarily charmed life that she'd forgotten? Surely not. Maybe he had a problem with the fact that she wasn't actually living in the attic apartment anymore. Although, was that really necessary? Main Street in Lovestruck seemed as safe as could be.

"Thanks for taking a few minutes to chat." A tiny furrow appeared between Brad's eyebrows.

"I hope this discussion doesn't prove to be too awkward—"

Felicity's stomach churned. Uh oh. This couldn't be good.

"—but we've had some interest in the space your yoga studio currently occupies."

Felicity's mouth opened and then closed again. What was he talking about? "I don't understand. Someone already wants to rent the space when my lease runs out?"

She'd just moved in a month ago. Who chose commercial space to rent nearly an entire year in advance?

Brad shook his head. "No. They want to rent the space sooner than that. Much sooner—just after the first of the year, as a matter of fact. Don't worry, the space is yours. You've got a contract and of course we'll stand by that, no matter what. But this client has made it clear that they'd be willing to buy out the rest of your lease." He shrugged. "I guess I felt like I had a responsibility to let you know."

"Oh, wow." Felicity swallowed. "I, um. I don't know what to say."

Not once had she considered that she might have an opportunity to get out of her lease. She'd made an impulsive decision based on a broken heart, a weekend yoga retreat and serving as Madison's maid of honor, and she'd thought she was stuck with it for life. A full calendar year, at minimum. And here was Brad, like an Armani-clad angel, offering her the most unexpected Christmas gift of all—a way out.

Once Christmas was over, Nick could be placed in a real home with real parents. She would be free to leave Wade's house and walk away from Lovestruck altogether, if that's what she wanted.

Is it what I want?

Felicity gave Brad a wobbly smile. She suddenly had no idea what she really wanted. Lovestruck had finally started to feel like home, but all of that would change after Christmas.

"You don't need to say anything." Brad held up his hands. "I'm just the messenger here."

"Can I ask what sort of business would take the studio's place?" She wasn't sure why she wanted to know. She couldn't imagine any type of shop or business in the pretty, serene space she'd created. She only set foot on the special bamboo flooring in her sock feet.

Maybe it was some sort of dance studio, though. Or a florist or vintage dress boutique. Someplace cheery and pretty.

"A hardware store," Brad said.

Her shoulders sagged. "Oh."

"A nice, stable hardware store, though. Part of a national chain."

Ugh, it was getting worse by the second.

What did she care, though? By the time they moved into her dreamy yoga studio, she could be back in New York, working at another slick fashion magazine. Back where people knew not to let their dogs gnaw on Birkin bags.

"Can I think about it?" she heard herself say.

Brad's eyebrows rose. "Sure. I honestly didn't think you'd be interested. I was just letting you know as a courtesy."

Felicity's gaze dropped to the melting whipped cream atop her coffee. "The studio has been more of a challenge than I anticipated."

Everything in Lovestruck had…almost everything, anyway.

"I see. Sorry to hear it." Brad reached into the interior pocket of his suit jacket and then slid a crisp, white business card toward her across the table. "Sleep on it for a few days and give me a call if you have any questions."

If she had any questions?

Right now, questions were pretty much all she had. What she really needed were answers.

"This can't be right." Wade squinted at his cell phone.

Clearly he'd typed the incorrect words into his search engine. Either that, or his results were popping up in some type of foreign currency.

"What?" Jack glanced over his shoulder at the neat grid of handbags on the screen of his iPhone and snorted. "Are you in the market for a handbag?"

"Duchess chewed on one of Felicity's purses." Wade sighed. "Her 'Birkin.' It's a thing, apparently."

A thing that cost ten thousand dollars on eBay, evidently. *Pre-owned*. How was that even possible? Wade's first car cost less than half that amount.

"Her Birkin?" Jack winced as he tossed the new edition of the *Lovestruck Bee* on the firehouse's big kitchen table and dropped into the chair beside Wade. "You're in big trouble, man. Huge. Do you have any idea how much those things cost?"

Wade glared at him. "Since when did you become an expert on Birkin bags? I'd never even heard of them until the other night."

"Since I married a fashion reporter." Jack shrugged and grabbed an apple from the big wooded bowl in the center of the table. "I've learned a few things in the past few months."

"Like what, exactly?"

"Like women wear nude-colored shoes because it's supposed to make their legs look longer, wearing white after Labor Day is now socially acceptable and Birkin bags are pretty much the most expensive handbag on the market." Jack snapped his fingers. "Oh, and those things you call your house socks are bad. Really, really bad."

Ouch.

Was everyone in Lovestruck talking about his socks? *You have much bigger problems than socks, my friend.* "Who even are you right now?"

"Madison loves this kind of stuff, and I'm a good listener." Jack bit into his apple with the carefree ease of a man who wasn't in the market for a ten-thousand-dollar handbag.

Wade envied him—possibly for more reasons than he wanted to contemplate. "I get it. You're husband-of-the-year. But how does that help me replace Felicity's bag?"

"I guess it doesn't," Jack said.

Wade sighed.

"Look, you're never going to be able to replace it. Not unless you've amassed a vast personal fortune that's somehow escaped my notice." Jack finished off his apple and stood to toss the core into the trash.

"I need to make it up to her somehow." Wade's gut churned.

Felicity had dozens of other handbags. Heck, he'd warned her about Duchess's naughty streak—several times. The first few pairs of chewed-up stilettos probably should have been a warning sign. He'd picked up that purse and put it out Duchess's reach himself on more than one occasion. This was *not* his fault.

Except Duchess was his dog now. Not his mom's, but his. He'd even begun to like the little devil, naughty streak and all. But even the fact that the dog was ultimately his responsibility didn't really matter. What mattered most was the look on Felicity's face when she'd found the teeth marks on the bag—the tears that glittered in her moody blue eyes. She'd just seemed so utterly defeated that all Wade wanted to do was make it right.

"So much drama," he muttered. "Over a purse."

"A twenty-five-thousand-dollar purse," Jack said, oh so helpfully.

"No." Wade shook his head. "No way. I just saw some online for half that price."

Jack nodded. "Ah, you must have been looking at used ones."

Wade stared at him for a long beat. "Seriously, you could not have picked up all of this fashion knowledge by osmosis."

There was no way he was *that* good of a listener. No one was.

The tips of Jack's ears turned cherry red. "Madison reads her copies of *Vogue* to the girls. They seem to like it, so…"

The truth at last.

Wade let out a bark of laughter at the thought of

his rough and tumble firefighting friend reading *Vogue* aloud to his twin baby daughters. Even so, a strange warmth seemed to grab hold of Wade's heart. He had to admit it was kind of sweet.

Jack busied himself scrubbing an invisible spot off the kitchen counter in an obvious effort to ignore Wade's amusement as Cap strolled into the room.

His gaze flitted back and forth between Wade and Jack. "You two are suspiciously quiet. What's going on? Anything I should know about?"

Jack glanced at Wade, and he confined the rest of his laughter to a single snort.

"Nothing," Jack said. "Nothing at all."

Cap clamped his hands on his hips. "I don't believe you for a minute, but I've got something to keep you both out of trouble for the next hour or so."

Wade pushed his chair away from the table and stood, as eager to get his mind off Duchess's expensive taste in snacks as he was to stop thinking about Felicity. His life had been ten thousand times easier when he'd lived alone. No dogs, no babies, no women.

No meaning.

He crossed his arms. "What's up, Cap?"

"One of the fireplugs on Main Street is broken. Either a kid decided to pull a prank or someone bumped into it in a car and bolted, but we've got water spewing all over the place." Cap sighed. "The intersection in front of the Bean is practically turning into an ice-skating rink."

"We're on it," Jack said. He nodded at Wade. "We're going to need salt—probably more than we've got on board the rig."

"Got it." Wade headed toward the locker room to climb into his turnout gear.

He was grateful for his job, and especially grateful for this non-life-threatening emergency that wasn't in any way baby-related. A little good old-fashioned manual labor was just what he needed to get his head screwed back on again. He'd been spending so much time doing yoga, washing his hair with "premium" shampoo and folding teeny-tiny baby clothes that he'd forgotten how much he used to enjoy his regular life.

Everything was going to be just fine when Christmas was over. He'd been a-okay before Nick and Felicity had moved in, and he'd be fine again once they left. Just peachy, thank you very much.

Within minutes, he and Jack were pulling up alongside the curb on Main Street. Wade snuck a quick glance at Nama-Stay Awhile, but it didn't look like Felicity had a class going on. He told himself that was for the best. If she'd been there, he would have no doubt been tempted to drop by and say hi after they dealt with the fire hydrant—

which was exactly the sort of thing he needed to stop doing. Just like he needed to stop thinking of Nick's middle-of-the-night feedings as some sort of cozy date-night experience. What the heck was wrong with him, anyway?

"You okay?" Jack shot him a concerned glance as they walked around to the back of the engine and lifted the hatch that contained gallons of rock salt.

"Fine," Wade said through gritted teeth.

Jack hauled a bucket out of the hatch and used his utility knife to slice open one of the bags of salt. "I've got this. Why don't you go take a look at the fireplug and see if you can get the valve shut off?"

"Can do."

Wade grabbed a wrench and stalked toward the hydrant, situated right in front of the Bean's big picture windows. *Relax, man.* Snow flurries swirled all around him, and the lush swags of evergreen hanging from the coffee shop's white gingerbread trim smelled almost as good as the Christmas candles Felicity liked so much. He basically lived in a freaking snow globe. There was no reason whatsoever to feel so out of sorts.

Water gushed out of the plug—by all appearances at the standard rate of one thousand gallons per minute. It sloshed over Wade's boots and drenched the ankles of his bunker pants.

He stepped out of the way of the deluge as best he could, attached the wrench to the top of the hydrant and pulled hard to the right. The water slowed to a trickle and then a full stop. Onlookers gathered outside the Bean applauded as if he'd just done something miraculous.

Wade smiled to himself as he fished around, searching for the steamer cap in the frigid water. Thankfully, it seemed to be intact. In a few swift moves, he replaced it and sealed it shut.

Disaster averted. He'd help Jack with the rock salt, and in no time, the intersection would look exactly at it had before the flood. The afternoon coffee crowd would never even know what happened.

Life goes on, Wade thought. His hometown was as predictable as the setting sun. That should be a comfort, shouldn't it? Come January, he'd still be here, wearing the same uniform, riding in the back of the same shiny red firetruck. The only thing that would be different would be the gaping hole in his heart.

Not necessarily, though. There was still time. He could stop the damage before it happened. It's what he did—he fixed things. He saved the day for Lovestruck. Surely he could save his own.

Someone in the small crowd outside the Bean yelled a thank-you, and Wade glanced up. He smiled and lifted a gloved hand to wave, but his arm froze midair as his gaze snagged on one of Bean's windows.

Frost clung to the edges of the windowpane, making the quaint small-town coffee shop look like something out of a porcelain Christmas village. But he wasn't standing in the middle of a fairy tale, no matter how perfect his make-believe homelife sometimes felt. This wasn't pretend— this was reality, and in the imperfect present, Felicity was sitting at a cozy table inside the Bean, smiling and sipping coffee with another man.

Chapter Eleven

Wade reminded himself to breathe. He reminded himself that he was currently ankle-deep in a slushy deluge on Lovestruck's most public corner. He reminded himself that Felicity wasn't his girlfriend, his wife or the mother of his child. She wasn't *his*, and neither was Nick.

None of those very significant details seemed to matter, though. His stomach hardened, and his ears roared. Every cell in his body tensed as if prepared for battle.

"Wade," Jack called from the middle of the intersection, no doubt wondering why he'd suddenly turned to stone instead of heading back to the rig to grab another bucket of rock salt now that he'd gotten the fire hydrant taken care of.

Wade didn't much care, though. He'd been taken over by some sort of bizarre, propriety need to see what exactly was going on at Felicity's booth inside the Bean.

"I'll be right back." His grip tightened around his wrench as he stepped out of the muck and onto the sidewalk.

The onlookers exchanged puzzled glances, giddy smiles fading.

"Excuse me," Wade said, touching the brim of his helmet and nodding while he made his way to the Bean's double doors.

He stomped his messy boots on the welcome mat and then pushed his way inside. A rush of warm, coffee-scented air greeted him, which seemed to make the terrible churning in his gut ten times worse.

Was Felicity on a *date*? Granted, they hadn't actually promised not to date other people. But Wade hadn't even considered spending time with another woman. He'd assumed Felicity felt the same way. Big mistake, apparently.

The crush of people crowded around the register parted for him, and Wade tried his best not to make eye contact with anyone. In his turnout gear and helmet, he felt immediately, woefully out of place—a bulky, awkward mess in a sea of reindeer sweaters.

Except for Felicity's date, of course. The first thing to come into focus as Wade drew near the cozy corner booth was the sleek business suit that the man was wearing. And a tie? No one in Lovestruck dressed like that. Except...

"Brad?" Wade said, glaring down at the man— Brad Walker, Lovestruck's resident real estate mogul. His family owned half of Main Street.

"Wade?" Felicity's gaze traveled slowly from his helmet to the tips of his grimy boots, lingering briefly on the wrench in his hand as it dripped water onto the Bean's polished walnut floor.

"Hey, Wade," Brad said, smile freezing into place. He glanced back and forth between Wade and Felicity, then stood and smoothed down his tie.

Wade glared at the pristine strip of silk and thought about his favorite socks, heaped at the bottom of the dryer in a pathetic, gaudy lump. He had no one to blame for this situation but himself.

Brad cleared his throat. "I should probably get going. It was lovely chatting with you, Felicity. I'll be in touch."

I'll be in touch?

Wade had the sudden urge to conk Brad over the head with his wrench.

"Thanks so much, Brad," Felicity said, beaming as if Brad knew exactly what a Birkin bag was without having to Google it.

"Bye, Wade. Good to see you." Brad lingered just long enough to realize Wade wasn't going to respond, and then he walked away in his immaculate wing tip shoes.

Wade felt like a hulking idiot as he slid into Brad's vacated seat. The fact that Felicity was staring daggers at him didn't help.

He glanced at Nick, tucked beneath a flannel blanket decorated with tiny fire trucks in his bouncy seat, and his heart gave a bittersweet tug. Wade had never seen the blanket before. It could have been a hand-me-down from Jack's twins, but somehow he doubted it. Just last night Felicity had come home with a gingham-checked shopping bag from the children's boutique across the street from her yoga studio.

Wade swallowed hard.

"Do you mind telling me what just happened?" Felicity said, her tone razor sharp.

Wade nodded his head in the direction of Main Street. "A fire hydrant burst outside."

"I wasn't talking about a fire hydrant, and you know it." She lifted a single eyebrow. "Duchess would have been less subtle about marking her territory than you were just now."

Wade wasn't entirely sure girl dogs did that sort of thing. It seemed more like male dog behavior, but now didn't seem like the time to drive that point home. Nor did he want to inject Duchess the Destroyer into this particular conversation.

"I didn't realize you were dating," he said, trying his best not to sound jealous even though he could practically feel himself turning green.

"I'm not," Felicity said flatly.

Wade felt himself frown. "I don't understand."

There were two coffee cups sitting on the table, and only one of them was marked with Felicity's pretty pink lipstick.

"I'd never even met Brad Walker until ten minutes ago. We were *not* on a date. He wanted to talk to me about a hardware store moving into the yoga studio." She sat back in her seat and crossed her arms. It was his move, apparently.

"I see," he said. Actually, he *didn't* see. What was she talking about? "Wait, why would a hardware store move into the yoga studio? Don't you have a lease?"

Felicity shifted on the leather bench seat of the booth, not quite meeting his gaze all of a sudden. "Yes, but Brad's client really likes the space, apparently. They've offered to buy out the rest of my lease if I'm interested."

"Are you?" Wade growled. "Interested, I mean?"

Felicity's yoga studio wasn't his business any more than her dating life was, but he hated the thought of her closing up shop. She loved that

place. Come to think of it, so did he. He was starting to enjoy her early-morning yoga class. The
knitters and firefighters had even begun talking
about having a joint Christmas party.

"Maybe." She shrugged a single, elegant shoulder, and the wide collar of the fuzzy Angora
sweater she was wearing slid out of place just
enough to afford Wade a glimpse of her delicate
collar bone and the warm curve of her neck.

His chest tightened into a bruised and battered
knot. This was bad—really bad. Worse than if
she'd actually been on a date. If she gave up her
yoga studio, there would be nothing in Lovestruck
keeping her here after she moved out of his house.
Not Nick. Not her crowded little attic apartment.
Certainly not the gossamer thread of connection
holding them together. Wade wasn't even sure if
it was real. He wasn't sure of anything anymore.

"Can I ask you a question?" he said.

Felicity nodded, but her eyes grew wary. He
was losing her already. He could feel it.

Not yet, damn it.

It wasn't supposed to happen like this. He was
supposed to have more time—more days with Felicity and Nick to make sense of what he wanted.
They were supposed to be his until Christmas.

"Does this have anything to do with the
Birkin?" he asked.

It was a cop-out and he knew it. There were a

million agonizing questions swirling in his head, and none of them had anything to do with handbags.

"That's what you want to ask me about? My purse?" She let out a soft snicker, but the laughter didn't quite reach her eyes. They'd turned into bottomless pools of blue, as sad as he'd ever seen them before. "No, Wade. It has nothing to do with that. The studio is struggling. I'm not sure how much longer it can hang on. You've been such a huge help, and I appreciate it more than I can say, but my business can't survive on just the firemen and Alice's knitting club. I keep thinking I'll get really serious about trying to fill the classes after Christmas, but now Brad's offer just kind of fell in my lap. I think I should probably think about it."

"Right." No. Wrong, wrong, wrong.

He should say something, offer to help somehow. He'd stand in tree pose on every street corner if necessary, twirling a sign for Nama-Stay Awhile. Anything to get her to commit to staying in Lovestruck.

She leaned forward, narrowing her gaze before he could get the words out. "Now it's my turn to ask a question."

Wade nodded as his pulse kicked up a notch. "Fair enough."

"Would it have bothered you if coffee with

Brad just now *had* been a date?" Felicity arched an eyebrow, and one corner of her perfect mouth quirked into the subtlest of smiles.

It was the same sort of smile she gave him sometimes in the middle of the night when they were both too sleep-deprived and too vulnerable to keep their guards up. The same smile that sent warmth coursing through every inch of his body, slow and sweet.

She had his number. How could she not? He'd just come marching in here and made a fool of himself in front of Brad Walker and his perfectly fashioned Windsor knot. All he had to do was say it out loud.

Let's throw the rules out the window...starting right now.

The air between them felt electric, alive with all the things they'd never said. Wade wanted to kiss her right there in the middle of the Bean, in front of the whole damn town. Let them talk. He didn't care anymore. He didn't want privacy. He wanted her. He wanted *them*—Felicity and Nick, both. For real, not just for pretend.

You don't know the first thing about being a family man.

The voice in the back of his head sounded just like his father's, same as it always did. But it was growing quieter by the day, and right now, with

Felicity's lips only a breath away, it was little more than a whisper.

They could do this, couldn't they? They could make it work.

He reached to cup her face in one hand, drawing the pad of his thumb along the beautiful swell of her lower lip. How long had he dreamed about touching her like this? It felt like too many days and nights to count.

"Just the thought of it made me crazy," he whispered and then he leaned forward ever so slightly, closing the space between them.

Felicity let out a whimper of surrender, as soft as a kitten, when his lips nearly brushed against hers. It took every ounce of self-control Wade possessed not to rush. It was bad enough that their first real kiss was about to take place in public— he wanted it to be good. *Memorable.* Like a perfect mistletoe moment.

But the very real lack of actual mistletoe must have thrown a wrench in things, because the kiss ended before it began when Jack suddenly appeared at their table.

"You'll be right back, huh?" he said tersely.

Wade and Felicity sprang apart as if they were two teenagers who'd just been interrupted by an angry parent.

"Um." Felicity's face went pink. "Hi, Jack."

"Yeah, hello." Wade glared at his friend. *Seriously? Now?*

Okay, sure. He'd left Jack in the middle of the street with a bucket of rock salt and a fire truck blocking the intersection, which—now that he thought about it—was really bad. By far the most unprofessional thing he'd ever done. But it would have been great if Jack could have waited just one more minute to come inside and drag him away. So, *so* great.

"Look, I hope I'm not interrupting anything—" Jack glanced back and forth between them "—significant."

Neither of them said a word.

Jack winced. "Oh, man. I am, aren't I?"

"You're fine. I was just leaving, actually," Felicity said, gathering Nick and his baby seat into her arms in record speed. "Bye, Jack."

She slid out of the booth and murmured a goodbye to Wade without meeting his gaze, and then she was gone…just like the moment of intimacy they'd come so close to sharing.

At long last.

Almost.

"That can't be the end of the story," Madison said later that night as she swirled her glass of red wine.

"Oh, but it is." Felicity sighed, then reached for her own glass of garnet-hued Frontenac.

After almost being kissed by Wade, Felicity had gone home and replayed the events of the afternoon over and over in her mind. He'd been jealous when he'd spotted her having coffee in the Bean with Brad Walker—that much was obvious. She still hadn't gotten over the shock of seeing him stalk toward their booth dressed in full firefighter gear. As much as she'd wanted to be furious at him for acting like a complete and total caveman, she couldn't. The butterflies she always seemed to get when he was around had gone into overdrive.

But what did it mean?

Felicity had no idea. Wade had clearly been upset when he'd thought she was on a date, and he didn't seem to like the idea of closing the yoga studio any better. But was her impromptu coffee date with Brad the only reason he'd almost kissed her?

Eight hours later, she still didn't have an answer to that question. Hence, an impromptu girls' night at Lovestruck's one and only wine bar.

Actually, calling it a wine bar was a bit of a stretch. Uncorked operated out of the local bookstore. During the day, the bar at Pages on Main served fruit smoothies, but after dark, the bookshop dimmed its lights, set candles in mason jars all along the bar and offered a modest selection of wines and cheeses—all of which were from vineyards and cheese farms local to Vermont, of course. Felicity had never tasted anything so delicious, not even in Manhattan. Then again, her tastes had definitely been evolving lately.

"It's a good thing Jack interrupted us before we did something we might regret." She forced a smile and stacked a generous slice of Vermont peppered white cheddar atop a cracker.

Madison drained her glass and pushed it toward the bartender/bookseller for another pour. "You're a terrible liar."

"Who says I'm lying?"

"Come on." Madison gave Felicity a once-over. "You seriously asked me to come drink wine and eat cheese with you because you're *glad* you and Wade didn't kiss?"

Well, when she put it that way...

"Fine. I wanted to kiss him, okay?" Felicity plunked her glass down onto the bar's smooth service and glanced around to make sure no one was in earshot. After all, tonight was one of the off-nights for the Christmas festival. Otherwise, Felicity would probably be dressed as a Biblical character right about now.

The store was almost empty, though, save for a few people browsing the cozy mystery section.

Felicity and Madison had the entire bar to themselves.

"I'm just saying it's a good thing we didn't. Wade and I can't go around kissing each other. It would just complicate things, especially with Nick," Felicity said.

"Or not. Jack and I kiss all the time, and we have two babies at home." Madison held up two fingers for emphasis.

But both of those babies belong to you...and so does Jack.

"Well, it doesn't matter, anyway. When Wade came home from the station tonight, it was like nothing ever happened." Granted, that might have been Felicity's fault. She'd done her level best to act like everything was normal when he'd come through the door, even though his very presence had made her weak in the knees.

And then she'd done what she always did when she got scared. She'd fled.

She'd told Wade that Nick was already down for the night, and then she'd grabbed her purse and headed straight for Main Street without any sort of plan whatsoever. As usual, Madison had come to her rescue, suggesting they meet at Uncorked after Felicity's half a dozen panicked text messages.

"This is fun, though, isn't it? We haven't had

a real girls' night in ages." Madison smiled, but the soft glimmer of her eyes went bittersweet.

Felicity pretended not to notice that her best friend felt sorry for her. Of course she felt that way. Felicity had gone and developed feelings for the man everyone in town was already head over heels in love with. She wasn't the only woman in Lovestruck who wanted Wade to kiss her. That particular list was longer than Santa's naughty-and-nice roster. If Felicity wasn't careful, she was going to start greeting him at the door with covered dishes full of King Ranch chicken and tuna noodle au gratin.

It's finally happened. I've become one of them. Felicity took a gulp of wine. *I'm a casserole queen.*

As if she could read Felicity's mind, Madison gasped in horror. "Oh, no!"

"Don't say it." Felicity held up a hand. She was going to need more wine for this conversation. More, as in *all* of it. All of the wine. Every last drop.

But Madison had switched gears already. She wasn't talking about Wade, apparently. Every bit of her attention was aimed squarely at Felicity's handbag, resting on the bar just an arm's length away.

"Your Birkin!" Madison pointed at the bite marks Duchess's eager little teeth had left in the smooth bubblegum-pink leather. "What *happened*?"

Felicity barely glanced at the bag. "Oh, that."

Madison gaped at her as if her dismissive response was the equivalent of fashion blasphemy. Probably because it was.

"Duchess tried to eat it," she said.

"And you're not upset?" Madison reached for the bag and stroked it with the utmost care, as if it were an injured kitten.

"Of course, but…" Felicity's voice drifted off as she realized she wasn't entirely sure what she was trying to say.

Her Birkin bag was her pride and joy—the one enduring trophy she still had to show for all the hard work she'd done at *Fashionista*. All the money she'd managed to save had been poured into the yoga studio, and look where that had gotten her. Even her fancy beauty products were starting to run low—again, thanks to Duchess.

But she couldn't seem to muster much indignation over her French shampoo anymore. And she'd almost forgotten entirely about the bag. How was that possible?

"It just doesn't seem all that important anymore," she finally said.

"Wow." Madison blinked. "Pardon me while I drain my glass as I try to absorb what you just said."

Felicity laughed, and it felt so good to let go of

some of the emotions she'd been trying to hold on to for so long. She wasn't any closer to knowing what to do about the studio and Brad Walker's offer than she'd been a few hours ago, but she felt a tiny bit better than when she'd sent her panicked text to Madison.

Felicity moved a fingertip in a slow circle along the rim of her wineglass. The Frontenac was clearly going to her head. Why else would she suddenly not care about the destruction of her most valuable possession?

Because you've found something that matters more. Two somethings, in particular. Wade and Nick.

She made another cheese-and-cracker sandwich and sat on the bar stool beside Madison, sipping wine and laughing until the stars glittered against the velvety Vermont sky. Just because she was ready to admit her feelings about Wade to herself didn't mean she was ready to confess them to *him*. No way. Just…no.

She just needed to wait things out. Surely it would pass. She just had a crush, that's all. She couldn't actually be falling in love with Wade Ericson.

Felicity breathed a sigh of relief when she tip-toed back inside Wade's quiet little cottage. All the lights were out, save for the dreamy glow of the Christmas tree. Nick was sleeping soundly, and Wade had already gone to bed, just as she'd hoped.

But as she made her way to the guest room, she spotted a wrapped package sitting in the center of the coffee table. Wade's video game consoles were nowhere to be seen. The twinkling red-and-green lights from the tree moved over the gift's shiny gold paper in a kaleidoscope of colors. Her heart thumped hard as she read the note taped to the top of the present.

For Felicity,
I'm sorry...for everything.
Wade.

Chapter Twelve

Felicity knew she should probably wait to open Wade's gift on Christmas morning—or Christmas Eve, at least. When she was a little girl, her family had strict rules about such things. She and her siblings were allowed to open one gift each on Christmas Eve. On Christmas Day, the living room was always a minefield of torn wrapping paper, discarded ribbon and upended boxes. It was a tradition so deeply ingrained in Felicity's consciousness that, at first, she picked up the prettily wrapped present fully intending to place it beneath the tree.

But once it was in her hands, she couldn't quite

bring herself to let go of it. After all, Wade could
have placed it on the tree skirt himself if he'd
wanted her to wait and open it on Christmas.
And the note he'd attached to it fully indicated
it was an apology gift. For better or worse, she
was convinced.

Within a matter of seconds, she was sitting on
the sofa, surrounded by crumpled gold wrapping.
She gingerly peeled back layer upon a layer of
delicate tissue paper to reveal a beautiful leather
handbag.

It was pale pink, the exact shade of a puff of
cotton candy. There was no fancy designer label,
but the bag had an embossed stamp near the top,
with traces of gold leafing. Felicity could just
make out the word *Firenze*. She turned the bag
over in her hands and took a peek inside, heart
hammering hard in her chest. Clearly the purse
was vintage, but she couldn't imagine where
Wade could have possibly found something like
it here in Lovestruck. With its supple leather and
exquisite ballet-pink hue, it seemed like something that would be found in one of the Florentine
markets she'd so much read about on the pages
of *Fashionista*. They'd done a story once on the
Mercato Nuovo in Florence, where leather mer-
chants had been selling their wares beneath a
grand loggia since the Renaissance. The photo-
graphs of the colorful stalls, as bright and varied

as a jumbo box of crayons, had taken Felicity's breath away.

She ran her fingertips over the bag, taking in the impossible softness of the pale pink leather until a nearby snuffling sound pulled her out of her trance.

"Oh." Felicity glanced down at Duchess, sitting politely at her feet. "You."

The spaniel blinked up at Felicity with her big brown eyes and then pawed at her shin like she always did to Wade.

"What? Are you suggesting some sort of truce, or are you already eyeballing my new bag?" Felicity did her best to sound stern but caved and bent down to pet one of Duchess's soft ears. "Don't even think about it. I'm serious."

The little dog licked Felicity's hand.

Ugh, why did she have to be so adorable? And sweet? It was really hard to stay mad at an animal that was basically the canine version of a marshmallow, naughty streak and all.

"Fine. You can come up here with me, but don't you dare touch the bag. Got it?"

Duchess jumped onto the sofa, dug at the tissue paper until she'd managed to move it out of the way and then plopped into Felicity's lap. Within seconds, her soft, tiny body was rising and falling in a relaxed, sleepy rhythm.

Felicity leaned over as slowly as possible and

placed her new handbag on the coffee table, safely out of the dog's reach. She might be a pushover, but she'd definitely learned her lesson.

Then she leaned back against the sofa cushions and ran her hand slowly over Duchess's furry little head while she looked at her gift in the soft glow of the Christmas lights. A lump made its way to her throat. This bag was far more special than her Birkin. It was bag with a story behind it. It had meant something to someone once—someone who'd treated it with tender loving care.

And now it was hers.

My, my, Wade Ericson. She brushed a tear from the corner of her eye. Thank goodness she'd opened his present in private. If Wade thought she'd been silly for getting upset when Duchess left bite marks on her Birkin, he'd probably mock her endlessly for crying over a vintage bag. *You've surprised me once again.*

The sound of Nick's soft cries coming through the baby monitor woke Wade up right around three in the morning, just like clockwork.

He rolled onto his back and scrubbed his face with his hands, readying himself to stumble out of bed and prepare a bottle for Nick. Within seconds, he realized something was missing—namely, the warm ball of fur that typically liked to make itself at home on his pillow, butting his head so far out of the way that he often woke with a crick in his neck.

He opened his eyes. Duchess wasn't anywhere to be seen.

Wade groaned and untangled himself from his bedsheets, wondering what sort of trouble the dog had gotten herself into this time around. He hoped she hadn't snuck into Felicity's room again. He'd done the best he could to replace the Birkin. He didn't know what he was going to do if he had another fashion casualty on his hands.

Nick let out another whimper, so Wade dashed to the baby's room first. The night-light clicked on as he entered, and he changed Nick's diaper in the semi-darkness while the infant kicked his chubby little legs. He'd gotten so much stronger in the days since he'd been dropped at the fire station. So much happier.

The tiny furrow in Nick's brow had all but disappeared. Wade knew he was just a newborn and couldn't possibly be aware of what exactly he'd been through at such an early age—and for that, Wade was immensely grateful. But he still couldn't help but sense that Nick's easy expression and the way he melted into Wade and Felicity's arms every time one of them held him meant that he was no longer fighting for a place in this world. Was it possible that he somehow knew he'd landed in a place where he was loved and wanted?

Wade hoped so. God, how he hoped.

"Hungry, little man?" Wade nestled the infant against his shoulder and breathed in his tender, baby powder scent as he made his way quietly toward the kitchen.

The Christmas tree was still aglow when he reached the living room, which surprised him. He'd left it on so Felicity wouldn't come home to a dark house, but as a firefighter, he was pretty fanatical about turning the tree lights off when everyone went to bed. Felicity teased him sometimes about being so safety conscious, but she felt the same way—especially where Nick was concerned. She watched over him with such intensity that it was almost as if she expected him to vanish into thin air.

The house was so quiet. Worry bloomed in Wade's chest. Had Felicity not made it home?

But just as his adrenaline spiked, he caught sight of her handbag on the coffee table, unwrapped and placed just so, as if it were some kind of precious centerpiece.

A warm sensation took over the panicked ache that had formed behind his sternum as his gaze shifted to the couch. Felicity sat nestled in the corner of sofa cushions with her legs tucked beside her. Her head was tipped back, eyes closed, and her lush blond hair fanned around her lovely face like a halo. Wade had never seen such a beautiful sleeping woman, but the thing that most struck him about the sweet sight of her sleeping in the twinkling light of the Christmas tree was the dog curled into a tight ball behind the tender curve of her knees.

As usual, Duchess was snoring at a volume so loud it defied belief—a sure sign she was content. Wade couldn't help but smile. The two most important females in his life were finally getting along.

"It looks like you've been forgiven," he said, and Duchess's ears twitched ever so slightly. "I guess that makes one of us."

Wade knew better, though. Felicity wasn't the type to hold a grudge. But he didn't want to be a roommate she tolerated. He knew that now. He'd probably known as much all along, but now he was aware of little else. All he could seem to think about was the fact that she might walk away from her yoga studio. From Lovestruck. *From me.*

Nick's downy little head rested against Wade's shoulder, and Wade wished he hadn't made such an idiot out of himself at the Bean. He had no business being angry at Brad Walker. He didn't even want to be mad at his father anymore. If anyone was holding him back from the life he truly wanted, it was Wade himself.

No more, he thought.

Time was running out. Wasn't that the way it

always went during the holidays? They seemed to pass in a whirl of frosted peppermint and tinsel. When Wade was a kid, Christmas Eve had been his favorite day of the year. A sense of melancholy always clung to Christmas Day, because once the presents beneath the tree had been unwrapped and the wreaths came down from Lovestruck's wide front porches, it meant the most joyful time of the year was officially over.

He was an adult now, obviously. It had been years since Wade had thought about Christmas that way. Except this year, he'd become overly aware of every passing minute. Today, especially. And now, seeing Felicity and Duchess curled up together on the sofa made him realize the truth. He'd never be ready for this holiday season to end. *This* is what he wanted. Felicity, Nick and Duchess, all three of them here with him... forever. If his mom's headstrong little dog could let her guard down, maybe Wade finally could, too.

Felicity's eyelashes fluttered open while he was still standing there, bouncing little Nick in his arms. She gave him a slow smile that built as they looked at one another and the lights from the Christmas tree glittered around them like starlight. Wade's throat grew thick with all the things he wanted to tell her. They hadn't even kissed yet, and he wanted to ask her to stay. How could he ask her to be a family when they'd never even kissed? It seemed insane.

Then again, he and Felicity had always done things backward. How did the old rhyme go? *First comes love, then comes marriage, then comes the baby in the baby carriage.*

He let out a quiet laugh. They'd started at the finish line, and here he was, yearning to ask her for a new beginning. A real one this time, and as permanent as Christmas itself.

"What are you smiling at?" Felicity said quietly, eyes shining in the darkness.

"You look beautiful," he whispered.

Her lips curved into a bashful smile, then she reached for the pink purse and held it close to her chest. "I can't believe you did this. It's gorgeous. Thank you."

"You're welcome," he said, as Nick's tiny fingers closed around one of his ears.

"You didn't have to. I mean, I know I was a little upset when Duchess tried to eat my Birkin…"

Wade arched a brow.

Felicity winced. "Okay, a lot upset."

Wade flashed her a wink, but then he felt his smile fade. He didn't want to hide behind flirty banter anymore. For once in his life, he wanted to be real and open with a woman. Now, before it was too late.

He glanced at Duchess, still tucked fast asleep

beside Felicity, and a stab of envy pierced his heart. How much easier would things be if all he had to do was lie down next to Felicity to let her know what he was thinking and feeling? Whatever was happening between them was too important for that, though. She deserved more. They both did.

"I wasn't just apologizing for the handbag, you know," he said, rocking gently from one foot to the other and patting Nick's narrow back.

"Sit." Felicity shifted, scooting over to make room for him on the sofa, and patted the cushion beside her. "Can I hold him for a minute?"

"Of course. I'll go get his bottle ready." Wade handed her the baby, and her face lit up as Nick settled into her arms.

Wade took extra care preparing the bottle, heating the water to just the right temperature, leveling off the scoops of formula with the edge of a butter knife and testing the results on the inside of his wrist. He'd done this so many times by now that it seemed inconceivable he'd only just mastered it. So much in his life had changed— for the better—and all the while he'd been telling himself not to hold on too tightly to it. This wasn't real. This wasn't his future, but just a fleeting Christmas fantasy.

Not anymore. Seeing Felicity share coffee with Brad Walker had rattled him to his core, and now he was ready to fight for what he wanted. Felicity and Nick weren't just a fantasy. They were his family. All he needed to do was convince Felicity she felt the same way.

Wade took a deep breath. He could do this. He was certain Felicity wanted the same thing. He could see it in the tenderness in her eyes every time she looked at Nick. He could feel it in the way the air between them always seemed to swirl with heat and adoration and all the words they'd both been too afraid to say.

And Wade felt it again when he walked back into the living room and heard Felicity's sweet voice, as soft as an angel as she sung Nick another Christmas lullaby.

Hushaby, hushaby.
Christmas night.
Lullaby, lullaby.
Angel in white.

His throat closed as he stood in the doorway, clutching the bottle and watching them together. Had he honestly thought he could just do this temporarily and walk away unscathed when it was over? What a fool he'd been.

Felicity glanced up at him. She stopped singing and tilted her head. "You look like you want to say something."

So many things. There were a million things he

wanted to say, but in the end, all he could manage was a single word. "Stay."

Her smile dimmed, beautiful blue eyes narrowing as if she was having trouble understanding his meaning. "I'm right here. Don't worry—I wasn't planning on going anywhere anytime soon."

But Wade could see the slight flash of panic glittering in her gaze. And as he moved to sit down beside her, he could see the boom of her pulse galloping into overdrive along the graceful curve of her neck.

He took a deep breath. "I think you know what I mean, sweetheart."

Her eyes went immediately glassy at his use of an endearment. It had just slipped out. *Slow down, she's not ready.*

But Wade couldn't have reeled the words back in, even if he'd tried.

"He needs you." *I need you.* He very nearly said it, but something about the look in her eyes stopped him. "Let's do this, you and me. For real."

Forever.

"I…I…" She handed Nick over to him so she could wrap her arms around herself, and Wade got the definite sense it was some sort of primitive instinct to try to hold herself together.

What had he done, damn it?

"It's okay. Whatever is wrong, we can deal with it. I want this, and I know you want it, too,"

Wade said as evenly as he could. He just needed to stay calm, and everything would be all right. Felicity had been caught off guard, but once she realized he was serious, they'd work things out.

"I can't." She shook her head just as Nick started to cry. "Wade, please don't ask me. You don't understand."

He gave Nick the bottle and did his best to calm the panicked beating of his heart. "Then talk to me, sweetheart. Help me understand."

"It's not that I don't want to, Wade. I do. I promise I do." She shook her head as her bottom lip began to tremble—an aching hint of tender vulnerability that nearly tore Wade's heart in two. He wanted to take her in his arms and kiss it away. He wanted to promise her that they could do this. Whatever was wrong, it would be all right. Wade would *make it* right. He'd do anything.

"We both want it. That's all that matters—we can figure out the rest." He smiled at her, but it just seemed to make her more upset.

"No, we can't. I know it seems easy to you, but it's not. Trust me. I've been down this road before, and there's nothing but heartbreak at the end of it." She stood and started pacing back and forth in front of the Christmas tree.

She was afraid—clearly—and Wade desperately needed to know why. He couldn't fix things until he understood what had gone wrong. "Tell me? Please?"

Felicity stopped pacing and took a few deep breaths the way she always did in yoga class. "Remember the Christmas card that came a few days ago? The one with the picture of my cousin Lori and her baby?"

Of course he remembered. She'd gone completely pale when he'd noticed the card fall out of the pocket of her sweater. It was as if she'd seen a ghost.

Oh, no. He closed his eyes and dropped his head as the painful truth dawned on him. Felicity *had* seen a ghost when she looked at the picture— the ghost of her Christmas past.

Wade looked up at her, heart twisting in his chest as Nick kept tugging gently on his bottle. "That was the baby, wasn't it? The one you fostered?"

She nodded, blinking back tears. "I had her for six months, since the day she was born. The adoption papers had all been filled out. All we had left was one final court date—a formality. Or so I thought. Lori changed her mind, and it was like everything that had happened since the moment I first held little Ariel had just been a dream. I had to give her up, right then and there in the courtroom."

"Oh, Felicity." No wonder she'd said no when

the social worker first asked her to care for Nick. He'd known Felicity had connected with the sweet baby right from the start, and he'd never been able to figure out why she'd gotten so spooked and run away from the firehouse the night he'd been abandoned.

Everything was clicking into place now, though.

"I'm sorry," he said. "That must have been really hard."

"You have no idea." She inhaled a shuddering breath. "I gave my cousin a place to stay while she was pregnant because her parents had kicked her out. I took her to each and every doctor appointment. She wanted to give the baby up and asked me to take her. I said yes right from the start."

She paused for a minute, then shook her head. "I never saw it coming. If she'd changed her mind earlier or given me any hint she was having second thoughts, I might have been prepared. But I was completely blindsided."

"When exactly did this happen, again?" Wade asked, but he had a feeling he already knew.

"Just a few months before I came to Lovestruck," she said, confirming his suspicions. "I needed a fresh start. I needed space to breathe. I couldn't stay in New York. Lori and Ariel are still my family, and I'll always love them both. But seeing them at family dinners and holiday celebrations hurt too much. Lovestruck seemed lovely when I was here for Madison and Jack's wedding, so I decided to start over right here in Vermont."

And within weeks, another helpless baby had been thrust into her arms.

The timing was admittedly terrible. Wade wished he could take it back, but they'd gone too far down this road together. They were both too attached to Nick. No matter what Felicity tried to tell herself, she was in love with that child. Wade knew that better than anyone—maybe even better than Felicity herself did.

"If we tried to adopt Nick, it could happen all over again. You know that, right?" Felicity choked on a sob. "I couldn't handle it. Not again."

"Felicity, sweetheart." Wade set the bottle down on the table and stood to wrap his free arm around her, but she stiffened and turned her face away from the baby in the crook of his other elbow. "Listen to me. The three of us belong together. I know we do. It's not going to happen again."

And if it does, you won't have to go through it alone this time. I'll be here.

Wade pressed a kiss to the top of her head, and as the seconds passed, she melted into him. Her arms slipped around him, and she balled the back of his ratty old LFD T-shirt into her fists as if she were holding on to him for dear life.

Then she tipped her face upward, and for a sweet, sublime moment, he could see beyond the fear in her expression. There was nothing but love shining back at him from the depths of her cornflower blue eyes—and a yearning that somehow mirrored how he felt inside every time he looked at her. She let out the softest of sighs, and his gaze dropped to her mouth. Her lips were just a whisper away, pink and perfect, and in an instant he knew that all the waiting and all the wanting had been leading up to this moment—when he could seal his promise to her with a kiss. Their first…

"It's all going to be okay," he whispered. "I promise."

A tear slipped down her cheek, but at the same time, her hand splayed against his back, pulling him closer and closer as she rose up on her tiptoes. Every part of Wade's body and soul ached for her. He groaned under his breath, and then dipped his head, but in the aching second before his mouth crashed down on hers, Nick let out a happy little cry.

Felicity's eyes flew open. She froze, and as every last bit of color drained from her face, Wade could feel the magic in the air between them slip away, like a swirl of snow with no place to land.

She shook her head and backed away. "Please, Wade, please. Don't make promises you know you can't keep."

Chapter Thirteen

She'd done the right thing.

It really hadn't been a choice, no matter how much Wade had tried to make it seem like one. He knew he couldn't promise that everything would turn out all right. Nick didn't belong to him any more than he belonged to Felicity. The truth of the matter was that they'd just been playing house. It might have looked real from the outside, and it had certainly *felt* real at times, but it wasn't.

Saying no to him had been the right thing— the *only* thing, as far as Felicity was concerned. It was just too bad that she kept having to remind herself that walking away hadn't been the biggest mistake of her life.

"Felicity, honey? Is everything okay?"

She glanced up and found Alice looking at her, features etched with concern. All the knitting ladies were spread around the room on their yoga mats, sitting cross-legged as they waited for class to begin. The older ladies were always early birds, while the firefighters tended to breeze inside at the last possible minute. Felicity wasn't even sure they'd show up today, though—Wade, in particular.

"Sorry." She forced a smile. "I guess I just zoned out for a minute."

She'd been doing that a lot in the two days since Wade had told her he thought they should adopt Nick. One minute, she'd be standing at the counter in the Bean, about to place her order. And the next, the barista would be clearing his throat repeatedly, prompting her to snap out of her trance and tell him what she wanted. It was getting a little unsettling.

Not as unsettling as playing her part in the living nativity scene alongside Wade at the Christmas festival, though. Felicity hadn't known what to expect the day after their heartfelt moment in front of the Christmas tree. Wade had left early for work the following morning, and she hadn't heard a word from him all day. She'd half expected to arrive at the festival in her Mary robes and find that he'd gotten a substitute to play the part of Joseph. She'd almost hoped he would.

But when he'd come running up to the make-shift crèche, the relief coursing through her veins had been almost debilitating. She'd gone quite literally weak in the knees. And when he'd smiled at her and kissed her lightly on the cheek before taking his place beside her, she'd had to blink back tears.

What was she supposed to think? He hadn't mentioned their middle-of-the-night conversation at all in the past two days. It was almost as though it had never taken place. She wasn't sure whether to feel relieved or disappointed.

Relieved, obviously. At least he wasn't trying to change her mind.

"Morning, ladies." Wade flashed a wave as he entered the studio with his yoga mat tucked under his arm and four other firefighters following on his heels. "I hope we're not too late."

Alice and the knitting club members all cast expectant glances at Felicity. Every last one of them.

How many times was Felicity going to have to tell the people of Lovestruck that she and Wade weren't a couple? The entire town seemed to be holding its breath, waiting for them to announce they were secretly engaged or something. It was getting harder and harder to convince anyone otherwise. Felicity wasn't sure how much longer she could keep insisting she wasn't in love with Wade Ericson and that they weren't a couple and never would be.

Probably because every time she had to repeat such sentiments she felt like she was lying through her teeth. Damn Wade and his foolishly optimistic heart.

"You're right on time," she said as her heart twisted into a thoroughly confused knot.

Wade crossed to the front of the room to give Nick a tender kiss hello. Felicity had set him up just a few feet away on a pile of soft quilts with his favorite portable mobile hanging overhead. He lit up at the sight of Wade and fumbled at his tiny feet, a potential natural at happy baby pose

For the following hour, Felicity did her best to act like a proper yoga teacher and live in the moment. No more looking back. She had to stop reliving the painful conversation with Wade, unless she was willing to change her mind and try to make it work as a family—which she was *not*.

The number of things that could go wrong was endless, and nothing about Wade's charm and enthusiasm could stop them.

Also, she and Wade had never even kissed, for goodness' sake. People who committed to raising a baby together—for *life*—should be in love, shouldn't they?

Am I in love? Is he? Felicity pressed her face against her knees in the forward fold position and blamed the butterflies swirling around her belly on the lack of blood flow to her brain. No one was in love. Clearly.

If Wade loved her, he would have told her so. *I love you* would have been a great intro to a conversation about being a family. The best, really. Not that anything about her relationship with Wade had gone according to plan or proper order. They'd been doing things backward all along. Why change things up now?

"Downward dog, everyone!" Felicity peeked under her arm for a glimpse of Wade.

He wasn't a family man. He'd told her so himself on numerous occasions. He'd simply inhaled too much baby powder or something and forgotten who he really was. Wade didn't really want them to adopt Nick together. It was a crazy idea.

As he moved into position, his biceps flexed in the same way they always did when he lifted Nick out of his crib. Felicity's ovaries practically sighed. She squeezed her eyes shut and led the class straight into a gentle upward dog or cobra position, yogi's choice.

"Just remember to open your heart," she said, forcing her eyes open so she could check everyone's form in the mirrored wall at the front of the room. "That's the most important part."

The yoga ladies smiled back at her. Their flexibility had improved so much in the past few weeks. It warmed Felicity's heart to think about how much stronger each one of them was getting, day by day. The firemen all seemed so much more relaxed than they had when they rushed in for class. Most of them had their eyes shut.

Not Wade, though. When Felicity's gaze snagged on his reflection, his eyes locked with hers. For a brief, unguarded moment, his trademark lopsided grin slipped, and the look in his eyes became so achingly bittersweet and reminiscent of how he'd looked in the glow of the Christmas lights two night ago, that she forgot how to breathe. It was the most basic rule of yoga—breathe. In, out, in, out. And then the second…

Open your heart.

She looked away, because nothing had changed. She still couldn't do it. She just wasn't ready. She might *never* be ready, and the longer she let Wade hold on to hope, the worse she'd feel after Christmas when they turned Nick over to a new family—hopefully a permanent one this time. There was only one way to put an end to this emotional torture for both of them.

It was time to call Brad Walker.

* * *

According to the chirpy receptionist at Love-struck Real Estate, Brad was out of the office for the morning. But less than ten minutes after Felicity left her name and number, his assistant called her back. Would she be available to meet Mr. Walker at the Bean around two in the afternoon?

Yes. Yes, she would.

Felicity was slightly surprised he wanted to meet at the Bean, of all places, given what had happened the last time they'd had coffee there together. But why shouldn't they meet at the Bean? She wasn't doing anything wrong. The studio was *her* business, and closing it was the smart thing to do.

The only problem was that the weather was looking a little ominous. Wade had been called into work, even though it was supposed to be his day off. Cap was anticipating traffic-related problems due to heavy snowfall, and he wanted all hands on deck until late afternoon when the storm warning was over. Felicity didn't want to take Nick outside if she could avoid it, even though the Bean was just a short walk from the yoga studio. Luckily, Alice was delighted when Felicity asked if she could leave Nick with her at the yarn store next door.

"Thank you so much for this, Alice. I won't be gone long. I just have a quick business meeting this afternoon." Felicity tucked Nick into his bouncy seat behind the front counter, where he smiled from ear to ear when he caught sight of Alice's little dog, Toby.

A hairless Chinese crested, Toby looked more like a cartoon character than an actual canine. He had delicate little legs, smooth gray skin and a dramatic swoop of long hair on the tip-top of his head. The only other fur on his body was the white fringe around his ankles, Shetland pony–style. Alice dressed him up every day in sweaters she knit herself. Felicity had never seen him in the same one twice, which made her love him all the more. Toby was a true fashionista. She was certain he'd rather die of starvation than eat a Birkin bag.

"Of course, dear. I just love little Nicky." Alice glanced at her antique wristwatch. "I've got a crochet class starting in just a little bit, and most of the students are new moms. He's sure to be doted on. Take your time, and be careful. The snow is really coming down out there."

"Thanks so much. It should only take a few minutes, though."

There wasn't much to say to Brad Walker, really. *I give up. The studio is yours. Where do I sign?*

She forced a smile but felt a little sick to her stomach as Alice's gaze narrowed.

"Are you sure everything is okay? I'm always

here if you need to chat." The older woman's face creased into a benevolent grin, and Felicity almost felt like crying. She remembered Madison once saying that her aunt seemed like a mind reader, and Felicity finally understood what she'd meant.

Was it really so obvious that she was on the verge of falling apart?

Felicity cleared her throat and shifted her gaze over Alice's right shoulder. Who knew what would happen if she kept looking into Alice's kind eyes? She might accidentally tell all, and that was the last thing she needed to do. She could practically see the headline on tomorrow's edition of the *Lovestruck Bee* already.

Felicity Hart turns down Wade Ericson, Lovestruck's most desirable bachelor!

"I'm fine," she said. But the second the words were out of her mouth, she spied something hanging on the wall behind the yarn store's front counter that stunned her into silence.

Right there, pinned to a bulletin board with colorful scalloped trim, were a pair of knitted socks that were remarkably similar to the ones that Wade wore around the house all the time. The pair on display in Alice's shop clearly weren't as well-worn as Wade's. The multicolored yarn was crisp and bright, and Alice's socks still held their shape instead of being saggy and stretched out like the ones she found so amusing every time she spied them on Wade's feet. How had she described them to Madison?

Hideous. Albeit, sort of adorably so. It was kind of a relief to see the nerdier side of the man who every single woman in town wanted to marry.

"Those socks." She pointed at the bulletin board. The words *Upcoming Craft Projects* were printed on a card near the top of the corkboard in the kind of swirly hand lettering that was currently all the rage on Instagram. "Wade has a pair just like them."

Alice turned to glance over her shoulder at the socks and then nodded. "That's right. His mother took the rainbow socks knitting class a while back. I offer it once a year."

Wade's mother? "Oh, I hadn't realized the socks were handmade."

"They are, yes." Alice's brow furrowed. "If I'm remembering correctly, that was the last knitting class Evelyn Ericson took before she got sick, the poor dear. She made several pairs."

Felicity couldn't speak all of a sudden. All she could seem to do was stare at the socks as Nick babbled happily in his bouncy seat.

"Class starts the day after tomorrow if you're interested in joining us. No knitting experience necessary. I can always help you with the more challenging parts." Alice's gaze turned hopeful.

"I'm sorry. I don't think so," Felicity said. Now wasn't the time to be putting down more roots in Lovestruck when she knew she'd be leaving right after Christmas.

And why would she want to torture herself by taking knitted rainbow socks with her when she left? Every time she wore them she'd think of Wade...

And his mother.

She'd obviously meant the world to him. He doted on her mischievous dog and he wore the socks she'd made every night, no matter how many times Felicity teased him about sending his picture to her friends at *Fashionista* for the *Fashion Faux Pas* section.

Her heart gave a tug, and she pressed the heel of her hand to her chest to try to get ahold of herself. Now wasn't the time to go all aflutter over Wade—not when she was minutes away from giving up her future in Lovestruck. Even so, her head spun with the sudden realization that she'd been wrong about Wade all along. So had he, actually.

My, my, my. Look who's a family man, after all.

"Are you sure you don't want to sign up for the class? The socks make lovely Christmas gifts." Alice reached into a drawer behind the counter and pulled out a sheet of pink paper. "Here's the schedule. No need to commit right now. You know you're always welcome here, dear. We'll save you a seat, just in case."

"Thank you." Felicity blinked hard. What was happening? Was she going to cry now? In one of the busiest shops on Main Street?

Over a pair of ugly socks?

"Wade and his mom were really close, you know. His father wasn't the nicest man, and I think Wade spent most of his life trying to make his mother realize how much she was loved. He felt very protective of her. She would be so glad to know that Wade has you and Nick now." Alice placed her hand on top of Felicity's as her fist tightened around the pink flyer, nearly crumpling it into a ball.

She shook her head and blinked ferociously as she denied their relationship yet again. "But it's not like that between Wade and me. We're not..."

She couldn't finish, not this time. The words just wouldn't come.

So she took a deep breath and bent to pick up her handbag so she could tuck the pink flyer away inside of it. Out of sight and—hopefully—out of mind. "Anyway, thanks again for watching Nick. I really should be going."

But Alice wasn't paying attention to what she was saying. Her attention was fixed squarely on Felicity's pink handbag, sitting on the counter-top between them.

"Oh, goodness." Her hand fluttered to her throat as she angled her head for a closer look at the purse. "That's not… It can't be, can it?"

Felicity's heart beat hard in her chest—so hard that she could hear her pulse throbbing in her ears. "Alice?"

"That's her bag," Alice said, nodding.

"Whose bag?" Felicity said, but somewhere deep down, she already knew.

"Evelyn's. She bought it on her trip to Italy. It was her pride and joy." Alice let out a dreamy sigh, and then her eyes welled up. "May I ask where you got it?"

Felicity started trembling so hard she could barely force the words out. "Wade gave it to me."

Alice flashed her a knowing smile. "That's an awfully special Christmas gift, don't you think?"

Felicity couldn't seem to look Alice in the eyes anymore. Her gaze darted to the pretty pink leather bag, but that made her feel even worse. Good gravy, what was happening? "It wasn't exactly a Christmas gift. It was…something else."

An apology.

She'd been so upset about her stupid Birkin that Wade had given her his mother's bag. He'd told her he wanted to build a life with her—a family—and how had she'd reacted?

By telling everyone within earshot that there was nothing special going on between them. Over and over and over again. She'd just kept on saying it, even when she knew good and well that it wasn't true. She had feelings for Wade. She'd had them for a long time now. She'd just been too afraid to admit—so afraid that she was about to give up her yoga studio and her fresh new start in Lovestruck.

She inhaled a shaky breath.

Open your heart.

Maybe it was time to do some apologizing of her own.

Chapter Fourteen

"It's going to be a white Christmas," Jack said as the fire engine heaved to a stop alongside Main Street.

"You think?" Wade stared out the windshield toward the heaps of snow piled up on either side of the road. Even after a lifetime spent in Lovestruck, he couldn't quite tell where Main Street stopped and the sidewalk began. "Any other grand predictions? I'm all ears."

Jack shot him a sidelong glance. "You really want me to go there?"

Wade sighed. He'd walked right into that one. "Not about my personal life. I've got that under control, thank you very much."

"Under control? *Really*?" Jack nodded. The windows of the fire engine started fogging up with steam, but neither of them moved. "I suppose that's why Felicity could barely look at you this morning at yoga. Or last night at the living nativity."

Point taken. Things were strained between the two of them, but that wasn't Wade's fault. He'd been the one to put his heart on the line. He'd asked her to start a family with him—he'd wanted a real, *permanent* arrangement, and she'd soundly rejected him. There was no way Jack could blame the lingering awkwardness hovering over his fragile home life on Wade.

He couldn't even blame things on the casserole queens.

"It's not what you think," Wade said quietly.

Jack shrugged. "How do you know what I'm thinking?"

"I just do." Wade's jaw clenched. They were supposed to be digging the fire hydrants up and down Main Street out of the snow, not hunkering down in the engine for a heart-to-heart. "You think I screwed up. You think I've done something to push Felicity away, and that couldn't be further from the truth. In fact, the other night I suggested that we officially adopt Nick after Christmas—together—and she said no. So, there you go. I tried to make it work. I tried to make *us* work, but it's not what she wants."

Wade still wasn't convinced that was the whole truth. Deep down, he had a feeling he knew exactly what Felicity wanted. But what Felicity wanted and what she was willing to give were two different things.

Wade couldn't blame her, really. Felicity was heartbroken. Anyone could see that—heck, he'd spotted the hollow look in her eyes right from the start. Strangely enough, it was only now that he knew her whole story that he realized her tender vulnerability was one of the things that had attracted him to her in the first place. When everyone in town had been showering him with pizza parties and casseroles, she'd been the one person who somehow seemed to understand how he felt after delivering a baby to a lost and lonely teenager. He hadn't felt like a hero at all. Something inside of him had broken that day—a part of his heart would belong to that sweet, innocent baby for as long as Wade lived. No one could understand that like Felicity could.

And now, by some strange twist of fate, he had a chance to reclaim that tender piece of himself. He could give Nick the sort of home he deserved. But could he do it without Felicity?

Jack's eyebrows rose. "Seriously? You told her you were in love with her?"

"Yes." Something hardened deep in the pit of Wade's stomach. That's not quite what he'd said. "Well, no. Not in so many words."

"Dare I ask what words were actually involved?"

Wade glared at Jack. He was starting to regret all the times he'd butted into his closest friend's personal life. Turnabout was fair play, after all. "Listen, it's not that simple. The situation is far more complicated than it seems."

He didn't want to betray Felicity's confidence and spill all the details surrounding the baby she'd almost adopted. But Jack needed to understand what he was dealing with. This was real life with real problems, not some crazy episode of *The Bachelor* where all he needed to do was pick a woman, give her a rose and live happily-ever-after.

Jack shook his head. "If you love her, it's as simple as three little words."

That couldn't possibly be true.

Could it?

Wade's bones ached. He was tired—exhausted to his core. It had taken every ounce of strength he had to tear down the brick wall around his heart and let someone in. First Nick, and then Felicity. Or maybe it had been the other way around. He was no longer sure where one of them ended and the other began. He just knew that they felt like they were his. It seemed impossible that it would never be true, but he was doing his level best to accept it.

"I can't force her to stay," he said. "I can't, and I won't."

"I get that. I do, but don't you think you should at least be honest with her?" Jack gave him a bittersweet smile—one that Wade recognized in an instant. He hadn't seen that particular expression on Jack's face since the time he'd nearly lost Madison for good. "Learn from my mistakes, man."

Wade let out a long, slow exhale and shook his head. "It's just not the same."

Wasn't it, though? Wade had watched Jack try to get Madison to stay in Lovestruck by offering her the best of himself without being open about who he really was. It had been so obvious to anyone watching from the outside that it would never work. And it hadn't...not until Jack had opened himself up in the most raw and real way possible.

Wade hadn't done that with Felicity. He'd only torn the wall halfway down, and now there was even more he hadn't told her.

"I applied to adopt Nick—not as a couple, but on my own." Wade dropped his gaze to his lap. The world beyond the windshield was too bright, too full of holiday cheer for him to take right now.

He should have talked to Felicity again before he filled out the paperwork. He knew he should have, but he'd managed to convince himself that doing so would have made her feel pressured. And now here he was, trying to glue his fragile family together by any means possible.

There's nothing between Wade and me.

Felicity's voice rang in the back of his head. How many times had he told himself it wasn't true? There was plenty going on between him and Felicity, more than either of them wanted to admit. And now the space between them was filled with secrets—one that had the potential to bind them together, and another that would tear them apart.

Jack went still beside him. After a long, quiet moment, he finally nodded. "You'll make a great dad, Wade. I know you will, just as surely as I know Nick belongs with you. But you have to talk to Felicity. She deserves the truth—all of it, just like Nick deserves the both of you. And that will never happen unless you tell her you love her. I have a feeling that once you do that, the rest will sort itself out."

Wade tried to take a deep breath, but a weight had settled on his heart that made it difficult to take in a lungful of air. He wanted to believe Jack, but he was almost afraid to hope. Jack hadn't seen the anguish in Felicity's eyes two night ago. Pain like that didn't just work itself out. The best Wade could do was wait and be patient.

It was too late for that now, though. He'd already emailed the social worker. He knew he should have waited, but he'd sent the message in the wee hours of the morning after Felicity had shut him out. Nothing good came from decisions made at four a.m. Wade should have known better. He'd fought enough late-night fires to know people didn't think straight in the middle of the night.

Christmas was only two days away. He needed more time—or better yet, a Christmas miracle.

He fixed his attention once again on the frosty windshield and the gentle swirl of snowflakes beyond the glass, craving the wind on his face. What he really wanted—*needed*—right now wasn't a romantic pep talk, but the bitter wind on his face and snow crunching beneath his feet. He wanted the inevitable numbness that came with performing manual labor in the middle of a winter snowstorm while carrying seventy-five pounds of gear on his body. He wanted to just not feel for a while.

"Let's get to work," he said, reaching for the door handle. "Those fire hydrants aren't going to dig themselves out."

And then he stepped out into the cold. Alone.

Felicity pulled her coat more snugly around her frame as she left Main Street Yarn and blinked against a ferocious swirl of snow.

It was really coming down. No wonder Alice

and the knitting ladies had warned her against taking Nick outside today. She hadn't seen a snowstorm quite like this one in a long time, and she couldn't remember the last time she'd had a white Christmas in Manhattan.

But, of course, she wasn't in New York anymore. She was in Vermont, where winter—and the holidays, in particular—were larger than life. Of course Lovestruck would have a white Christmas. She'd probably wake up on Christmas morning and see reindeer prints in a blanket of glittering white in front of Wade's cozy cottage.

And then the next day, we'll turn Nick over to the social worker and I'll be free to go. Free of Wade. Free of babies...for good.

A shiver coursed through her as she headed toward the Bean. If she planned on staying in Vermont, she'd probably need a better winter coat. One of those full-length puffy ones that were all the rage with the Lovestruck moms. They were about as glamorous as Wade's rainbow socks, but a puffer coat sounded pretty good about now. And she'd definitely developed a soft spot for his socks.

Don't think about the socks right now. Or the handbag. Or Wade, for heaven's sake. There will be plenty of time to apologize after the papers are signed.

She could tell him she was sorry for mocking

his socks and thank him profusely for the bag at the same time she broke the news about giving up the yoga studio. It would be like ripping off a Band-Aid. Or like ripping her heart straight out of her chest, one of those things for sure. Probably the latter.

Felicity paused outside the Bean, lingering on the sidewalk and waiting for a gust of wind to pick her up and carry her far, far away from Brad Walker and his paperwork. She wasn't sure she could do this, especially after what she'd just learned about Wade. But every time she thought about staying and trying to make things with Wade permanent—and real—she remembered how she'd felt that day in the courtroom. In the blink of an eye, everything about her future had changed. It had been hard enough to go home to an empty crib all by herself. She couldn't imagine losing a partner at the same time, and Wade hadn't said a word about the two of them staying together if they weren't able to adopt Nick.

Listen to me. The three of us belong together. I know we do.

Those were the words he'd said, and as dreamy and wonderful as that belief seemed, Felicity couldn't help wondering what might happen if one of them went missing from that equation. He loved that baby down to the deepest part of his soul. She'd seen it in his eyes the moment he'd seen her holding Nick in her arms outside the firehouse. Even before that, she'd known he'd fallen in love with the child everyone in town was celebrating with casseroles and pizza parties. His reluctance to talk about delivering Nick spoke volumes. Some things were just too personal and precious to talk about out loud. Felicity knew that better than anyone.

She wanted to believe that was why he'd never told her he loved her. Because of all the wonderful things he'd said two night ago, he'd never uttered the three little words that might have convinced her that the beautiful future he described could actually be their destiny. *I love you*. Maybe if he'd said it, she wouldn't be standing in the middle of a snowstorm with her face pressed against the window of the Bean, hoping against hope that Brad Walker would be a no-show.

He wasn't, of course. He was sitting right there, in the same booth where they'd had coffee a few days ago—right where Wade had interrupted them and dripped all over the floor while he'd stood there hulking over them like a wrench-wielding caveman.

He'd been jealous. Of course he had. He'd nearly kissed her in the middle of the Bean, while the entire town had watched. And Felicity hadn't cared a bit, because she'd thought it had meant something. Maybe it had. The handbag certainly made her see things in a whole new light.

Her breath clouded the window just as Brad glanced at his watch. She was already late by at least ten minutes. It was now or never. Felicity turned around, pressed her back to the window, closed her eyes and counted to ten. After ten steady breaths in and out, she'd go inside. Breathing always calmed her down. *Thank you, yoga.*

1, 2...

Was it crazy that what she wished for most of all in this moment was for some sort of Christmas magic to intervene and show her what to do? Probably, but she wished for it all the same.

3, 4, 5...

Seriously, where was Santa or Rudolph or Clarence the angel from *It's a Wonderful Life* when someone really needed them?

6, 7, 8...

She'd even welcome Bumble, that silly abominable snowman character from that super old, vintage reindeer movie at this point. Anyone, really.

9...

Was this what it felt like to lose her mind? It had to be.

10.

Her eyes fluttered open, and a stab of disappointment pierced her soul. Of course she hadn't magically conjured a Christmas character to save her from herself. It was just her on the sidewalk, all alone. She might as well get used to it.

She straightened, squared her shoulders and turned toward the entrance to the Bean. It was time to quit stalling and make a decision. But just as she grabbed the door handle, she spied something strange through the whirl of snowflakes clouding her vision. Something big and bulky and white. Something that looked an awful lot like...

"Bumble?" Felicity blinked. Hard.

No way was she seeing a ridiculous abominable snowman from a stop-motion animation film made before she was born. It just wasn't possible. Her knees went a little weak as she narrowed her gaze, studying the snowy form as it bent over something on the sidewalk. She spied a flash of silver—a shovel, maybe? And in an instant, the snow monster dug away the mound on the sidewalk until something familiar appeared beneath the layer of frosty white.

A fire hydrant.

Felicity gasped, and her mind went completely blank. She forgot all about Brad Walker waiting for her inside the Bean. She forgot about his paperwork, her dwindling savings account and her struggling yoga studio. She even forgot about Duchess the dog's literal appetite for fine fashion. The bulky white figure just up ahead wasn't a snow monster—of course it wasn't. It was a firefighter, braving a Vermont snowstorm to make sure the fire hydrants didn't get buried. Safety first!

Wade.

Felicity's breath seemed to bottle up in her chest, along with all of her hopes and dreams. It was him. It had to be, and seeing him here, now, when she needed him most, was all the Christmas magic she needed.

The world around her felt like it was moving in slow motion as she let go of the doorknob to the Bean and started running down the sidewalk. Someone yelled for her to be careful as her ballet flats slid on a patch of ice. Felicity didn't know who, and for once she didn't care who was watching. Let all of Lovestruck talk. She was tired of denying the truth and lying to everyone in town. Most of all, she was tired of lying to herself. She wanted to be with Wade, for real. For real and maybe even forever.

As she drew closer, the firefighter's uniform slowly began to take shape, barely visible through its heavy layer of snow—the heavy black coat and pants, the yellow reflective stripes around the wrists and ankles of the turnout gear, the helmet pulled down low over his eyes. Eyes that had seen her when no one else had. Eyes that knew her like no one in else in the world.

He was scraping the ground around the fire-plug with his long-handled shovel and glanced up just as she reached him. And when she got her first clear look at him, her legs nearly buckled beneath her from sheer relief. Everything went liquid, like a watercolor painting of a heartwarming Christmas scene as tears swam in her eyes. She'd known it was him! She'd know that beautiful, heroic man anywhere.

"Felicity?" Wade's eyes glittered with a breathtaking combination of wonder and happiness. He seemed as surprised to find her there as she'd been to spot him there on Main Street.

He was absolutely covered in snow. No wonder she'd mistaken him for Bumble.

"You must be freezing," she said, teeth chattering.

"I'm fine." He dropped his shovel and ran his hands up and down her arms. "But you're shaking from head to toe. What are you doing out in this mess? Is Nick okay?"

"Nick is fine. He's great, actually. He's at Alice's, being doted on by her new mothers class. I was on my way to the Bean, but then I saw you out here, and…"

Her hands found their way to his chest, and before she knew what was happening, she'd wrapped her arms around his neck, pulling him closer and closer…craving his warmth, his charm, his hope. And when his heartbeat crashed against hers, she thought she might just be able to believe the promise he'd tried to make two nights ago.

It's all going to be okay. I promise.

She smiled up at him. "You didn't tell me the handbag belonged to your mother."

His big palms slid up to cup her face, and he brushed the snow flurries from her cheek with a gentle swipe of his thumb. "There's something I should have told you, too, something more important than a pink handbag."

"Says the man who'd never heard of a Birkin until a few days ago," she said as hope—hope so huge it felt impossible—blossomed inside her.

"I'm in love with you, sweetheart. I should have told you—"

She cut him off by rising up on tiptoe and pressing her lips to his. It didn't matter what either of them should have said or what they should have done. The past was the past, and if Wade was going to be her Christmas future, it was time to leave the past behind. All of it. What mattered most was the here and now, and she wasn't going to let another second go by without kissing Wade Ericson.

His mouth was frosty cold from being out in the snowstorm, but as she opened for him and their kiss grew deeper, she was swept up in a lovely wave of crackling heat, like a bonfire shining on a hillside on a cold winter's night. Wade was warmth and comfort, love and longing. He was everything she'd always wanted, but never imagined she'd find. And maybe, just maybe, he was hers.

Her head spun so fiercely that she had to pull back for a second and catch her breath, and when she did, Wade pressed his forehead against hers and grinned at her with that flirty, lopsided grin she'd loved right from the very start. Had she really thought she could stick to their no-romance rule? What a fool she'd been.

"Felicity Hart, did you just kiss me on Main Street, for all the world to see?" Wade's hand slid back to cradle her neck, and he pressed a tender, innocent kiss to the corner of her mouth.

"I think I did," she murmured.

"People will talk, you know." He brushed his lips slowly, reverently, over hers and pressed another gentle kiss to the opposite side of her mouth.

What was he doing? She was going to melt right at the feet of his snow-covered boots.

Happiness sparkled inside her, as dazzling as new fallen snow. "Let them. After all, we already have a baby together."

The crinkles near the corners of Wade's eyes vanished, and his eyes turned serious. "Do we?"

He was asking her again. He was asking her

to place her trust in him—to trust in *them* and the future they could build together with Nick.

She still wasn't absolutely sure she could do it. But as long as Wade loved her, she was willing to try. She had to.

"We do." She nodded.

Then Wade let out a whoop as he swept her clear off her feet and spun her around and around. Felicity tipped her head back, closed her eyes and laughed. She was giving him what he wanted most of all—the best Christmas gift either of them could have asked for. And in that snow-swept moment of pure and perfect bliss, Felicity believed.

She believed in Christmas magic. She believed in new beginnings. She believed in love.

Chapter Fifteen

They needed to celebrate. Wade was adamant, and even though Felicity never would have ordinarily agreed to celebrate something that wasn't yet official, she couldn't help but acquiesce. His joy was infectious, and even though there was a a tiny voice whispering somewhere in the back of her head that things could still go sideways, she decided to ignore it. Happiness was a choice, after all—a choice she was willing to make, so long as Wade was by her side.

He had enough hope for the both of them. That's what he told her again and again when he finally set her back down on the ground and kissed her until she saw stars.

"You just wait, sweetheart," he whispered into her hair. "I'm going to sweep you off your feet."

She laughed. "I think you just did that."

"I mean it. Tonight we're going on our first real date. Prepare to be romanced." He took her hand and spun her around like a ballerina. She felt airy and light, like she was part of the "Waltz of the Snowflakes" in *The Nutcracker.*

Felicity laughed as he drew her back into his arms and kissed the top of her head. "We have a baby, remember? We can't go anywhere."

"That's right. We do, don't we?" He flashed her a wink. "Pizza and champagne by the Christmas tree, then?"

Felicity had never heard of anything so romantic. She might even have to break down and make him a casserole tomorrow. "I can get on board with that kind of picnic."

"Excellent." He scooped his shovel up off the ground and used it to motion across the street, where Jack stood waving at them. "I should probably get back to work so I don't leave Jack on his own, like the last time I wanted to kiss you silly."

"Sounds good. I'll pick up Nick from the yarn shop and get things ready at home." *Home.* That word had never sounded quite so wonderful.

He winked at her. "See you tonight, sweetheart."

Her heart did a little flip-flop. "It's a date."

* * *

As Felicity expected, Alice's crochet class had fallen completely in love with Nick. The new moms had taken turns holding him, and there were even a pair of brand-new knitted baby bootees on his feet when Felicity darted back inside the yarn shop. They were bright red with fuzzy white trim, like tiny little Santa boots. No one would tell her who'd made them, but Felicity's bets were on Alice.

Even Toby the dog had become a fast friend, and every time the slender, hairless little pup pranced into view in his fancy snowflake sweater, Nick would let out a gleeful stream of babble. She and Wade were going to have to get him his own puppy someday, weren't they? Maybe a goofy, affectionate retriever mix, so long as Duchess didn't mind. If they were going to be a family, they might as well really do it right. What went better with a white picket fence than a boy and his puppy?

Slow down, she told herself, pressing a hand to her abdomen. *Just breathe.*

But everything was suddenly happening so fast. Wade was in love with her, and whenever she was around him, he had a way of truly making her feel like everything would be all right. She just had to hold on to that feeling as hard as she could and let him carry all her doubts and fears on his broad, beautiful shoulders. It was all going to be just fine. Wade and Nick were her Christmas miracle—she could feel it.

"Thanks so much for watching him for a little while." Felicity scooped Nick into her arms while he kicked his tiny feet, Santa bootees moving in a happy little blur.

"Oh, please. It was only a matter of minutes. I'd be happy to watch him anytime," Alice said as she walked Felicity to the door of the yarn shop. "In fact, I've been wanting to talk to you about that very thing."

"You've been wanting to talk to me about babysitting?"

"I couldn't help noticing that the firefighter and knitting club yoga class seems to be the only time that Nama-Stay Awhile is full." Alice's kind face curved into a sympathetic smile. "I hope you don't mind my mentioning it."

"Oh." Felicity shook her head. For a few blissful minutes, she'd forgotten all about her yoga studio. And her checkbook. And Brad Walker, whom she'd just stood up for their meeting at the Bean. "Um, it's fine. Believe me, I've noticed it myself."

"Well, I was thinking that what you really need over there is a nursery."

Felicity blinked. "A nursery?"

"For babies and small children. I just know some of the moms in town would come try a class if they could bring their little ones along." Alice's gaze darted meaningfully to the group of new moms seated around the craft table in the center of the yarn shop.

"Alice, you're a genius." The sidewalks of Lovestruck were crammed with women in Lululemon leggings pushing baby strollers every morning. Why on earth hadn't Felicity thought of such an idea herself? *Oh, right. Probably because I was too busy trying to hide from those same moms and their precious children.* "I'll need to get some partitions to section off part of the studio to be a nursery area. Baby gates, maybe? And I'll need some toys, too. A few rocking chairs…"

It was a lot, but doable. Her savings would be down to zero once she made the necessary changes, but she had a feeling it just might work, apart from one significant detail.

"I'll just need to figure out where to find a few babysitters," Felicity said, running her hand in gentle circles over Nick's slender back.

The few times she and Wade had left the baby with anyone else, Alice or Madison and Jack had watched him. Felicity wasn't sure she'd trust anyone else with him quite yet.

"That's the best part." Alice beamed.

Felicity felt herself smile. "You don't mean…"

"Me!" Alice held her arms open wide. As if on cue, Toby scrambled off his dog bed by the register and came trotting toward them to dance and woof at their feet.

Felicity couldn't help but laugh. No one could ask for a better babysitter. It would be like having Mrs. Claus herself run the nursery. The Lovestruck moms would line up around the block to sign up for class.

"Are you sure you truly want to add part-time babysitter to your list of responsibilities? I'm not sure I could ask you to take that on. It's sure to be a lot of work."

Alice waved a hand. "Don't be silly. I'd love it. And I don't plan on doing it alone. I just know the knitting club ladies would love it. We could take turns and do it in pairs. Some of those women live alone, you know. Ethel's grandchildren live down in Texas, and Berta just lost her husband last year. You'd be doing them a favor, honestly. They need you as much as you need them."

Felicity's eyes welled up again. How many times was she going to cry today? "I haven't thought of things that way before."

She'd tried so, so hard to keep to herself since moving to Vermont. She'd imagined a calm, quiet life of yoga, covered bridges, fresh maple syrup and really great cheese. But as lovely as it seemed, every time she'd imagined such a life, she'd pictured herself alone. Safe. Content…if not quite happy.

But no matter how hard she tried, Lovestruck kept working its magic. Slowly but surely the town and its people were making their way into her heart.

"That's just how Lovestruck works. It always has, and it always will. We help each other." Alice reached for one of Nick's tiny feet and gave it a tender squeeze. "Think about it, and let me know. We're here for you, dear. All of us."

Felicity nodded, blinking back tears. She wanted to say thank you, but she didn't quite trust herself to speak. And as she made her way back to Wade's cottage, she couldn't help feeling that Christmas had come just a few days early. One by one, all her Christmas wishes were coming true.

Even the wishes she'd tried her best to keep locked away deep inside her heart, too precious and perfect to hope for.

Wade paused at the gate of the white picket fence in front of his cottage, lingering for a moment before opening it and making his way up the final few steps to the porch. The yard was heaped with snow, and a ribbon of smoke curled up from the chimney. Frosted windows glowed gold in the darkness, and beyond the sparkling silhouette of the Christmas tree, he could see stockings hanging from the mantle of the fireplace in a tidy little row—four of them, arranged from biggest to smallest. Wade, Felicity, Nick and, lastly, a tiny stocking for Duchess, decorated with a white felt paw print.

If Felicity's surprise kiss in the middle of downtown Lovestruck hadn't convinced him that she was ready to try to make their fragile little family permanent, the stockings sealed the deal. They hadn't been there when he'd left for the firehouse earlier. She must have put them up sometime after they'd found each other in the blizzard, and the sight of them filled his chest with such unexpected joy that it hurt.

He clutched at his heart. Felicity was trying. Those stockings were proof that she was ready to go all in. A foursome of red-and-white-striped socks hanging from a mantelpiece shouldn't have been enough to make a grown man cry, but Wade found his throat growing thick all the same.

He swallowed hard and made his way to the porch in three easy strides, bounding up the steps with all the enthusiasm of a kid on Christmas morning. The front door opened with a creak and, as he spotted the flannel blanket spread neatly on the floor beside the decorated blue spruce and the silver ice bucket carrying a bottle of Moët & Chandon at a jaunty, celebratory angle, one word echoed in the back of his head.

Home.

He felt his face split into a grin as he dropped

his duffel bag on the floor by the front door, where it hit the wooden planks with a thud. Wade had lived in this house for almost five years, and somehow right now, standing on the threshold, he felt as if he were teetering on the edge of some sort of precipice. Life before, and life after.

After. He chose *after. After* was what he wanted, what he needed. Jack had been right. Once Wade had told Felicity how he felt about her a whole new world had opened up to them—a whole new life.

He still needed to tell her about the adoption application, which he'd do right away. They'd have to get in touch with the social worker and add Felicity's name to the paperwork, but they could deal with that tomorrow. Christmas Eve. Tonight belonged to the two of them, just him and Felicity. Besides, officially filling out the paperwork to become a family on the day before Christmas had a certain poetic ring to it. It would be something they could celebrate every year as a family, along with Christmas Eve.

Wade glanced again at the stockings hanging from the mantel and then headed to the kitchen, expecting to find Felicity warming up a bedtime bottle for Nick. But just as he reached for the swinging kitchen door, she bustled right through it, nearly crashing into him.

"You're home. I just put Nick down for the night, and Duchess is happily gnawing on a soup bone in the nursery, so she won't crash our picnic." Felicity's cheeks went pink as he took in the cute little Christmas apron she was wearing. It had ruffles and was printed in swirling red-and-white stripes, like a Starlight peppermint candy. "It's silly, I know, especially since all I had to do was call and order a pizza. It's not like I'm actually cooking, but I did a little shopping this afternoon. I guess I'm feeling especially Christmassy."

"I can see that," he said, casting a meaningful glance at the stockings.

"I had the best day. I can't wait to tell you all about the conversation I had with Alice this afternoon."

Wade tugged the frilly strings of her apron and reeled her toward him while she let out a playful little yelp.

"The apron is perfect. You're adorable, and I want you to tell me all about your day—every last detail," he murmured against the side of her neck as his hands slid into her tumbling waves of hair. She was softness and light, and when she melted into him with a sigh, he could hardly believe his luck.

He should have known, though. When he'd exited the firehouse on the opening night of the living nativity and first saw her standing there wrapped in miles of blue silk with a baby in her arms and tears in her eyes, he should have known. That was the moment his life had changed—the moment he'd lost his heart to Felicity and Nick both. He just hadn't realized it yet.

No, that wasn't quite right. Somewhere deep down—somewhere in the very pit of his being, tangled up with all the other thoughts and feelings he did his level best not to think about—he'd known. How could he not have? It was never a coincidence that the baby had turned up at his fire station. He'd been dreaming about little Nick for fourteen nights in a row, wondering why he'd been the one who'd answered the call that night. Of all the firefighters in the LFD, why him?

And then the baby had made his way back to Wade, cradled in the arms of the only woman in town who could possibly know what it felt like to care so much about someone so tiny and so vulnerable and still be utterly powerless to have any sort of real impact on their future. It had terrified Wade as much as it had stunned him. Nick deserved better than him. He deserved a man who knew what it meant to be a father.

But with Felicity beside him, Wade felt like he could be that man. Christmas had brought them together this year for a reason, and that reason wasn't just Nick. It was because they made each other whole.

I want to marry this woman.

Wade's mouth moved from Felicity's neck to the tender spot behind her ear, where he could feel the boom of her pulse against his lips. She felt so alive when he touched her, like a glorious, shimmering force of nature. It was like holding sunshine in his hands.

"Felicity," he murmured.

"Yes?" she said, in a breathy, tremulous voice that nearly brought him to his knees.

Marry me. Let's do this right. He couldn't just blurt it out, though. He still hadn't told her about the adoption application yet. That should come first, shouldn't it?

He still had time to come up with a special Christmas proposal. Why did he feel so panicked, like he had to get the words out as quickly as possible? It wasn't now or never.

"There's something I need to tell you, too," he said.

She pulled back to smile at him. "I hope it's not that you don't like pepperoni, because that could be a deal breaker. I'm willing to negotiate when it comes to extra cheese, but only a monster turns down a pepperoni pizza."

"I'm not a monster," he said, and for maybe the first time in his adult life he truly believed it. Just because he shared his father's last name didn't mean he was Fred Ericson's son.

"That's a relief." Felicity's eyes danced, and before Wade could change the topic of conversation from pepperoni to adoption papers or even marriage, the doorbell rang.

"Oh! That must be the pizza. Can you get it while I go grab some champagne glasses from the kitchen?" She headed back toward the kitchen.

Wade's heart hammered hard in his chest. "Absolutely."

Felicity aimed a final glance at him over her shoulder as she pushed through the swinging door. "Just so you know, this is already the best first date I've ever had."

And just like that, the riot in Wade's soul found its calm. A storm might still be brewing outside, but he and Felicity were home now. They were together. While snow pattered against the windowpanes, they'd sip champagne beneath the boughs of the big blue spruce and plan their future. This Christmas would be the first of many. Next year, they'd probably take Nick to have his picture taken with Santa Claus. The year after that, he'd be old enough to set out a plate of cookies and milk before he went to bed on Christmas Eve. Soon afterward, Wade and Felicity would be up all night every Christmas putting together bicycles and complicated toys, and Wade would love every second of it. He could see the years playing out in his head like a favorite holiday movie—the kind people never grew tired of, no matter how many times they'd seen it.

And it all started right here, right now.

Joy welled inside Wade's heart as he strode to the front door, but when he swung it open, adrenaline shot through his system, fast and hard. His limbs grew twitchy, and all of his senses went razor sharp, the same way they always did when he arrived at the scene of fire. He could hear the snowflakes landing on the pavement in soft, delicate whispers. He could smell the cheery, holiday scents of evergreen and frost, but they seemed cloying all of a sudden. Too fragrant, too sweet. And the panic roiling inside him was so thick he could taste it.

He gripped the doorknob tight, blinking as he tried to make sense of why the teenager on his doorstep wasn't carrying a pizza box or wearing one of the signature red-checkered hats from Lovestruck Pizza. There was no car in the driveway with a pepperoni pie decal emblazoned on its side—just a young girl on his porch dressed in an oversize hoodie and a pair of salt-stained Converse sneakers with a hole in the toe.

Nick's biological mother.

* * *

Felicity couldn't find any proper champagne flutes in Wade's kitchen cabinets, so she grabbed two wineglasses instead. Then she paused, thought better of it and switched them out for two chunky ceramic mugs with reindeer faces and peppermint-striped handles. It just seemed like it might be more fun to drink out of Christmas cups. So she gathered them in one hand, slid two plates in her other and pushed through the swinging door with what felt like a smile as big and silly as the reindeer-faced mugs.

Then the world seemed to tilt sideways.

Felicity recognized the young girl standing in the entryway at once. The scene outside the firehouse was seared into Felicity's memory with such clarity that she'd never forget the teenager who'd banged on the car window while she'd been waiting for Wade to change into his costume for the living nativity. She couldn't, no matter how hard she tried.

And she'd definitely tried...oh, how she'd tried. For days afterward, she'd done her best to shake the memory of how helpless and frail the infant had looked in the girl's arms, how frightened the teen seemed...the tremble in her voice and her awestruck expression as she'd thrust the baby at Felicity.

Look at you. You're the Virgin Mary, right? It's like a sign.

Bile rose up the back of Felicity's throat. The reindeer mugs clanged together in her grasp as she started shaking violently from head to toe. *A sign.* Right. She'd actually let herself believe that moment had been fated, and here she was…about to get her heart ripped completely out of her chest.

Again.

"Felicity, sweetheart," Wade said, turning slightly toward her as his gaze flitted back and forth between Felicity and the girl. "This is—"

"Nick's mother," Felicity said, finishing for him. She set the mugs and plates down on the closest surface—she wasn't even sure what it was. An end table? A bookshelf? Everything had gone blurry and terrible. Spots swam before her eyes, and she'd known if she didn't rid herself of the dishes, they'd eventually crash to the floor.

Why couldn't she breathe? Why couldn't she hang on to anything? Everything she tried to grab hold of always seemed to slip away. The mugs. The plates. Ariel… Baby Nick.

"Why don't we all sit down and talk?" Wade said, motioning for the girl to step farther inside and take a seat on the sofa.

She moved past him, fiddling with the strings of her hoodie as she sat down. She looked almost as lost and cold as she had that night outside the fire station. Where was her coat? Where were her *parents*? Felicity wanted to wrap her in a blanket and make her a cup of hot cocoa almost as much as she wanted to tell her to leave and never come back.

What was wrong with her? She wasn't cut out to handle this. She'd tried to warn Wade. She'd tried to explain it to him. She'd flat-out begged.

Please, Wade, please. Don't make promises you know you can't keep.

He looked at her, imploring her with his soulful gaze. "Felicity?"

She shook her head. *Don't.* How could he ask her to sit down with them as if this was just a normal social call? As if Nick's mother wasn't there to take her baby back?

That had to be the reason. Why else would she turn up out of the blue, right before Christmas?

"I, um…" Felicity bit her bottom lip to keep it from trembling as she took a sharp inhale. She probably needed to sit down before she collapsed, but she couldn't seem to take a single step toward the sofa. "There's something I should take care of."

"Wait," Wade said, and the ache in his eyes became too much for Felicity to take. He looked completely torn, unsure whether to stay and find out what the girl wanted or to follow Felicity and make sure she was okay. "Please?"

She *wasn't* okay. She'd probably never be okay again.

She couldn't believe she'd let him convince her that everything would be all right…that they were a family. She knew better. She'd already learned this lesson once before. What made this time any different?

This time, you're in love.

She loved Wade just as much as she loved Nick, and she'd foolishly believed that being in love would protect her somehow. Oh, how wrong she'd been.

"It's fine." She took a backward step, focusing intently on the Christmas tree so she wouldn't have to look at Wade. Or the girl. Or the stockings hanging from the mantel. But then her gaze homed in on the ornament Wade bought a few nights ago at the Christmas festival—a porcelain teddy bear with a baby blue banner strung from one paw to the other that read *Baby's First Christmas*.

There was nowhere safe to look. The graceful boughs of the tree went liquid as tears swam in her eyes.

"I'll be right back," she lied.

Instinct told her to go straight to the nursery and scoop Nick out of his crib so she could hold him one last time. She needed to memorize the feel of his warm, tiny body pressed against her chest, the little kitten sounds he always made when he slept, his soft baby powder scent and the feel of his fine, wispy hair against her lips when she kissed the top of his head. But she couldn't.

If she did, she'd never let him go. So on shaky legs, she went directly to the guest room instead, and while Wade sat in the living room with Nick's mother, Felicity dragged her empty suitcase out from under the bed and started to pack.

Chapter Sixteen

"Felicity?" Madison looked her up and down and then cast a glance over Felicity's shoulder as if in total disbelief to find her alone on the doorstep of the home she shared with Jack and the twins.

Not *technically* alone, actually.

"Is that the Birkin-eater?" Madison said, gaze narrowing at the dog in Felicity's arms.

Madison hefted the little spaniel higher into her grip. Duchess was quite a bit heavier than she looked—probably because of all that fancy canned food Wade insisted on buying for her. And also probably because Felicity had just carried the little beast five long blocks while also dragging her wheeled suitcase behind her.

Good gravy, what a mess I've made.

"Of course it's Duchess." Honestly, what other Cavalier King Charles spaniel would Felicity be dragging all over Lovestruck? "I sort of dognapped her just now. Not on purpose—it kind of just happened."

She sniffed.

"What on earth is happening right now?" Madison said as night fell around them in swirl of velvety darkness and snow flurries. When she finally caught sight of the luggage at Felicity's feet, her eyes went wide. "Did you walk all the way here from Wade's house?"

Felicity nodded without further elaboration, and her teeth started chattering again. Since the second she'd set eyes on Nick's mother, she'd been unable to stop trembling. Everyone in Lovestruck could probably hear her bones rattling by now.

"It's freezing out there. Come inside." Madison hooked an arm through Felicity's and led her into the house as if she were incapable of taking another step on her own.

Maybe she was. Felicity didn't even know. All she knew was that she'd needed to get as far away from Wade and Nick as possible before she became broken beyond repair.

"But keep that dog away from my handbags.

And my shoes." Madison rubbed her hands up and Felicity's arms. "You're shaking like a leaf. What happened? Did you and Wade have an argument?"

No—but they would once Wade discovered that Felicity had slipped out the back door without saying a word. Not to mention the accidental dog-napping.

What should she have done? Leave the poor dog behind? Duchess had abandoned her soup bone, plopped onto the guest bed and proceeded to pout the entire time Felicity stuffed things into her suitcase. Felicity hadn't been able to look the spaniel in the eyes. Those melting brown irises were just too much to take, especially once Felicity had finishing tossing things into her bag and tiptoed to the back door of Wade's cottage.

Duchess had inserted herself in Felicity's path and refused to budge. Felicity had done her best to explain things to the dog in desperate whispers, but it hadn't helped matters at all. In fact, it had only made things worse. Duchess had started whimpering, and Felicity had no choice but to grab the poor distressed pup and take her along on her impromptu getaway.

"We didn't have an argument. It was worse than that." Felicity shook her head, and Duchess swiped at one of the tears on her face with a dainty pink tongue.

So much worse.

"Who was at the door, babe?" Jack said, strolling into the room wearing a green sweatshirt with the words *Feliz Navi DAD* emblazoned across the front of it.

Felicity tried to laugh—dorky dad fashion was always funny, no matter the circumstances—but it came out as a strangled sob.

"Look, hon. It's Felicity," Madison said, leading her to an overstuffed recliner and tucking a blanket around her legs while Duchess's tail wagged back and forth. "Her bags are on the porch. Can you run and get them? And maybe heat up some water for tea?"

Jack stared for a beat, clearly not understanding what Felicity and Wade's dog were doing in his living room—with luggage—until Madison shot him a meaningful glance, propelling him into motion.

He nodded and beat a hasty trail toward the porch. "Absolutely, babe. No problem."

Madison sat down on an ottoman across from Felicity and gave her knee a squeeze. "We got the best cinnamon spice tea at the Christmas festival the other day. You'll just love it. It's like Christmas in a cup."

"Thanks," Felicity said, even though Christmas was the last thing she wanted to think about at the moment. She didn't want to think about anything, really. What she really wanted was for everything to go completely blank. She didn't want to think, and more important, she didn't want to *feel*, anything at all.

She'd been so close to starting a new life in a new town. A simple, safe life with no strings attached—nothing and no one to hurt her, ever again. Then she'd made the fatal mistake of letting her guard down. After weeks of hiding in her protective little shell, she'd mistaken Wade Ericson for a nutty Christmas character and let herself believe in happy-ever-afters, and look where it had gotten her. She was a trembling, devastated mess. A perpetrator of canine crimes. The type of person who snuck out the back door instead of facing heartache like an adult.

Maybe things had worked out for the best. She probably didn't deserve to be anyone's mother.

Felicity wasn't even altogether certain how or why she'd ended up at Jack and Madison's house. Her main objective had been to go someplace where Wade wouldn't be able to find her. The apartment above the yoga studio would be the first place he checked once he realized she'd slipped quietly out the back door while he'd been talking to Nick's mother. She hadn't known where else to go, and her footsteps had somehow carried her here.

She couldn't stay, obviously. For starters, she

was intruding on their holiday plans. Tomorrow was Christmas Eve. Plus, there were two very important reasons she and Duchess couldn't hide out here longer than one night. And those reasons were named Emma and Ella.

Felicity's gaze flitted toward the corner of the room where presents were piled beneath the Christmas tree in identical, matching pairs. A nearby end table boasted a giant framed photo of both girls, dressed in precious, coordinating tartan ruffles as they sat on Santa's lap. Two stuffed snowmen toys lay discarded on the sofa. Signs of the babies were everywhere. Her throat closed up tight as she spotted four Christmas stockings lined up on the mantel, so similar to the ones she'd bought earlier this afternoon…back when she'd been part of a family.

Felicity stood, hanging on to Duchess as if the dog was a security blanket. "Can we go someplace else?"

Madison followed her gaze, wincing as she saw the stockings. "Something's happened with Nick, hasn't it? Oh, Felicity. I'm so sorry. Yes, let's go to the kitchen. Forget the tea. I'll make us some hot toddies."

Jack came in from outside as they headed toward the kitchen. He smiled at Felicity and told her he'd put her bag in the guest room.

"I'm sorry," she told Madison as she slumped

into a chair at the kitchen table. "I should have called first. Tell Jack he doesn't need to get the guest room ready. I can go to a hotel."

"Don't be ridiculous." Madison opened a cabinet, pulled out a bottle of whiskey and set it down on the kitchen counter next to a bear-shaped bottle of honey. "You're clearly upset. I'm not letting you go anywhere."

Madison snatched a pacifier off the counter and attempted to shove it into a drawer before Felicity caught sight of it. She'd noticed, though. It was impossible not to. This house wasn't safe—not even the kitchen. The drying rack beside the sink was filled with baby bottles and toddler spoons. A baby monitor sat right in the center of the kitchen table. Everything about the place screamed *babies, twins, motherhood*. It made Felicity want to curl into a ball on the floor.

She might have done it if she hadn't been so afraid she might bump her head on a matching pair of Tickle Me Elmos. Instead, she took a deep breath and counted to ten while Madison poured water into an electric kettle and sliced open a sunny yellow lemon. Duchess settled into a snoring lump on Felicity's lap.

Within seconds, Madison slid a steaming drink in front of Felicity and sat down beside her. "Okay, now tell me everything."

Where to start?

Felicity took a sip of her hot toddy and closed her eyes as the whiskey warmed her body. She toyed with her locket, purely out of habit, and then looked down at the dainty gold heart. The best place to start was probably back at the beginning.

Madison was her closest friend in Lovestruck. It was time she knew the truth about the framed baby picture Felicity kept on her desk back when they worked together at *Fashionista*. Maybe if Felicity had been more open about what she'd been going through and tried to share the burden of her heartbreak, she would have been able to move past it. But did anyone ever truly get over losing a child? Even a child that was still safe and sound, but simply no longer a part of their everyday life?

Felicity didn't think so. It seemed impossible.

Madison waited patiently for her to say something as Felicity took another gulp of hot toddy. Sweet lemony fire blossomed in her chest, loosening her limbs. And for the first time, she realized that the pain she'd been carrying around for the past six months—the constant ache that had become her faithful companion since that long lonely day in a Manhattan courtroom—was probably the same sort of pain that had stopped her cousin from going through with the adoption. It was the same pain that had brought Nick's young mother to Wade's door tonight.

She finally understood she wasn't alone in

this. They were all mothers in one way or another, and a mother's love was a rare and precious thing. Sometimes it was just too strong to release, no matter what sort of promises had been made. No matter if the mother had been forced to hand over the baby she'd thought she was adopting or whether she'd changed her mind about a decision she'd thought would be permanent. Broken promises and broken hearts all around.

It was time for Felicity to forgive her cousin. Until she did, she'd never be able to call another baby her own. Not even Nick, although she was sure she'd already lost him, too.

Felicity ran a shaky hand over Duchess's warm back and blinked away tears as she finally met Madison's gaze. "You really want me to tell you everything?"

Madison nodded.

"It started just like Christmas," Felicity said, voice breaking. Then slowly—carefully—she slipped the gold chain over her head and opened the heart-shaped locket to reveal a tiny photograph of Ariel. "It started with a baby."

Wade wasn't sure when he first realized that Felicity had left and wasn't coming back.

The minutes ticked by as he sat beside the young girl on his sofa, and he did his best to concentrate on what she was saying. But he felt like he was about come apart at the seams, burst right through his skin. It was the same feeling he got on the rare occasion when he arrived on the scene of a fire that was already too far gone to wrestle under control. There was nothing he could do but stand by and watch it burn until it was over, the damage was done and the flames had reduced everything around him to ash.

Felicity's absence was a given. She'd checked out the very second she'd walked into the room and seen Nick's biological mother standing in the living room. The life had drained right out of her, and there hadn't been a thing Wade could do to stop it. He'd known better than to try to make her stay and find out what exactly the troubled teen had wanted. Every cell in his body screamed to go after her, to protect her. But he needed to talk to the girl. He couldn't very well leave her out in the cold.

Marcie—that was her name. It was printed in neat block lettering on the birth certificate she'd handed to Wade before she left, along with a baby blanket and a Christmas-themed storybook. *Goodbye presents*, she'd called them. Tomorrow she'd be moving to Texas with her family, and before she left Vermont, she'd wanted to thank Wade for all he'd done for her son. Then she'd promised to never come back again.

Wade stood in the doorway and watched her

walk toward the bus stop around the corner, hoodie pulled snug around her face. He'd offered to drive her, but she'd turned him down, and on some soul-deep level, Wade knew why—she wanted to leave before he could ask if she wanted to see Nick.

In the end, he wasn't sure whether to feel relieved or sad by the unexpected turn of events. The pang in his chest felt like some strange combination of both, but as the snow swallowed up the footsteps that Marcie left behind, he also got the sense of one story ending and another beginning—a brand-new story filled with hope and promise, untethered from the past.

He had to tell Felicity.

The walls of his little cottage practically vibrated with her absence. Still, he tried to tell himself he was only imagining things. She'd been rattled. Of course she had, but she wouldn't just leave, would she?

Yes, apparently. The truth sank into his bones as he ran from room to room calling her name. He couldn't even find Duchess. Was he losing his mind? They'd both been there twenty minutes ago.

The nursery was the last room he checked, and relief coursed through Wade hot and fast when he caught sight of Nick sleeping in his crib with his tiny hands curled into fists, as if trying his best to hold on tight to his new, fragile family.

Rest easy, son. Wade blinked hard, tears stinging the backs of his eyes. *You're home for good.*

Then Wade's cell phone rang, and he tripped on every single piece of furniture in his path as he raced back to the living room to pick it up. His heart slammed around his chest as he answered without bothering to check the display.

"Felicity?" he panted into the phone. He knew it was her. It *had* to be.

"Sorry, friend. It's me," Jack said on the other end.

"Oh." Wade tried his best to swallow his disappointment, but it settled at the back of his throat, black and bitter like tar. "Hey."

It wasn't exactly the warmest greeting, but Wade couldn't even think straight. He had to get off the phone and bundle Nick up in his snowsuit so they could get down to the yoga studio. He wasn't sure where else Felicity would have gone. Just the thought of her sitting all alone in that sad, small attic apartment with that even sadder, smaller Christmas tree made him sick to his stomach.

"Now's not a really good time, Jack. I—"

"She's here," Jack said, cutting him off.

"What?" Wade was pretty sure he'd heard correctly, but he couldn't be sure. Jack's tone was awfully low, barely above a whisper.

"Felicity. She's here at our house. With your dog, I might add." Jack cleared his throat. "She seems upset, and I should probably be minding my own business, but I thought you'd want to know."

"Definitely." Wade dragged a hand through his hair, tugging hard on the ends in an effort to kick his rear into gear. He needed to get over there. Now. "Thanks, man. You have no idea. I'm coming over right now. Whatever you do, don't let her leave."

"I'll try, but I can't make any promises. She and Madison are in the kitchen right now, and I'm pretty certain there's whiskey involved." Jack let out a gravelly laugh. "Besides, I know better than to try to control a woman."

So did Wade, obviously. And he'd never want to, either. But she had to know that Marcie hadn't changed her mind about giving Nick up. If she had, Wade would've accepted it. Her rights as a parent hadn't yet been terminated by the courts, and people made mistakes. Bad ones. It would have killed Wade to give Nick up, but he would have done it, just as Felicity had given up Ariel six months ago.

He hadn't fully understood how painful that must have been for her until now...until he'd

swung open the door and seen the familiar teenager standing on his front porch, clutching a baby
blanket. Felicity might never come back. What had
just happened in Wade's living room may have
felt like closure, but there were no guarantees—
not until the court approved an adoption. Would
she wait by his side until things were official?
Could she?

He honestly didn't know. But she deserved to
know where things stood. She deserved the truth,
in all its complicated, joyful uncertainty.

He took a deep breath. "I'll be there as soon
as I can."

"Wow." Madison drained what was left off-
her hot toddy and dabbed at the corners of her
eyes with a napkin as she looked at Felicity from
across the table. "That's…a lot. Why didn't you
tell me any of this before? You shouldn't be dealing with such heartbreak all on your own."

Felicity blew out a shaky breath. "I don't know.
I think I thought if I didn't talk about or dwell on
it that the pain would just go away. I thought I
could start a new life in a new place and it would
be as if it had never happened."

Looking back, she'd been hopelessly naive. If she
could just go back in time to the very beginning—
before she ever moved to Lovestruck—she'd do so
many things differently. But of course that wasn't

possible. This wasn't a Christmas movie, it was real life. *Her* life, which, at the moment, was as messy as it could possibly be.

"Have you told anyone?" Madison asked. "Anyone at all?"

Felicity's gaze fixed with her friend's, and she nodded. "Wade."

A smile made its way to her lips before wobbling off her face. *Wade.* Of all the things she wished she could go back and do differently, she wouldn't have changed a minute she'd spent with Wade. Not a second—not even the horrible moment earlier that had caused her to steal his dog and run away.

"Hon." Madison reached forward and gave Felicity's hand a comforting squeeze. "Why don't you call him? He's got to be worried sick."

Felicity shook her head. "I just can't."

She was too ashamed. She'd had a chance to be strong—to stay and do the right thing—and she'd done the exact opposite. A real couple would have handled things together. A real *mother* would have stayed to see things through.

"He'll understand why you left. I promise he will," Madison said as if she could read Felicity's mind.

Would he, though? Felicity wasn't so sure. He'd asked her to trust him, to trust in *them*, and at the first sign of trouble, she'd left. On top of it all, she'd stolen his dog.

Madison's eyebrows rose. "Besides, you don't know for certain that Nick's biological mother came back because she changed her mind. The truth might not be as bad as you think it is."

Felicity shook her head. She didn't want to hope. She couldn't. She didn't have a drop of hope left inside her. It was better to just accept the fact that their temporary family was exactly what it had always been—temporary.

Her fingers burrowed deeper into Duchess's soft fur. What was she going to do?

"Excuse me." Jack opened the door to the kitchen but lingered in the doorway without stepping inside the room. "I'm sorry to interrupt, but I need to borrow Madison for a quick sec. Okay, babe?"

Madison frowned at him. "Seriously, now?"

"Yes, now. Right now. It's super urgent." Jack's gaze flicked to Felicity and then back to Madison. He cleared his throat.

"You're acting really weird, but okay." Madison squeezed Felicity's hand, harder this time. "I'll be right back. Don't go anywhere."

Right. Because that's what Felicity did when things got uncomfortable, wasn't it? She ran.

Jack was probably thinking the same thing. No doubt he was in such a hurry to talk to Madison because he was wondering how long they were going to have to harbor Felicity and her canine fugitive.

"Take your time," she said. No more running, starting right now. It was time to stay and deal with her problems head-on.

Stay.

Every time that word spun through her mind, she heard it in Wade's voice, the exact way he'd said it when he'd told her he wanted to adopt Nick together and be a family. He'd said it in his three-in-the-morning voice—sleepy and low, and she'd loved the way it had settled so deliciously deep in her belly.

The baby monitor on the table crackled to life, pulling her out of the memory. At first, she assumed that Jack and Madison must have gone to Emma and Ella's room to check on the twins. But then the voice that came through the little speaker was identical to the one she'd just been thinking about…yearning for…

"Hey, little man. Don't cry. Everything's going to be just fine," he said.

Felicity went still as stone and stared at the baby monitor. It was Wade. There was no mistaking that voice—she'd know it anywhere. And he was using his favorite nickname for Nick, little man. Was Wade here, in Jack and Madison's house? With Nick?

"That's right," Wade said, and hearing him speak so soothingly to Nick, so lovingly, was such a balm to Felicity's battered heart that she felt like she might float right off the kitchen chair. "Your birth mother came to say goodbye one last time because she loves you. How could she not? You're perfect. And you know what else you are? You're mine…mine and Felicity's. We're your parents, little man."

Duchess's ears twitched, and she sat up to cock her head as she tried to figure out how Wade's voice was coming from the little white box on the table. Felicity probably would have found it adorable if she hadn't been too stunned by Wade's words to think about anything besides baby Nick.

His birth mother hadn't come to take him away, but to say goodbye. The truth was almost too impossible to believe. Felicity pressed a hand to her chest because her heart felt like it might pound right out of her. And then a slow smile rose up inside her when she realized what was happening… what Wade was doing.

He was speaking to Nick, yes, but he was talking to *her*. He was letting her know how he felt in the same way she'd done when she'd told Duchess how charming she'd found him. Everything was coming full circle.

"Don't you worry about a thing. I might not seem like the best choice for a dad. She probably doesn't think I'm ready or that I haven't thought things through. But I've never been so certain of anything in my life. I've known since the second I saw her standing in the snow in a swirl of snowflakes and blue silk with you in her arms. You're my future, my destiny. You both are."

He paused to clear his throat as hot tears spilled down Felicity's cheeks.

"If she'll have me, that is."

And then he pushed through the kitchen door, where he stood on the threshold with Nick strapped to his chest in a baby sling and the other baby monitor gripped firmly in his hand. The smile he gave her wasn't like any of the ones she'd seen on his handsome face before. It wasn't his trademark flirty grin or the sheepish one he always had when she poked fun at his socks. It wasn't the least bit guarded or forced. This smile was a rare and precious gift—open, honest and brimming with promise. Promises of hope. And a future too wonderful to fathom, like Christmas every day.

Duchess hopped off Felicity's lap and ran to paw at Wade's shins. Felicity followed. It took every ounce of willpower she possessed not to throw her arms around him and Nick and hold on for the rest of her life. But there were things she needed to say first—important things. Or as Jack might say, *super urgent*.

"I know you're ready, and I know you've thought

things through. I never doubted you for a second."
She pressed a hand to her heart. "It's me. I'm the
one I didn't believe in."

"What about now?" he said, gaze lowering to
her lips.

Nick's tiny eyelashes fluttered open, and when
he caught sight of Felicity, he kicked his tiny feet
and let out a happy squeal.

And all the hope that Felicity had been so
afraid to feel came flooding back to her heart
tenfold. She didn't even try to push it away. *No
more running*, she told herself. No matter what
the future held, she was here to stay. Lovestruck
was her home, and so was the man standing in
front of her.

"Now I believe," she said. "I believe in Christmas, I believe in family and I believe in us."

Wade swept her into his arms with Nick tucked
snugly between them and Duchess prancing at
their feet, and as he brushed away each and every
one of her tears, Felicity looked up at him and
smiled.

"I love you, Smokey, and I'm yours. Not just
until Christmas, but always and forever."

Epilogue

Dear Nick,

Today's the day your daddy and I have been waiting for since the moment we first saw you. It's the day you'll officially become ours in a Lovestruck courtroom surrounded by family and friends.

There are so many people who love you and want to welcome you into their hearts as the judge signs the papers making you an Ericson—Jack and Madison, Emma and Ella, Aunt Alice and Cap from your daddy's firehouse, of course. Your grandpar-

ents even made the trip from Manhattan, and so did your cousin, Lori. She's brought her sweet one-year-old daughter, Ariel, and we both hope you'll grow up to be great friends someday.

Years from now, when we tell you the story of how you came into our lives during one snowy Christmas in Vermont, we'll probably say we were on the way to play Joseph and Mary in a living nativity scene at the Christmas festival. We might say that unlike Mary and Joseph, we had no idea that a baby was about to change everything we thought we knew about life and love. But it did, and that baby was you.

It's been six months since that fateful night outside the firehouse—six months of diapers and late-night feedings, six months of trying to keep Duchess the dog from stealing all your baby toys, six months of falling more in love with you each and every day. So much has changed during that time, and there's so much I can't wait to tell you, like how the ladies from Alice's knitting club love to dote on you at the nursery they've taken over when I'm teaching at the yoga studio every morning. And how your daddy proposed to me on Christmas Eve during the living nativity scene by sneaking an en-

gagement ring into the box the wise men carried. And also how I tried to knit him a pair of striped socks for Christmas and they turned into a complete disaster, but he wears them all the time, anyway. Likewise, I always wear the locket with your picture in it that he gave me on Christmas morning. The one I used to wear is tucked away in a jewelry box, along with all the precious memories it holds. Because this past Christmas marked a new beginning. Not just for you, but for all three of us...together.

Right now you're too young to understand any of those things, but I wanted to write them down so that when the time is right, we will give you this letter and you'll know how much these past six months have meant to us, your parents.

When I first came to Vermont, I never expected to be a mother. It still seems strange to call myself that, because being your mom seems too good to be true. It is, though. You're ours now, and we're yours. Please know we'll always be here for you, and we'll answer any questions you might have someday about your birth mother, who loved you very much but wanted you to have a better life than she was prepared to give you. Your favorite baby blanket was a gift from her, and the Christmas book that always makes you smile came from her, too. I know it might be hard to understand why she made the choices she did, but never doubt that she loved you with all her heart.

Yes, you are loved, little Nick. You are loved and you are wanted, more than you can possibly know.

All my love,
Mommy

* * * * *

#2809 HER TEXAS NEW YEAR'S WISH
The Fortunes of Texas: The Hotel Fortune • by Michelle Major
When Grace Williams topples from the balcony at the new Hotel Fortune, the last thing she expects is to find love with her new bosses' brother. Wiley Fortune has looks, money and charm to spare. But Grace's past makes her wary of investing her heart. This time, she is holding out for the real deal...

#2810 WHAT HAPPENS AT THE RANCH...
Twin Kings Ranch • by Christy Jeffries
All Secret Service agent Grayson Wyatt has to do is protect Tessa King, the VP's daughter, and stay low profile. But Tessa is guarding her own secret. And her attraction to the undercover cowboy breaks every protocol. With the media hot on a story, their taboo relationship could put everything Tessa and Grayson have fought for at risk...

#2811 THE CHILD WHO CHANGED THEM
The Parent Portal • by Tara Taylor Quinn
Dr. Greg Adams knows he can't have children. But when colleague Dr. Elaina Alexander announces she's pregnant with his miracle child, Greg finds his life turned upside down. But can the good doctor convince widow Elaina that their happiness lies within reach—and with each other?

#2812 THE MARINE MAKES AMENDS
The Camdens of Montana • by Victoria Pade
Micah Camden ruined Lexie Parker's life years ago, but now that she's back in Merritt to care for her grandmother—who was hurt due to Micah's negligence—she has no plans to forgive him. But Micah knows that he made mistakes back then and hopes to make amends with Lexie, if only so they can both move on from the past. Everyone says Micah's changed since joining the marines, but it's going to take more than someone's word to convince her...

#2813 SNOWBOUND WITH THE SHERIFF
Sutter Creek, Montana • by Laurel Greer
Stella Reid has been gone from Sutter Creek long enough and is determined to mend fences...but immediately comes face-to-face with the man who broke her heart: Sheriff Ryan Rafferty. But as she opens herself up bit by bit, can Stella find the happily-ever-after she was denied years ago—in his arms?

#2814 THE MARRIAGE MOMENT
Paradise Animal Clinic • by Katie Meyer
Deputy Jessica Santiago will let nothing—not even a surprise pregnancy—get in the way of her job. Determined to solve several problems at once—getting her hands on her inheritance *and* creating a family—Jessica convinces colleague Ryan Sullivan to partake in a marriage of convenience. But what's a deputy to do when love blooms?

HSECNM1220

"I didn't fall," she announced with a wide smile as he
returned the crutches.

"You did great." He looked at her with a huge smile.

"That was silly," she said as they started down the walk
toward his car. "Maneuvering down a few steps isn't a
big deal, but this is the farthest I've gone on my own
since the accident. If my parents had their way, they'd
encase me in Bubble Wrap for the rest of my life to make
sure I stayed safe."

"It's an understandable sentiment from people who
care about you."

"But not what I want."

He opened the car door for her, and she gave him the
crutches to stow in the back seat. The whole process

was slow and awkward. By the time Grace was buckled in next to Wiley, sweat dripped between her shoulder blades, and she felt like she'd run a marathon. How could less than a week of inactivity make her feel like such an invalid?

As if sensing her frustration, Wiley placed a gentle hand on her arm. "You've been through a lot, Grace. Your ankle and the cast are the biggest outward signs of the accident, but you fell from the second story."

She offered a wan smile. "I have the bruises to prove it."

"Give yourself a bit of…well, grace."

"I never thought of attorneys as naturally comforting people," she admitted. "But you're good at giving support."

"It's a hidden skill." He released her hand and pulled away from the curb. "We lawyers don't like to let anyone know about our human side. It ruins the reputation of being coldhearted, and then people aren't afraid of us."

"You're the opposite of scary."

"Where are we headed?" he asked when he got to the stop sign at the end of the block.

"The highway," she said without hesitation. "As much as I love Rambling Rose, I need a break. Let's get out of this town, Wiley."

Don't miss
Her Texas New Year's Wish *by Michelle Major,*
available January 2021 wherever
Harlequin Special Edition books and ebooks are sold.

Harlequin.com